Hammerstrike

by Walter Winward

SIMON AND SCHUSTER
NEW YORK

DESIGNED BY IRVING PERKINS

MANUFACTURED IN THE UNITED STATES OF AMERICA

LIBRARY OF CONGRESS CATALOGING IN PUBLICATION DATA

WINWARD, WALTER.
HAMMERSTRIKE.

I. WORLD WAR, 1939–1945—FICTION.   I. TITLE.
PZ4.W7945HAM   1979   [PR6073.I58]   823'.9'14   78-25746

ISBN 0-671-24668-2

For my good friends Keith and Pearl

Author's Note

1. Skiddaw Camp is an invention. Because its fictitious location is near that of an actual camp—Grizedale Hall (POW Camp Number 1)—there may be a temptation to think that they are one and the same. This would be wrong. Neither captors nor captive in Skiddaw are other than imaginary.

2. Although Germans use the metric system of weight and measurement, for ease of reference the English system has been employed more or less throughout. The only exceptions are where I have deemed it dramatically advisable.

3. In writing this book I consulted a number of individuals and organizations. The staff of the Somerset County Library were most helpful in obtaining books long out of print. Several members of the Embassy of the Federal German Republic, who prefer to remain unnamed, assisted me with wartime ranks and the Luftwaffe chain of command. The Imperial War Museum was, as always, untiring in its efforts to oblige, in particular Mr. T. C. Charman, who furnished me with the words of German war songs. And finally the family and friends of the late Oberleutnant Hans-Dieter Mueller were unfailingly courteous in answering my many questions. To all of the above I give my thanks. Any errors of fact are my own, as are the opinions expressed.

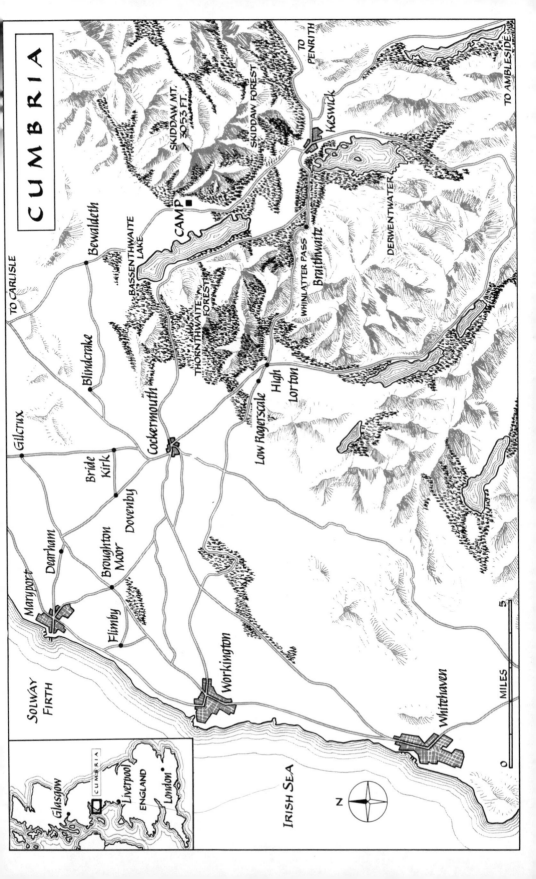

SKIDDAW CAMP

A
ROUGH PLAN
SHOWING MAIN
FEATURES

• NOT TO SCALE

600 YARDS

30 FEET

350 YARDS

WORKSHOP

STORE

POW KITCHEN

POW CANTEEN

LIBRARY

BRITISH OTHER RANKS' QUARTERS

POW ACCOMMODATION

21	22	23	24	25
16	17	18	19	20
11	12	13	14	15
6	7	8	9	10
1	2	3	4	5

SICK BAY

OFFICERS' BATH & HEADS

BRITISH OFFICERS' QUARTERS

BOILER ROOM

GERMAN MESS

INNER PERIMETER FENCE

OUTER PERIMETER FENCE

MOTOR POOL & BICYCLE SHED

EXERCISE YARD

50 YARDS SQUARE

ADMINISTRATION BLOCK

GUARD-ROOM

INNER GATES

WORKSHOP

ARMORY

CHAPEL

OUTER GATES

N

Watchtowers

You must either conquer and rule or lose and serve,
suffer or triumph, and be the anvil or the hammer.
—GOETHE

Prologue

NOVEMBER 12, 1942

Hitler nodded to indicate that the meeting was at an end. Taking his cue, Generalmajor Kurt von Stuerzbecher collected his briefcase from the planning table and backed out of the Operations Room, leaving the Fuehrer, Reichsmarschall Goering, Field Marshals Keitel and Kesselring and their aides to get on with the next business. This was von Stuerzbecher's first visit to the Fuehrerbunker, but he had been warned that Hitler liked to keep protocol to a minimum. Thus there were no Roman salutes, no affirmations of continued loyalty.

Outside in the corridor he collided with General Jodl, going the other way. As usual, Alfred Jodl was late. Hitler's closest military adviser raised his eyebrows when he saw von Stuerzbecher's uniform.

"Demoted, Stuerzbecher?"

"No, an accident."

He had arrived by plane just as the air-raid sirens began wailing. It turned out to be a false alarm, but in his anxiety to get to hell out of it he had slipped and fallen, covering his uniform with mud and oil. There had been nothing to do but borrow his pilot's spare, and von Stuerzbecher was now dressed as a Luftwaffe *Oberleutnant*. Hitler had thought it a great joke.

"What's his mood?" asked Jodl.

Although there was considerable difference in both age and rank between the two officers, they had known each other since before the war. It would have been an overstatement to call them friends, but neither did each have to watch his back in the other's presence.

"Good enough, considering the news from North Africa."

"He has stronger nerves than I have, then. Is Himmler in there?"

"No. It seems the SS has been excluded from this meeting."

"But not junior Luftwaffe generals apparently. What's going on? Is the Reichsmarschall trying to obtain permission to bomb Geneva?"

Von Stuerzbecher did not reply. These days it was hard to know who was privy to what. There was little doubt that Reichsmarschall Goering had convinced Hitler that Reichsfuehrer Himmler's attendance would not be required at the discussions, which had been going on since midafternoon, and possibly the same applied to Jodl. If Jodl was in, he'd be told; if he wasn't, it was better to say nothing.

Jodl laughed at his subordinate's caution.

"Secrets, eh? Well, every state needs its secrets and us more than most. Look after Holland for us, Stuerzbecher."

Jodl thrust back his shoulders and went into the Operations Room. Before the door closed behind him, von Stuerzbecher heard Goering say, with undisguised sarcasm, "I hope we didn't keep you from anything, Herr General."

Von Stuerzbecher made his way to street level, where, at the entrance to the Fuehrerbunker, he surrendered his pass. The SS NCO who accepted it took in the Knight's Cross with Oak Leaves at von Stuerzbecher's throat and stiffened to attention.

"Heil Hitler."

"Heil Hitler," murmured von Stuerzbecher, and he went out into the cold Berlin night, glancing skyward, as all old fighter pilots did, to check the weather. It was perfect: a three-quarter moon above some low-lying cloud. They'd be over again tonight, the *Tommis*, but whether the target would be Berlin was anybody's guess for the moment.

Von Stuerzbecher's driver peeled himself away from a group of other drivers and stamped out his cigarette as his passenger approached. He opened the staff-car door and stood at attention until von Stuerzbecher was inside and seated.

"Back to the airfield."

Von Stuerzbecher settled himself in a corner and selected a fat cigar from a leather case. No shortage of those yet, thank God. And what a pleasure to light up! There was no smoking near Hitler.

He fingered the briefcase on his lap but made no attempt to open it. There was a reading light in the back of the Mercedes, but he had no desire to read. He knew the contents by heart. From the moment Goering had given him the problem 'way back in August, he had spent most of his waking hours planning and replanning. He had not referred to his notes once throughout the whole meeting.

"If it becomes necessary, we shall hammer their hands to a cross," Goering had said, recognizing, by his relative silence, that Hitler approved of the scheme.

It was not difficult to deduce that Keitel and Kesselring did not; they had heard that sort of vainglorious comment from Goering before. In 1940, for example, during the *Kanalkampf*, the "Battle of Britain," as Churchill called it. And it had come to nothing. They had heard it again when the Reichsmarschall had bragged that not a single bomb would fall on Berlin. He had been wrong about that, too, and a single glance out the window of the moving staff car was more than enough to see how wrong.

Like most fighter pilots, former or current, Generalmajor von Stuerzbecher was on the small side, five feet eight, and stockily built. A native of Hamburg, with his dark hair and somewhat swarthy features he looked anything but the archetypal blond Aryan flier who used to gaze down from the recruiting posters. Most women would have called him handsome. One in particular had thought him special enough to accept his proposal of marriage. But she had died a long time ago, and since then there had been no one who meant more than any of the others. In peacetime and at his age, thirty-four, he would have considered himself fortunate to have achieved the rank of major, let alone his present status. But this was November 1942, and youthful brigadier generals were thick on the ground.

He rapped on the communicating window.

"Faster!"

Von Stuerzbecher glanced at the phosphorescent dial of his wrist watch. Almost 2200 hours. With luck and good winds, the flying time between Berlin and Amsterdam in the Ju 188 he had commandeered for the trip was less than a couple of hours. Nevertheless, he was cutting it a bit fine. The last thing he needed was to run into six or seven hundred Lancasters and Halifaxes heading the other way.

He grinned at the irony of his thoughts. How times changed, and how with them changed men. There was a period, about five years, from his early days in the Condor Legion to the latter half of 1941, when he had gone looking for enemy aircraft. The hours on the ground had been resented and he had driven more than one maintenance crew to despair by his insistence that the Me 109 be ready for takeoff whenever he demanded. They had been heady days, those, when every young *Leutnant* wanted his own *Staffel* and every *Staffelkapitaen* his own *Geschwader* and the coveted Knight's Cross.

He fingered the sheet-metal tie, as it was irreverently called among air crew. Thirty-one enemy bombers and fighters had earned him that. The Knight's Cross itself bestowed by Reichsmarschall Goering at Karinhall; the Oak Leaves that followed by the Fuehrer in person at

Berchtesgaden. Talk had had it, and he was, if immodestly, enough of a realist to believe it, that the "knives and forks," the Swords to the Ritterkreuz, would not have been far behind if he had been left in command of a fighter station. But Goering had put a stop to that, just over a year ago.

A face-to-face meeting with the Luftwaffe chief, even for an *Oberst* commanding a fighter station, was an unusual event. If it wasn't for a decoration, it generally meant trouble. But on this occasion it was neither.

The Reichsmarschall was looking tired, von Stuerzbecher observed. He hadn't lost any weight; if anything, he had gained a few kilos. But the flesh hung sadly now.

Goering got straight down to business.

"First of all the pleasant part," he said, reading from an official document. "With effect from October 1, 1941 you are promoted to the rank of *Generalmajor*."

Von Stuerzbecher was startled. It wasn't four months since he was promoted to *Oberst*.

"Thank you, Herr Reichsmarschall," he managed.

"Don't thank me yet. You haven't heard the rest of it. As from 0800 hours tomorrow you are relieved of your duties as officer commanding—" He threw the document to one side. "To hell with that formal jargon. From tomorrow morning, Stuerzbecher, you're grounded."

"Then I refuse the promotion, Herr Reichsmarschall."

Goering slammed the desk with his fist.

"*You* obey orders, Herr Generalmajor. You neither accept nor refuse. You do as you are told. Is that clear?"

Biting his lower lip, von Stuerzbecher nodded. Goering's flash of temper vanished as quickly as it had appeared. He pushed across a heavy wooden box containing a dozen Romeo y Julietas. Von Stuerzbecher declined.

"You've been a lucky man so far," said Goering, peering at what was obviously von Stuerzbecher's dossier. "You've limped home half a dozen times with your machine shot to rags, but you've never suffered more than a scratch yourself. How long do you think that sort of luck can last? I haven't always sat in a chair. I know what it's like on a station. In a crisis—and crises are becoming commonplace these days—you break the rules and take up an aircraft yourself. That is not a criticism; nine out of ten station commanders do the same. But it's a dangerous practice. The air war is a young man's game. I've had it proved to my own satisfaction that after the age of twenty-four or twenty-five a pilot's reflexes slow down. You're an ace, Stuerzbecher, and aces are far too hard to come by to risk losing them to a lucky burst from a novice Spitfire pilot.

"I could have given you a Group. I could have given you Galland's job or Kammhuber's, but I need you here. I'm putting you on my staff. You may have to cool your heels for a few months, but I'll find a use for you, sooner or later. But no more combat flying. That's an order."

Cooling his heels rated high as the understatement of the war, thought von Stuerzbecher, tapping an inch of ash onto the luxurious carpeting of the staff car. Three months doing nothing except signing chits and giving speeches; a further five months with a training unit, giving advice to youngsters barely out of school on the best way to stay alive. And then, in August this year, there had been another meeting with Goering.

"Wehrmacht prisoners of war held by the British," began the Reichsmarschall. "Have you any idea what the figures are?"

Von Stuerzbecher hadn't, and he said so.

"Neither have we," confessed Goering, presumably referring to the OKW. "Not an exact count anyway. The problem is, every so often the British send shiploads of them to Canada, which militates against us in two ways. First, until letters from them begin arriving home we've no idea who is where. Second, it makes it difficult for Doenitz's U-boat crews to torpedo indiscriminately. They could well be sending their own comrades to the bottom.

"But at a rough guess we've come up with a figure of

eight thousand. We could be many thousands out in either direction, but that's our working total. The majority are Luftwaffe, with a sprinkling of Army and Navy." He paused for effect. "I want you to engineer a scheme for getting them out."

Von Stuerzbecher thought he was going mad.

"All of them?"

"All of them," affirmed Goering.

"But you're asking the impossible, Herr Reichsmarschall," protested von Stuerzbecher. "No one's ever successfully escaped from the British Isles. In fact, only one man has ever succeeded in escaping from what could be loosely termed British jurisdiction. Leutnant von Werra— and that was from Canada. And it didn't do him much good," he added.

"Nevertheless, he got home," said Goering. "That he was killed on the Russian Front has no bearing on the matter. The one has nothing to do with the other. Good God, man, Allied airmen escape from camps even such as Colditz with monotonous regularity and the manpower involved in tracking down even half a dozen of them is enormous."

"With due respect, Reichsmarschall, Britain is an island and Germany is not. Furthermore, Allied prisoners on the run receive help from the various underground movements in all occupied countries. Our own prisoners would have no such assistance."

"But if it could be done, Stuerzbecher, if it could be done." Goering slapped his pudgy hands together in an attitude of prayer. "Imagine that. If it takes a couple of regiments of German soldiers to recapture half a dozen escaping Allies, imagine eight thousand German POWs on the move. From Devizes Camp in Wiltshire to Comrie Camp in Scotland, eight thousand men on the run. Even if only a fraction of them ever got home, think of the chaos the escape alone would cause on that wretched little island."

Goering came out of his reverie and was suddenly efficient again.

"There is also another consideration. By itself, the mass escape of German POWs would tie down the British home-based security forces for two weeks, perhaps four. They would create something of a nuisance value, but we need more than that.

"I don't have to tell you, my dear Stuerzbecher, that the war is not going well for us. Certainly, on paper, it looks as if we are holding our own, but a counteroffensive by the Russians or an Allied push in North Africa would be catastrophic. What's more, the High Command think that either or both are possibilities, and should that become the case the invasion of Europe can only be a matter of time. We should need the pressure taken off us, which is where you come in.

"If you can devise a plan for the escape of our POWs, we intend to coordinate it with a massive movement of troops and armor, all that can be spared, to the Channel ports— give the Allies the impression that we have resurrected Sea Lion and intend to invade Britain. What then will Churchill do? It is the Fuehrer's opinion that he will add two and two together and come up with the only logical answer: that the POWs have escaped to commit sabotage, disrupt communications to assist our *own* invasion force. He may believe that such an invasion is impossible, but dare he take a chance? He will be compelled to withdraw troops from other theaters, hopefully North Africa. At the very least he will think twice before sending reinforcements.

"The whole exercise will be no more than a gigantic bluff, of course, but wars have been won with less. If you can do your part we shall have gained valuable breathing space, time to hammer the Allies into the ground—into defeat."

And so from that chance remark of Goering's, Operation Hammer was given its name.

At first von Stuerzbecher considered the whole idea to be an advanced case of lunacy, but the more he examined

22

the setup of the British POW camps, the comparative caliber of prisoners and captors, the more he became convinced of its feasibility. On paper it worked—enough, anyway, for the Fuehrer to have given the go-ahead signal that very afternoon. There were, of course, a thousand minor details still to be finalized, but it was nowhere near the madman's scheme it had first appeared.

The Mercedes turned off the main highway. Papers were scrutinized and salutes exchanged. The driver coasted to within feet of the waiting Ju 188.

Apart from being granted the highest security classification, Operation Hammer was now a matter of some urgency. Von Stuerzbecher had wanted six months' further preparation; Hitler allowed three. On reflection, the *Generalmajor* could well understand why. Slowly but surely the tide was turning against the Reich, though God help anyone who dared voice such treason. Just three weeks after the meeting with Goering at Karinhall, the Wehrmacht had come to a grinding halt outside Stalingrad, and as of this moment Army Group Don was in big trouble. Six weeks after the impasse at Stalingrad that at El Alamein had occurred, another bitter blow. And finally, four days ago, the High Command's August predictions had come true when the Allies invaded North Africa.

Urgent indeed.

Von Stuerzbecher left the staff car, buttoning up his leather coat against the icy November wind.

The pilot of the Ju 188, a young *Oberleutnant* by the name of Moenke, was standing beneath the port wing. Judging by the smell of aviation fuel and oil, the machine had been warmed up and was ready to go. Moenke smiled to himself when he saw that von Stuerzbecher was still wearing, beneath the leather coat, his own spare uniform. He trusted the Generalmajor would not forget to whom it belonged.

Under his flying leathers, pinned to his left breast, Moenke wore the Iron Cross. But because of his preoccupation with the meeting in the Fuehrerbunker during the

23

flight up, that fact and the youngster's name were the sum total of von Stuerzbecher's knowledge. Once in the air and on course, he decided to dig a little deeper.

"Thanks for the loan of the uniform. I hope the lack of it didn't prevent you from keeping an engagement."

Both men were wearing flying helmets and throat microphones, but even so the noise generated by the twin 1776-h.p. Jumo-213A engines was enormous. Von Stuerzbecher, in the observer's seat, had to remind himself not to shout.

"Not at all, sir. I always carry a spare in case I'm lucky enough to be invited to a cocktail party at the Adlon."

Von Stuerzbecher couldn't tell whether or not Moenke was being sarcastic. He decided not. The Adlon Hotel in the Wilhelmstrasse was the scene of many prewar junkets, but they were a thing of the past. Moenke was bright enough to know this.

"The last I saw of it they were sweeping up the rubble. You'd be lucky to get a cold beer there nowadays."

"I expect so. Is the Generalmajor's parachute harness quite comfortable?"

The youngster was being ridiculously stiff and von Stuerzbecher thought he knew why.

"Quite comfortable, thank you. You don't much care for acting as chauffeur, do you?"

"May I answer truthfully?"

"Of course."

"Then with all courtesy, I should prefer to be doing something more constructive toward winning the war."

"And ferrying generals around the countryside is not your idea of constructive war effort?"

If von Stuerzbecher had expected Moenke to be embarrassed, he was mistaken.

"Tonight, Herr Generalmajor, the terror fliers will be over again. The winter war is not like the summer war. In summer, we can expect them in the early hours so that they can be landing in England in daylight. In winter they come over at any time. Tonight my *Staffel* will be hunting

24

Lancasters. I should be with them. If, when we get nearer the Dutch coast, you will permit me to switch frequency to one of the radar beacons, you will understand why I should be with my *Staffel*."

Damned impudence, thought von Stuerzbecher.

"I too have fought the *Tommis,* you know, Oberleutnant."

"I know, sir. And, if you will forgive me, you use the correct tense, the past. It is now my turn."

Good Christ, thought von Stuerzbecher, he makes me sound like an old man. Which I suppose I am to him. He'd still have been studying geography when I was shooting down my first Spitfire.

In response to a command from a controller south of them at Dortmund, Moenke took the Ju 188 too close to its operational ceiling of 33,000 feet. The thinness of the atmosphere at this altitude made the controls mushy in his hands. There was little he could do with the aeroplane at this height except keep it pointing in the right direction.

The cloud base thickened as they neared the Dutch border, rendering the ground invisible. But six miles above the earth the Junkers was bathed in moonlight. It was, thought Moenke, perfect bombing weather. With the cloud dense up to 17,000 feet, even the Stirlings, with a pitiful ceiling of just over 20,000, would be able to fly where the flak could not get at them until they were well into German territory. It had its disadvantages, of course; the bombing stream would not be able to see its own ground markers. But the Pathfinder squadrons had developed aerial marking to such a degree that such a minus factor would have no more than a slight nuisance value.

It was definitely a night when only fighters would be able to prevent further devastation of German cities.

"How old are you?" asked von Stuerzbecher.

"I shall be twenty next month, sir, the week before Christmas."

"And have you had many successes?"

"In twenty-two sorties I have scored three confirmed

25

victories. All Lancasters. It's not much, but it's a beginning."

They crossed the Dutch border at Enschede. A few minutes later, passing over Apeldoorn, von Stuerzbecher sensed that his pilot was becoming fidgety.

"All right," he said, "change frequency."

It took only a few moments' listening to the wireless traffic passing between ground and air to realize that the *Tommis* were on their way and the night fighters had been scrambled. Radar controllers never said, and probably didn't know, the full strength of a bombing fleet, but to an experienced listener like von Stuerzbecher, the number of fighters being given directions could only mean an enemy task force of between seven and eight hundred. And if he were any judge the Ruhr would again be the target. The *Tommis* had been knocking hell out of the heart of industrial Germany in recent weeks and it seemed they would not stop until the last factory was razed to the ground. It was hard to know which was preferable, if preference in such matters could be expressed. Whether it was better that the R.A.F. concentrated on industrial targets or better that they left the factories alone and dropped their death on cities that had no strategic importance, only a demoralizing factor.

In the time it took von Stuerzbecher to think these thoughts, the Ju 188, traveling at a speed in excess of 300 m.p.h., had covered five miles. They were now some forty miles east of Amsterdam and about fifty from the Dutch coast. Soon, Oberleutnant Moenke would need to begin his descent. Unless. . . .

The Ju 188 had undergone many modifications and performed many roles since it started life as the Ju 88, a *Schnellbomber*. The infinite flexibility of its design had proved so adaptable that it had served as a reconnaissance fighter, heavy day fighter, torpedo bomber, conversion trainer and antitank aircraft. But as a night fighter it was unsurpassed. With a top speed of over 320 m.p.h. and equipped with two 20mm cannons, one 13mm machine gun and two 7.96mm machine guns, it could outgun and outrun any bomber the British put up. Moreover, Oberleutnant Moenke was trained as a night-fighter pilot.

Judging by the wireless traffic, the night fighters had not been scrambled long, which probably meant the long-range Freya radar had only just picked up the bombing leaders crossing the British coast. Von Stuerzbecher had long held the opinion that it was poor strategy to wait until the bombers were on top of continental European soil before attacking. If they could be hit on their side of the North Sea, so much the better. Any Luftwaffe pilot who was forced to bail out would just have to take his chances.

Moenke's Junkers was not equipped with radar; the heavy nose aerials caused a serious drop in speed and maneuverability, and the Luftwaffe liked to think that major generals got to where they were going without incident. But lack of radar was only a minor drawback. More often than not it didn't function and pilots relied upon a visual for the final attack.

Von Stuerzbecher felt a tremor of excitement. It was over a year since he had been involved in a scrap.

"How are we off for fuel?" he asked.

"Three quarters, sir."

"Then let's get some of that aggression out of your system. Stay on this heading but take her down to twenty-six thousand. I won't be able to do much except act as observer, but in view of what you said earlier maybe that's all I'm fit for at my age. Listen to the radar controllers but don't respond or ask for a fix. We'll bag what we can and go home. Have you got all that?"

Moenke did not need telling twice. "Thank you, Herr Generalmajor."

"Don't thank me. If Goering ever finds out what happened, I'll claim you kidnapped me."

Oberleutnant Moenke put the nose down. The twin Jumos roared appreciatively as the atmosphere became less rare and the propellers began to bite.

A Lancaster, the fastest of the R.A.F.'s heavy bombers,

had a cruising speed of around 260 m.p.h. Crossing the Dutch coast at 26,000 feet, Moenke's Junkers was flat out at 323 m.p.h. Thus, the bombing fleet and the Ju 188 were approaching each other at close on 600 m.p.h. With a mean distance of 150 miles between East Anglia and Holland, they should sight the Pathfinders in a little over ten minutes, von Stuerzbecher estimated.

But the sky is a big place, and after a quarter of an hour they had seen nothing.

Von Stuerzbecher was about to instruct Moenke to swing north when the boy anticipated him. Good. The youngster could think for himself. There was a possibility they'd both get home this night.

A minute passed. Two . . . Three . . . Fifteen, twenty miles covered.

A further two minutes, another ten miles.

And then von Stuerzbecher saw them.

Four or five thousand feet below and a mile to starboard, squadron after squadron of them, silhouetted against the clouds. He had no field glasses and it was hard to tell from the distance, but it seemed that most of them were Lancasters, possibly Halifaxes. They were an awe-inspiring sight.

There was no need to say anything to Moenke. Already he was making a low sweeping dive to come up below and behind. Height was everything at the beginning of a sortie, but useless once a sighting had been made. Underneath, that was the place to strike, at the Lancaster's unprotected belly.

They were not the only German aircraft in the sky. Although still well out over the North Sea, they were now nearer the Dutch coastline and other night fighters had been dispatched on an interceptor course. Even as they watched, one of the leading bombers took a direct hit in the fuel tanks and exploded in mid-air.

As Moenke leveled out at 19,000 feet some of the bombers were already taking evasive action. The pretty airborne pattern, which had started in England, was now

28

breaking up as the R.A.F. pilots fought to stay alive and keep out of reach of the night fighters. The apogee of the cloud formation was at 18,000, but many of the *Tommis* were ignoring their natural distrust of cloud and putting their noses down. Von Stuerzbecher spotted one such fugitive half a mile ahead and at roughly the same altitude.

"Lancaster," shouted von Stuerzbecher, but Moenke was already firing.

Then a succession of events took place so quickly that the brain hardly had time to record one before it was assailed by another.

Oberleutnant Moenke's kill rate of three out of twenty-two sorties was about average, so it was probably excitement or nerves which made him shoot too early. In either case, he was not close enough or low enough to bring his score up to four, and he saw his ammunition wasting itself at eight hundred meters. Simultaneously, the Lancaster's rear gunner returned the fire.

"Christ," said Moenke, and side-slipped to port. Which brought him into the sights of a second night fighter.

The radar controller for this sector had seen Moenke's Junkers edge on to his screen and knew that it was not a German aircraft allocated to him. It should therefore be a *Tommi*, but the screen was now full of *Tommis*. In any case, he was an experienced officer and something about the way the blip was dancing about told him that it was a friendly stray from another sector. The pilot of the second night fighter saw it differently.

There is not much similarity between a Wellington bomber and a Ju 188. Apart from markings, the Wellington is larger in every respect. But both are two-motor aircraft and to the inexperienced eye, with aircraft weaving and twisting all over the sky at hundreds of miles an hour, they look somewhat alike. It was Moenke's fatal luck that the pilot of the other night fighter was on only his third mission.

A fraction of a second after the Ju 188 side-slipped to port, the novice pilot opened up with cannons and machine guns. It would be inaccurate to say that Moenke was hit by the novice pilot; it was more of a case of his aircraft running into the 20mm cannon shells. Eighteen struck home, roughly half and half high-explosive and incendiary, and they were enough to ensure that Oberleutnant Moenke would not be celebrating his twentieth birthday in Christmas week.

Suddenly the cockpit was filled with the smell of oil and death. Momentarily shocked into a state of immobility, von Stuerzbecher forced himself by an effort of will to examine the situation. He was not hit, that was the first thing he decided. The blood on the instrument panel was not his. But Moenke was dead and the Junkers had received a mortal blow. He had to get out. Already the aircraft was dropping into a deadly spiral. A few more seconds and gravity would guarantee that the cockpit became his coffin.

Desperately he reached across Moenke and jerked the lever that released the cockpit canopy. It flew off with a terrifying roar. In spite of his predicament he wasted valuable seconds jettisoning everything that could possibly give away his true rank and status. He was over the sea, and if he didn't die of cold first it was just as likely he would be picked up by a British ship as by a German.

The contents of his pockets went fluttering out into the bitterly cold night. Papers, matches, cigars, wallet. He got rid of everything, even money; there was no time to think selectively. The last item to go was his briefcase, which he threw out open.

Between the time he sighted the Lancaster to the time he spilled out of the doomed Junkers, only half a minute had elapsed. Apart from practice jumps, he had never bailed out of an aircraft before, and his greatest fear as he tumbled through the clouds was colliding with another plane.

The sea looked rough and uncompromising, and hitting it feet first was like jumping off a high wall. He ditched his parachute immediately. Some pilots swore that air in the canopy helped to keep them afloat, others that the canopy could fill with water and drag a man under. He was taking no chances on the latter. His life-jacket would keep him buoyant, at least for a time.

The cold was terrible. Within minutes he could no longer feel his legs. He had no idea how long he was in the water and he reckoned later that he must have passed out. The first thing he remembered was willing hands dragging him from the sea. And a voice saying: "Looks like we've copped ourselves a Jerry."

Part 1

One

NOVEMBER 15, 1942

A thin fall of new snow covered Skiddaw Camp. It was going to be cold that winter. Cold enough anyway, as the third week in November finally ushered out autumn, for Oberleutnant Franz Mohr to make a mental note on the subject of fuel for Hut 9's stove.

Crossing the compound from north to south, from the ablutions to the long wooden hut that served as the German Officers' Mess, Mohr threw an anxious glance in the direction of the guardroom and the main gates. There was no sign of activity, which probably meant that, so far, Naumann had got away with it. Though God only knew whether he had survived the night. In the small hours before dawn the temperature had been below zero Fahrenheit.

When level with that section of the camp that the British called the Exercise Yard and the German prisoners the Pig Pen, Mohr stopped for a moment. It was early, not yet 9 A.M., but already a dozen officers had got together a scratch game of volleyball. Playing in an area fifty yards square and mesh wired, broken in places, in the manner

35

of a park tennis court, the officers had knotted together a dozen scarves to act as a makeshift net. At present it was obviously not serving its purpose, as there was an argument in progress regarding whether the previous shot had gone under or over the scarves.

Willi Schneider called across to him.

"Come and join us, Franz. Perhaps you can teach these buffoons the rules."

Mohr shook his head.

"You'll get fat."

"It's the diet."

Willi Schneider could play with only one arm, his right. The muscles in the shoulder of his left had been badly injured when his parachute inexplicably flared thirty feet from the ground after he bailed out of his Me 109 over Dover. That was two years ago, in the autumn of 1940. Before that Willi had notched up seven assorted kills. He was, now, just twenty-one.

Franz Mohr continued across the compound, the reason for his earlier anxiety uppermost in his mind.

The previous day, evidently immune to irony, the Camp Commandant, Major Mitchell, had organized a belated Armistice Day ceremony for the dead of the previous war. It was laughable, really; here they were, three-and-a-bit years into another European war, and he was taking time out to remember the last skirmish. Still, most of the POWs attended, and the morning had its bright spot. Taking advantage of the lull in normal camp surveillance, Emil Naumann escaped.

At first no one knew how it had been done. When an escape attempt was in the cards, normally the camp was buzzing like a saw both immediately before and afterward. Which was natural enough, as the escaper usually asked his friends to cover for him during the first few hours. But the rules didn't apply to Naumann. He was a loner, a solo artist. In the last six months, he had been under, over or through the wire three times. Which was pretty good, considering that each unsuccessful attempt

36

was punished by twenty-eight days in solitary. He hardly gave his captors chance to draw breath before he was on the move again. Mohr wondered why the *Tommis* didn't put a permanent special watch on him, especially as he generally walked around the compound with a pencil and paper in his hands. Whatever he was measuring, it wasn't the dimensions of a football field.

Naumann had answered his name at the 8:30 A.M. roll call and was missing at the afternoon head count. Captain Thorogood, the adjutant to the camp's commanding officer, called an immediate *Sonderappell*, a special roll call, but the tally still came out one man short. Naumann was *spurlos verschwunden*, had vanished without trace. It was evening before news began to circulate of the civilian workman found bound and gagged in the rear of the workshop at the eastern end of the camp. Oberleutnant Naumann had overpowered him, taken his overalls and tool bag, and calmly walked out through the main gates.

Major Mitchell threw an apoplectic fit and gave Otto Breithaupt, the senior German officer, a severe reprimand. Thorogood took it even further and threatened all sorts of vengeance if Naumann wasn't recaptured soon. But that was nothing new. Thorogood hated Germans with a venom that was almost psychopathic. He hated Naumann most of all.

Apart from being a pain in the neck to the British, Emil Naumann was the one real ace in the camp, though technically many of the POWs were so classified. But Naumann was in a bracket of his own. Not quite twenty-two years old, at the time he crash-landed in the sea off Yarmouth when low on fuel his total confirmed haul was forty-four *Tommi* aircraft. He had Swords to his Knight's Cross, a very rare honor indeed. A law student in 1939, he had found in the war, as had many others, a chance to find his true vocation.

Oberleutnant Franz Mohr paused before the entrance to the Mess to light a cigarette, his second of the day's ration of eight. At five feet ten he was a tall man for a fighter pilot, and he was now in his nineteenth month of captivity. Two of those months he had spent in solitary confinement after the same number of escape bids. As in any other walk of life, there are men who can accept and profit by solitude and there are others who cannot. Franz Mohr fell somewhere between the two categories.

He had viewed the twenty-eight days' punishment following his first attempt with equanimity. It was every POW's clear duty to escape, and it was equally the duty of the captors to punish the miscreants. That was one of the rules of the game. A month in the cooler was nothing. In many ways it was a relief not to have to share quarters with eight or nine others. But the fourth week was hard; he began muttering to himself halfway through it.

All of his second term, which had ended on the last day of October, was murder, and hunger was his constant companion. The general diet in the camp was poor enough, but the diet in solitary was barely sustaining. He knew he had lost weight from the way his clothes hung, but he was quite shocked when he caught sight of himself the day of his release. Where once his hair had been fair and thick and carefully trimmed, now it was graying, thinning and badly in need of attention. Where his eyes had been clear and his face unlined, now the whites were a dull shade of gray and he had the wrinkles of a man of forty. But Franz Mohr was just twenty-four.

Being a prisoner of war, Oberleutnant Mohr missed many things: a glass of real malt whisky, concerts, books that were not vetted to see if they were suitable. Most of all he missed women. But in Skiddaw Camp that was one commodity very definitely not on the menu, and the alternatives were practiced by very few.

Built in haste in 1941 to take the overspill from Grizedale Hall on Lake Windemere, Skiddaw Camp housed over two hundred POWs, most of them Luftwaffe officers but with a sprinkling of commissioned personnel from the German Army and Navy, together with a number of other ranks who acted, in part, as officers' servants. Disregarding the "old" men such as Mohr and Major Breithaupt, who was twenty-six, the average age of the internees was twenty-two.

Located at the edge of Skiddaw Forest between the 3,000-odd feet of Skiddaw Mountain to the east and Bassenthwaite Lake to the west, the camp was a nightmare for potential escapees. The nearest town was Keswick, five miles to the south, while east there was nothing of size closer than Penrith. The coast was twenty hard miles away, as were the only two ports worth the name, Workington and Whitehaven. But reaching either was only the start of the problem. Beyond Workington and Whitehaven was the Irish Sea.

In choosing Skiddaw as the site for a POW camp, the authorities had used their heads. There was no point in getting out if the coast was the end of the line.

A rough rectangle in shape, the compound measured six hundred yards long by three hundred and fifty wide at its broadest point. In the early days, when the overspill from Grizedale Hall was numbered in tens, a single perimeter fence of rolled barbed wire, eight feet high, was considered sufficient to deter would-be wanderlusts. It was not until the summer evening that the then commandant, Lieutenant Colonel Makepeace, discovered a flock of sheep contentedly grazing near the sick bay and his complement of prisoners reduced by four, that both an inner and an outer fence were deemed necessary, with a thirty-foot open stretch in between. Taking into consideration that there were eight watchtowers equipped with searchlights along the length and breadth of the compound, in spite of a mere doubling of the fencing, getting out became much more than twice as difficult.

The main gates were a hundred yards off the Keswick road, shielded from the gaze of curious motorists by trees and scrub. The authorities had debated leveling this area, but eventually decided against it. Escaping via the main entrance was accepted as impossible and had been until Emil Naumann took his morning stroll. To get out, a pris-

39

oner had to pass two lots of sentries. The first pair guarded the gate set in the inner perimeter fence and had keys only to that. Once through the inner gate a man had to pass a second pair of sentries on the outer perimeter fence, who, too, had keys only to their own exit. Thus it was impossible for a prisoner or prisoners to overpower the first pair of sentries and force them to open both gates.

Arriving from the outside, once through the gates a new POW was confronted with a baffling number of buildings, all built with the object of keeping him in and healthy, if not happy. Armory, Bathhouse and Heads, Chapel, Dry-goods Store, Exercise Yard, Fuel Store, Guardroom, Hospital, Interrogation Room, Jail, Kitchens, Library, M.T. Pool, NCO's Mess, Officers' Mess, Prisoners' Accommodation, QM Stores, Recreation Room, Sick Bay, Tailor's Shop, Upper Watchtowers, Vehicle Maintenance Section, Wireless Room. So much for A to W. X, Y and Z were absent. The nearest X-ray facilities were in Penrith, there was no room or need for a Y.M.C.A., and not even the Army had found a use for the letter Z.

Apart from time spent in the German Mess, the majority of prisoners spent most of their waking hours in their own huts. During the dark winter months this was unavoidable; curfew was at four-thirty, right after the final roll call, and reveille not until six the following morning. For sanitary reasons doors were not locked, but any POW found wandering around the compound during the curfew hours had to have a damn good reason or be charged with attempting to escape and held twenty-eight days in solitary.

But even in summer months it was always possible to find half a dozen prisoners from each hut lying on their bunks. It was difficult to understand why. Certainly no tunnel-escape bids ever emanated from the huts. They were too far from the wire.

The huts were in rows of five, and each was not much bigger than a large garage. Each housed ten men in two-tiered bunks, a pair against each longitudinal wall and the remaining one against the wall opposite the door. A wood-burning stove occupied the middle of the floor, its chimney going up and out through the roof. This method of heating was far from efficient. Those close to the stove fried and those six feet away froze. Next to the stove was a trestle table and two wooden benches. Beside each bunk was a small locker for personal effects. Lighting was by a single naked bulb hanging from the ceiling. This was controlled from the guardroom and remained lit during the hours of darkness. Blackout material covered the windows.

These were the officers' quarters, and paradoxically the enlisted men fared better. Because they were fewer and because protocol dictated that they should live apart from their superiors, they had been allocated six huts for thirty of them on the south side of the compound. With only five men per hut, each had a two-tiered bunk to himself, and so far as the majority of them were concerned life here was a damn sight better than fighting on the Eastern Front. With the exception of several of the air crew NCOs, none of them had made an escape attempt. What the hell was the point? Apart from farm work in the summer and snow clearing in the winter, here they had nominal duties and were subject to very little military discipline. Over there, they could be killed. It was better to sit tight until the war was over. In the meantime they had their cards and dice, occasionally some poisonous alcohol made from potato peelings on an illicit still, and their pin-ups. Even in the Wehrmacht Betty Grable was popular that year, and a glossy magazine picture of the million-dollar legs was about as close as any of them was going to get to a woman this side of war's end.

Mohr pinched out his cigarette, carefully packed away the stub in his tobacco tin, and pushed open the door of the Mess.

Situated near the southern perimeter wire, but visible from a watchtower, the British had provided the structure and no more: four walls, a roof and a stove. But, as under a reciprocal agreement with the British, captured German officers received two thirds of their active service pay, certain purchases had been made. What could not be bought had been manufactured, and what could not be manufactured had been stolen.

There was a table-tennis table, battered but serviceable, together with half a dozen paddles. Balls were harder to come by, and anyone who broke one with a fierce hit was fined and banned from the table for a month. In consequence, the game was somewhat ladylike. At the moment, Leutnants Peter Kaehler and Johann Preiss were engaged in a match that looked as though it would last until roll call.

Across the Mess, Skiddaw's snooker champion, Oberleutnant Emke, was engaged in making a marathon run on the moth-eaten baize, while his opponent looked on gloomily.

Aged twenty-three and a big bear of a man, Theodor Emke, when not destroying egos and winning cigarette rations, was the camp comic and tall-story teller. Shot down over Hull on his tenth mission as pilot of a Dornier 217, Emke swore by everything he held sacred that, after bailing out and before managing to pull the ripcord of his parachute, he had landed on the tail plane of a Hurricane and ridden it for several miles before being thrown off. He also swore that he had succeeded in buckling the tail fin and that he had last seen the Hurricane spiraling to the ground, out of control. It was his considered opinion that he deserved the Ritterkreuz for being the only member of the Luftwaffe to make a "kill" using biceps alone.

A single-time escaper, Emke was forever coming to the Escape Committee with weird and wonderful ideas for getting out. Whether he was serious or not no one ever ascertained. August's suggestion was for vaulting the barbed wire with a vaulting pole, which he planned to make in the workshop. The latest idea was to construct a hot-air balloon from rifled inner tubes and float out.

But for all his levity, Emke was a great morale booster

and a man of indefatigable courage. There were few in Skiddaw who knew it, but at least twice he had brought home a badly mauled aircraft when the intelligent action would have been to bail out. But this would have entailed leaving injured crew members to their fate, and this Emke had refused to do.

He grinned cheerfully and waved his cue in greeting as Mohr sat down in the armchair he had purchased from the British Mess for six pounds. He had been cheated, he knew; the armchair was heading for the garbage dump before he stepped in. The stuffing was coming out of the sides and a wayward spring made comfort a hazardous business, but it was the only decent chair in the Mess, and he was proud of it.

On the other side of the table Otto Breithaupt was reading a year-old magazine and Fritz Uhde, Leutnant, was writing a letter to his wife.

Dear God, thought Mohr with weary amusement, we look like a bunch of refugees from the soup kitchens.

If that was an exaggeration, certainly the clothing of most of the POWs was a long way from elegance. The emphasis here was on warmth, although in this respect Luftwaffe personnel fared less well than their counterparts in the Army and Navy. Naval officers were generally wearing their heavy woolen sweaters when taken prisoner, and from the highest to the lowest among the Army ranks a greatcoat was usually seen. But in order to be captured at all, a Luftwaffe officer either bailed out or crashed, and his flying suit invariably suffered as a result. Consequently they wore anything they could beg, borrow or steal. The longer a man had been in captivity, the poorer his apparel became. Mohr's was very old.

"How many does that make this week?" he asked Uhde.

"Six." Uhde did not look up from his scribbling.

"But you're only allowed to send out four a month."

"I like to keep ahead. They might change the regulations. Besides, Emke never writes to anyone. I use his quota."

"Don't the censors think it odd, Emke signing his name to endearments to your wife?"

"I never give it a thought."

"And what about your little wife?" put in Breithaupt. "Doesn't she think it strange, receiving protestations of love from a man named Theodor Emke?"

"I never thought of that, either." Uhde frowned. "As a matter of fact, she thinks Emke's letters are better than mine. I can't understand it, seeing as how I write them all."

Mohr chuckled and Breithaupt laughed openly. Uhde had been married a week when shot down over Scotland in 1940. He had celebrated his twenty-first birthday last July and spent most of his waking hours with a pencil in his hand.

Their game at an end, Peter Kaehler and Johann Preiss relinquished the table to other players and strolled across. Inseparable companions since they completed flying training together, they even looked alike, both being slim and blond, and they had their twentieth birthdays within a month of each other earlier in the year. To complete the coincidence, they had been shot down in separate aircraft within hours of each other and arrived at Skiddaw on different trains but the same day.

An only child, Kaehler had lost his parents in one of the first bombing raids of the war, and subsequently he spent his leaves with the Preiss family in Dresden. To no one's surprise, a firm relationship had formed between the young pilot and Johann's sister, and it was taken for granted that he and Hannah Preiss would marry when the war was over. Hannah's letters to her brother were full of solicitous inquiries concerning Peter's health, and Johann often complained lightheartedly that nowadays his sister hardly knew her brother existed.

"Perhaps you can settle an argument for us, Herr Major," said Kaehler.

"Oh God." Breithaupt pulled a long face. "I'll bet this is about medals again."

44

"I don't know why they bother," said Mohr. "The High Command does not award Knight's Crosses for table tennis."

"Perhaps we'll escape one day," said Preiss. "Then you'll see Galland and Kammhuber run for cover."

"Pigs might fly," muttered Mohr. "All right, what's the problem?"

"The problem, Herr Oberleutnant," said Peter Kaehler with mock formality, "is that my idiotic friend here is suffering from *Stacheldrahtkoller*." Mohr smiled to himself at the reference to barbed-wire madness. "In his ignorance, my foolish brother officer suggests that it is necessary to destroy thirteen Lancasters and a Wellington to get the Knight's Cross."

"And you say?"

"I say ten Lancasters and an escort."

"Is there a wager on this?"

"Four Players cigarettes."

"Then pay the man, Leutnant Kaehler. A minimum of forty points are needed for the Knight's Cross. A Lancaster is three points and the twin-motor Wellington two. So if your arithmetic is better than your ability to gamble, you'll find you need thirteen Lancasters and a twin."

"Yes, but—"

"Pay up, Peter."

"And continue this elsewhere, for God's sake," interjected Uhde. "I'm trying to concentrate."

"But Herr Oberleutnant, Franz . . ." protested Kaehler.

Mohr heaved himself to his feet. "Let's leave these two to fight it out among themselves, Otto. I'll play white."

"Done."

Breithaupt set up the chess pieces. Mohr moved P-K4. Breithaupt countered with P-K3.

"The French Defense," muttered Mohr. "No wonder you always lose."

"There's nothing wrong with the strategy. It's just unfortunately named, that's all."

"Yes. I often think the French Defense should comprise

knocking over the king and surrendering before a shot's fired."

Breithaupt laughed. Mohr moved P-Q4.

"Was anything happening outside?" asked Breithaupt.

"Nothing that I could see. Perhaps he's got away with it."

"I'll be more inclined to believe that in another forty-eight hours. If they haven't got him by then I'll think he's in with a chance. Your move."

"You think he's a fool to keep going solo, don't you?"

"Not really. I just wish to God he'd let some of us in on what he plans. For all he knows we could have a major break-out pending. If he went the day before we'd all be in the soup."

"Perhaps so. On the other hand, you can't blame him for keeping himself to himself."

Major Breithaupt studied the board and shook his head.

"I know your theory, but I just can't believe we have an informer amongst us."

"More likely you don't want to believe it."

"No, it's not that."

Mohr eased forward his king's bishop.

"You've got to face facts, Otto. We all have. In the past six months we've had three attempts foiled at the last moment."

"Maybe the British are getting cleverer."

"That's possible but unlikely. I don't underestimate them, believe me, but the bathhouse scheme was too much of a coincidence for me."

"Not at all. It's one of the obvious places to look. Close to the wire, constant to-ing and fro-ing. They'd be fools not to keep an eye on it."

"I'd be more inclined to believe you if they hadn't pounced two days before we planned to go."

"It's logical that they'd leave it so late. Planning escapes keeps us happy, and when we're happy we're not a bloody nuisance. They keep us quiet for a couple of months and jump when we're ready."

46

"Yes, but what bothers me is precisely how they know when we're ready. You're in check, incidentally."

"Damn."

Breithaupt covered the endangered king with his knight. "Your move."

Mohr paid no attention. Breithaupt looked up.

"Your move, Franz."

But Mohr was looking toward the entrance to the Mess. Breithaupt glanced over his shoulder. Captain Thorogood stood in the doorway, his uniform beautifully pressed, his Sam Browne gleaming. He looked like a wealthy patron visiting a workhouse.

"Permission to enter?" he asked in German.

"Permission granted, Herr Hauptmann," answered Theo Emke, who was closest.

Thorogood walked slowly over to where Breithaupt and Mohr were seated. Neither German got to his feet. The adjutant studied the chessboard for a moment.

"Some news for you, Major Breithaupt," he said. "The civilian police have just been on the phone. They've picked up Naumann. He hadn't even got as far as Keswick." Thorogood tapped the table with his cane. "I suppose you chaps will realize sooner or later that there's no way home. One of the advantages of being a wretched little island, as I believe Goering put it. Just thought I'd let you know."

Thorogood turned to leave. He had raised his voice slightly in order that the whole Mess might hear, and there were long faces everywhere. Naumann had been caught before, as had others, but each time they hoped for the best.

"Damn," murmured Breithaupt.

"By the way," called Thorogood from the door, "if you're playing black, Major, you're in trouble. Mate in two."

Breithaupt stared unseeingly at the board.

47

Two

NOVEMBER 15

"The Fuehrer is beside himself!"

Reichsmarschall Goering drummed his thick fingers nervously on the massive desk top and addressed his three senior commanders: Field Marshals Albert Kesselring, known behind his back as Smiling Albert, Hugo Sperrle, and Hans-Jurgen Stumpff. Strictly speaking, Sperrle and Stumpff were not as yet privy to Operation Hammer, but Goering felt he needed all the wise heads he could get.

"I thought he was going to throw one of his fits," the Reichsmarschall went on. "Did I have so little control over my junior generals that they went joy-riding whenever they wished? Hadn't I made it quite clear to Stuerzbecher that combat flying was out? Well, he was guessing there, of course, but as usual it was a damned good guess. Stuerzbecher wasn't shot down over occupied territory, therefore he must have been shot down over the North Sea. And what was he doing over the North Sea when his destination was Amsterdam? The Fuehrer added that it would be better for all of us if Stuerzbecher was

49

dead. Well, gentlemen, we now know that that is not the case."

The three senior officers looked at one another. Kesselring voiced their thoughts.

"You are quite sure of that, Herr Reichsmarschall?"

Goering eyed him with contempt. Good God, would he have summoned them just three days after Stuerzbecher's disappearance if he were certain the man was dead?

"Of course I'm sure. The BBC fliers program announced this afternoon that it had captured, *inter alia,* 'Oberleutnant Stuerzbecher.' "

"*Oberleutnant* Stuerzbecher?" queried Sperrle, the missing general's former commanding officer in the Condor Legion. "How do you know Oberleutnant Stuerzbecher and Generalmajor von Stuerzbecher are one and the same?"

"Because I checked, man, that's how I know. Stuerzbecher, with or without the *von* is not exactly a common or garden name. To be precise we have, or rather had, seven of them on our strength, of which three are *Oberleutnants*. But I had them all investigated, just in case the British had made a mistake in the rank and their Stuerzbecher is not our Stuerzbecher. Two are dead. Two are on the Eastern Front. One is in Norway and the sixth is right here in Berlin. The seventh is Generalmajor von Stuerzbecher. Make no mistake, gentlemen, the officer the British have taken prisoner is our man. The date of his capture and the other details tally with what we know. We also know that he was wearing the uniform of a Luftwaffe *Oberleutnant* when he left the Fuehrerbunker on the eveing of the twelfth."

"But why did he risk using his own name?" asked Stumpff. "As you rightly say, there aren't many Stuerzbechers about and the British must have it on record that a senior officer exists with that name."

"It was probably a chance he had to take," said Kesselring. "Otherwise, how would we know he was in enemy hands? He would realize that the names of captured fliers are broadcast by the BBC and he was hoping we would put two and two together."

"Precisely," intoned Goering. "Though I don't have to tell you what will happen if the British also put two and two together and discover that Oberleutnant Stuerzbecher is really Generalmajor von Stuerzbecher. They'll put him through the mincer. They'll roast his balls until he breaks. And when he breaks so does Operation Hammer—and much else besides."

The silence hung heavily in the room. Outside, it looked as if it might snow. Finally, it was Sperrle who spoke.

"We'll have to get him out."

"Good God, man, do you realize what you're saying?" Goering's voice rose an octave. "It'll be three weeks before we even know which camp he's in. And get him out how? With an airborne division? With the Leibstandarte Adolf Hitler Division? Tell him to walk out the front door, saying he's sorry but he has urgent business in Berlin? You don't know what you're asking."

"There is an alternative." Kesselring studied his fingernails for a moment. "Have him killed. When we know which camp he's in, get a message through to the senior German officer saying that he's a traitor and potential informer and that he's to be executed without delay. I know that Hammer is his brain child and that his death will set us back a year, but I see no other way out. If we can't rescue him we must ensure that he is not in a position to reveal what he knows."

"Out of the question," said Goering. "Apart from other considerations, no airman is going to believe that Stuerzbecher is a traitor. He's a hero, a Knight's Cross holder. They would no more believe him to be capable of a treacherous act than they would me."

"Perhaps," said Sperrle cunningly, "they would not believe Generalmajor von Stuerzbecher to be capable of treason, but about *Oberleutnant* Stuerzbecher, who knows?"

"No," said Goering emphatically. "Good God, Sperrle, you're asking me to pass the death sentence on one of my best officers for the sake of expediency. I won't have it. What are we, barbarians?"

"It's been done before."

"Not in my name. And not now, not ever."

"Then we have to get him out, it's as simple as that."

Goering toyed nervously with a paper knife. Nothing but trouble, these days.

"Hitler will have to be told," he said finally. "I cannot take the responsibility for something of this magnitude on my own shoulders."

Kesselring was astonished. "You mean the Fuehrer doesn't know?"

"Not about Stuerzbecher being alive, no. The Fuehrer has more to do than listen to the BBC."

The three field marshals exchanged glances, each hoping that Goering was not about to ask one, or all three, of them to accompany him. This was one meeting they felt readily able to miss.

"I don't envy you, Herr Reichsmarschall," said Sperrle eventually. "I don't envy you one bit."

The meeting between Hitler, Martin Bormann, Hitler's Deputy, and Reichsmarschall Goering took place in the Chancellery on the evening of the fifteenth of November 1942. No stenographer was present and no records were kept.

It lasted fewer than ten minutes, and for once Hitler was almost reasonable. He accepted Goering's hypothesis that Generalmajor von Stuerzbecher and Oberleutnant Stuerzbecher were one and the same, and that at least removed the uncertainty from the situation. Stuerzbecher was alive, Stuerzbecher was needed in the Reich; it was just a question of strategy.

He peered over the spectacles he wore only in the presence of his senior commanders and confidantes.

"This is not the happiest of affairs, my dear Reichsmarschall, but wishing matters were different will not alter the facts. Tell me, is Stuerzbecher reliable?"

"Completely."

"Then we need have no fear that he will be loose-tongued."

Goering hesitated too long. Hitler pounced.

"We do have such a fear?"

"Not as long as he is accepted as a mere *Oberleutnant*. But if it were thought otherwise . . . There are drugs. . . ."

Hitler dismissed the suggestion with an airy wave of his hand.

"The British do not use such methods. However, it would be inadvisable to leave him in their hands for too long. You have considered the alternative to rescue, I suppose?"

"Yes."

"And rejected it, I can see that. Well, you know your own business best."

"If I may make a suggestion, Fuehrer," put in Reichsleiter Bormann.

"Please do."

"The Luftwaffe is not competent to organize a rescue attempt. By definition its sphere of influence is the air. This will undoubtedly require something more subtle than five hundred bombers. It might be advisable for the Reichsmarschall to consult Reichsfuehrer Himmler."

Goering glared at the Deputy Leader with something akin to hatred. The bastard. As Bormann well knew, there was no love lost between himself and Himmler.

"With due respect, Fuehrer—" But Hitler cut him off.

"No, I think Bormann's idea is an excellent one. Himmler is undoubtedly the man to see. And I suggest you do it quickly."

It was both a dismissal and an order. There was no arguing with Hitler when his mind was made up.

"It will be done immediately."

"I sometimes wonder about the Reichsmarschall," said Bormann after Goering had left the room.

53

"Then don't. Perhaps he is not the man in adversity he once was, but he is still someone I prefer to have with me than against me."

"Of course."

Reichsfuehrer-SS Heinrich Himmler was unavailable until much later that same evening, but by eleven-thirty he knew the whole story. By eleven forty-five Goering had gone and Himmler was fastidiously rinsing the Reichsmarschall's herb-tea glass. The niceties were observed even among sworn enemies.

Making himself comfortable in front of an open fire, Himmler smiled behind his thick glasses. This was a real bonus, Goering coming cap in hand after being instrumental in excluding the SS from the Hammer conference in the Fuehrerbunker. That his exclusion had been the fat Reichsmarschall's work he had no doubt. But now the boot was on the other foot. If the SS could rescue one of Goering's generals, what a pill that would be for the overweight buffoon to swallow.

The only real question was, should he involve the SS? They were not trained for a commando operation, which was what snatching von Stuerzbecher would involve. A small force, probably three or four men. No more.

There was also the question of failure to be considered. No one had ever succeeded in escaping from Britain and getting home. The odds were therefore against it this time. On the other hand, it would be as well to be involved somewhere along the line. If it came off, he would take the credit. If it failed, someone else could shoulder the blame.

The decision taken, he walked quickly to his desk and picked up the telephone.

"Find Standartenfuehrer Weil and send him to me immediately," he ordered.

Three

NOVEMBER 15

It was just after 4:30 P.M. when Oberleutnant Emil Naumann was returned to Skiddaw Camp under guard. The Military Police had planned to hustle him quickly through the gates and into the guardroom before a demonstration could take place, but the timing of the closed one-tonner's arrival was unfortunate. The last roll call of the day took roughly half an hour, beginning at four, and the last of the POWs had just answered his name. Roll calls, special or otherwise, were held in the Pig Pen, which was at the western end of the compound, in full view of the guardroom and administration offices. There was therefore no chance that Naumann's return would pass unnoticed.

Theo Emke was among the first to spot him, and within seconds a roar went up and ranks were broken as more than two hundred prisoners surged forward to slap Naumann on the back. He looked exhausted, but he was grinning broadly.

Finally the MPs beat a path to the guardroom door, but not before two of them, in the jostling, had lost their caps, two their cigarettes, and one a brand-new lighter fashioned out of gun metal.

Before he disappeared Naumann clasped his hands in the air in the manner of a victorious prizefighter. "Don't try the hills, it's too bloody cold."

Gradually the compound emptied, though not all the POWs went back to their huts. Keeping well within the shadows to avoid the watchtower searchlights, Obergefreiter Willi Braune and Unteroffizier Hans Geith made for the boiler room in the southern sector of the camp. Each had a pilfered packet of cigarettes tucked inside his battle-dress blouse, but Willi had kept the lighter for himself. They usually worked as a team. Braune would swipe whatever was going and quickly slip the stolen goods to Geith. Later they would split the booty, fifty-fifty.

In the British Army there is no exact equivalent to the Wehrmacht ranks of *Unteroffizier* and *Obergefreiter,* but roughly one is a lance sergeant and the other a corporal first class. Thus Geith marginally outranked Braune and as such had wangled the job of orderly to Major Breithaupt. Willi was Oberleutnant Mohr's orderly, and the two NCOs were virtually inseparable. They didn't quarrel often, but when they did it was over a woman, and the same woman at that.

During a leave taken together early in the war in Berlin, they both fell for the same girl, Lotti Kreipe. Lotti was blond, bubbly, eighteen, and a barmaid in a middle-bracket hotel. She was also a first-class prick-teaser. Now they were POWs she wrote to them both regularly but never at the same time. Thus when one had a letter, the other did not.

A *Schusterjunge,* a Berlin street urchin, throughout most of his childhood and adolescence, Willi Braune was what the Germans call *dreikäsehoch* ("three cheeses high"). In other words, very short. Early deprivation showed in every line of his workhouse-brat's face, but like most poor and underprivileged children he had learned the art of survival almost before he could walk. There was nothing Willi could not scrounge or steal if he put his mind to it, which was the one reason Oberleutnant Mohr prized him as an orderly. There could scarcely be another. Willi's coffee tasted like paint stripper and cleaning a pair of boots was beyond him. But whatever the German Mess was low on, Willi would provide. As a thief he was incomparable.

Twenty years of age now, he had been captured in the Australian push on Tobruk in 1941. Although a POW for almost two years, he had no desire to get back into the fray.

By way of contrast, Hans Geith talked of little else but escape, though talking was as far as his schemes got. In his imagination he saw himself leading a daring breakout and returning triumphantly to Berlin, where his heroism would be rewarded by Lotti in bed.

In his more rational moments, however, he realized that being a prisoner was a whole lot better than shivering in some freezing fox hole under a barrage of enemy mortars. POW for a year less, Hans Geith was a strapping five feet eleven with the physique of a light-heavyweight boxer. Add to this his Nordic good looks and an easy manner with women and it might well be asked why Lotti Kreipe had difficulty in making up her mind. But this was to do an injustice to Willi's quick mind and indefatigable sense of fun. A Valentino he was not, but women were never bored in his company.

Glancing quickly over his shoulder to make sure they were not under observation, Willi pushed open the boiler-room door. With Hans at his heels like a faithful retriever, he ducked inside and locked the door by the simple device of jamming a length of iron bar under the handle.

Lance Corporal Harry Cade was already there, sitting on an upturned tea chest, swigging a bottle of beer. In front of him, covered with an army blanket, two more tea chests served as a makeshift table, a candle flickering at either end. A jug of hot coffee bubbled noisily on top of the furnace. On a cold November evening in the Lake District, there could hardly be a better hideaway.

57

"You buggers are late," said Cade.

After two years and one year respectively in POW camps, neither Willi nor Hans had much difficulty in understanding or speaking basic English.

"Sorry, Harry," said Willi. "Some trouble at the guardroom." He looked around at the seating arrangements. As well as the chest Cade was sitting on, three others had been set up. "Who is the fourth?"

"Harpo Cook. He'll be along later." Cade fished around at his feet and produced two full bottles of beer. "Three bob each."

"They were two shillings last week," protested Hans.

"There's a war on, mate. Besides, I had to give a couple to the duty corporal so I'm already out of pocket. Three bob or you drink coffee."

Willi paid for both of them. It didn't matter. Harry Cade was a lousy card player and he'd have the six shillings and more back before the evening closed.

"We'll play just the three of us until Harpo arrives?"

"Sure. Cut for deal."

Across the compound in Hut 9 it was freezing. Compared with the luxury currently being enjoyed by Willi Braune and Hans Geith, the officers' conditions in this hut were miserable. The stove had gone on the blink again, spewing out puffs of black, evil-smelling smoke. There was nothing to be done with the offending flue until the following morning, and it was a question of either shivering or choking to death. The residents had opted for the cold.

Oberleutnant Theo Emke had gone to bed, as had most of the others. Fully clothed from head to foot and wearing a balaclava helmet and woolen gloves, Emke was trying to read and keep warm at the same time. The book was *A Farewell to Arms* by Hemingway, one of the volumes permitted by the camp authorities. It was well thumbed and in French, and Emke was having trouble with some of the sentences. But he was determined to plow on. Tomorrow it had to be returned to Oberleutnant Herburg, the camp librarian, and Emke was not due another volume for ten days.

At one end of the trestle-table, also muffled to the gills, Peter Kaehler and Johann Preiss were arguing the relative merits of the Messerschmitt Bf 109Es and the Spitfire. Kaehler was for the Spitfire, Preiss for the Me, and both were getting on Major Breithaupt's nerves.

"Will you two kindly keep it down?" he snapped from the other end of the table.

Huddled in a whispered conversation with Franz Mohr, Breithaupt was unusually edgy. But Naumann's recapture had depressed him. Besides, he was an outsider in Hut 9. By rights, after curfew, he should have been tucked up in his own quarters, Hut 5. It only meant a snap check by a bad-tempered guard for him to be in trouble.

"So, twenty-eight more days in the cooler for Emil," said Mohr. "Frankly, I don't know how he stands it."

"He's tough," said Breithaupt. "No criticism intended."

"And none taken. I freely admit I couldn't take another term of solitary. For me it's either all the way home next time or a bullet in the head."

"That's foolish talk, Franz. Let's put it down to tiredness."

"As you wish."

Franz Mohr lit his penultimate cigarette of the day. Quite true, he was tired. Perhaps tomorrow he'd see things differently.

"The trouble with Naumann being in the cooler right now," said Breithaupt, "is that he won't be in circulation again until December 14 or 15. If we're to make our attempt on the twelfth as planned, it would have been helpful to know what conditions are like on the outside."

"We're still going, then—regardless of what the weather does?"

"Of course we are. Everything is set for that day. Why, you're not thinking of backing out, are you?"

Mohr smiled and shrugged his shoulders. "I doubt it.

59

Anyway, we're no worse off, Naumann being recaptured. If he had got clean away we'd still be in the dark."

"True enough. But I'd still like to have spoken to him."

"Perhaps we'll get lucky, Otto. Perhaps Mitchell will be feeling in a benevolent mood and let young Naumann off with a caution."

"And perhaps Reichsmarschall Goering will send us all a box of cigars for Christmas."

Seated in his office, sucking thoughtfully at an unlit pipe, Major David Mitchell, M. C., was feeling anything but benevolent. He was normally a mild-mannered individual, but the combination of the pain in his left leg and the business of Naumann had brought on a fit of irritability that he was finding difficult to shake. The pain was the result of a wound suffered at Dunkirk, which had rendered him unfit for active service, a fact that pleased his wife no end. He had done his bit, she was fond of telling him; the ribbon on his breast proved it. If he had to spend the remainder of the war as a policeman, that was fine with her. In his more rational moments he could see her point of view and accept it. She had no wish to become a widow or have to tell their two children that they were now fatherless. She had married an accountant, not a soldier. The sooner he could get back to his civilian profession, the better she would like it.

David Mitchell sighed deeply and audibly. Which was all very well for her. Somewhere along the line she had got the idea that all he did every day was count heads and keep the gates locked. But there was a damned sight more to it than that.

"Well, sir?"

Mitchell became aware that Captain Thorogood was still awaiting an answer to his last question. Perched on the edge of a chair on the opposite side of the desk, the adjutant tapped the floor impatiently with his cane.

"In a minute, Adrian. Let me think about it."

A rangy, bespectacled man in his middle thirties, David Mitchell knew that he was regarded as soft by many of the officers and men, not least among them Adrian Thorogood. Perhaps they were right. No doubt he did see his role more as a keeper of the peace than as a winged nemesis, though maybe that would have to change. The camp's record for escapes and attempted escapes was a poor one. Not worse than a lot of others but nowhere near the best. Not altogether his fault, however. It seemed to him that when the transfer of the overspill POWs from Grizedale Hall took place, the C.O. there had seized the opportunity to get rid of most of the bad hats in one fell swoop. After that, it snowballed. Skiddaw became known as the camp where the regular escapers were incarcerated and so anyone with a bad record was sent there.

"Look, sir." Thorogood decided he'd have to force the pace or the matter would never be resolved. "What it amounts to is this. If you sentence Naumann tonight, his spell in the cooler begins from today. If you let him sweat it out in the guardroom until tomorrow, we get an extra day out of him. God knows, the way he carries on he'll be escaping again before Christmas in any case."

"Not strictly within the rules, Adrian. Habeas corpus and all that."

"*Rules*, sir." Adrian Thorogood raised his eyes to the ceiling. "Do you think the Nazis obey the rules when one of our chaps goes over the wire? Not likely. He'd be lucky not to face a firing squad."

"The Germans signed the Geneva Convention just as we did—before we did, as a matter of fact—and the Convention clearly states that twenty-eight days' solitary confinement is the punishment for an escape attempt. Not twenty-nine days, note. And I do wish you wouldn't call them Nazis. It's inaccurate. Not every German belongs to the Party."

"Every officer in this camp took an oath of loyalty to Hitler and in my book that makes them Nazis."

"Technically, perhaps. But our men take an oath of loyalty to the King, yet I can name you half a dozen individuals right off the cuff who are antiroyalist."

Thorogood groaned inwardly. What the hell was the

matter with the man? At this very moment there were British soldiers, sailors and airmen being blown to smithereens and this old duffer was worried about the bloody rules.

Not yet having attained his twenty-seventh birthday, Adrian Thorogood felt well within his rights to think of his C.O. as old and a duffer. Although they wore the same uniform and Thorogood too had the purple and white ribbon of the Military Cross sewn to his left breast, there the resemblance between the two officers ended. Mitchell was glad to be out of the firing line and Thorogood could not wait to get back in. He regarded his posting to Skiddaw with distaste, but he was determined to perform his duties efficiently until the brass concluded he was better suited as officer in command of a rifle company.

Although his dark good looks and fancy name seemed to indicate an upper class background, Adrian Thorogood was far removed from that. The son of a plumber and a chambermaid, he was christened Adrian because his mother, an incurable romantic, had read the name in a magazine story during her confinement. Tougher than she looked, she dug in her heels and argued her husband out of Frank and William. The name caused Thorogood a lot of trouble in his grammar school and was partly the reason he was so handy with his fists. But even the schoolboy scrapping paid dividends. For two years running he won the regimental boxing championship as a middleweight.

Before the war he had worked as a clerk to a jobbing builder, but he seized the outbreak of hostilities as the perfect opportunity to get out of the rut. No sooner did he complete his basic training than he applied for a commission. To his great delight he was accepted and proved to be a natural. His plan now was to make the Army his career, but he was bright enough to realize that a lot of working-class lads who had stepped a couple of rungs up the ladder would have the same idea. The ones who made it would have a good record behind them. His decoration was a start, as was his fluency in German, but he knew that everything an officer does is taken note of and follows him around for the rest of his days. It was therefore no earthly use lamenting his stint at Skiddaw. It had to be done and done well until a better opportunity appeared.

He got to his feet. "Then I'm to take it, sir, that you wish to see Oberleutnant Naumann right away?"

"You are, Adrian, but before you go I should like to remind you of one or two things. The first is that not only am I commandant of this camp, I am also your senior officer. You sometimes seem to forget it. The second is that while I appreciate your war record to date and your ambition, the way to get on in the Army—in life, for that matter—is to heed the rules, in spite of your dislike of the word. They were designed by men much wiser than either of us. Thirdly, and lastly, it is what I write on your service sheet that helps or hinders your promotion chances. It's worth bearing in mind. Now I'll see Oberleutnant Naumann."

Flushing at the reprimand, Captain Thorogood donned his cap, saluted and went out.

Alone in his cell in the guardroom but aware that he was being watched carefully in case he suddenly sprouted wings and flew out, Oberleutnant Emil Naumann rubbed his kidneys gingerly. He had taken a dozen punches and knew he'd be pissing blood for a week. Not from the MPs, whose only concern had been to get him off their hands as quickly as possible, but from Corporal Napley. Napley was a very bribable man and terrified that his blind eye to the escape would be discovered and punished. The beating was to remind Naumann what else could happen if he opened his mouth. As if he would. There were few enough corrupt individuals in Skiddaw without losing one to a military prison.

Although normally a good-looking youngster, Emil Naumann was showing signs of wear and tear after a night in the open and thirty-six hours without a shave. Even so, his was the sort of character that took adversity in stride.

The *Tommis* might put him down but he wouldn't stay down for long.

On the other side of the bars James Napley, duty corporal, was indeed a worried man, and it was starting to show. A Londoner born and bred, he possessed the sort of greasy handsomeness that made him popular with certain types of women. Too much so, in fact. Five years earlier at the age of seventeen, with three burly brothers threatening all manner of mayhem unless he did the honorable thing, he married the young girl who was expecting his child. The marriage didn't last twelve months, but neither he nor his estranged wife had bothered about a divorce. Which was something he had omitted to tell the Carlisle girl with whom he had undergone an identical ceremony during the first days of October. And now his new wife was champing at the bit, wanting to go to London with him and "meet the family" on his next leave.

Jesus Christ, it never rained but it poured. First the wife and now this bastard German getting caught. Well, he could only hope that those digs in the kidneys had been taken to heart.

Corporal Napley's bribe-taking normally involved small items. Money for keeping his eyes shut while somebody swiped a hammer and some nails; a quid for not reporting a German officer caught red-handed in the wrong hut after curfew; a little black-marketeering on the side—coffee, eggs, whatever the bastards wanted and could pay for. But nothing of the magnitude of, when gate NCO, waving Emil Naumann through when he knew full well Naumann was not the workman he purported to be. Twenty pounds in notes that had earned him, and it had seemed like easy money at the time. A rocket from that bastard Thorogood, sure, but nothing more. And now Naumann had got his bloody stupid self caught again.

"Corporal Napley!"

The guardroom rocketed to attention as Captain Thorogood burst in. Napley was the last to get to his feet. Christ, pull yourself together.

64

"Sir!"

"Get the prisoner over to the C.O.'s office at the double."

"Very good, sir. You, you and you." Napley stabbed a forefinger at the nearest three soldiers. "Get fell in."

Napley unlocked the door to the cell.

"All right, Sunshine, let's go."

Although it was against regulations for other ranks to address captured officers in such a manner, Naumann had spent enough time in this particular guardroom to realize that protest was useless. It was a fact of life that some British soldiers, like some German soldiers, were ill-bred.

He grinned impudently. Christ, thought Napley, he's going to blow the gaff. Very close to Naumann he whispered: "One word out of you, mate, and I'm going to see you buried." To add emphasis, he punctuated the threat with a push in the back.

It was Naumann's fatal error to object to being treated like a pig in a pen. He whipped round on Napley and struck him openhanded across the face.

"You will not touch me," he snarled. "You will never lay your hands on me again."

And then things happened so fast that even at the inquiry later there were arguments over the exact sequence of events. Some witnesses swore that Corporal Napley stood his ground and did nothing. Others were equally convinced that he jabbed Naumann with his rifle and that to get out of the way the German officer ran for the door. In either case, the next thing anyone could recall with any clarity was Naumann outside the guardroom and Napley at the door, swearing he would shoot if Naumann did not stand absolutely still. Yet a third group of witnesses were convinced that Naumann, with nothing to look forward to save twenty-eight days in solitary, was having a last bit of fun at Napley's expense. But the ones who supported the duty corporal's version of the incident vowed that Naumann was making for the gates.

Whatever the facts, no one was in any doubt regarding

what happened next. Napley shouted "Halt or I shoot." And Naumann didn't halt. In the relative quiet of the postcurfew compound, the shot from the Lee-Enfield was deafening. Naumann fell to the ground, most of his face blown away.

The shot was heard as far away as Hut 9, where Major Breithaupt was preparing to return to his own quarters. It was followed by a fusillade from the northeast as a nervous watchtower guard fired at shadows. After a moment's stunned silence, Peter Kaehler made for the door.

"Sit down, you bloody young fool," rasped Franz Mohr. "They'll shoot at anything that moves."

The volley was heard in the boiler room, where Lance Corporal Cade had just taken a hammering from Willi Braune for the third time running.

"What the bloody hell—" began Cade, knocking over a couple of empty bottles in his haste to get to the door.

But Willi was wiser. "If you go out there, my friend, you might have to answer a lot of awkward questions."

It was heard in the C.O.'s office, where Major Mitchell was rehearsing his set speech. Later he was never quite sure how he knew, but he was not surprised when Adrian Thorogood rushed in to tell him Naumann was dead.

They buried the young *Oberleutnant* the following day. In war there is no time for decent intervals between death and interment. For the German POWs, a sad collection in their old and battered clothes, it was the supreme irony that one of the most decorated officers in the Luftwaffe, veteran of a thousand dogfights, should be shot down while unarmed by a trigger-happy *Tommi*. But they accepted Major Mitchell's explanation, given in person to the senior men, that the whole affair had been a ghastly accident. Mitchell might be their warder-in-chief but they knew him to be an honorable man. It was just another tragedy in a war full of tragedies.

Mitchell himself was not quite sure about his personal honor. In the hastily constituted inquiry the morning after

66

Naumann's death, there was not enough evidence to suggest that the shooting had been deliberate or malicious. Especially as Corporal Napley found a strange ally in Adrian Thorogood, who professed to have seen most of the incident and what else could the corporal do? Though if Mitchell had overheard the conversation which took place later between his adjutant and Napley, he might have been more concerned.

"I'm not against shooting Jerries, Napley, and I'm certainly not going to have a British soldier court-martialed for doing so. Perhaps if we shot a few more of the buggers the war would be over a damn sight quicker. But I find it odd that it was not only you who pulled the trigger, it was also you who allowed Naumann to escape. So just bear it in mind that I'm not a fool."

The final act was for the C.O. to send the papers to Division with the recommendation that no further action be taken. Forty-eight hours later the matter was history.

Four

Christian Eicke awoke slowly, every muscle in his body
aching. His mouth tasted like the innards of an old boot.
Cautiously he opened his eyes. He was in a cell, no doubt
about it. Even if, in the half-light, he could barely see the
heavy iron door with the grille in it, there was no mistaking the fetid smell of prison. But why? And much more to
the point, where?

He tried sitting up and made it at the second attempt.
But the effort proved too much for his stomach and he just
made the latrine bucket before puking.

He felt a little better after that. Perching himself on the
edge of the planks that served as a bed, he fished in his
tunic pockets for a packet of crumpled cigarettes. With the
cigarette alight, he made his mind a blank, knowing from
past experience that it was useless to make a conscious
effort at recall, that the events of the previous night would
percolate through in their own time.

Unless he had done something completely idiotic, he
was still in Cologne, a very bad place to be, what with the
Tommis bombing the shit out of it at regular intervals.

69

Early in the evening he had gone out and started hitting the bars. By nine, with no food inside him, he was three parts drunk. It was around then that he got into the argument about the camps.

"We Germans are a civilized race. The camps are Allied propaganda."

"You haven't been east. I have. I've seen them."

"You're drunk, Oberleutnant."

"Probably."

Later on he had picked up a little blond *Fräulein*—a *Fräulein* who turned out to be a *Frau*. Though maybe she had told him she was married and he had been too drunk to care. Either way, to the best of his recollection, her husband had chosen to arrive home at an inopportune moment, while the blonde's heels were drumming a tattoo on Christian's back. The fight hadn't lasted more than a couple of punches. The husband opted for discretion when he realized that Christian, drunk as he was, was much younger and decidedly stronger. But he returned half an hour later with three bully boys in tow. And that was that. Christian thought he remembered hitting the street in an untidy heap, but the rest was a blank.

He touched his ribs gingerly. They hadn't settled for just tossing him out. They had made sure he stayed out by kicking him.

He got to his feet, doused the cigarette, and hammered on the cell door. His wrist watch had stopped at twenty minutes after midnight, but he judged, from the muted sounds he could hear, that it was early morning and the prison was coming alive.

Finally, after five minutes' banging, the grille was pulled open and the face and shoulders of a young *Gefreiter* appeared.

"Yes, Herr Oberleutnant?"

"Never mind yes. Let me out of here."

"I regret that is not possible."

"It had better be. If this door isn't open in ten seconds you'll be spending the rest of the war in Russia."

"I have my orders. If the Oberleutnant will be good enough to wait." The *Gefreiter* started to close the grille.

"Hold it." The youngster studied Christian patiently. "Look, I'm sorry. Forget about the threats. Put them down to a hangover. But I have to get out of here."

"I understand that, Oberleutnant. But until my orders are changed I can't release you."

"Okay, go and get them changed. Where am I incidentally, civilian or military lock-up?"

In spite of the *Gefreiter*'s uniform, it was not impossible for Christian to be in a civilian prison. But he was relieved when he was given the name of the barracks.

"Bring some coffee back with you."

Christian returned to the plank bed. Being in a military prison wasn't too bad. He could easily have been picked up by the Gestapo or the Kripo, and that wouldn't have been funny at all. Mind you, he told himself, don't go hoisting the flags too soon. The OKW doesn't welcome its officers being picked up in a bloodied, drunken heap.

It was ten minutes before he heard the sound of feet in the corridor and the rattle of keys. The door swung open and the *Gefreiter* came in, carrying a wooden platter containing some black bread and cheese and a large mug of coffee. Behind him stood a *Hauptmann* wearing the white *Waffenfarbe* and the letter *L,* which designated an Infantry training regiment. His uniform was so immaculate that it must never, surely, have been anywhere near a battle. Crumpled, unwashed and unshaven as he was, Christian felt a moment of shame.

The *Gefreiter* placed the coffee and cheese on the bed and retreated. Christian seized the mug and drank half the contents in one swallow. The *Hauptmann* stepped forward again and sniffed distastefully. Christian eyed him over the rim of the mug.

"Oberleutnant Eicke?" Christian nodded at the inane question. "Hauptmann Westerhoff. It's customary to get to one's feet when a senior officer enters the room."

"Add it to the charges."

71

"We'll see about that later. In the meantime, kindly finish your coffee quickly and get cleaned up. Gefreiter Wecke will show you where. He'll bring you to me when you're respectable. You are, of course, to consider yourself under open arrest."

"Of course."

Hauptmann Westerhoff clicked his heels and went out.

"Is he always that efficient this early in the morning?" Christian asked Gefreiter Wecke. "What in God's name is the time, anyway?"

"It's twenty-five minutes to seven, sir. And if you'll forgive me I think it would be wise to make a move. Hauptmann Westerhoff does not like to be kept waiting."

"Too goddam bad for Hauptmann Westerhoff," said Christian, but he finished his coffee in a single mouthful and followed the NCO to the washroom.

Shaving kit, soap and a towel, together with toothpaste and a toothbrush, had been laid out for him. A shower and a change of uniform would have made him feel as good as new. Even so, after fifteen minutes' scrubbing, scrapping and brushing, he was ready to face whatever lay ahead.

"Okay," he said, "lead on."

Gefreiter Wecke preceded him along a series of passages before stopping in front of an unmarked door. He knocked timidly. "Good luck, sir."

Christian went inside, closing the door behind him. Hauptmann Westerhoff was behind the desk, smoking a foul-smelling French cigarette in a holder. Feeling less surly now, Christian stood loosely at attention until summoned closer and instructed to sit down. Hauptmann Westerhoff studied him closely.

He didn't look like much, this Oberleutnant Eicke. He didn't even look German. More like Irish with that dark curly hair and almost black eyes. His papers gave his age as twenty-five, but that was either a mistake or he had had a lot of nights like last night. Closer to thirty would have been Hauptmann Westerhoff's guess, though the external evidence of the fight, the bruised cheekbone and cut upper lip, could have had something to do with that.

Christian waited as long as he thought necessary before asking, "What are the charges?"

"Insubordination will be another one unless I start hearing Herr Hauptmann at the end of such questions."

Casually, Christian fumbled in his breast pocket for the Knight's Cross. He rarely wore it where it should be worn, around his neck, but he frequently found its display useful in getting him off the hook.

Hauptmann Westerhoff goggled at it. The Ritterkreuz, this oaf? Good God.

There was no further mention of insubordination, and his tone contained a little more respect as he read from a document in front of him.

"Let's see. The lady's husband is an *Oberst,* so we can begin with assaulting a senior, very senior, officer. Of the three men who . . . helped . . . you into the street, one has a fractured jaw, another a couple of cracked ribs, and the third cannot see this morning out of either eye. Then there's the drunkenness in a public place, the obscene language, and the stealing of a military vehicle."

"The *what?*"

"While the Military Police who picked you up dusted themselves off—you gave them trouble as well, by the way—you snatched the keys of their vehicle and drove away. You were singing '*Stille Nacht, Heilige Nacht.*' A little early for Christmas carols, I would have thought. You'd probably still be going if you hadn't rammed a street lamp."

"Jesus Christ."

"When they caught up with you, you—"

"No more," groaned Christian. "They'll throw the book at me."

"I'm afraid the book isn't big enough, Eicke," said Westerhoff. "You're a one-man Panzer division. There are things you've done that aren't even in the wretched book." He returned the document to the desk. "But no one's going to throw anything at you."

"I don't understand."

"No more do I." Westerhoff smacked his lips in disap-

73

proval. "But those are my instructions. I got in touch with your unit when you were brought in and was ordered to put you on the first plane for Berlin. You have friends in high places evidently."

"Not that I know of," said Christian, unable to believe his luck.

"Nevertheless, no one is pressing charges. Your bags have been packed and are waiting for you, together with your orders, at the aircraft. If I were you, I'd get on my way before someone changes his mind."

Utterly bewildered, Christian stood up and made for the door. From behind him, despairing of ever receiving a salute or any other form of recognized courtesy from this officer, Westerhoff called out: "Also if I were you, Oberleutnant, I'd take time out to get myself a bath. Really, you smell quite appalling."

The orders were unequivocal. Oberleutnant Eicke was to present himself to SS Standartenfeuhrer Weil in Berlin on November 18, 1942, at 4:30 in the afternoon. Which puzzled Christian even more. What the hell did the SS want with him? Unless in shooting off his big fat drunken mouth last evening on the subject of the camps he had been overheard. Those bloody camps—would he never be rid of them?

He remembered vividly that day on the Eastern Front. A bright, sunny afternoon, full of hope. The vanguard of the division had outstripped its supply lines and dug in, consolidating the position. There wasn't much activity from the Ivans, and Obersturmbannfuehrer Hoess had said: "Come on, Christian. Let's go and wangle some tea."

They drove seventy or eighty kilometers before reaching the camp. It seemed much like the others he had seen except that it was more heavily guarded, and the inmates, mainly Slavs and Polish and Russian Jews, were more undernourished. There was also a peculiar, not entirely unpleasant, smell he couldn't put a name to.

The commandant was an old friend of Hoess's and they took wine and cake in his pretty little house far away from the main compound. The commandant's wife was the perfect hostess, keeping the conversation general and flowing. With the wine beautifully cool and the cake delicious, the war seemed a long way off.

"Goebbels appears to think the Russians will be crushed before winter," remarked the commandant, when the talk finally got around to the fighting.

"Don't believe everything you read in the *Voelkischer Beobachter*," said Hoess. "I sometimes think Goebbels isn't talking about the same war the rest of us are in. We take a beating up front and Old Clubfoot turns it into a magnificent victory."

"I should have you shot for treason," grinned the commandant.

"Save your bullets. Let the Ivans use theirs."

"You sound fatalistic, Erich," said the commandant's wife.

"Realistic. Neither Christian nor I expect to survive the year. No matter what you read, casualties are reaching an unacceptable level."

"Is that true, Herr Sturmbannfuehrer?" Christian was asked.

"It's an opinion, anyway," he answered, "and one a lot of us subscribe to. The Ivan is far tougher than we were led to believe, and Russia is a massive country. Even if we beat them on the ground, an occupying army would find it enormously difficult to administer such a vast territory. I think it was Nicholas the First who said he had two generals in whom he could confide—Generals January and February. We're going flat out, but unless we make even better progress the weather will beat us if the Ivans don't."

"Dear me," tutted the commandant, "more treasonable speeches. I'm getting very worried about the SS."

The talk drifted to other topics, and then it was time to go.

75

"I'd show you around," said the commandant, "but I'm afraid I have work to do. However, if I can grab hold of a junior officer—"

"No, no," said Hoess hastily. "I've seen it all before, and I don't think I need a repeat performance."

They thanked their host and hostess and took their leave. Traveling back toward the main gates in the staff car, Christian suddenly pointed.

"Good God, look at that."

Two guards were systematically beating a young girl, obviously Jewish. She couldn't have been more than fifteen, and they were belaboring her with fists and boots, ignoring her screams, trying to get her to join a long queue of other inmates who were apparently awaiting their turn in the showers. A wizened old man, possibly a relative, looked on helplessly.

"Stop the car," ordered Christian, and he was out before Hoess could stop him.

Angrily he strode over to the guards, pushing them to one side. He held out a hand to the girl. She cowered before him, her eyes filled with terror.

"Come on," he said, "no one's going to harm you." But the girl remained transfixed. Christian turned on the guards. "I ought to have you shot. You're a disgrace to the uniform you wear."

Neither guard was much impressed by Christian's rank or his anger.

"We are merely doing our duty, Herr Sturmbannfuehrer. The girl cannot work. She has sickness in her lungs. She must go with the others."

"Go where?"

For the first time Christian saw that the shower queue consisted mostly of the very old and the very young. The few in-betweens looked ill.

"Go where?"

The guards exchanged glances. Was it possible that this SS major was as ignorant as he appeared?

"For the love of God, Christian," called Hoess, "get back in the car."

Hoess's shouting triggered some response in the girl. She began to cry and sobbed something in a tongue Christian did not understand.

"What is it, girl? Do you speak German?"

"She says that she is going to be killed and that she does not wish to die," murmured the old man.

"Killed? What d'you mean, killed? From the disease in her lungs? Is it tuberculosis? They have doctors here."

"Ah yes, doctors," said the old man.

"For Christ's sake, Herr Sturmbannfuehrer," screamed Hoess, "get back in this damned car! That's an order!"

Confused, realizing he had walked into a situation that was beyond him, Christian returned to the car. It moved off immediately. Looking over his shoulder he saw the girl being pushed into line. She had stopped struggling.

"You'll have us both up against a wall," barked Hoess, red-faced with anger. "This is a *Vernichtungslager.*"

Christian sat stunned. *Vernichtungslager.* Extermination camp. He had heard rumors of such places but had put it down to propaganda. But it was true, all true. The commandant and his pretty wife, with their cold Rhine wine and home-baked cakes, were overseers of death. The meaning of the sickly sweet smell he had been unable to identify became clear.

That same afternoon, after drinking a bottle of brandy, he was placed under close arrest for attempting to strike a superior officer.

And so on, thought Christian, as the aircraft crossed the river north of Magdeburg. One bottle of brandy had led to another and another. But it would be dishonest to say that his heavy drinking was still the fault of what he had seen in the east. That may have started it, but now he enjoyed the habit for its own sake. He was sliding down the slippery path to alcoholism and he couldn't get off. He needed something to force him off, but he didn't know what.

At precisely 4:30 P.M. Christian was ushered into the *Standartenfuehrer*'s office, though really, pulling rank, Weil had turned it into more of a sitting room. It contained

77

a desk and filing cabinets, but they were almost out of place. Drawn up on either side of an open fire were two high-backed leather armchairs. Between the armchairs a small table held a silver coffee service and china cups and saucers. Beside the tray was a bottle of French brandy and two goblets. It was hard to believe that this was Berlin and that outside they were still clearing up the dead and dousing the fires from last night's raid.

Seated in the chair facing the door, Weil barely glanced up from the papers on his knee when Christian came in. In looks he was not unlike his chief, Reichsfuehrer Himmler: the same close-cropped head, the same thick spectacles through which he peered myopically. On the wall above the fireplace hung photographs of Himmler and Hitler, while near the window, on either side of the desk, stood the furled standards of the premier Waffen-SS divisions—the Leibstandarte Adolf Hitler and Das Reich. On the wall opposite the fireplace, beautifully worked in gold thread on a piece of damask cloth, was the SS motto—*Meine Ehre heisst Treue* ("Loyalty is my honor").

Two paces inside the door Christian, now bathed and in a clean uniform, stood rigidly to attention. It was one thing to be impolite to lowly Hauptmanns, quite another not to show courtesy to a Standartenfuehrer.

Weil glanced up. "Come in, Eicke, come in. Come in and sit down."

Christian walked the length of the room and took the second armchair, sitting erect, his cap on his lap.

"And for God's sake relax, Oberleutnant. No one can see you here. If we're to gain anything from this meeting I don't want you to feel you're on the parade ground. I was about to have some coffee and brandy. Would you care to join me?"

Christian stammered his acceptance. The *Standartenfuehrer* poured for both.

"Help yourself to cream and sugar. And brandy. Don't be bashful. I know from your dossier that you're a drinking man."

To hell with it, thought Christian. If he wants to treat me like Martin Bormann, I'm not going to say no.

He poured himself a massive slug. By comparison Weil's glass looked empty.

"Your very good health, Oberleutnant." Weil smacked his lips. "Even if the French cannot do anything else, they know the secret of manufacturing brandy. I often think that all ethnic groups—perhaps I mean nationalities— have things they do well and things they do not do well, and that they should concentrate on their strengths. The French, for example, are peerless in making wine, the Americans are magnificent businessmen. The English should stick to managing colonies, under proper supervision, of course. The Italians . . ." He paused and smiled, not unpleasantly. "Well, perhaps not every nation has a gift."

"The Germans, sir?" Emboldened by the brandy and the congenial atmosphere, Christian didn't give the question a second's thought.

"The Germans? We are the world's conquerors. Or don't you listen to the Fuehrer's speeches?"

Standartenfuehrer Weil was still smiling. My God, thought Christian, that's almost treason!

"I can speak to you in that somewhat disrespectful manner," went on Weil, reading Christian's mind, "because I understand that you too are frequently guilty of disparaging comment and outrageous action. That is so, is it not?"

It's a trap, Christian decided. The coffee, the brandy, the avuncular attitude. One word out of place and I'll be dangling by my balls.

"I'm not sure what the Standartenfuehrer is referring to," he said carefully.

"Come, come, Eicke." Weil drummed his fingers irritably. "It's all here, in the dossier. Would you like me to read some of it to you?" He flicked open the cardboard cover. "Oberleutnant Christian Eicke, formally Sturmbannfuehrer Eicke of the SS Panzer Division Totenkopf. Quite a drop in rank and status there, Eicke. From a *Sturmbann-*

fuehrer in the crack Death's Head Division to an *Ober-leutnant* on garrison duty. Iron Cross First Class, Poland 1939; Knight's Cross, Russian Front 1941. I hear you think a lot of the Ivans as soldiers. Well, no matter, no matter. So do we all. Now."

Weil skipped a couple of paragraphs.

"Ah, here's an interesting snippet. Drunk and striking a superior officer, April 1942. Severely reprimanded. You were lucky to have Obersturmbannfuehrer Hoess speak up for you there. May 1942, drunk and disorderly, contra-vening Section so-and-so. May again, drunk. Then there's a gap. I imagine the clerk got sick of the repetition. July 1942, court-martialed for striking an NCO. Again only a severe reprimand. You were damned lucky, Eicke. They could have shot you. I would have done. Drunk, drunk, drunk and disorderly. Fighting, abusive to senior officers. And the last entry: Demoted to the ranks and dishonorably discharged from the SS on the orders of Reichsfuehrer Himmler personally. Reenlisted in the ranks of the 131st Infantry Regiment almost immediately. Promoted *Ober-leutnant* October 1942. Currently based in Cologne."

Weil tossed the file to one side.

"A pretty sorry record, eh, Eicke. Sturmbannfuehrer at the age of twenty-three and Oberleutnant putting out fires and arresting black-marketeers two years later. A pretty miserable decline for a man of your previous record. What the hell happened? I've looked and looked, but nowhere here does it say directly, only hints."

Christian gripped the brandy goblet until his knuckles whitened. "If the Standartenfuehrer will forgive me I choose not to answer."

Weil brought his fist down with a crash on the arm of the chair. In spite of being several feet away, the coffee table jumped a couple of inches.

"No!" he roared. "The Standartenfuehrer will not for-give you! Where the hell do you think you are, Oberleut-nant? There's a bloody war on and it's no place for prima donnas. So pour yourself another brandy and listen to me.

Because you'll answer civilly when I ask you a question. And unless you watch your manners very carefully, your next stop will be the firing squad you've luckily escaped for so long."

Christian did as he was told and poured himself a second brandy. He sipped it gingerly. Weil's anger disappeared as quickly as it had begun. Many high-ranking officers had learned that trick from Hitler, whose rages were invariably stage-managed.

"I'll rephrase my question," said Weil. "Your service record tells me of a sudden change of character. One day you're a bemedaled officer with a crack SS division, traveling rapidly up the promotion ladder. The next you're on your way to becoming an alcoholic with psychopathic tendencies. I want to know why."

"Psychopathic tendencies?" Christian felt lightheaded and wondered if Weil had put something in the drink. "A phrase from a Jewish science. Perhaps you should consult Freud, Herr Standartenfuehrer."

"If that remark is meant to annoy me, Eicke, you haven't succeeded. The Theory of Relativity is a Jewish phrase, but I can't ignore it because of that. Very well, if you won't give me a straight answer, I'll do it for you. It was the camps, wasn't it? You saw the camps?"

It seemed a long time ago and strangely irrelevant now. "Yes."

"Good," said Weil, "we progress. You saw something you neither liked nor approved of, and took the adolescent escape route of booze. Very well, I'm not going to defend the camps. It might surprise you to learn that many people in a much higher position than you feel the same. If the war goes badly for us, every German, whatever the color of his uniform, is going to pay a terrible price for the work of a handful of madmen. But I want to know more about you, Eicke, so I'll ask you another question. Was it the systematic slaughter of civilians that disgusted you? If so, what do you think the R.A.F. does when it bombs our cities? Does every bomb only hit a target of strategic im-

81

portance, a factory, a steel mill? Is that even the intention? Are German civilians immune from being blown to pieces? Perhaps you'd care to explain your theory to some soldiers who are both widowers and childless. It is a regrettable fact of war, Oberleutnant, that innocent people suffer, the weak suffer.

"Have you ever attacked an entrenched position of fifty men with fifty of your own? Of course you haven't. Such an act would deserve you a place in an asylum. You either wait until you outnumber them five to one or soften them up first with artillery. That's rather like five bullies in a school playground ganging up on one boy. But it is war. Perhaps you've read Macaulay on the subject. 'He knew that the essence of war is violence and that moderation in war is imbecility.' "

"Quotations," sneered Christian. He was no longer intimidated by Weil. "I'll give you one. 'There is such a thing as legitimate warfare; war has its laws. There are things which may be fairly done and things which may not be done.' Cardinal Newman. Bombing cities or opposing an inferior force with a superior one are legitimate tactics. The camps are another thing. I understand war, Herr Standartenfuehrer."

"Good. I'm glad of it. I may yet find a use for you."

Christian wished to God he'd get on with it and not treat him as an enemy of the Reich, which he wasn't. He was a German soldier and he wanted a German victory. Things would be different then. The criminals would be hanged and honest men put in their places. But either Weil could give him something to do that was worth doing or let him get back to Cologne and a fresh bottle.

The *Standartenfuehrer* reached for Christian's dossier and flicked through it until he found the entry he was looking for.

"It says here that you were educated in England and that you speak English fluently."

"I was there for six years, sir—from 1930 to 1936. My father's business obliged him to spend almost as much time in England as he did at home and it was decided that I should go to school there."

"Why was that? We have excellent schools and universities right here in Germany."

"I believe it was because he wanted me to understand the British way of thinking. He's in shipping and it's his opinion—" Christian paused, embarrassed—"it's his opinion that the British build the finest ships in the world."

"I think Admiral Raeder would probably agree with you," said Weil wryly. He studied Christian for a moment before going on. "And your sister, how did she take all this? You gallivanting around England while she was stuck at home?"

"My sister, sir?" Christian hadn't thought of Heidi in years. "My sister was a semi-invalid from adolescence on. She died in 1936, which was one of the reasons I returned home."

"Ah yes, here it is. Cause of death, leukemia."

Christ, thought Christian, there wasn't much missing from SS files.

"And how is it now, the English?" asked Weil.

Christian shrugged. "I'm probably a bit rusty, but a language is not something one forgets easily."

"Good, excellent." Weil placed the dossier on the floor beside his chair. "You're a lucky man, Oberleutnant, as I've said before. Not many of us are granted second chances but you're about to get one. How would you like to do some real soldiering, the kind you're obviously well suited for, instead of rotting in Cologne?"

Christian did not hesitate, though later he thought that the charges Hauptmann Westerhoff had itemized had something to do with his decision. "I'd like that very much, sir."

Ten minutes later he was not so sure. He listened in astonished silence as Weil explained, leaving out only the name of the officer, that a Luftwaffe general had been captured by the *Tommis* and Germany needed him back. As of this moment they did not know where the officer was being held, in which camp, if indeed he had reached a camp, but that information would be available via normal POW channels in the near future. When it arrived, with a tiny handful of men, probably not more than two or three, Oberleutnant Eicke was to go in and snatch the general.

Christian thought he was going out of his mind. Take two or three men and invade a British POW camp, rescue some bloody fool who had got himself caught, and get that same bloody fool home to Germany. Impossible.

"If the Standartenfuehrer will forgive me," he said, "the Standartenfuehrer is mistaken. It can't be done."

"Good. I'll tell Generalmajor von Stuerzbecher's mother."

"Stuerzbecher? *Kurt* von Stuerzbecher?"

"The same." Weil looked up innocently. "You know the general?"

The bastard, thought Christian. Now he understood the reference to Heidi. For five years, from the summer of '31 until Heidi's death, Kurt von Stuerzbecher had courted Christian's sister. He tried everything in his power to persuade Heidi to marry him, but Heidi said no, not until she was better, which they all knew would never be. But Kurt refused to give up. He was a guest in the Eicke house in Hamburg whenever an opportunity arose. During the long summer vacations from school in England, while Heidi was resting, Kurt and Christian would spend their afternoons together. It was Kurt who had taught Christian how to catch the fattest trout and how to bring down the highest-flying pheasant. In spite of the difference in their ages, nothing was too much trouble. If Kurt could not spend as much time as he wished with the sister, he was determined to spend it with the brother.

They saw little of each other after Heidi's death. Kurt joined the Luftwaffe and became an ace with the Condor Legion; Christian had his studies to complete. They tried keeping in touch, but the bond that had held them together was broken. They bumped into one another from time to time, drank together, talked about the old days;

and it was enough. To Christian, Kurt was like a brother; it wasn't necessary to constantly reaffirm old loyalties.

"Would the Standartenfuehrer mind answering a question of mine?" asked Christian slowly.

"Go ahead."

"Why was all this necessary?" He indicated the brandy, the coffee in the china cups. "You could have given me a direct order. As a soldier, I would have had to obey it."

"It's one thing to give an order, Oberleutnant. It's quite another to know that the order will be carried out in the best possible way. A simple reading of your dossier was not encouraging. I wanted to see if you were the man the file says you are now or the one you used to be."

"And?"

"You're one of the few available men with the qualifications to pull this off. You speak English and you know England. Your record shows that this is the sort of operation that used to appeal to you. You need to lose about ten pounds in weight and throw away the bottle, but if anyone can do it, you can. If you succeed, you'll have rendered the Reich an inestimable service."

"And if I fail? It's still impossible, whether the officer is Kurt von Stuerzbecher or not."

"Perhaps it is. But you'll at least try and find a way now, won't you? There's a lot at stake. Success will ensure that your former rank is restored and that your file reads less like that of a convicted felon. You might even get the oak leaves added to that Knight's Cross of yours."

"I'll need time," said Christian.

"That you have. It'll be two weeks, perhaps three, before we know in which camp von Stuerzbecher is being held."

"And I'll want a free hand in picking my own team. I won't have any interference in that, no SS thugs palmed off on me just because they have a good killing record."

"Granted. You'll almost certainly be in civilian clothes, of course, so don't choose anyone who looks too German. But apart from that you can recruit anyone you wish. Let me have their names and I'll see to it that they're released from their present duties. The same applies to you, naturally. Cologne will be told that you have been assigned to my office. I suggest you make your headquarters here in Berlin. If you have any trouble finding suitable accommodations, let me know. We have special arrangements for important personnel."

Alone, Standartenfuehrer Weil walked to the window and watched Christian cross the street below. Soon he was lost in the crowds.

He hoped he had made the right decision, selecting Eicke. It was a gamble, but he had the best qualifications. More to the point, he fitted the specification the *Reichsfuehrer* had stipulated. An SS man who was no longer SS. Himmler could claim success for a victory and shrug off a defeat. On balance, it was an hour well spent.

Five

Throughout the war the London Cage was housed at 8, Kensington Palace Gardens. Officially known as the Prisoner of War Interrogation Section (PWIS), it was, as the title implies, a preliminary interrogation center for captured Germans.

In the early days of the war, when no German flier expected the conflict to last longer than a few more weeks, the downed pilots unwittingly gave their interrogators more intelligence than the latter could have dared hope for. Apart from name, rank and serial number on the questionnaire that all new arrivals were obliged to fill in, all kinds of other questions were posed: home address, unit, nature of mission, and so on. Although it may seem incredible, these were frequently answered in detail. The apparent ingenuousness of the approach was partly responsible; a simple form to complete instead of rubber truncheons in a cellar. But more than that the fliers had received very little instruction in security. In its arrogance the Luftwaffe did not expect many of its pilots to be shot down. It was not until Franz von Werra's escape and debriefing that lectures on the method of dealing with interrogation were made mandatory. In consequence, by 1942 the interrogator's job had become much more difficult. Of necessity, therefore, he became more subtle.

Normally a POW could expect to spend no more than a day or so at the Cage before being dispatched to a regular POW camp such as Grizedale Hall, Skiddaw, Devizes, Lodge Moor, Sheffield, or Comrie, Scotland. Some were held longer and some sent elsewhere for further grilling. It all depended upon what value the limited resources of British Intelligence placed on the captured individual. In Kurt von Stuerzbecher's case, he had been there for six days.

After being put ashore at Harwich in the early hours of the thirteenth, he was taken under escort to London, arriving at Liverpool Street Station as dawn was breaking. In the usual manner he was given a questionnaire to complete. After scanning it briefly he filled in the barest details. His name, dropping the *von* and changing his first name to Karl; his rank, demoting himself six grades to *Oberleutnant;* and a fictitious serial number.

"You haven't finished," the Staff Sergeant said when he collected the document.

Many afternoons spent with Christian Eicke had given von Stuerzbecher a good command of the English language. But he affected only partial understanding and made his accent more guttural than it actually was. It was possible at a later date that a hidden knowledge of English would be of value.

"It is all that is permitted."

The Staff Sergeant shrugged. It was the stock answer. In any case, it was none of his business. He was merely the office boy.

Alone, von Stuerzbecher examined his surroundings. The room was small, fifteen feet by twelve, and the window barred and shuttered. The only furniture was a wooden table, a couple of chairs, and a camp bed.

He made his mind go blank. By this time the Luftwaffe High Command would know that he was missing and the telephone lines would be buzzing. But there was nothing he could do about it. More than likely he would spend the remainder of the war as a prisoner, but as long as that was the worst that happened he would put up with it. He had committed a criminally negligent act by flying into the *Tommi* bomber stream, and now he would have to pay for it. While the British believed him to be a mere *Oberleutnant*, however, incarceration would be tolerable. If they ever found out his true rank—well, it didn't bear thinking about. In one respect the Geneva Convention worked in his favor, more so than normally. Giving only his name, rank and serial number precluded any awkward and unanswerable questions regarding his unit.

The door opened and a youthful British captain entered, carrying von Stuerzbecher's questionnaire and a notebook and pen.

"Good morning, Oberleutnant," he said breezily and in German, and introduced himself as Captain Harrison.

"Good morning," answered von Stuerzbecher, getting to his feet. Christ, those were details he'd have to remember. With his assumed rank of *Oberleutnant,* the British captain was senior to him.

"Sit down, please."

Captain Harrison took the chair on the other side of the table. He looked at von Stuerzbecher thoughtfully before tapping the questionnaire.

"This won't do, you know," he said. "If we're to let your people know you're safe, I'll need more information than this."

"I'm not allowed to divulge any more than I have, as you well know."

"Oh, I agree that those are the rules, but like most rules they're unrealistic. I'm not asking you to reveal the strength of your squadron or its position. But if you'll simply give me your home address I'll see that your wife and family are informed."

"I'm sorry, that can't be done." Von Stuerzbecher shook his head firmly.

Harrison frowned. "Surely your home address can't be

of strategic importance." He tried a joke. "Not unless it's in the Wilhelmstrasse."

"I'm sorry, Herr Hauptmann, but you know as well as I do that my home address *does* have strategic importance. Alone, perhaps not. But pieced together with information obtained from other prisoners from the same town might tell you whether or not your bombing sorties are having any success."

"Rubbish, Stuerzbecher. I'm merely trying to be helpful. I'd have thought a man of your age would have realized that." He scribbled something in the notebook. "How old are you, anyway? Thirty-five, thirty-six? A bit old to be an *Oberleutnant*, I would have thought."

Von Stuerzbecher remained silent.

"A bit old, anyway," continued Harrison, "to be an *Oberleutnant* on operational duties. I could understand it if you were behind a desk, but flying over the North Sea? That I find puzzling."

"Nothing puzzling about it at all. I am an experienced flier. Germany needs experienced fliers. Q.E.D."

"Well, that's something, anyway." Captain Harrison made a note. "You're a pilot, not an observer or radar man."

Von Stuerzbecher cursed inwardly. God, he'd have to watch his tongue. The slightest slip and he was done.

"My name is Karl Stuerzbecher, my rank is *Oberleutnant*—"

"Yes, yes," said Harrison testily. "I have all that. But it's still puzzling. Most of your pilots we shoot down are in their late teens or early twenties. You're in your middle thirties. So either Germany is running short of youngsters more quickly than we thought or you're not what you purport to be."

Von Stuerzbecher said nothing.

"And another thing that intrigues me," Harrison continued, "according to the fellows who brought you in, when you were picked up you were carrying almost nothing that could be termed personal effects. I find that very strange, particularly the absence of cigarettes, lighter or matches. I can see from your fingers that you smoke."

"When one is bailing out of a damaged aircraft, one does not bother with such trivia as cigarettes and matches."

"True enough. On the other hand, one normally keeps cigarettes and matches in a side pocket."

"Not in my case. In any event, you were the one who suggested cigarettes, not I. I'm a cigar smoker. One cigar would last me a whole sortie. I don't need to carry spares."

"Cigars, eh? I would have thought cigars were difficult to come by in Germany, especially for the lower ranks. If your armed forces are anything like ours, brigadiers and above grab the best of whatever's going."

Abruptly Captain Harrison stood up.

"Would you like some coffee, Stuerzbecher? Sorry I can't manage breakfast but that won't be for several hours yet."

"Coffee would be most welcome."

"I'll arrange it."

After telling the staff sergeant to rustle up a mug of coffee for the prisoner, Captain Harrison descended a floor, walked a short distance along the corridor and rapped lightly on an unmarked door. Half a minute later he was explaining his misgivings about the new POW to a full colonel.

"Something very fishy, sir. He's far too old to be an *Oberleutnant* on active service and he tells me he smokes cigars. We might have caught a mackerel here."

The colonel was unconvinced. Still, he could afford to overlook nothing, at least for a day or so.

"Put a few political questions to him, then leave him on ice for twenty-four hours."

Von Stuerzbecher was in the process of draining the mug when Harrison returned.

"Coffee all right?"

"Excellent, thank you. May I ask when I shall be assigned to a camp?"

"Oh, soon, soon. Just a few more questions. I need the answers to these to make sure you're put in the correct camp. We try not to mix the ordinary German with the hard-core Nazi. We find there's more blood spilt by doing that than anywhere on the front."

Harrison spread open his notebook, as though preparing for a lengthy session.

"You're not a Nazi, I suppose, are you?"

Von Stuerzbecher was puzzled but saw no reason to answer untruthfully.

"But of course I am. I have no reason to be ashamed of that."

"I see." Harrison made a note. "Then you agree that the *Anschluss* of Austria and the invasion of Czechoslovakia and Poland were legitimate acts."

"Of course," answered von Stuerzbecher without hesitation. "As you would no doubt agree that the colonization of India, Africa and much of the rest of the world were legitimate acts. It may come as an unpalatable shock to you, Herr Hauptmann, but empires, British or German, are not founded on the principle of charity."

Whether Captain Harrison took the bait as a ploy or he was genuinely annoyed that von Stuerzbecher had the temerity to compare Germany with Mother England, the Luftwaffe officer was never later quite certain.

"You're not seriously trying to compare our methods with yours?"

"Cause no, effect yes. The ethnic African didn't greet you with open arms. He fought you. You were stronger and therefore won. It matters little to a conquered people that they are subjugated by the sword or the tank. The end product remains the same."

"Philosophy, Herr Oberleutnant?"

"Geopolitics, Herr Hauptmann. Britain became a maritime power and acquired a far-flung empire because she is a tiny, isolated island with a genius for administration. Germany's empire will be contiguous with her present borders. Germany has no interest in overseas British possessions. It was a mistake to try to colonize parts of Africa. Germany's destiny lies to the east, the rest of Europe and Asia."

"*Lebensraum?*"

"If you wish. And it is pointless to turn up your nose at it, Herr Hauptmann. *Lebensraum* is no longer an idea; it is a reality."

"You obviously haven't been reading the latest reports from Stalingrad."

"A temporary setback. We've had them before; we shall no doubt have them again. But be clear about one thing: the German people are far too dynamic to be limited to territory assigned by the Treaty of Versailles."

"That old chestnut."

"Chestnut perhaps. But if you attempt to emasculate a nation, you'd better make sure you get both balls."

Captain Harrison smiled. "You don't talk like a mere *Oberleutnant*, Stuerzbecher."

"Perhaps mere *Oberleutnants* in the Wehrmacht have a better perspective of history than their equivalent in the British armed forces," retorted von Stuerzbecher.

Nevertheless, he said no more. This apparently harmless debate was not taking place because Captain Harrison wanted an early-morning argument. The British officer was a skilled interrogator. God knows how many times he had had similar conversations. One slip of the tongue would reveal that von Stuerzbecher had been in the Fuehrer's presence less than twelve hours previously, and an audience like that did not happen to mere *Oberleutnants*.

It was time to shut up.

"I think we are getting beyond the bounds of our respective roles," he said lightly. "Our personal beliefs and philosophies are irrelevant to my present status."

Captain Harrison did not attempt to argue. Unhurriedly he closed the notebook and pocketed his pen.

"I agree. I think I've heard enough."

"Which means I'll be sent to a camp?"

"You seem very anxious to leave us."

93

Von Stuerzbecher said what any *Oberleutnant* would have said.

"Herr Hauptmann, you know as well as I do that even lowly *Oberleutnants* possess information that you would be glad to have. My base, the strength of my unit, new aircraft, conditions in Germany, morale. Of course I am anxious to leave you. What German officer wouldn't be?"

"Well, we'll have to wait and see."

Harrison paused with his hand on the doorknob.

"The Medical Officer will visit you shortly, to ensure that you've suffered no ill-effects from your ducking. Your meals will be brought to you here. I know what the Geneva Convention says about exercise and fresh air for POWs, but you'll forgive me if, for the moment, we do not obey the letter of the law. We'll have another chat tomorrow."

In the event, "tomorrow" took place at 3 A.M. the following morning, November 14.

Von Stuerzbecher was sleeping fitfully on the camp bed. Apart from the orderly who brought his meals, he had seen no one but the Medical Officer for almost twenty-four hours.

The Medical Officer had given him a thorough examination. This was due less to concern for a fellow human being than to a desire to discover the general state of his health. Medical Officers were a vital cog in an Intelligence unit, as their reports could frequently indicate the sort of diet a prisoner had been getting prior to his capture. Any form of malnutrition could indicate food shortages in the Reich, and that kind of information was of incalculable value to the British.

Von Stuerzbecher was fully awake the minute the door was flung open. This time it wasn't Captain Harrison but an R.A.F. squadron leader in full uniform. He sat on the far side of the wooden table and produced the ubiquitous notebook and pen.

"Good morning, Herr Oberleutnant," he said cheerfully in good and accentless German. "I am Squadron Leader

Manson. Sorry about the miserable hour, but I'm sure you people of the *Nachtjagdgeschwader* are used to getting up at uncivilized hours."

Von Stuerzbecher rubbed his eyes to clear them. The Luftwaffe equivalent of squadron leader was *Major,* and this was how he addressed his new interrogator.

"Please don't apologize, Herr Major. I could do with a bit of company."

"Good, good. Well, just a few more questions and you'll be seeing the last of us." Abruptly he switched to English. "It was a Ju 88 night fighter you bailed out of, wasn't it?"

Von Stuerzbecher understood the question perfectly but faked bewilderment.

"I'm sorry, Herr Major, but I didn't catch that."

Manson repeated the question in German.

"I'm afraid I can't answer that. If you've found any of the pieces you'll know and if you haven't I'm not at liberty to tell you."

Manson smiled his understanding and produced his cigarettes. Hesitating only briefly, von Stuerzbecher accepted one with thanks.

They puffed away in silence for a couple of minutes before Manson said, "You know, when I was first told that we'd captured an *Oberleutnant* who is my age, I was most anxious to meet you. Promotion's slow in our bloody mob, but it must be murder in the Luftwaffe. Unless you've been a bad boy, of course. We've got a couple of those in the R.A.F.; wing commander one day, cleaning the latrines the next. Was that it?"

Von Stuerzbecher held his peace. Manson changed tack.

"Look, old man, you've got to answer some of my questions or you'll be in this room for the duration. I'm not asking you to betray any military secrets. Good God, I'd have no respect for you if you did. But my C.O. has given me a job to do and he won't take no for an answer."

"I'm permitted only to give my name, rank and serial number. Anything more is forbidden."

"As you wish." Manson put down his pen and closed the notebook. "I can see I'm not going to get much out of you. Still, I admire you for it. Not many of your chaps see it that way. They're only too happy to sing like canaries and get the hell out of here."

"I don't believe that, Herr Major."

"Don't you, by God. You've obviously got a great deal more faith in your fellow fliers than I have. I tell you frankly, Stuerzbecher, sometimes there's so much baring of souls going on in this room that I feel like a bloody priest. Most of it's guilt, I suppose. When your pilots see the devastation they've inflicted on London they're filled with remorse. Inevitable, don't you think?"

"The R.A.F. are not exactly dropping feathers on our cities."

"Come, come, there's no comparison. We aim for strategic targets; you chaps aim for civilians."

"That's not true, Herr Major."

"Not true my foot. Apart from anything else, those radar-equipped JU 188s give our heavy bombers a hell of a problem. The aerials might cut down their air speed, but they're still very fast for a night fighter. Far faster than a Lanc, anyway. How do you find landing them? Surely the aerials give the plane a very dangerous stalling speed."

"I wouldn't know, Herr Major. Aerials? Radar-equipped Auntie Jus? This is all a mystery to me."

Manson nodded, as though coming to a conclusion. Then without a word he got up and left the room.

Von Stuerzbecher sighed with relief. Round One to him.

Apart from meals, they left him alone throughout the fifteenth and sixteenth of November, and on the seventeenth they tried a plant, a German-speaking British officer in the uniform of a Luftwaffe Leutnant. He had been ushered into the room just after lunch as a newly captured flier, and it took von Stuerzbecher less than a quarter of an hour to judge the man to be a fake. He was too garrulous. Suspecting hidden microphones, no German officer would be that talkative.

96

They removed him in the late afternoon, on the pretext of a separate interrogation, and that was the last von Stuerzbecher saw of him.

In the small hours of the eighteenth Captain Harrison returned, accompanied this time by a full colonel. Although weary through irregular hours and lack of proper exercise and ventilation, von Stuerzbecher was immediately on the alert. Under normal circumstances the interrogator's rank was just one grade higher than the prisoner being questioned. A Luftwaffe *Oberleutnant,* therefore, rated a British captain. (The Squadron Leader was an exception, belonging to R.A.F. Intelligence, whose questions were, or would have been with encouragement, on technical subjects beyond the ken of Army officers.) But this, a full colonel—there couldn't be many of those around.

Von Stuerzbecher got to his feet in a hurry and stood rigidly at attention. The colonel introduced himself as Wilkin.

"All right, Jamie," he said to Captain Harrison, "you can leave us. I don't think Oberleutnant Stuerzbecher is likely to attack me."

Alone with Colonel Wilkin, whose German had a Bavarian lilt, von Stuerzbecher was given permission to sit, which he did with an air of resignation. He had not yet been permitted to shave or to bathe, and he felt filthy. By way of contrast, Wilkin looked as if he had just stepped from the fitting room of a military tailor. His uniform was clean and beautifully pressed, his Sam Browne dazzling. He was not much older than von Stuerzbecher, but already his hair was graying.

"I must ask your forgiveness for what must appear to be gross discourtesy," he began. "Normally, we are not so inhospitable to our guests. In fact, the majority of them don't stay with us this long. But you puzzle us, Oberleutnant. You puzzled Squadron Leader Manson, you puzzled Captain Harrison, and their reports have puzzled me. What, we are all asking ourselves, is a German officer in his middle thirties doing with the rank of *Oberleutnant?*

By rights you should be my equivalent, an *Oberst,* perhaps higher. We're very curious, to say the least. We've talked about it and we've come up with several alternatives." He enumerated them on his fingers. "One, you're not a pilot at all but a desk officer who for some reason found himself in an aircraft; two, your rank is not what you state it to be; or three, and much more important, you are not military personnel. You are, in effect, a spy."

"Ridiculous. I was in uniform."

"True, but why were you in uniform, why were you not wearing a regulation flying suit? It's Captain Harrison's theory that you had civilian clothes in a suitcase, which you were forced to abandon when you were shot down."

"Absurd. A fairy tale."

"Oh, I agree it's an uncomfortable thought," said Wilkin smoothly, "and the consequences are even more unpleasant still. But you were found not only in walking-out dress but without any documentation whatever, not even identity discs. We only have your word that you are Oberleutnant Karl Stuerzbecher of the Luftwaffe. You see our problem, don't you? If you are the officer you claim to be we need proof. If you're not an officer at all, I'm afraid your next interview will be with a firing squad."

Von Stuerzbecher thought as quickly as his tired brain would permit. Whether or not the firing-squad threat was a bluff, he would have to treat it as being serious. The alternative was to reveal his true rank and name, and that was out of the question. But thirdly, he had to get out of this wretched London Cage as soon as possible. The longer they kept him here, the more likely they were to discover his true identity. He decided to try a bluff of his own.

"Perhaps you've heard of Leutnant Franz von Werra, Herr Oberst," he said.

"I have indeed," answered Wilkin. "In fact, I had the pleasure of interrogating him myself. A rather pompous young man, I thought, full of his own self-importance. And some of his claims for aircraft destroyed were pure fiction."

"Nevertheless, Herr Oberst, Werra escaped and got home to Germany. Before being posted to a new *Staffel* he was debriefed at length by our own Intelligence people, and from him we learned much of your methods. For example," von Stuerzbecher lied, "he told us that it was not unusual for British Intelligence to judge a pilot to be a civilian and therefore a spy, and threaten the firing squad. You know as well as I do that it is every officer's duty to rid himself of documents which may be of value to the enemy. I had more time than most and threw away everything. We do not underestimate you, Herr Oberst. A cigarette lighter made in a certain city might tell you more than any imprudent statement; a packet of cigarettes with a girl's telephone number scribbled hastily on the back; a newspaper cutting. These items could tell you more than we wish you to know.

"My fellow officers have frequently accused me of being a cautious individual, and perhaps they are right. But in an emergency there's no time to select what one will keep and what one will dispose of. It's better to get rid of it all."

Von Stuerzbecher drew a deep breath and hurried on.

"I am who I say I am, Herr Oberst—Oberleutnant Karl Stuerzbecher of the Luftwaffe." He allowed a trace of bitterness to creep into his words. "If I have been passed over for promotion, if I am not the flier Adolf Galland is, or Werra, that is not for me to judge. To call me a spy is ridiculous and to send me before a firing squad with no more than an unsubstantiated presumption is an act unworthy of the uniform you wear and the rank you hold."

Colonel Wilkin twiddled his thumbs for several minutes after von Stuerzbecher finished speaking. "Very well," he said finally, "very well."

He stood up, rapped on the door for the guard to open it, and went out. Von Stuerzbecher heaved a long sigh and shut his eyes.

Captain Harrison was waiting for Wilkin in the colonel's own office.

"Well, sir?"

99

"I don't know, Jamie, I just don't know. He's either a brilliant liar or he's telling the truth."

"I think he's lying, sir."

"They're all lying, Jamie, they've all got something to hide. Anyway, we can't keep him here any longer. This is a busy hotel and we've already wasted enough time on him. I think you'd better make arrangements to send him on."

"We could move him out to Cockfosters, sir, let them have a crack."

"No, they're up to their eyes too. Send him to a camp. If we've made a mistake, that's our bad luck. There are still plenty of other fish to fry."

And so early in the morning of the nineteenth of November, Generalmajor Kurt von Stuerzbecher was at last given shaving implements and a sliver of soap and told to prepare to move out in half an hour.

With two other prisoners he had never seen before he was driven through bomb-torn London in a closed one-tonner and handed over to his traveling escort at Euston Station. Twenty minutes later he was on his way north.

Part II

Six

NOVEMBER 19

For the third time that week it had snowed overnight in the Lake District, and Skiddaw Camp was covered with an inch or two of new powder. There was more on the way, too, judging by the temperature in the compound and the fat-bellied clouds glowering over the Cumbrian Mountains. Not that the weather affected the volleyball players. In the Pig Pen they were already at it, although it was barely 9 A.M.

Crazy, thought Private George Cook, who was on early duty as compound picket and who was shivering uncontrollably as he made his rounds. He watched one-armed Willi Schneider miss a strike, fall in a heap, and jump up laughing. Like a bunch of school kids.

Which was some comment, coming from someone who was hardly more than a school kid himself.

At nineteen, George Cook needed a razor less than twice a week, and his temperament matched his cherubic features. The results of his induction exams had labeled him below average. He wasn't clinically stupid, but he was very slow. Slow to understand an order, slow to carry it out. Nicknamed Harpo by the Germans because of his blond curls, he prayed only that he would never be sent overseas or be asked to point his rifle in earnest.

Out of the corner of his eye he saw Corporal Napley approaching and decided to make himself scarce. For some reason he couldn't fathom, Napley seemed to take a sadistic delight in making his life a misery.

On the veranda outside his office in the Administration Section, Company Sergeant Major Bernard Purser also saw Napley crossing the compound and Cook's reaction. One day, he told himself, he would have to have a word with Napley. There was once a time when a man had to earn his stripes and work to keep them. Nowadays, any fool with a loud voice had two up before he was dry behind the ears.

CSM Purser returned to his office and resumed checking the sick list.

With the C.O. away at a meeting and Captain Thorogood taking the opportunity to do some shopping in Carlisle, Bernard Purser was effectively in charge of the camp. There were junior officers on Skiddaw's strength, of course, but like most old soldiers the CSM's opinion of junior officers was nil. They were good for nothing except scrounging cigarettes and tea.

CSM Purser scratched his initials on the sick list and tossed it onto the "out" tray for Captain Thorogood to endorse on his return.

Now aged forty-three, Bernard Purser was the archetypal professional soldier from the top of his closely cropped head to the tip of his highly polished boots. He had been in the Army most of his adult life and had won the Military Medal in France in 1918. Now that *had* been a war, he was fond of saying to anyone who had never witnessed it personally. Men stuck in trenches and told to stay there, regardless, until it was time to be relieved or to advance. And there was precious little relief. Knee-deep in mud for weeks on end and covered with lice so familiar they had names, that was the role of Tommy Atkins. He was a fighting man through and through, as hard as nails. He'd have eaten most of the present-day armies of either side for breakfast and still have found room for a snack.

Not an unkind man by any means, CSM Purser was nevertheless known as a terror on the parade ground, capable of throwing the most violent rages if so much as a speck of dust were discovered on a soldier's rifle. Only he knew that the rages were faked. The way he saw it, the senior NCO in a camp was father, mother and wet nurse to the other ranks. A soldier might be put on report for rust on his bayonet, but afterward it would become second nature to respect his weapon, and one day he would be glad of it.

To the Germans he was known as Sergeant Major Tomorrow, after his habit of answering any question with that word. ("When are the Red Cross parcels due?" "Tomorrow." "When are we going to get more blankets?" "Tomorrow." "When will the war be over?" "Tomorrow." With a grin.) The Germans, as far as was possible, liked and respected him because they knew he was too wise to hate them simply for being Germans. Before she was killed in the Blitz, his wife had also respected him. Neither of them were people of great emotion, so love was out of the question. But respect, yes, even though she never fully understood why his job was his whole life. He still missed her.

CSM Purser had suffered two major disappointments in his life. The first was that he had never made Regimental Sergeant Major. He did an RSM's job in all but name, but he had never been granted the title. In the field or even with a training battalion, he felt he would have made it. As it was, he knew he had reached the end of the promotion road.

The second disappointment was that his only son—only child, for that matter—had elected to join the Royal Navy. With the boy now on convoy duty somewhere in the North Atlantic, it somehow gave them less in common.

He checked the desk alarm and compared it with his

wrist watch. It was almost nine-thirty, time to put on the kettle and get out the board. In a couple of minutes Ober-feldwebel Ernst Reitlinger would be knocking at the door, carrying a sheaf of papers. The documents were a blind. Whenever the C.O. and the adjutant were away, Oberfeld-webel Reitlinger and CSM Purser got stuck into a game of checkers. The setup had bothered Purser at first; it could have been called fraternizing with the enemy. But when young Tom Hastings, the only officer on the British side to know of the meetings, told him that *fraternization* came from the Latin word for "brother," the CSM had felt better about it.

Although not much given to self-examination, Purser sometimes wondered about his relationship with Reit-linger. Here they were, on different sides of the fence, yet it would be true to say that the *Oberfeldwebel* was the best friend he had. Admittedly they were roughly the same age, held similar rank, and had both fought with distinc-tion in the 1914–18 conflict; but it was nevertheless an odd situation made odder by the fact that neither spoke much of the other's language. Enough to get by; enough to say "Good morning" and "How are you" and "What lousy weather." But no more. Their only real means of communication was through the universal medium of the checkerboard—that, and a cup of hot, sweet tea. But that was how it should be with old soldiers.

Across the compound in Hut 5, Major Breithaupt's hut, the Escape Committee was in session. Or rather, for the moment, it was not. The four members had reached an impasse, divided as to whether the snow would affect, even postpone, the break planned for December 12. Major Breithaupt and Oberleutnant Franz Mohr were of the opinion that if the snow continued to fall between now and then, the whole venture would have to be rethought. The other two were all for going whatever the conditions.

"Good God, if we let the weather put us off we don't deserve to get out." Those were the sentiments of Kapi-

106

taenleutnant Heydt of the German Navy. "If we miss this opportunity we won't get another crack until the spring. It was the same last year; once the snow sets in this early it'll be with us until March. By the time we get home the whole bloody country will be run by Jews and Gypsies."

"Defeatist talk, Wilhelm?" smiled Mohr.

"You know bloody well it's nothing of the sort." Heydt flushed angrily. "But we're German officers and we're doing no damned good penned up over here. If the Luftwaffe hasn't got the balls for it, the Navy has."

"It'll be a committee decision," said Breithaupt firmly. "There'll be no more unauthorized attempts."

"Then for God's sake make the decision, man, or we'll be here forever."

Otto Breithaupt eyed Kapitaenleutnant Heydt with distaste. Heydt was what the propagandists meant when they talked of "real" Nazis; blond, blue-eyed and fanatical in the extreme. As the commander of a U-boat operating out of the French submarine base at Lorient, Heydt had sunk 80,000 tons of Allied shipping before he was twenty-three, two years ago. He would still have been at it if his ship had not developed engine trouble and been caught on the surface by a Coastal Command Mosquito. He had surrendered without firing a shot and remained bitter about it. In any other commander, not scuttling the U-boat and leaving his crew to their fate would have earned the tag of coward. But Heydt's courage was a matter of record, as was his intense dislike of the Luftwaffe, whom he considered to be overfed and underemployed.

"Let's go over the pros and cons once more," said Breithaupt patiently. "The twelfth is three weeks away and all our arrangements are geared to being completed by that date. If we don't go then, we don't go at all, and we're likely to have a dozen very disgruntled officers on our hands. If we do go, we're up against the weather. Let's assume it's actually snowing on the twelfth. Admittedly that will hamper our pursuers, but it's not going to help us much either. We won't be able to stick to the roads. Nor-

mal people do not wander around in such conditions. We
shall therefore have to go across country, and I don't have
to tell any of you what the terrain is like between here and
the coast. It's rugged, even for fully fit men who have
trained on a proper diet. The snow will make the going
twice as difficult—not to mention the tracks we'll leave.
Those are indisputable facts."

Mohr nodded his agreement; Heydt shook his head fu-
riously; Hauptmann Heinrich Weiss merely looked bored.

The question of escape was academic to Weiss, whose
face was hideously scarred. The pilot of a Ju 88 shot down
over London in 1940, Weiss was the only member of the
crew to have survived. An antiaircraft battery had made
the kill, a lucky shot hitting the bomber amidships and
setting it on fire. Weiss had bailed out with his flying overalls ablaze. The initial free fall, far from putting the fire
out, had only fanned the flames upward into his face. Civilian surgeons had done their best, but plastic surgery
was in its infancy and there was none to spare for the
enemy. Apart from the scars on his cheeks and jaw, he
had virtually lost the sight of one eye, over which he now
wore a patch. There was no way he was going to be able
to walk through twenty miles of enemy territory without
being spotted.

Not yet twenty-four, Hauptmann Weiss was as fanatical
a Nazi as Heydt, though it was hard to tell whether the
hatred that burned inside him was due to political convic-
tion or bitterness because of his disfigurement. Somewhere in Germany he had a wife, who wrote to him regularly. He never replied to the letters. For him, that part of
his life was over.

"What's your opinion on the subject?" Breithaupt asked
him.

Weiss took his time answering.

"I think we're putting the cart before the horse, Herr
Major," he said eventually.

"How so?"

"We're talking about whether the escape should go

ahead as planned. Like Heydt, I'm all for it. Even if we don't succeed, or only partly succeed, we'll cause the British a hell of a lot of trouble, and in no small respect that's a contribution to the war effort. But I'm assuming, of course, that the *Tommis* don't already know of our plans for the twelfth."

Breithaupt groaned out loud. "Not that again."

"Yes, Herr Major, that again. I'm not alone in thinking we have an informer among us—though I exclude those at this table, naturally. I believe Oberleutnant Mohr subscribes to the same theory."

Mohr nodded. It was something of a fixation with him, and he was glad Weiss had raised it.

"As I told you the other day, Otto, the three attempts we've had foiled at the last minute must be more than coincidence."

"And, as I said," intoned Breithaupt, "we mustn't underestimate the British. They're not fools, they know we're going to try and get out. All they've got to do is keep their eyes open."

"Using that as a working hypothesis," said Weiss, "we're being absurdly optimistic to attempt an escape at all. We might just as well sit back and wait for the war to end. I agree with Mohr; coincidence must be ruled out. As head of security I know just how careful we are. Unacceptable though it may be to you, Herr Major, I have come to the conclusion that we're being sold out."

Breithaupt gnawed at the end of his pencil stub. Weiss was correct in one respect: he, Otto Breithaupt, didn't want to believe that there was a traitor in the camp.

"I assume that theorizing is not the end of it, Hauptmann Weiss," he said finally. "You have something practical in mind to root out this so-called informer."

"I have."

"For God's sake," broke in Heydt, who was tired of this talk of treachery. "Do we go ahead on the twelfth or not?"

"I suggest we shelve that decision until we hear what Hauptmann Weiss has to say," said Mohr. "It's no use us giving the green signal if we get no further than the wire."

Breithaupt concurred. "Let's hear your scheme, Heinrich."

"It's really quite simple," said Weiss. "I'm sure we all have our own ideas about who the alleged traitor is, but whether we are justified in our suspicions we don't know. I have therefore devised a method that will give us the answer once and for all.

"To begin with, I suggest we each write down three or four names here and now. Any name that appears more than once will mean we're all thinking along the same lines. Once that is established we can proceed."

It was a positive suggestion and even Breithaupt agreed that it could do no real harm. "Do we include NCOs?"

"Only the more senior ones, those who have actively participated in escapes or have shown their willingness to do so. We can forget about the very junior ranks; they're more interested in comfort than betrayal."

Each man thought carefully before condemning a fellow officer or senior NCO. When the lists were completed they were handed to Weiss, who spread them out on the table in front of him.

"It seems we have two common denominators, gentlemen," he announced. "Two names that are common to several lists. One appears three times, the other four. Although Kapitaenleutnant Heydt evidently trusts his own officers and ratings implicitly."

"There are only a dozen of us," snapped Heydt, "and I know them all as well as I know myself. You asked my opinion, you've got it."

"Get on with it, man," Mohr urged.

"Very well. The name that appears three times is Oberfeldwebel Reitlinger."

"Nonsense," said Breithaupt, who had considered Reitlinger before dismissing the notion as absurd.

"Nevertheless," said Heydt, "he and CSM Tomorrow are as thick as thieves. If I didn't know Reitlinger to be a family man I'd suspect they were lovers."

"They play checkers, that's all. If you're going to use that as a basis of treachery, this whole exercise is a waste of time."

"He has opportunity, Herr Major," put in Weiss. "Three of us think he's a possibility. We can't afford to overlook him."

"And Martin Bormann's Joe Stalin's cousin," muttered Breithaupt.

"And the other name?" asked Mohr.

"The other name is much more interesting. Oberleutnant Kapp."

Each of them had an immediate mental image of Oberleutnant Kapp, late of the 186th Artillery Regiment, and Franz Mohr at least wondered if he had put the name on the list because he, personally, didn't like the man. There was very little to like. Kapp was *dreikäsehoch*, bespectacled and skinny, and one of the very few German officers to be captured during the British rout at Dunkirk. No one could prove it, but it was thought that Kapp had surrendered at the first available opportunity. How he had even got his commission was a mystery to most of them; Party influence, it was suspected. But apart from being physically unattractive, Kapp was the camp complainer. As far as he was concerned food parcels were always late, mail was misdirected, and the standard of cooking and hygiene was abysmal. Even the handful of fellow army officers shunned his company and sometimes he would disappear for hours on end. This latter was far from being proof of his guilt; a clever informer would make it his business to be seen. But it was something to be considered.

"So, Kapp," said Heydt.

"We haven't proved anything yet," Breithaupt interrupted quickly. "I for one doubt that it is Kapp even though I put his name on my list."

"Well, that's my business from now on." Weiss threw the lists into the stove. "We'll soon know, one way or another."

"How do you propose to go about it?" Mohr asked.

"I intend to set a trap. I shall leak information, gradually, over the next few days, that an escape is being planned for, shall we say, two weeks from now. Naturally, Kapp and Reitlinger will be given different information. On the due date we shall keep a careful watch. If the *Tommis* turn up in force at one of the supposed exits, we'll know which is our *Spitzel*."

"And then?" asked Heydt.

Weiss drew a hand across his throat. But Breithaupt was having none of that.

"There'll be no drumhead courts-martial while I'm senior officer," he warned. People like Weiss tended to forget that courts-martial were forbidden; only the *Tommis* could mete out disciplinary action—in theory, that is; in practice, it was somewhat different.

"Well, we haven't caught our rabbit yet, have we?" Weiss smiled his twisted smile. "The scheme might not work. If it doesn't, we'll have to try again."

Breithaupt shook his head. "Sometimes, Heinrich, I swear to Christ, you enjoy this sort of thing."

"It's a contribution, Herr Major. What else can a man in my position do?"

Breithaupt got to his feet.

"As far as I'm concerned that's all for today. We'll see how Heinrich's plan works out, then discuss the twelfth again. Let's get to hell out of here. My chaps must be freezing outside. Walk with me, Franz?"

It was snowing again and they huddled deep inside their threadbare clothes.

"What about the new batch of POWs?" asked Mohr. "Would you like me to meet them?"

"If you wouldn't mind. I've got a hundred other things to do." He chuckled. "Besides, the train's bound to be late."

"Don't grumble about the trains, Otto. It means our bombers are still doing the job."

Seven

NOVEMBER 19

During the Second World War most escapes from POW camps, on either side, were made via tunnels, and the one planned from Skiddaw for the twelfth of December was no exception. In one respect the porosity of the soil in that part of northern England, while hindering progress, helped the POWs. Few tunnel escapes had been tried from Skiddaw and none had succeeded, which led the British to believe that it could not be done. Mostly, escapees got out by using sheer bluff, as Emil Naumann had done, or by stowing away in the back of civilian refuse carts or delivery trucks. In the early days, before the doubling of the perimeter fence, two officers won temporary freedom by throwing a makeshift rope ladder over the barbed wire, which was not electrified, and scrambling out in that manner. When such schemes worked they were a great morale booster, but they had one obvious drawback: only one POW, at the most a couple, could get out at any one time. Breithaupt's plan for the twelfth involved a dozen.

Although he had no way of knowing whether or not Major Mitchell and his staff, via an informer or by keeping their eyes open, were aware of the tunnel, Breithaupt was pretty sure that, either way, the commandant wouldn't pounce until the last moment. As he had pointed out to Oberleutnant Mohr, this had the dual effect of keeping the POWs happy and untroublesome while they were digging and demoralizing them when their efforts proved valueless at the eleventh hour. That had been Mitchell's *modus operandi* in the past and there was no reason to think he would change a winning pattern.

Getting under the wire was only a fraction of the problem for would-be escapees. On the outside they needed clothes that would pass casual scrutiny, money for emergencies, provisions; they needed maps, compasses, a knowledge of the terrain. It was not the slightest use building a tunnel to rival the Simplon if they were discovered sitting at the side of the road, wondering which way was west. For this reason Skiddaw was invariably a hotbed of clandestine cottage industries.

Clothes were the most important item. The majority of POWs looked like POWs, either because they still wore some of their flying gear or because of the regulation overalls issued by their captors. So the first thing was to change the color and shape of their clothing, which was the responsibility of an *Oberleutnant* who was a tailor in civilian life. Dyes were obtained from berries, collected during the autumn and squirreled away, and ordinary ink. The bark from some trees, too, when soaked in hot water, produced a reliable brown pigment. Thus, a pair of gray-blue Luftwaffe trousers, which against regulations many of the air crew wore in combat, would be transformed. Admittedly not every attempt proved successful and what should have been dark blue or brown turned out to resemble something like camouflage netting. But this was wartime Britain and many of the indigenous population wore what looked like castoffs.

Once dyed, trousers were restyled, reassembled and pressed. But not too well. Several fugitives had been spotted for what they were because of a knife-edge crease in their trousers.

Tunics proved more difficult. There was no way that, without proper equipment, the military cut could be disguised and the tunic turned into a civilian jacket. But at least the color could be altered and, under a dyed overcoat (a doctored greatcoat), would not be too noticeable.

After clothing the second-most important item was money; money for fares if the going got rough; for purchases if the provisions ran out; and for bribes if an escapee was fortunate enough to reach a port and find a corruptible skipper. It was a curious paradox of camp life that money for bribes had first of all to be obtained by bribery. POWs were paid in scrip, not currency, and scrip was useless outside the camp. The amount varied according to rank, but an *Oberleutnant* in 1942 would obtain roughly the equivalent of six pounds sterling per month. The black-market exchange rate was four for one.

Apart from Corporal Napley there were other guards in the exchange market. Although it was a indictable offense and the punishment severe if discovered, it went on all the time. Many of the captured fliers possessed expensive wrist watches, pocket watches, fountain pens, and other items capable of being converted to hard cash. The going rate varied according to the natural laws of supply and demand, but any POW who could hang on to his possessions for long enough was assured of a respectable price. And legitimate currency was of course smuggled in by new arrivals, sometimes in a very odd manner. Mostly it was concealed in book-bindings and suchlike, but the *Hauptmann* who swallowed ten one-pound notes after bailing out and waited for nature to take its course was very disappointed when he found no takers for the end-product.

After money came provisions, usually chocolate. An alert observer should always have been able to tell that an escape was in the cards when few of the POWs were seen eating their rations.

Penultimately it was a matter of knowing in which direction to go and what to avoid. Recaptured POWs were an invaluable source of information in this. A route that was passable in June was sometimes out of the question in December; a house where someone had obtained a glass of water in August could well be a temporary billet for troops in November. These were things to know.

In view of the camp's proximity to the coast, maps and rough compasses were not considered essential equipment for potential runaways from Skiddaw. Nevertheless, they were provided if required—if, for example, a prisoner decided to head not for Workington or Whitehaven but inland. Each recaptured flier, after his twenty-eight days in the cooler, was thoroughly debriefed by the Escape Committee and a reservoir of intelligence assembled from which maps were drawn. Most of the POWs got no farther than a few miles, so there was an embarrassing plethora of knowledge concerning the hills and roads within the immediate vicinity of the camp. Further on was more of an unknown quantity, but even so the disposition of the major roads was known.

Lastly there was the question of attitude once out of Skiddaw, and on this, lectures were given by officers who knew something of England and the English, standing room only.

Many POWs were recaptured because they looked and behaved like POWs. An ignorance of the language was not in itself a drawback; the English, it was pointed out, are a secretive race not much given to social intercourse. They are reserved in attitude and demeanor. Not for nothing did the proverb originate of an Englishman's home being his castle. Once inside, with the portcullis down and the drawbridge up, he is not interested in callers and neighbors. He's not much interested in them outside the castle, either. Therefore, the POWs were told, even if you have a working knowledge of English, don't be too chatty; don't try to curry favor by tossing out "good mornings" at random, if by some misfortune your route takes you through a town or village. More important still, don't skulk. The Englishman is a proud individual who makes way for no man. And here, usually, the story was told of the English spy in Cairo during the First World War. His disguise as an Arab was perfect, his accent faultless. Yet he walked through the bazaar as if he owned it, something no Arab would ever do. So keep your head up and never run, unless it's for a bus.

But all of the foregoing presupposed that a POW was on the loose, and as yet none was.

As senior German officer, Major Breithaupt, in consultation with the remainder of the Escape Committee, had given long and careful thought to the positioning of the tunnel. From the inner perimeter wire to the outer was a standard thirty feet, nine and a fraction meters the way the Germans calculated it, so at first glance it mattered little where the tunnelers started, all other things being equal. But the western boundary housed, as well as the guardroom, the administration offices and the armory, which was always heavily guarded. The opposite end of the compound was also out, which was a pity as quite close to the inner perimeter wire stood the POWs' kitchen, canteen and a room that served as the library. The snag here was that the nearest cover beyond the outer wire, a clump of trees leading into a copse, was seventy yards away, over sixty-four meters. Unless a prisoner wanted to run that far in full view of the watchtower guards, tunneling anywhere close to the trees would take the rest of this war and most of the next.

The best idea had been the officers' bathhouse and heads, on the north side. With all the comings and goings from that building, an escape burrow there had been considered foolproof. But two days before a projected attempt, Captain Thorogood descended with half a company of armed men, and that was that. A second tunnel anywhere in that region would have to wait a while.

Which left the south side, though really there was nothing there save the Motor Pool (again heavily guarded), the British officers' quarters (definitely not), the long wooden hut that served as the German officers' Mess (too obvious), and the all-denominational chapel. Breithaupt had not even considered this as a possibility until an afternoon in August when young Peter Kaehler rushed into Hut 5.

"Sir, I've just come from the chapel—"

"Congratulations. I've been saying for a long time that what we need around here is more religion and less griping. What are you trying to do, Kaehler, pray your way out?"

"Of course not, sir. But it's one of the coolest places in the camp on a day like this, and the chaplain's hardly ever there except on Sundays, so he doesn't mind—"

"Will you kindly slow down, Kaehler, and get to the point. I have work to do even if junior officers do not."

"I'm trying to, sir." Kaehler took a couple of deep breaths. "There's a way out from there, Herr Major, I swear to God there is. It's just a wooden structure, the chapel, like the Mess, but through lack of space or something they've pushed one end of the altar right up against the south wall. And it *moves*, sir."

"Moves? Have you and Preiss been making that potato wine again?"

"No, sir. But it does. I tried it."

"Tried what? What moves, you dunderhead?"

"The altar, sir. I leaned against it and it damn near toppled over, God knows why."

"God indeed, Leutnant Kaehler. Show me."

In purpose-built Skiddaw the chapel appeared to have been erected as an afterthought. It wasn't difficult to imagine the military planners, in their anxiety to take care of the overspill from Grizedale Hall, omitting it from their original drawings and then, as the camp took shape, thinking, Oh Lord, isn't there something in the Geneva Convention about a place of worship for POWs? Can't find the precise reference, old man, but we've got a few hundred square feet doing nothing down there on the southwest perimeter; that'll have to do. Nothing too fancy, though; we're not competing with Sir Christopher Wren. Didn't know the Jerries prayed, anyway.

And nothing too fancy was what the POWs got; a

wooden structure with a wooden floor seventy or eighty feet long by thirty wide, with benches as pews and an altar like an oversized desk.

Kaehler was right, Breithaupt saw immediately; no one had bothered to nail the altar down, perhaps thinking that its own weight would keep it in place, and what was the point in going to more trouble than was necessary for POWs? Furthermore, the altar was hollow, just a big box really, large enough to take a man. Underneath its base were only the floorboards.

"Grab a couple of reliable men and keep watch," he ordered Kaehler. "I'm going to take a look."

It took Otto Breithaupt the rest of the afternoon to pry loose a couple of boards, but what he saw when he had finished, via the dim light of a pencil torch, gave him immense satisfaction. There were no solid foundations. The corner posts had each been sunk into a bed of concrete, but that was all; the rest was just earth. And the gap between the beams supporting the floorboards and the earth itself was a good five feet, almost high enough to stand up in. In their haste to get the camp completed on schedule, the *Tommis* had made a mistake which was going to cost them dear.

Back in his hut Breithaupt did some rapid calculation. The tunnel could be started just inside the south wall of the chapel, which was some twenty feet, or six meters, from the inner perimeter wire. The distance between the inner and outer wires was thirty feet, about nine meters, and from the outer wire to the cover of the trees, much closer on this side of the compound than at the eastern boundary, about fifty feet, or a little over fifteen meters. Allowing for the fact that the tunnel would have to be approximately a meter wide by a meter high, the quantity of earth they would need to shift was around thirty cubic meters. The space beneath the floorboards of the chapel was six or seven times as big, so there would be no problem getting rid of the excavated soil. Just dump it, it was as simple as that.

A relay of good tunnelers, allowing for shoring up and laboring under arduous and exhausting conditions, could shift half a cubic meter a day. In theory, therefore, in sixty working days they should be in a position to attempt the break. Not every day could be a working day, of course; too great an interest in the chapel by too many POWs would raise suspicions. Three or four days a week should be about average, say fifteen weeks from the time they started. The second or third week in December would see them ready to go.

A major problem to be overcome before digging could get under way was finding a pretext for heavy traffic between the main compound and the chapel, and here Breithaupt had an inspiration. He formed a choir and asked permission to hold choir practices in the chapel. The commandant welcomed the idea; anything that kept the prisoners out of his hair without interfering with the routine of the camp could only be beneficial. Captain Thorogood wasn't so sure.

"They're up to something, sir. Good grief, why do they want to stay indoors when the sun's cracking the flags?"

"Nonsense, Adrian. But if it'll make you any happier, keep an eye on them."

The adjutant did just that, but Breithaupt outfoxed him. For the first two weeks of choir practice not a cubic centimeter of earth was moved, not a spade lifted; the choir did precisely what all choirs do: rehearsed. And if the rendering of the various hymns was less than holy, well, that only meant more homework.

Captain Thorogood eventually gave up. If the bloody Jerries were up to something, he'd find out about it sooner or later.

Gradually the tunnel progressed. While the choir sang hosannas above them, the duty diggers burrowed away, not the least of their problems being ventilation. But there was little to be done about that. It simply meant stopping once every five or ten minutes and sometimes crawling backward to breathe the (comparatively) fresh air beneath the chapel.

The pattern of digging never varied. By feeble torch-light, the POWs worked in teams of two. While the lead man of the pair chipped away at the earth in front of him with implements fashioned from old cans, pilfered chisels, even sharpened messtins, the second man filled a cut-off trouser leg, tied with string at one end. When the "sack" was full he retraced his steps until he was underneath the chapel and dumped the contents. The exercise was then repeated.

Shoring up was the most difficult and unpopular task, as on those days no forward movement was made. The POWs were always on the prowl for planks, bits of iron, or anything else that could be used. The end product would have given a mining engineer heart failure, but it worked—for the most part.

The days it didn't work were toward the end of the summer, when the rains came and soaked the desiccated soil, causing minor falls and snaillike progress. The roof of the tunnel was a good two meters below the surface of the compound, and the chances of a gaping hole suddenly appearing were remote. Still, they had to be careful. No one knew what the effects of a heavy downpour would be. Breithaupt's estimate of half a cubic meter a day proved to be about average, though it was sometimes less, never more.

Nevertheless, by the end of September they were under the inner perimeter wire, and by the last day of the following month outside the compound itself. Now, as November ran toward its wintry close, they were reaching the end of the trail. The Escape Committee had calculated that the last sackful of earth would be removed on December 11, and the break was planned for the following night.

With luck, the POWs who had worked on the tunnel were thinking. Provided that nothing went wrong at the last minute; provided that the roof didn't cave in or Captain Thorogood develop second sight or somebody rat on them; provided that . . .

Each of them knew that what they were attempting had never succeeded before and that every tunnel took on a personality of its own, sometimes friendly, sometimes hostile. This one, nicknamed *Kaninchenbau*—"Rabbit Warren" or "Rabbit Run"—had been lucky for them. Only one minor upset had occurred, though that could easily have become a disaster.

It took place one morning when the chaplain walked into his domain just as the tunneling crew were emerging from beneath the altar. Leutnant Uhde, who was supposed to be door guard, had let his mind wander to his young wife and had not seen the chaplain until it was too late. Franz Mohr saved the situation by rallying the POWs around the altar and getting them to sing an impromptu rendering of "Stille Nacht, Heilige Nacht" ("Silent Night"). When the chaplain remarked that wasn't it a bit early to be practicing carols, Mohr responded that the choir needed all the rehearsal it could get. The chaplain, somewhat shortsighted, was compelled to agree and left them to it.

So the tunnel was a lucky one, but with only three weeks or so to go now before K-Day (for *Kaninchenbau*), the men occasionally showed signs of strain. Friends snapped at one another for no apparent reason, and those who had been selected to make the attempt found themselves drawing further and further apart from those who were to stay behind. No one argued with the decision regarding who should go; that was up to the Escape Committee and final. But it was hard for those not on the list to watch those who were, checking and rechecking their iron rations, clothing, maps. It was also hard to understand why Breithaupt had limited the number to an even dozen, though most of them accepted that twelve missing in a snap head count would create only confusion, while fifty or sixty would instantly sound the alarm.

Leutnants Kaehler and Preiss were going. Kaehler was a must, because it was his alertness that had set the whole scheme in motion. And where Peter Kaehler went, Johann Preiss went. Franz Mohr was going, though Otto Breithaupt debated the wisdom of this at first. If this escape did not succeed, Franz could well go to pieces with a further twenty-eight days in the cooler. But he had worked hard on the digging and deserved his chance.

Kapitaenleutnant Wilhelm Heydt was going and taking with him four of his naval officers. Heydt had put forward his own name and those of his subordinates, and there was no arguing with him. It would have been difficult to negate his claims, in any case. Whether Breithaupt liked the man or not, the fact remained that Heydt had served on the Escape Committee for a year without asking for a place on previous runs. It was his due, and Otto Breithaupt could not deny it.

Leutnant Fritz Uhde was going. He was one of the lucky ones. At the beginning of any escape bid, the officer who originated the idea plus any one other POW he nominated were first on the list. After that, depending on what the method of egress was, the Escape Committee chose a further eighty percent. With a tunnel attempt it would be the strongest—those who could dig without showing strain— as, naturally enough, only the individuals who worked on the tunnel could expect to use it. The remaining two or three places were chosen by lot, scraps of paper in a cap, the successful ones marked with a cross. Fritz Uhde had drawn a cross and was already smelling his young wife's scent.

Oberleutnant Werner Herburg was going—by accident. Nominally the camp librarian with no more arduous a duty than ensuring that books, a great prize, were fairly distributed, it was Herburg who owned the chess set Franz Mohr and Otto Breithaupt usually played with. It had been received the previous Christmas, 1941, sent by Herburg's mother via the Red Cross. The British examined it with a fine-tooth comb for contraband, and finding nothing, passed it on to the officer concerned. It was used regularly without incident until July 1942, when it was accidentally dropped by Peter Kaehler at the end of a session. It broke into four layers. Between layers, carefully folded, were ten English five-pound notes, a total of one hundred and fifty pounds, a fortune. Further examination failed to reveal any more treasure, but it was obvious that Frau Herburg was a clever lady. She had overlooked the obvious hiding places and opted for the obscure, hoping that somehow the money would be discovered. As it rightfully belonged to her son, who without hesitation put it into the common fund, there was no way the committee could exclude him from the next serious break-out.

The penultimate place went to Oberleutnant Theo Emke. It was impossible to leave Emke out. In spite of his hugeness, which gave him great difficulty in the tunnel, he had twice the work rate of any other officer. Those huge biceps and hands could virtually dig a tunnel by themselves, and he never grumbled. He would be sadly missed by all save the would-be snooker champions, but his place was on the outside.

For the final spot to make up the round dozen, Major Breithaupt first of all suggested Hauptmann Weiss. Weiss declined. "In the Reich I will be given a desk job; here I am useful." No one argued.

Breithaupt then considered himself, but quickly rejected the idea. He wanted to get home and into the fight again as much as anybody, but his place was in Skiddaw, coordinating. It might be presumptuous and arrogant of him, but here he had a value greater than his value to Germany in the air. Many of the POWs were only kids; they needed guidance; he had a duty to see they did nothing foolish. His self-imposed task (he refused to think of it as self-sacrifice) could keep him in Skiddaw for the rest of the war, but that was the luck of the draw.

So the twelfth and final place was left open. There was no obvious candidate, but one never knew when one might appear.

At three o'clock that same afternoon Oberleutnant Mohr was summoned from his hut by his orderly, Obergefreiter Willi Braune. The expected batch of new POWs had arrived. Normally this was treated as a gala event by the old-timers, all anxious to see if they knew anyone amongst the new arrivals. But today the weather kept them huddling around their stoves. Blobs of snow the size of fists, driven by a rising wind, had been falling since noon and it was impossible to see further than a few feet.

"The perfect day for an escape, Herr Oberleutnant," said Willi. "The *Tommis* would never find us."

Mohr smiled to himself. "Us, Willi? When was the last time you went under the wire?"

"I've never been given the opportunity. It's always the officers who make the breaks."

"Then I'll see to it that you're included in the next. It's a bit tricky though. We're charging the main gates in broad daylight."

"Herr Oberleutnant—?"

"We need someone to fling himself at the guard's bayonet while the others get out."

"Perhaps I'll wait for something better."

"Perhaps you will. All right, Willi, you can get back to whatever you were doing. There's no point in us both catching pneumonia."

Willi made his way across the compound to the boiler room. With any luck Harry Cade would already be there, coffee bubbling. Charging the main gates, for Christ's sake. What did the *Oberleutnant* take him for, a lunatic? It was all very well for the officers; if they got home it was a full-page spread in the *Voelkischer Beobachter* and tea with the Fuehrer. For other ranks it was back to the front line. There was a lot to be said for being a prisoner.

Emerging himself, Franz Mohr wrapped his threadbare coat more tightly about him and put his head down. God, but it was a wicked day. Kapitaenleutnant Heydt or no, if the weather was like this on the twelfth, no one was going anywhere.

At the door to the guardroom CSM Purser was waiting for him. Mohr stamped his feet and shook himself like a terrier.

"Good afternoon, Sergeant Major," he said in English.

"I trust if this weather continues you will not be taking roll call in the open."

"I really couldn't say, sir, though I think it's unlikely. We'll probably just do a head count in the huts."

"I should hope so. Well, by how many bodies have you depleted the Wehrmacht this time?"

"Just three, sir, all Luftwaffe *Oberleutnants*. They've seen Major Mitchell, but the M.O. is busy. Their examination will have to wait."

"Very well. Lead me to them."

Mohr followed the CSM into the guardroom. The three captured officers were standing in a line, facing the door. Mohr looked them up and down. His eyes widened in astonishment and it was all he could do not to click his heels.

On the far left of the trio, von Stuerzbecher saw instant recognition pictured on the face of the newcomer.

"Oberleutnant Karl Stuerzbecher, Luftwaffe," he barked. "Good to see you again, Hans."

It took a moment or two, but Mohr got the message.

"Good to see you, Karl, though your memory fails you. It's Franz, not Hans."

"Of course, Forgive me. It was such a brief meeting."

This conversation, for the apparent benefit of the other two POWs, was conducted in German and the CSM did not understand a word of it.

"All right," he said, "that's enough of that. You can chat as much as you like outside. Get going."

"Of course, Herr Feldwebel." Mohr beckoned the others. "Follow me, gentlemen."

Outside, Franz Mohr thought quickly. For obvious reasons von Stuerzbecher did not want the British to know who he was, but less obviously he didn't want his two companions to know either. Mohr had to get rid of them.

"Look," he said, "I'd like to have a word with my old friend Karl before the others commandeer him for news of home, so I'll leave you to find your own way to the Mess." He pointed. "Go diagonally across the compound and it's

126

the first wooden structure you see after you pass the Motor Pool. Welcome to Skiddaw, by the way. I hope you won't be here long."

The other two were only too glad to get out of the cold and within a few strides had disappeared behind a curtain of snow. In spite of himself Franz Mohr now came to attention.

"Herr Generalmajor," he said respectfully.

"None of that," warned von Stuerzbecher. "I'm Oberleutnant Stuerzbecher without the *von* from now on and don't you forget it. Let's keep walking. Who are you and where did we meet, incidentally? I seem to know you."

Mohr introduced himself. "We met at a party in Paris in the summer of 1940. You were only an *Oberstleutnant* then, but needless to say we heard of your subsequent promotions. Is it true that the *Tommis* don't know who you are?"

"As far as I know. And it's essential, Franz, that they don't find out. I can't tell you how essential, but believe me, a great many German lives depend on it."

"You're safe as far as I'm concerned, sir."

"I expect so, but what about the others? Is there anyone else here likely to recognize me?"

"Hard to say, Herr—I mean, Karl. There are a couple of hundred of us here and it's possible you've met some of them before. Then again, I wouldn't have recognized you myself except for the fact that you were good enough to talk tactics to me for half an hour. If you'll forgive me, you've changed."

"We all have, Franz. Who's the senior officer?"

"Major Breithaupt."

"Breithaupt, Breithaupt. No, I don't think I know him, but we had better remedy that as soon as possible. Also, I've got to get a message home right away, letting them know where I am. Not the normal POW's letter, though that will have to do if there's no alternative."

"The Navy has a code, sir—I'm sorry—Karl. They're a bit jealous about letting anyone use it, but I'm sure they'll

make an exception in your case. It'll mean letting Kapitaenleutnant Heydt in on it, though."

"Can't be helped. All right, Major Breithaupt first, and
then Kapitaenleutnant Heydt. And I know you must have
a thousand questions you want to ask me, Franz, but
much later if you don't mind."

"Of course."

Eight

The same weather conditions that were creating havoc in northern England were also being felt in Germany. Not that the Berliners were worried; it could snow from now till Armageddon for all they cared. It might be nasty, squelchy stuff in peacetime, but in wartime it was a gift from the gods. It made the young girls' faces bright and hid the bomb-torn buildings. More important, it kept the *Tommis* grounded. Even the terror fliers couldn't take off in weather such as this. The current joke was that Goebbels would shortly announce in the *Voelkischer Beobachter* that the snow was the result of a new secret weapon. It was cold, bloody cold, but cold was better than dead.

Inside Oberleutnant Christian Eicke's rented apartment it was far from cold, not all of the heat being generated by the roaring fire.

"You're out of your mind, Christian." Feldwebel Josef Schelling looked from the map of England spread out across the table to his superior officer and friend. "When the SS came and grabbed me from the front I thought my time was up. Now I know I was right. A division couldn't do it. You've got one Ritterkreuz, for the love of God; what the hell do you want with another? We wouldn't stand a chance."

Christian ran a hand through his dark hair. "It's precisely because fourteen thousand men couldn't do it that the three of us can." He grinned disarmingly. "Anyway, you're forgetting something. I'm not asking you, I'm telling you."

"That's below the belt, Christian." The third member of the trio, Obergefreiter Wolfgang Schultz, pulled a long face. "When we arrived you said this was a volunteer operation."

"So it is. But I'm the volunteer. You two are conscripted."

"Bloody hell."

"You mean there's no way I can get back to somewhere nice and safe like Stalingrad?"

"None."

Josef Schelling shrugged. "In that case I volunteer. But you might have chosen someone other than Schultz here. If the British don't kill us, he will."

"Balls."

As a matter of fact, since he had come to the conclusion that three was the optimum number for the operation, Christian had given both other members of the team considerable thought. To begin with, he had listed everyone he could think of, officers and other ranks, who were in any way suitable for the task at hand. He had examined their qualifications carefully and only with the greatest reluctance rejected them. The list finally narrowed down to the two men opposite him. NCOs or not, Feldwebel Schelling and Obergefreiter Schultz had, in effect, chosen themselves. There was no one with whom Christian would rather work, no one he would trust more with his neck. Though to look at them they were a most unlikely couple.

Born in 1904 in Düsseldorf (though now he was approaching forty, he sometimes gave his year of birth as

1908), Josef Schelling was a giant of a man, three full inches over six feet with shoulders to match and a chest that threatened to burst out of his regulation tunic. A mechanic by trade, he had supplemented his income between the wars by prize-fighting in fairgrounds. His face still bore the marks of those days, though he swore that his broken nose was due to a fall after too much beer. Drinking beer was his favorite pastime and he had been known to put away three crates in an evening.

On loan from an Infantry unit and attached to the Engineer Battalion of the Totenkopf SS Division, his fondness for the bottle was the source of much trouble in the early days. Promoted *Oberfeldwebel* three times, three times Schelling had been demoted before Christian took him in hand. As his immediate superior officer, Christian was responsible for two of the demotions and he was at a loss regarding what to do with the big fellow. He could have him shot, that was one solution. Getting drunk anywhere near the front was not treated as a joke in the SS, even for NCOs on attachment. He could toss him into a military prison for the duration. But that didn't appeal either. There seemed too much good in the man to take the easy way out.

The second time Schelling appeared before him, Christian had the answer.

"It seems to me," he said, "that you're always in trouble because you have too much time on your hands. I've therefore arranged with the Battalion *Hauptscharfuehrer* for you to be drilled every moment you're not actually eating, sleeping or on patrol. What's more, whatever the ground conditions, you will be required to parade in full uniform, which must, of course, be cleaned and pressed. Let's see if a little fresh air and exercise can't cure you of your addiction to beer."

It took ten days, but eventually Schelling realized he couldn't beat the system, and Christian was not surprised when the ex-*Feldwebel* requested an interview. He was only amazed that it had taken so long. Drilling under the beady eye of the *Hauptscharfuehrer* for five hours a day on normal days and all day on rest days wasn't funny; neither was scraping inches of mud off a uniform and boots in preparation for the next inspection.

"Permission to speak, Herr Sturmbannfuehrer?"

"Permission granted."

"I respectfully request to be taken off punishment. As the Sturmbannfuehrer rightly predicted, fresh air and exercise takes away a man's appetite for beer."

"Good." Christian reached in his desk drawer and produced a bottle and two glasses. "But not schnapps, I trust. Sit down."

They finished the bottle together, and Schelling gave no more trouble after that. And, being a natural leader of men, he gradually worked his way up the promotion ladder again.

When Christian was transferred to the Recco Battalion of the Totenkopf Division, he took Feldwebel Schelling with him. Reconnaissance was a dangerous business, with the battalion sometimes operating half a dozen miles ahead of the rest of the division. On such occasions it was comforting to know that he had at least one NCO who was both reliable and courageous. Or in this case two, for included in the transfer was Wolf Schultz.

Obergefreiter Wolfgang Schultz had been a long-time friend of Josef Schelling's before Christian met either of them. A fully accredited hero, Schultz wore with pride one of the army's most coveted awards, the *Panzervernichtungsabzeichen*, the badge for the single-handed destruction of a tank. Or, rather, he wore two, for on two separate occasions he had taken out a Russian tank without using an antitank weapon.

There were some who sniggered at the sight of the huge Schelling and the diminutive Schultz going out on the town together, and who nicknamed them Lennie and George after the two characters in John Steinbeck's *Of Mice and Men*. But sarcastic comments were always made in private, for in spite of his size Wolf Schultz was a fighter of renown. What he lacked in weight and height he made up for in speed and guts, going at an opponent with arms flailing like miniature windmills. In order to put him down and make him stay down, you had to knock him out; anything less, regardless of the state he was in, simply enraged him and put him back into the fight with twice as much energy and venom as before. Many a man who fought Wolf Schultz was beaten because his arms grew too heavy to deliver the *coup de grâce*.

Schultz openly confessed to wishing he was six feet four with the looks of Clark Gable. Instead he was five feet eight, weighed 140 pounds, and resembled a recalcitrant cherub with a bad case of rabbit teeth. But this drawback in no way prevented him from pursuing one of the most active sex lives anyone in the Totenkopf Division, not renowned for its celibacy, had ever known. If the division was miles from anywhere and the nearest female company a nanny goat, Schultz would somehow find a willing woman. He put it down to an acute sense of smell, which he said was the equal of a stallion's at breeding time. Others put it down to luck and indefatigable energy.

On transfer to the Reconnaissance Battalion, Christian took him on at Schelling's request. At first Christian had his doubts, only slightly mollified by sight of the tank badges. What on earth could this skinny individual do? Schultz answered the unposed question with a vengeance on their first sortie by taking out, alone, a Russian machine-gun nest that was holding up the advance. Christian's misgivings disappeared in a flash at the sight of the *Obergefreiter* racing up a heavily defended slope with the speed and agility of an Olympic sprinter.

Subsequently, prior to Christian's ignominious dismissal from the SS, the three of them did everything together, in battle and out of it. If it was dangerous, it was for them. And it was a measure of the deep friendship that existed between them that neither commented on Christian's new rank of *Oberleutnant*. They knew some of the story; the rest would be told if and when Christian elected to tell it. In the meantime, they thought it completely natural that, faced with his present problem, Christian had sent for them. They would have felt insulted had he done otherwise. They would respect and calculate the hazards, of course, and they would grumble; but that was just part of being an old soldier.

"It's still impossible, Christian, whether I volunteer or whether I'm dragooned." Feldwebel Schelling frowned at the map of England. "The British aren't going to let us walk calmly in, free the general, and walk out again."

"First of all," said Christian, "forget Stuerzbecher's rank. If the British knew that, they'd stick him in a special camp and we'd never get at him. But as far as we can gather he's got away with posing as an *Oberleutnant*."

"Don't the *Tommis* have lists of names of senior officers?" asked Schultz. "I thought we did."

"We do. So do they. But they can't update them with any degree of regularity or accuracy. As the war goes on, promotions are made weekly. It's impossible to keep track of every junior general in the Luftwaffe. Aces like Galland and Kammhuber, yes. They'd be as well known in England as they are here. But Kurt von Stuerzbecher is not exactly of the front rank. If he were, he'd have Kammhuber's job or Adolf Galland's."

"It's still impossible," said Schelling.

"I wish to God you'd stop using that word," said Christian irritably. "Although I must admit I said exactly the same to Standartenfuehrer Weil. But that was before I knew where the camp was."

He could see they were not convinced.

"Look," he said, "the *Tommis* expect POWs to make escape attempts. That's why they guard the camps. I've no exact figures, of course, but I was allowed to see Werra's account of his bids and it seems to me that more POWs get out than we ever knew. What they don't do is get home. They're normally caught within hours of going under the wire, and that's because they have only the vaguest idea of where they're going and what they're going to do when they get there. The *Tommis* rely heavily on the fact that England is an island. There's virtually no

134

way off for an escape bid organized from the inside. But one organized from the outside, that's different. Because it's never happened before, the *Tommis* won't be ready for it. That's our advantage."

"Christ," muttered Schultz, "you mean we've actually got to get him out of the camp as well as bring him home?"

"How the hell else d'you think we're going to snatch him?" demanded Christian. "I can't go up to the commandant and ask him if it's okay for Stuerzbecher to take a walk, see you Christmas."

"But it's im—" began Schelling—"Sorry, Christian, but it's ludicrous. There are just three of us. We know approximately where the camp is but we don't know what its defenses are, what the surrounding countryside is like. We know Stuerzbecher's inside, but we don't know where. There must be hundreds of POWs in there. We don't know what his routine is. We don't know what time he gets up and what time he goes to bed. We've no way of getting a message to him, telling him to be ready at a certain hour. Wear a blue carnation so we'll recognize him. With all due respect, Christian, this is the most arrant piece of nonsense I've ever heard."

Christian nodded. "Except for the last sentence I'm inclined to agree with everything you say. We don't know what the camp's defenses are, we don't know where Stuerzbecher is, we don't know what routine he follows. I also accept that there's probably very little chance of getting a message to him, but I can't solve any of these problems over here. I won't have a clue to what's going on in Skiddaw until I've taken a look inside."

"Now I know I'm going mad or deaf," groaned Schelling. "Correct me if I'm wrong, Wolf, but I thought I heard our so-called superior officer say he was going to take a look *inside* a British POW camp. Like a tourist."

"That's what comes of being stationed in Cologne. All that bombing has sent him crazy."

Christian grinned. "All right, all right, but examine it logically. I can't make any concrete plans for getting Stuerzbecher out until I know where he is and what security is like. And I can only find that out by paying them a visit. I speak fluent English don't forget, which was partly the reason Standartenfuehrer Weil pulled my name from the hat."

"And we speak none."

"Let's hope you won't have to."

"And let's hope Generalmajor von Stuerzbecher starts broadcasting for the *Tommis* so that we can call this whole thing off," said Schelling. "What's so special about him anyway, or aren't we supposed to ask that?"

"I'm not sure myself," admitted Christian. "All I know is that somebody wants him back."

"Beautiful." Schelling shook his head at the prospect. "Three German soldiers marching along the country roads in northern England. Hasn't it occurred to anyone that we might be a bit conspicuous?" Christian said nothing. Schelling's eyes narrowed. "We will be in uniform, I suppose?"

"Er, not exactly."

"What does not exactly mean?"

"It means we'll be in plain clothes."

Schultz held his head in mock despair. "Oh Christ, let me off. Do you know what the British do to German soldiers caught wandering around in plain clothes, Christian? They put them up against a wall and shoot them. No messing, no formalities, just a firing squad."

"I've thought of all that," said Christian, "but there's no way round it. It's twenty miles from coast to camp and twenty miles back again. Uniforms are out."

"We could drop in at night, on a regular bombing run, and be on our way before sunup," suggested Schelling.

"That's out. There'll be no dropping in and dropping out. We can't take a chance on somebody seeing a parachute and sounding the alarm before we've even started. We'll go in by U-boat." He jabbed a finger at the map. "Somewhere around here, Maryport, or maybe a little farther south. It'll depend what the Navy thinks. With any luck we'll come out the same way."

"Christ, submarines," said Schelling. "I hate the bloody things."

Christian was surprised. "You've traveled in one?"

"Of course I haven't. Why should I travel in something I hate?"

Christian didn't attempt to argue the logic of that.

"When are we due to leave?" asked Wolf Schultz.

"The sooner the better. The availability of a U-boat is a major factor, but there's no point in hanging around. Say a week or so, December eighth or ninth. In the meantime, you can bunk in the spare room."

"Where you can keep an eye on us."

"Where I can keep an eye on you," agreed Christian.

He checked the time and reached for his cap. He had an appointment with Weil at 8 P.M., and he did not want to be late.

"You'll notice the liquor cabinet is well stocked," he said, "courtesy of the management. Help yourselves, but take it easy. We may have a lot of cross-country hiking to do and I want you two to be up to it."

"If the Oberleutnant will excuse the impertinence," said Schultz cheekily, "the Oberleutnant is looking a bit overweight himself."

"The Oberleutnant," said Christian, "has lost two kilos in the last week and he intends to lose two more before we sail. I'm serious, Wolf," he added somberly. "The difference between spending Christmas in Berlin and not spending it at all could depend upon how fast you can run."

"Reminds me of old times," said Schultz, when the two NCOs were alone.

Schelling shook his head mournfully.

"I wish you hadn't said that. The only thing I remember about the old times is that whenever the three of us were billeted together, you could bet your life someone was going to start shooting at us."

Standartenfuehrer Weil was delighted to see that Christian looked much fitter than at their last meeting. He had lost some weight and his eyes were much clearer, the surroundings less puffy. Weil was far from happy, however, with Christian's choice of personnel for the venture.

"A *Feldwebel* and an *Obergefreiter*? Couldn't you have done better than that, Eicke?"

"I've worked with them before, sir. They're the best there is."

"I hope you're right. From a brief reading of your plan, if you can call half a page of outline a plan at all, you're going to need a couple of supermen."

"As I explained in my covering letter, sir, there's nothing more I can tell you until I've seen Skiddaw for myself. From what I can gather from Leutnant von Werra's account, Grizedale Hall, where he was interned, was no more than an English country house converted into a POW camp. Skiddaw seems to be somewhat different."

"Yes, I understand your difficulties." Weil picked up a document from his desk. "I have a message here from Admiral Doenitz. He has a U-boat undergoing minor repairs at Lorient in Brittany. It will be ready to sail at 0800 hours on the seventh. You and your party are to report on board at 2300 the previous day. The captain is Korvettenkapitaen Stieff.

"The U-boat will stand off your suggested landfall of Maryport, and you will be ferried ashore by dinghy. The exact spot will depend on weather conditions, enemy activity, the propensity of mines, and so forth, but you will be landed during the hours of darkness on December 9–10. So much for getting in."

The *Standartenfuehrer* studied Christian carefully before going on.

"On the direct orders of Admiral Doenitz, Korvettenkapitaen Stieff has been told that he is not to risk his ship in any way whatsoever. Do you understand that?" Christian said that he did. "In any way whatsoever," repeated Weil. "If there is any manner of danger prior to the landing he is to abandon the operation entirely, and he is to be the final arbiter as to what constitutes danger. The same ap-

138

plies once you are ashore. You will not be picked up if in doing so the safety of the U-boat is threatened."

Christian nodded his understanding. On the scales of relative values, one Luftwaffe *Generalmajor* did not equal one U-boat.

"It's been left to you," continued Weil, "to work out a system of signals with Korvettenkapitaen Stieff, but under no circumstances will he stand off Maryport later than the evening of the fourteenth. If you are not there by then, he is to assume you've failed and make for the Atlantic. Bear that in mind, Eicke. If you do not rendezvous with the U-boat by the fourteenth you will not get home. I'm sorry it has to be like that, but the U-boat is needed elsewhere."

"I understand, Herr Standartenfuehrer."

"Good. You will not, incidentally, be the senior non-naval officer aboard. I have arranged for Obersturmbann-fuehrer Kirdorff of the Prinz Eugen SS Division to act as liaison officer between Stieff and yourself. He is there as a precaution, to look after your interests—in case Stieff takes Admiral Doenitz's orders too literally. You do not know Kirdorff, I believe?"

"No, Herr Standartenfuehrer."

"Fine. That's how it should be."

Weil consulted his notes.

"Now looking down your list of requirements, most of this is easily arranged. Civilian clothes with appropriate labels, British identity papers, currency, English cigarettes, ticket stubs, et cetera. But I'm not sure that all you should be taking as a weapon is one 9mm Luger. It's not much of a defense."

"Our best defense will be to remain unseen," said Christian. "But if we are unfortunate enough to be asked to identify ourselves it's no use having perfect documents backed up by three machine guns. We'll have to bluff it out. The pistol is for emergencies only."

"Very well." Weil shut his notebook. "That seems to be it, Oberleutnant. I shall want to see you once more, on the morning of the sixth. You will then be given sealed orders, not to be opened until Stuerzbecher is safely out."

"Sealed orders, sir?"

"A contingency plan, Oberleutnant, for use if things do not work out as you anticipate."

Nine

DECEMBER 5

At 0630 on a bitterly cold but snowless morning, CSM Purser received a telegram from the Admiralty. The messenger who delivered it left quickly without waiting for a signature of receipt. *We regret to inform you that your son, David Ramsey Purser, was killed in action. . . .* Et cetera. It gave the date but not the time and, curiously, Bernard Purser felt he would have liked to know the precise hour of the boy's death. What was he doing then? Drinking beer in the Sergeants' Mess? Reprimanding a young soldier for sloppy dress? Sleeping? There was a lot missing from these official telegrams, though no doubt David's C.O. would write him a personal letter sooner or later. He would probably never be told, however, whether his son had died well or badly, quickly or slowly; whether a shell had put an end to his life instantly or whether he had drowned, calling for help, his lungs full of oil.

Bernard Purser stared at the yellow message form for a long time. Somehow a mug of sweet tea appeared miraculously by his bunk, but he did not recall drinking it. Even so, when he next looked, it was empty.

He wondered what they did with the bodies of youngsters killed at sea. He should know that. Good God, he was a senior NCO after all. A pretty pickle he'd be in if he were ever asked the question and didn't know the answer. Though it was different on dry land. There, a soldier killed in action was buried in firm soil as soon as there was a lull in the fighting, his identity discs placed with the others. He'd seen plenty of that in World War I. Sometimes the Orderly Room table would be piled high with discs, all awaiting a telegram. He supposed the Navy did it differently. Full honors and a canvas shroud and Union Jack if there was enough time. And if there was enough left of the body to put in a shroud.

Bernard Purser was not the sort of man to feel self-pity or to get instantly and incapably drunk and go hunting for the nearest German to beat senseless. Perhaps it didn't make him much of a soldier, but he knew full well that, on this very day, some father in Hamburg or Berlin or Dresden had received an identical telegram and that he too was bewildered at the insanity of it all. It was probably a capital charge to even think it, but he wondered if either the Imperial General Staff or the German High Command saw boys like Able Seaman Purser as anything more than units.

In the manner of these things the news of Sergeant Major Tomorrow's son's death spread quickly throughout the camp, and that morning, at early roll call, there was none of the usual skylarking. No one faked absence by refusing to answer his name. The POWs were soldiers also, and many of them had lost friends or relatives in three years of war.

At 0900, in spite of the fact that Major Mitchell and Captain Thorogood were in camp, Oberfeldwebel Ernst Reitlinger knocked timidly on CSM Purser's door, half expecting him not to be there. But the CSM was having none of that. "Take the day off, Sarnt Major. Take a week's compassionate." "No thank you, sir. I've got nowhere to go."

142

The *Oberfeldwebel* stood in the open doorway, clutching a piece of old newspaper tied with string. Inside were twenty-four new checkers, twelve black, twelve white, handmade since midsummer from castoff bits of wood. He had intended them as a Christmas gift for his friend, but this seemed as good a time as any to present them.

"Come in, Ernst. Sorry there's no tea on the boil this morning. Damn-fool orderly forgot to bring the milk."

Oberfeldwebel Reitlinger stammered that it was okay, that he couldn't stay in any case, that he just wanted to leave the parcel. For the first time since becoming a POW he felt bitterly his ignorance of English. What was adequate for playing checkers was quite useless for saying what was in his mind. So he said nothing. Instead he put his gift on the desk and left.

CSM Purser fingered the string binding it for a long time, but he did not open the parcel.

Shortly after 9 A.M. on the south side of the compound, Obergefreiter Willi Braune assisted by Unteroffizier Hans Geith pulled off his personal coup of the war by stealing a bicycle. Or rather by stealing the wheels; he already had a frame. He had found it the previous spring, rotting and rusting after a winter spent in the open. But the brake cables appeared intact, as did the chain and pedals, and Willi had hidden it under a mound of coke in the boiler room.

For several weeks now Willi's keen nose had told him that an escape was brewing, and he had pondered how to make a profit from it. What would an escapee need more than anything else, apart from a private airfield and a fully fueled airplane? Well, there was money, but that was unobtainable except in small amounts from the card games with Harry Cade and Harpo. In any case, that was profit in itself. There were weapons, but the armory was watched more closely than a Berlin brothelkeeper eyed his best girls for signs of lovesickness. Besides, no escaping

POW would risk being caught with a weapon, which meant a dawn meeting with the firing squad.

A vehicle, naturally, would be the stroke of the century, never mind the war, but the guard at the entrance to the M.T. Pool had the same instructions as the one on the armory: shoot to kill anyone who even looks like a car thief. A bicycle, however, was a different matter. There was no guard on the bicycle sheds, although the Motor Pool sentry was in a position to oversee both establishments.

Unless he could be distracted.

It shouldn't be difficult. A whole bicycle might be a problem, especially as they were usually padlocked to their racks, but all Willi needed was the wheels.

They tossed for it and Hans lost. He would do the thieving while Willi distracted the guard.

The usual method for filching from the *Tommis* was to create a diversion by starting a fight. But this would mean letting others in on the scheme and splitting the profits.

Willi thought about it for a couple of days and finally conceived the idea of *Stacheldrahtkoller*—barbed-wire madness. Right in front of the M.T. Pool guard, he would pretend to have gone insane.

Which is precisely what he did at 0906 hours on the morning of the fifth.

While the sentry looked on in amazement, Willi turned cartwheels and exclaimed that the rocks he dug out of the snow were gold, that he would pocket as many nuggets as he could carry; and that the sentry should do the same.

No older than Willi, the sentry was mesmerized. And while he watched the lunatic acrobatics, Hans Geith unscrewed the wing nuts of both wheels of a bicycle and escaped.

Willi then promptly recovered, dumped the rocks, which he declared were fool's gold, and rejoined Hans in the boiler room. Both were delighted with their success. Any one of the potential escapees would pay well for a working bicycle.

"Let's see if they fit," said Willi.

He took hold of the boiler-room shovel and began shifting coke. A minute later he said, "I could have sworn I put the frame here."

"A bit to your left," advised Hans, hunting through his pockets for the nuts and washers he had stolen with the wheels.

But the frame wasn't a bit to the left; neither was it a bit to the right. And after fifteen minutes' frantic shoveling they knew it wasn't there at all.

"Somebody's stolen it," said Willi, aghast at the thought. "Some bugger's been in and taken it. Of all the filthy thieves. . . ."

Hans Geith was more philosophical.

"Well, we've got the wheels now. All we need is a frame—Hey, don't throw lumps of coke at me."

Much later in the day in the German mess, Theo Emke read aloud to Oberleutnant Hans Baum the letter Baum's mother had sent her son. After three years of war most German civilians had got the message about censorship and careless talk, and Frau Baum's two closely written pages were a model of generalization; so much so that the blue pencil had hardly been used. She expressed the hope that her only son was well and that he was taking good care of his health, the most precious of God's gifts. His sister Helga asked after him all the time and was growing up into a lady, keen on her studies and with no interest in boys. She was making something for his birthday and was hoping she would be allowed to send it. ("I won't tell you what it is, it'll spoil the surprise.") Father had had a bad cold but was getting over it. It had, however, blocked his nose and Frau Baum was quite sure his snores could be heard ten kilometers away.

There was more in the same vein, quite a lot having to do with the health of Baum's relatives. An aunt had sprained her ankle, an uncle had developed some kind of rash. Another aunt thought she had lost her cat and was

145

very surprised when it returned, trailing half a dozen hungry kittens.

The letter was quite creased now, having been received a month earlier and read almost daily to Oberleutnant Baum. Theo Emke in no way objected to this self-imposed chore and was quite sure, if and when he escaped, someone else would take it over. For Hans Baum could not read himself. In the autumn of 1941, while on a night-bombing mission over southern England, his aircraft had received a direct hit from flak and he had watched the rest of his crew fry before some instinct for self-preservation forced him to bail out. He had not spoken during his interrogation, and he had not spoken since. He passed his days in the Mess or in his hut, carving crude figures of men from pieces of wood. He could not answer his name at rollcall, but the camp authorities understood. Strictly speaking, he should have been repatriated or, at the very least, transferred to a hospital for the mentally ill, but thanks to administrative red tape, he was still in Skiddaw.

Understanding that the reading was at an end, Oberleutnant Baum held out his hand. Emke folded the letter carefully and passed it over. Baum put it in a side pocket. From the other side of the table Leutnant Fritz Uhde looked at the pair with an expression of sadness and pity.

"I still say you're making a mistake, Emke. You're not doing Baum or Frau Baum any favors by kidding her."

"Shut up, Fritz," said Emke, not unkindly, and glanced anxiously across at Hans. None of them were ever quite sure how much he understood. Certainly he recognized the names of his sister and the others his mother wrote of, but that seemed to be the limit of his comprehension. However, Emke was taking no chances.

"She'll find out sooner or later," persisted Uhde. He was at a low point in one of his interminable letters to his young wife and wanted something to occupy his mind. "Even if the war goes on for another ten years she'll have to know in the end."

"So let her find out in ten years' time, then," retorted

146

Emke, though he was far from convinced that the action he was taking was the correct one.

Frau Baum knew it was Theo Emke who penned her son's letters, but she was under the impression that Hans dictated them. Without ever saying so directly, Emke had allowed her to believe that Hans had lost the use of his right hand when he was shot down and that he was too idle to learn to write with the other one. Whether Hans was noted for idleness at home or not Emke didn't know, but Frau Baum appeared to have accepted the story. ("And thank that kind Oberleutnant Emke from the bottom of my heart. I don't know what we would have done if we hadn't heard from you via him.")

Uhde was probably right on balance, Emke conjectured, but it was too late to do anything about it now. Having maintained the deception for over a year, he could hardly turn round and tell Frau Baum that her son was an imbecile and there must be doubts whether he would ever live a normal life again.

In any case, after the twelfth, with any luck, it would no longer be his problem. He had already spoken to Otto Breithaupt, and Breithaupt had promised to do what he could to find a replacement scribe. Frau Baum would wonder (because there was no way any censor would allow her to be told that Oberleutnant Emke had successfully escaped), but there was no helping that. Perhaps he could go and see her when he got home, break it to her gently. But he doubted that he had the courage. Rather face a hundred Spitfires in a crippled Ju 88 than tell a mother that her son would never be the same again.

Hans Baum shuffled his chair backward and got to his feet. For a moment he looked steadily at Emke, and Emke thought he was trying to convey his thanks. Then the moment passed and Hans walked slowly from the Mess.

Over in Hut 5, as dusk began to close in and the shouts of the guards, summoning the POWs to the last official roll call of the day, were heard in the distance, huddled around the stove Major Breithaupt, Oberleutnant Mohr and Kurt von Stuerzbecher were engaged in the argument they had been having, off and on, for the last ten days— that of wishing on von Stuerzbecher the twelfth and final place in the Rabbit Run. Otto Breithaupt and Franz Mohr were all for it; von Stuerzbecher was not so sure.

To his way of thinking, he should sit tight until someone in Germany got a message to him, possibly via Kapitaen- leutnant Heydt using the naval code. Then, and only then, would he be free to act, if act was indeed his instruction. It could well be that the High Command would wish him to stay put; that was not inconceivable. As Oberleutnant Stuerzbecher he was just one more anonymous POW; as an escaper, if he were recaptured, he could well be marked down as a troublemaker and subjected to further interrogation. He had survived the London Cage by the skin of his teeth; he might not survive, as an *Oberleut- nant*, a more lengthy examination.

Breithaupt and Mohr knew nothing of Operation Ham- mer, of course. Together with Hauptmann Weiss and Ka- pitaenleutnant Heydt they knew him only as a senior offi- cer successfully masquerading as an *Oberleutnant*. It was perfectly natural, therefore, that they were puzzled at his reluctance to escape.

"I don't understand you, Karl," said Breithaupt. Along with the three others who were privy to von Stuerz- becher's real identity, Breithaupt now called him Karl without second thoughts or deference. "If you don't get out now you may not get out for months, perhaps not ever. Whether we pull it off or not, just making an attempt on such a grand scale will force the *Tommis* to tighten up security all round. It will never again be possible to escape in more than ones and twos, and as an *Oberleutnant* and a newcomer, your name will be well down the list. Good God, the twelfth is only a week away and already hints are being dropped about the spare place. I can't hold it open much longer."

"I understand your difficulties, Otto," said von Stuerzbecher, "but appreciate mine. I must wait until I've heard from Germany."

"But that could take weeks," protested Breithaupt. "Heydt's letter will have only just arrived. There's not a snowball in hell's chance you'll get a reply before the twelfth."

"Then you must let the last place go to someone more deserving."

"You know I can't do that, either." Breithaupt shook his head. "If by some miracle a few succeed in getting home and it becomes known, as it will, that a general was left behind while mere lieutenants were given places, I'll be pilloried in my absence."

"You can get Franz here to tell the OKW that I gave you a direct order."

"That's exactly what he can't do," put in Mohr. "Otto's senior officer, in practice if not in fact. It matters not that you outrank him considerably. As head of the Escape Committee what he says goes. He can order you out or order you to stay behind, just as he pleases."

"Then he must order me to remain."

Abruptly, von Stuerzbecher reached a decision. Through no fault of his own, Otto Breithaupt was in an intolerable position. He would tell him, both of them, so much and no more, though even going that far might lay him wide open to a charge of indiscretion.

"Look, it must have occurred to the pair of you, as it must have occurred to Heydt and Weiss, that an officer of my rank possesses more war secrets than the rest of the camp put together. I was damn lucky that in all Skiddaw only Franz had met me before. But if I escape and get recaptured, there's a possibility I'll be transferred to another camp, where I may be recognized. If that happened I'd put my chances of remaining an anonymous *Oberleutnant* for more than a few days no greater than even.

"The colonel at the London Cage, as I told you, was very curious why someone of my age held such a lowly rank. No offense intended, Franz. If he had learned he had been

149

duped, he would have put me through the mincer. As the war progresses, interrogation techniques improve, and I have no way of knowing how long I could hold out before I said something I shouldn't." Von Stuerzbecher tapped the table to emphasize his next words. "And believe me, gentlemen, I am not exaggerating when I say that some of the intelligence I possess could mean the difference between victory and defeat. I must stay here until I am told what I have to do."

Breithaupt and Mohr exchanged glances. This put a different light on the matter.

"If that's your decision," said Breithaupt.

"It is. And I assure you—"

Von Stuerzbecher did not get a chance to finish. The door was flung open and Corporal Napley poked his head in.

"Come on, you three, are you deaf? *Appell*, roll-bloody-call. If you're not on parade in two minutes it's the cooler for you."

Toward midnight, in the peace and quiet of his quarters, CSM Purser poured the last of the whisky and fingered a couple of the checkers that Oberfeldwebel Reitlinger had made. He had been drinking heavily since 9 P.M. but felt in no way drunk, though a doctor would have diagnosed otherwise.

It was bloody nice of Ernst to have spent his leisure hours carving those; he must have been at it for months. He had months to spare of course, but it was still a handsome gesture. Usually when the POWs made something they tried to sell it; it was one of their few ways of earning extra money.

The telegram from the Admiralty lay on the table, and he read it for the hundredth time, the words dancing as he tried to focus. Christ, he had drunk more than he thought.

Poor young David, never really had a chance. Like so many of the youngsters the war was claiming, never had a chance to meet the proper girl, get married, have a few kids, build a home. If the chaplain was to be believed, David was okay now. But it was hard to accept that the same God who was now embracing David was apparently unconcerned about the living. That was the trouble with Christianity, something he had never considered before; everything was geared to death.

Leaving a quarter inch of whisky in his glass, Bernard Purser staggered to his bunk and, fully clothed, fell headlong onto it. By the time he was snoring, December 5 had passed into history.

Ten

Immediately after morning roll call Hauptmann Weiss collared the rest of the Escape Committee for an ad-hoc meeting at the southeast corner of the Pig Pen. The trap to catch the informer was to be sprung the following night.

"You've left it late enough," said Kapitaenleutnant Heydt sourly.

"These things take time," retorted Weiss. "I could hardly go up to Oberleutnant Kapp and tell him directly that an escape was being planned. He'd have smelled a rat instantly. Still less could I approach Oberfeldwebel Reitlinger. The information had to be filtered through to them."

"How are you working it?" asked Franz Mohr.

"Very simply. Kapp has been told that an attempt is to be made from the sick bay at nine o'clock tomorrow evening. If Thorogood operates according to the established pattern, he'll make his swoop then, trying to catch us in the act. If he moves before, he'll find nothing, because there is nothing. He'll have to be there at 2100 to see how we plan to get out."

"And Reitlinger?"

"He's been told the same time and date, but a different place; from behind the library. You'll notice that I've devised routes well away from each other, one on the north side and one on the east. That's a precaution in case there's a lot of running around tomorrow. We don't want any mistakes regarding the identity of our traitor."

"You're still assuming there is one," said Breithaupt.

"I'm convinced of it. In any event, we'll know one way or another tomorrow."

"What about lookouts?" asked Heydt.

"That'll have to be us, I'm afraid. I know there's a risk involved, wandering around the compound with Thorogood on the rampage, but you'll appreciate I couldn't let anyone else in on the deception. I suggest Heydt and myself watch the sick bay, and you, Herr Major, with Oberleutnant Mohr the library."

"On the assumption that Kapp is the better bet and you want to be in at the kill."

"On that assumption precisely, Herr Major." Weiss smiled his twisted smile.

Breithaupt nodded. "Very well, we'll do as you suggest—2100 it is, though I for one will not be disappointed if we have a wasted night."

"The Major has a touching belief in the goodness of his fellow man."

"It's what we're fighting for, isn't it? Now if you'll excuse us, Heinrich, the rest of us have a choir practice and we're late already."

"By all means, Herr Major."

From his office window Captain Thorogood saw the meeting break up. Although he had no concrete intelligence on the subject, he was fairly certain that what he had just witnessed was a gathering of the Skiddaw Escape Committee. As senior German officer, Breithaupt was bound to be on it. Breithaupt and Mohr were as thick as thieves, so the *Oberleutnant* would be a member too. Kapitaenleutnant Heydt was the ranking naval officer and there was little doubt, if Thorogood was any judge of men, that he'd insist on the *Kriegsmarine* being represented. One-eyed Hauptmann Weiss was an enigma, but a clever and fanatical enigma. They would need his brains and capacity for cold, unemotional assessment.

But what the hell were they plotting? They were undoubtedly up to something. With the exception of Naumann's solo run, the camp had been too quiet for months. It was unnatural.

Abruptly he left his own office and rapped on the door of Major Mitchell's. The commandant was studying the outgoing mail and wondering whether he should let a reference to "the good food and excellent working conditions" slip by before passing the letter on to the official censor. On balance he thought not; his German wasn't fluent enough to detect a hidden meaning in the sentence, but as it was patently untrue it must be regarded as suspect.

"Yes, Adrian?"

"Permission to hold a *Sonderappell*, sir."

"A special roll call?" Mitchell frowned and checked the time. "The normal one was only completed half an hour ago."

"Which is the time to nab them, sir. They won't be expecting it."

"Nab them? Nab who? What's going on?"

"Nothing, sir, which is what's bothering me. We've been too quiet for too long. They must be up to something."

"I thought you were always informed when trouble was brewing."

Mitchell smiled to himself at his adjutant's discomfort. He knew Thorogood liked to pretend that the forestalling of an escape bid was due to his own alertness.

"Not always, sir. Do I have your permission?"

"Is it snowing?"

155

"Sir?"

"If you're going to call a *Sonderappell* it will undoubtedly mean that you'll want to parade the prisoners in the Exercise Yard and keep them there until you've finished. If it's snowing I'll get all manner of flak from Major Breithaupt about maltreatment."

Adrian Thorogood held his temper. Bloody old fool. God knows how the Allies were expected to win the war if Mitchell's attitude were reflected in other camps.

"With due respect, sir, Major Breithaupt is a prisoner of war. I don't think we should pay too much attention to whether or not he thinks it's a good idea."

"He's also a human being. If the situations were reversed, if Major Breithaupt were in my shoes and you were in his, you'd have no hesitation in calling him a Nazi thug and sadist if he made you stand for hours in the snow. You'd certainly have something to say about that."

"Perhaps so, sir, but it's a part of war. It's his job to try to get out, it's ours to keep him in."

"Regardless of methods?"

"Absolutely . . . sir."

Mitchell made a pyramid of his fingers. "That's what the Nazis say, the real Nazis, I mean. Total war demands total abrogation of the rules."

Thorogood's jaw tightened. "I should like it placed on record that I resent that remark, Major Mitchell. I'm simply doing my job."

"They say that too. And you still haven't answered my question: Is it snowing?"

"No, sir."

"Then you have my permission."

Christ, thought Thorogood, and he went to find the CSM.

Gathered around the altar in the chapel and singing a carol with gusto, Major Breithaupt's choir were enjoying themselves when Thorogood struck. Theo Emke, whose stint it was as door guard, was the first to suspect that all was not well.

"There's something going on outside," he called out urgently.

The choir fell silent.

"Be a little more specific, Emke," said Breithaupt calmly.

"Sorry, sir, but there are *Tommis* running in all directions. Look out—one of them's heading this way."

"Get back over here," ordered Breithaupt. "And keep singing—all of you."

It was something he had always feared would happen and prayed never would: some kind of disturbance while two of his moles were underground. In this case, the moles were Peter Kaehler and Johann Preiss, and there was no chance of getting them out. They were two meters under and up to thirty meters away from the altar. Even so, he kicked its base in the hope that they would hear.

The chapel door was flung open and Lance Corporal Harry Cade shouldered his way in, bayonet fixed.

"All right, you lot, *Sonderappell* right away. Get over to the Pig Pen and get fell in. Right now. *Verstehen*?"

The choir looked fearfully at Breithaupt, awaiting his lead.

"What's the matter, Corporal? Somebody escaped?"

"Don't ask me, mate, I only work here. Come on now, let's move it."

Breithaupt stalled for time, hoping that Cade would leave them to make their own way across.

"All right, Corporal, we'll follow you."

But Harry Cade remained in the doorway.

"No chance, old son. I'll follow *you*. Now get going."

There was nothing they could do but obey. Harry Cade made sure everyone was out and shut the door behind him.

Throughout the remainder of the camp a minor panic set in among the POWs as they tried to secrete forbidden goods.

The Oberleutnant tailor lifted a floorboard in his hut and shoved in the tunic he was refashioning. Fortunately, the

157

tailoring system was geared to special roll calls, and whenever an article was finished it was passed on immediately to the POW concerned. Even so, if the tunic were discovered it would mean several wasted weeks as well as the loss of a cache.

In Hut 21 two of the camp forgers, working independently at the trestle table, each got rid of a set of identity documents by the simple expedient of placing them in a waterproof bag kept to one side for such occasions. Their pens and inks were placed in a separate bag. Once outside, both bags would be tossed into the nearest rain barrel, to be collected later.

Elsewhere, men were hiding currency they should not have, compasses, maps, hand-fashioned tools. It was most unlikely that a body search would be carried out, but it was better to be safe.

On Major Breithaupt's standing orders, certain minor items were left to be discovered. Captain Thorogood would consider it most odd if a hut search revealed nothing and he would continue looking until something turned up. It was as well to let him find a few unimportant bits and pieces.

In the boiler room Willi Braune and Hans Geith finished their morning coffee slowly. On learning of the *Sonderappell*, Harry Cade had made the boiler room his first port of call, and ten minutes after he cleared the chapel the POWs were assembled in the Exercise Yard, in hut order.

A *Sonderappell* usually took one of two forms. First there was the head count made by the junior NCOs under the supervision of CSM Purser. If that tallied with the total on the CSM's clip-board, the prisoners were kept standing in the Exercise Yard for another hour or so while squads of soldiers searched the huts and the German Mess for contraband. If it did not tally, every POW's name was called individually and a close watch kept to make sure prisoner A did not answer for prisoner B as well as for himself. When it was finally established who was missing, the fun really began.

158

Rarely did the head count tally, mainly due to the POWs' natural desire to cause as much trouble as possible for their captors. A hut that should have a complement of eight would be found to contain seven, the eighth having bent down to tie a bootlace. In the recount, a prisoner from an adjacent hut would move smartly to his right or left and make the total nine. But CSM Purser's NCOs were up to these dodges and the tocsin wasn't sounded until it was established beyond all doubt that someone had bolted.

Apart from the sick and bed-ridden, who were not expected to parade, there were 219 officers and enlisted men in Skiddaw, and the first count put the number at 212. That didn't matter. CSM Purser was accustomed to the prisoners fooling around. In any case, the total was increased to 214 when two Luftwaffe officers appeared from the direction of the heads, having been caught literally with their trousers down.

CSM Purser tried again. This time he made it 217 and there were no late arrivals. Either his NCOs were stupider than they looked or Skiddaw was minus two birds. There was nothing to do but call the roll.

Each junior NCO supervised three or four huts, and it was Hut 9's misfortune to be in Corporal Napley's domain. That Napley had not missed Kaehler or Preiss in any of the three head counts was excusable. Certainly he could see that where there should be eight bodies there were only six, but the CSM alone kept a full list of who was indisposed. It was not until the absentees were checked against that that their names would be known.

Against a background of shouting Corporal Napley called the roll, starting with the senior officer.

"Oberleutnant Mohr."

Franz Mohr clicked his heels and announced himself present.

"Leutnant Uhde."

"Ja."

"Oberleutnant Emke."

"Ja, Herr Brigadefuehrer."

159

Napley scowled. "That'll be enough out of you. Leutnant Kaehler." No reply. Napley looked up. "Leutnant Kaehler?"

"I think he's sick," said Mohr.

Napley made a mark on his pad and another against the absent Johann Preiss. Two of the bastards. Just two missing and both his.

He marched across to the CSM.

"Leutnants Kaehler and Preiss absent, Sarnt Major."

"Any explanation?"

"Oberleutnant Mohr thinks they're both sick."

"Not on my list they're not. All right, Corporal."

It took five more minutes to establish that only Leutnants Kaehler and Preiss were unofficially absent, and ordering his NCOs to keep the POWs where they were, the CSM went to report to the adjutant.

From his window in the administration block Adrian Thorogood had witnessed the various counts and the roll call, and he knew from experience that all was not as it should be. In some perverse manner he felt pleased. It was a black mark, of course, not to have a full complement, but his judgment in springing the *Sonderappell* had been vindicated.

He returned to his desk as Bernard Purser knocked and entered the office.

"Two prisoners missing, sir. Leutnants Kaehler and Preiss, Hut 9."

"I see. No explanation, I suppose."

"None, sir, but . . ."

"Yes?"

"I was going to say, sir, that if they've hopped it they've been damned quick about it."

"They *are* quick, Sarnt Major. Every German in Skiddaw is quick and prepared to take any opportunity to escape. It might sometimes be overlooked by other members of this establishment, but we have over two hundred dedicated Nazis out there whose only desire is to get back to the Fatherland and begin bombing our cities again. All

160

right, fetch Major Breithaupt and the senior officer from Hut 9 to me. The rest of them can stay out there and freeze."

"Very good, sir."

Alone, Adrian Thorogood debated the advisability of telling Major Mitchell he was short a couple of Germans. He decided against it. The commandant would doubtless invite Breithaupt into his office for a cozy chat and a cup of tea, and that was not the way Thorogood planned to handle the matter at all. If two of them had got under the wire Thorogood wanted to know how. To that end he would keep the POWs standing outside in the cold all night if necessary.

There was a tap on the door and CSM Purser ushered Breithaupt and Mohr into the office. The two Luftwaffe officers stood at attention, eyes to the front. Purser took up a position near the window.

"At ease, gentlemen," said Thorogood. Mohr and Breithaupt relaxed. "It seems two of our birds have fled the nest and I'd like to hear your views on the subject. You first, Oberleutnant; they're in your hut."

"I have nothing to say, Herr Hauptmann."

"You mean you don't know anything or you won't say anything?"

"I mean I know nothing."

"I see. You're trying to tell me that two officers under your supervision can disappear into thin air and you know nothing about it. If you ran your *Staffel* the way you run your hut, I'm surprised you shot down any aircraft at all. What about you, Herr Major? As senior German officer and head of the Escape Committee, surely you have something to contribute."

Breithaupt acted dumb. "Escape Committee? I'm sure I don't know what the adjutant is talking about."

"Your acting ability does you credit, Major. The theater lost a valuable recruit when you joined the Luftwaffe."

Thorogood lit a cigarette and studied the burning match thoughtfully for a moment or two before blowing it out.

161

"I'm going to make a couple of guesses, gentlemen. My first guess is that Leutnants Kaehler and Preiss are not outside the camp at all." He watched them for a reaction. There was none. "My second guess is that you, or some of you, are digging a tunnel or planning some other method of escape and that Kaehler and Preiss were trapped inside when the *Sonderappell* was called. If those two assumptions are anywhere near the truth, I'm going to turn this camp upside down until I find the prisoners and their place of concealment. When that happens, all of you will be allowed to return to your quarters. Until then you will remain in the Exercise Yard, in ranks. You will not be permitted to smoke and neither will you be released to eat. You will make that announcement to your men, Herr Major."

Breithaupt's jaw muscles tightened angrily at this flagrant violation of the regulations.

"I will make the announcement, Herr Hauptmann, but prior to doing so I formally request an interview with the commandant."

"Your request is noted and denied. You can make your own arrangements for seeing the commandant at a later date. In the meantime, let me remind you that I have German-speaking officers outside. You will tell your men exactly what I told you to say, and nothing more. Take them back, Sarnt Major."

In the meantime, Peter Kaehler and Johann Preiss were only just beginning to realize that they were trapped.

Working at the extremity of the Rabbit Run when the *Sonderappell* was called, neither had heard Major Breithaupt kick the altar. Even if he had made ten times the racket it was doubtful if the two young Leutnants would have paid much attention. Another meter, a meter and a half, three or four more days, and they'd be ready to break out. The excitement was more than they could bear, and they concentrated totally on the job at hand.

If it had been possible to see the diggings from an aerial

viewpoint, the POWs who had worked on the Rabbit Run would have marveled at their efforts. Operating purely by instinct and common sense they had tunneled almost in a straight line and were, in fact, several meters beyond their estimated position. Had they broken the surface now, their exit would have been hidden from the camp by the nearest of the trees. But Leutnants Kaehler and Preiss had no way of knowing this and continued excavating as though their lives depended upon it, fearful that the twelfth would arrive and they would not have dug far enough.

It was a filthy, debilitating business and most of the POWs were exhausted after an hour. Theo Emke could manage twice that, but Emke was an exception.

Neither the front man nor the rear man of each team had the easier task, though they changed positions as often as was necessary. The front man had only to dig and shovel the earth behind him, but he was working with primitive tools in almost total darkness with virtually no oxygen. Torn fingernails and bleeding hands were the least of his worries. Even after the war, POWs who had been involved in tunnel projects were subject to sudden, seemingly irrational fits of claustrophobia. The rear man had the advantage of breathing the comparatively fresh air beneath the chapel every so often, when he took a filled sack back to empty it, but he had to crawl, at an agonizingly slow pace, a total of sixty meters every trip. Sixty meters might not sound much, and it isn't much on the surface. But on bended knees in the cold December ground, with sudden falls of soil causing panic and always with a mouthful of dirt, it was far from a rest cure.

At the end of an hour, which most prisoners learned to gauge with uncanny accuracy, both members of the team would retrace their steps and wait until Breithaupt judged the coast to be clear and let them out. While waiting, they used a canvas bucket full of cold water to clean off most of the dirt. As they worked naked, leaving their camp clothes in a heap to be donned when they were finished, this chore took more than a few minutes. But it was essential they not rush it. The surest way for the *Tommis* to smell a rat was for a dozen POWs to go into the chapel looking like the choirboys they purported to be and emerging like coal miners. Once in the chapel, any grime that had been missed was removed from them until they looked as good as new. The only thing they could do little or nothing about was their hands and nails. No matter how hard they scrubbed, the dirt remained ingrained, the calluses immovable. It continues to be surprising that, throughout the war, POW camp authorities on neither side instituted a hand check as a matter of daily or weekly routine. One glance would have been sufficient to reveal which of the prisoners was working on a tunnel.

But it's the most obvious things that are frequently overlooked, as Kaehler and Preiss were beginning to realize. Without help from above there was no way of moving the altar and getting out.

"What the hell d'you think has happened?" Peter Kaehler kept his voice down to a whisper. They had both tried, without response, tapping the inside of the altar. Shouting was out of the question for fear a *Tommi* guard was on the prowl.

"Damned if I know." Preiss was shivering. "But I hope to God they get us out of here before I freeze to death."

"There must be some sort of panic on. Major Breithaupt wouldn't just walk off and leave us."

"Be just our bloody luck, wouldn't it, if someone else has gone under the wire and we're included in the missing. They'll stick us in the cooler whatever happens and bang goes our chance for the twelfth."

"Christ, I hadn't thought of that."

Preiss shone the torch up through the floorboards beneath the altar.

"Maybe if we got a plank or something and gave it a shove—"

"And it topples over just as Sergeant Major Tomorrow walks in through the front door. The Major would have

164

our guts for guitar strings. Forget it, Johann. We're stuck here until someone lets us out."

"Which might mean the rest of the day."

"Which might mean the rest of the bloody week."

Thoroughly depressed, they lapsed into silence.

Including the time spent on the head count and the roll call, the POWs had been standing in the Pig Pen for over an hour. To a man they were frozen stiff, but Major Breithaupt had ordered them not to break ranks. Most of them had now guessed why they were being punished en masse. Although the precise location of the tunnel and the exact date of departure was a secret known only to a handful, none of the prisoners was a fool.

"Bloody bad security," Breithaupt heard a naval officer in an adjacent rank mutter. He was not one of Heydt's men selected to make the escape, and he was feeling bitter. "I don't mind the bastards making a run for it, but they might at least make sure the rest of us don't suffer if they're caught in the act."

It was obvious that Breithaupt was meant to overhear the complaint, but he chose not to comment. It was an unjust accusation, but an understandable one. POWs were subject to the most intolerable stresses and deprivations, one of the least being loss of liberty. Not out of malice by their captors, but because there was a war on, they were fed inadequate food; the vitamins and minerals needed to keep the nervous system vital were largely absent. The majority of them knew that their homes and families were being bombed almost daily by the R.A.F. and the Americans; if a wife or child was killed they might not know about it for weeks. The absence of women was a further demoralizing factor. None of them had even been near, let alone made love to, a woman in two years. Given these circumstances it was perfectly natural that nerves became frayed and tempers were held in check only by an effort of will.

Three ranks away, Fritz Uhde had also overheard the

naval officer's criticism. "He's right, you know. We should have been prepared for something like this."

"Shut up, Fritz," said Franz Mohr pleasantly. "If you want to stay behind and take over as head of the Escape Committee, I'll see Otto Breithaupt gets your place in the tunnel."

Fritz Uhde shut up. He wasn't really being ungrateful, he told himself, but he was fearful that as a result of today's happenings something would go wrong with the escape.

"Sorry, Franz."

"That's all right."

But it was far from all right, thought Mohr. If Thorogood was as good as his word, he would keep them standing here until hell froze over.

He was wondering what to do about it when Theo Emke solved the problem for him. Only God and the Luftwaffe knew why Emke was still an *Oberleutnant;* he had all the qualities for much higher rank.

"What we need is a sing-song," he grunted, and immediately suited the action to the word. *"Unsere Flagge und die wehet auf dem Maste . . ."* His deep bass voice rang out across the compound. "Come on, you miserable bastards, let's hear it."

Within seconds a dozen voices joined in, and a moment later the whole compound was singing.

> *Unsere Flagge und die wehet auf dem Maste*
> *Sie verkundet unseres Reiches Macht;*
> *Denn wir wollen es nicht langer leiden*
> *Dass der Englischmann daruber lacht. . . .*

The *Tommis* knew this one well by now. It was a favorite German taunt—*Denn wir fahren gegen England* ("We're sailing against England"). Translated it went:

> Our flag waves as we march along
> It is the emblem of the power of our Reich;
> And we can no longer endure
> That the Englishman should mock it.

166

The NCO in charge of the Pig Pen detail tried a feeble, "Silence in the ranks," but no one could hear him and he soon gave up.

Another hour went by. And then two. Taking Captain Thorogood's orders literally, the squads of soldiers under the overall command of the CSM turned the German lines upside down. Some of them, like Lance Corporal Harry Cade and Harpo, acted within the spirit of the law and simply searched the obvious places; others, like Corporal James Napley, obeyed the law to the letter.

It was Napley's squad that turned over the German Mess. Franz Mohr's precious armchair was poked and prodded by Napley's bayonet until the stuffing was bulging from a dozen new slashes. The net on the table-tennis table was torn in two, and a ball, left lying around by mistake, was stamped on. The snooker table was pushed onto its side and kicked until it fractured. Priceless books, priceless to the POWs, were defaced. The prisoners had little, and that little Corporal Napley took a delight in destroying.

The bathhouse and heads, being the site of a previous break attempt, were given special attention. The prisoners' library was next on the list, followed by their canteen. Even the coke in the boiler room was moved and Willi Braune's two bicycle wheels impounded.

It was fortunate for the Germans and unfortunate for the British that the huts, being roughly in the middle of the compound and therefore far away from the perimeter wire, were considered unlikely bolt holes, and they were searched last. Bedding was pulled apart and the floors examined cursorily for loose boards. But by this time the troops were tired and fed up, and little of value was found.

The chapel was virtually ignored. Admittedly it was used as a place of worship by both captors and captive, and lately the choir had got more use out of it than anyone else; but unconsciously the troops did not see it as part of German territory, in much the same way as British front-line soldiers didn't believe that the God they prayed to would have much truck with Nazis. A couple of *Tommis* poked their heads in, but that was as far as it went. Some atavistic superstition warned them of sacrilege.

At the end of two and a half hours CSM Purser had to report almost total failure. The squads had missed the Oberleutnant tailor's cache and no one had even considered looking in the rain barrel. The haul was a few small coins, two torches, a sharpened nail file, the beginnings of a pencil-written journal, and a small-scale map of Greater London. It was enough to send Adrian Thorogood purple with rage.

"The men can't have searched thoroughly, Sarnt Major. If they had they'd have found Kaehler and Preiss."

"Perhaps they're already out, sir. It might be an idea to alert the civilian police and the Home Guard."

That was Major Mitchell's theory too, and Thorogood had already made the necessary telephone calls. He could still hear the police inspector's sarcastic voice.

"It's been done, Sarnt Major, though I'll stake ten years' promotion they're still in the camp. Even if they're not, how in God's name did they get out? They didn't do a Naumann and walk through the damned gates. You've already told me there are no gaps in the wire. So they must have gone under the bloody thing. Which means a tunnel. Which also means that if you can't find Kaehler and Preiss you should at least be able to find the tunnel."

"If you'll forgive me, sir, it's not logical that a tunnel would be constructed and only two POWs escape. If there were a tunnel we'd be missing a lot more than two."

"Not if it's still being dug and those two bastards were trapped in it at *Sonderappell*. Not then."

The CSM had an idea. "Then why not call off the search, sir. If Kaehler and Preiss turn up later today or tomorrow, you'll know you were right and we can begin looking for the tunnel. If they don't, we'll know they've got out somehow."

Thorogood thought about it. It was a reasonable suggestion. Two men could not survive underground for more than a few hours. If there was a tunnel, they'd have to emerge.

"All right, Sarnt Major Purser, that's not a bad idea. But before we put it into practice I want you to repeat the whole exercise and this time include our lines. I wouldn't put it past the bastards to be trying something there. If that doesn't work, we'll try it your way."

They were sitting in the dark now; flashlight batteries were at a premium and not to be wasted. Somewhere to their right they could hear water dripping and on several occasions some small animal or other had made scuffling noises. Johann Preiss hoped it wasn't a rat.

"What time do you think it is?" he asked.

"Don't know. One o'clock, maybe two."

Preiss shivered in the blackness and massaged his legs to keep the circulation going. His stomach told him that Peter's guess was a couple of hours out.

"I wish to Christ I knew what was going on up top."

"I'd be a lot happier if I knew what the hell we were going to do when we get out. Whatever the reason, there must be a *Sonderappell* on; there's no other explanation for Major Breithaupt leaving us down here. And when we turn up the *Tommis* are going to want to know where the hell we've been."

"Maybe we can tell them we escaped, didn't like the food rationing, and came back."

"I'm serious, Johann. We can't just appear from no-where like bloody pixies."

Preiss caught the drift. "Don't even think of it," he said. "Don't even suggest that we stay down here another six days."

"I don't see what else we can do. The best that can happen when we show ourselves is a couple of weeks in the cooler, which means we'll miss the twelfth anyway. The worst that can happen is that they'll comb the camp from end to end, looking for the tunnel. They're bound to find it sooner or later, which means no one else gets a chance either. It's better they think we're already over the hill and far away."

"But six days! What kind of a state do you think we'll be in to make a run for it then?"

"We'll manage. Breithaupt will get food to us and there's just enough room here to do exercises. We'll make it into a kind of competition, see who can do the most push-ups and knee-bends."

"You'll cheat," said Preiss, and laughed quietly at the absurdity of the statement. "You must want to get back to Hannah very much," he added.

"If she were not your sister I'd tell you just how much." Kaehler allowed himself a moment of fantasy. "Imagine it, Johann, a couple of weeks from now and we could be seeing her, your whole family. Think of those veal cutlets your mother cooks."

"Don't, for Christ's sake."

"And new potatoes running with butter."

"Peter, I'll cave your head in. I think I'd commit murder for a plate of new potatoes right now."

"Just keep thinking about them. The time'll pass quickly, you'll see."

When it started snowing at 3 P.M., Captain Thorogood opted to forestall Major Mitchell and call off the hounds. The men had been through the whole dreary business a second time and had come up empty-handed; searching the British lines had proved to be a complete waste of energy. Besides, the POWs in the Pig Pen were getting restless. The singing was sporadic and unenthusiastic now, but a rowdier element were starting to toss snowballs at the Pen guard. They had been out in the cold for almost six hours and they were hungry and tired. If he kept them any longer he'd have a riot on his hands. Tomorrow was another day. If Kaehler and Preiss turned up, he'd begin again. But part of him was already agreeing with the general consensus that, somehow, they had got away.

170

"All right, Sarnt Major, dismiss the prisoners. We might as well abandon the afternoon roll call as well."

When CSM Purser made this announcement and it was relayed in German by Breithaupt for the benefit of those who did not speak English, the POWs managed an ironic cheer and began to break ranks. They were stopped in their tracks by Breithaupt's next words.

"I know you're tired and hungry and that uppermost in your minds is the thought of hot drinks and food. You've been kept here all day by the British, but I want you to show them that if necessary you would have stayed here all night. German servicemen are not rag, tag and bobtail troops even when they're prisoners of war. So I want you to march out of here as though you were recruits on the drill square. Dismiss."

The CSM had not understood a word of it, but to his amazement he saw 217 Germans come to attention as a man and file smartly out of the Pig Pen.

The three other members of the Escape Committee waited at the exit for Breithaupt. Men like Theo Emke and Werner Herburg were also hanging around, but Breithaupt waved them off. Decisions first, inquest later.

"Bastards," said Franz Mohr when he saw the wreckage in the Mess. "Pointless bloody vandalism."

Breithaupt seemed to have expected something of the sort. "Don't blame them all, Franz. We've got people like that on our side too."

They gathered round a table at the far end, leaving others to clean up.

"All right," said Breithaupt, "before I say what I think, I'm open to suggestions."

"We can't do anything about them tonight." Heydt made his voice hard. This was no time for romantic rescue gestures. "It's a bad business, but if we go anywhere near that chapel the *Tommis* will descend like locusts."

Weiss concurred. "But it's worse than that," he added. "I've been thinking about it for the last three hours. We can't really let them out at all."

171

"Franz?"

"I'm afraid I agree with Hauptmann Weiss. If they suddenly reappear tomorrow the *Tommis* will know for certain we have a tunnel somewhere. If they don't, they'll think Kaehler and Preiss have escaped. There's no alternative; they've got to stay down there until the twelfth."

"I hope to God they've come to the same conclusion." Breithaupt hated the thought of subjecting the youngsters to a week's incarceration. "The question is, is it possible to survive that long?"

"They're young," said Mohr. "They're as healthy as any of us are. In any event, we have no choice. Either they take their chances or we lose the tunnel. Those are our options."

Breithaupt mulled it over. "All right, we'll put it to them. But pass it around that tomorrow morning I want every man on the escape to forfeit a quarter of his rations. They're going to be starving and they deserve every assistance we can give them. They'll also need blankets. Franz, I'll leave that to you. Every other man to give up one of his blankets. You might dig up some reading matter and give them one of the emergency torches as well. Christ, they've got to have something to do down there."

Peter Kaehler and Johann Preiss were in surprisingly good condition when Major Breithaupt reached them immediately after roll call the following day, though they fell upon the food wolfishly and didn't speak until their bellies were full.

They had slept fitfully, they both admitted, and they had completely lost track of time. It was also a bit macabre, being buried alive beneath a place of worship. But yes, they could stick it out until the twelfth, as long as the food kept coming. They had no option really, did they? Anyway, down here there were no parades. A few mice and worms and maybe a rat or two, but nothing they couldn't cope with. See you around, Major.

Breithaupt felt quite choked up when he left them.

Eleven

Fortunately it was still snowing, the flakes leaping and dancing in the cold north wind, half veiling the watchtower searchlights. In less inclement conditions it would have been possible for the guards to pick out four furtive shapes moving quietly across the compound.

At fifteen minutes before nine o'clock Franz Mohr and Otto Breithaupt slipped from their respective huts and met, as arranged, behind Hut 20, from where they had a more or less clear view of the library, a tiny wooden structure at the eastern end of the camp. Half a mile in front of them, though they could sense it rather than see it, the mountain which had given the camp its name rose into the night sky. A few minutes later, Kapitaenleutnant Heydt and Hauptmann Weiss took up a position opposite the sick bay.

Mohr rubbed his hands and blew on them to keep warm.

"I hope this isn't a waste of time. It's no night to be chasing wild geese."

"And I hope it *is* a waste of time." Breithaupt's voice was muffled by the black balaclava covering his head. "In

173

any case, don't grumble at the weather. If it's like this all over Europe there'll be many a family in Germany thanking God that the Lancasters are grounded."

"I don't know about that. Stuerzbecher hinted only this morning that the *Tommis'* new radar enables them to pinpoint a target with unerring accuracy, regardless of conditions."

Breithaupt grunted with annoyance. "He shouldn't talk about such things."

"Maybe I misunderstood," said Mohr hastily.

"No, you didn't." Breithaupt sighed the long sigh of the very weary. "I know it's difficult for him, playing a dual role. He has to think twice, three times, before he ever opens his mouth. Anyway, it's no secret the war's going badly."

"You called it treason when I suggested the same thing a couple of weeks ago."

"Whistling in the dark, Franz. You can't fight this sort of war on two fronts, and postwar historians will prove it. It either had to be the Russians or the Americans and the *Tommis*. It could never be both."

Franz Mohr was mildly shocked. "It sounds as if you've already accepted defeat. If so, why are we still fighting? Why are we even considering an escape?"

"We're still fighting, and you and the others are going to escape because no one's told us otherwise. We're soldiers, Franz; we do as we're told."

Breithaupt was silent for a moment.

"It's strange, isn't it, how victory or defeat can hang on such a slender thread as the whims or forgetfulness of a few individuals? There was a lot of talk—very private of course—that the Fuehrer never invaded England because he felt an instinctive empathy, as I suppose many of us do, with the British. If he had, it might be all over by now."

Mohr snorted quietly. "A better reason might be that we didn't command the air over the Channel and we hadn't enough landing craft. I'm afraid I don't subscribe to unconscious motivations."

"They exist, nevertheless. Do you recall the story, I don't

know how apocryphal it is, about Marshal Blücher's forces at Waterloo?" Mohr said he didn't. "It seems that a squadron of French cavalry fought its way through Blücher's lines and got as far as the cannon. When the officer in command asked who had the nails with which to spike the touch-holes, no one had bothered to bring them. They had all been so anxious to get on with the charge that they had forgotten the reason they were going."

"For want of a nail a horseshoe was lost, et cetera," said Mohr.

"Something like that. It seems to me that we Germans are like that squadron of French cavalry. We keep pressing forward but we're not quite sure where we're going or what we're going to do when we get there."

"Christ, that's a bit deep."

Breithaupt shook his head and grinned wryly.

"Sorry, Franz. I'm not long-suited in philosophy. But it's this sort of thing"—he gestured in the general direction of the library—"that gets me down. If we have to fight an enemy within as well as the *Tommis* . . ."

"You'll soon know," said Mohr, and placed a cautionary hand on Breithaupt's arm.

But it was only Obergefreiter Willi Braune heading for his card game in the boiler room. The door opened, revealing a momentary glow, then closed again.

"That was your bloody orderly, wasn't it?"

"It was. Yours is probably already inside. Didn't you know? Braune and Geith play cards most nights with a couple of *Tommis*."

"I did not know. I'll put a stop to that first thing in the morning."

"Not a good idea, Otto. It does no harm and the ratings don't have much to look forward to. Besides, let's not upset Braune and Geith; they're the best thieves in the camp."

"Perhaps you're right. Christ, I'm cold. If nothing happens in the next few minutes it looks as though Weiss was wrong."

But on the north side of the compound Hauptmann Weiss was feeling far from wrong. It was, he estimated later, approximately three or four minutes after nine o'clock when the watchtower searchlights at the northeast and northwest corners swung suddenly inward, as though at a prearranged signal, and illuminated the area around the sick bay. In an instant, that whole section was full of *Tommis,* making no attempt at stealth. Directing operations was Captain Thorogood in person, and Weiss picked out CSM Purser and several others he knew by name. In all, there were some fifteen or twenty armed soldiers in the vicinity.

But neither he nor Heydt stuck around to count them. Thorogood would soon discover there was nothing to be found and he might widen his area of search. It would go badly for any POW caught out in the open.

"We've seen enough," he whispered, making no effort to hide his exultation.

Mohr and Breithaupt had also heard the ruckus, and he drew the only conclusion possible.

"So Weiss was right after all."

Breithaupt's voice was full of bitterness. "Yes. Tomorrow we shall have to have a word with Oberleutnant Kapp."

In March 1941 Kapitaenleutnant Otto Kretschmer's submarine, the U 99, was sunk by a British destroyer, HMS *Walker,* and Kretschmer himself was taken prisoner and incarcerated at Grizedale Hall. Apart from keeping in touch with Admiral Doenitz using a code devised prior to the war, before being transferred to a Canadian POW camp in May 1942 Kapitaenleutnant Kretschmer found a way to circumvent the regulations governing courts-martial.

Under the Geneva Convention prisoners were not allowed to sit as a court-martial board on other prisoners; punishment, whatever the nature of the offense, could only be meted out by the captors. Kretschmer got round this by setting up what he called a Secret Council of Honor to try those whose courage or loyalty was in doubt. In all but name it was a drumhead trial, but Major Breithaupt, in spite of earlier misgivings, was determined to use the artifice in the case of Oberleutnant Kapp.

At 0930 on the morning of the eighth, after a roll call that revealed Leutnants Kaehler and Preiss still to be missing, Oberleutnant Kapp was summoned to Major Breithaupt's hut, Hut 5. The regular occupants were told to make themselves scarce, and a guard was placed on the door, both inside and out. Because of the secret nature of the proceedings, Breithaupt selected Emke to watch the inside and Werner Herburg the outside.

It had occurred to the Escape Committee that if their suspicions regarding Kapp were correct, Captain Thorogood would be looking for an explanation from him before long. Breithaupt wanted the Council of Honor out of the way before that event took place, if he allowed it to take place at all. However, in spite of the seemingly damning evidence against the bespectacled artillery officer, Breithaupt had no intention of countenancing a kangaroo court or assuming him guilty until that fact had been proven beyond all doubt. To begin with, therefore, he invited Kapp to sit at one end of the trestle table. Breithaupt sat at the other, flanked by Mohr on his right and Heydt and Weiss on his left. It had been decided to call evidence only in written form, and each man had in front of him a signed deposition from the officers who had fed Kapp the false information.

Breithaupt called the meeting to order and addressed Kapp directly.

"Last night," he began, "an escape attempt from the sick bay was thwarted at the last moment by the appearance of Captain Thorogood. We are making inquiries into how Thorogood could possibly have known of the time and place of the attempt, and we believe you can help us in this."

"I, Herr Major?" Kapp's face was a picture of innocence. "How should I be able to help you?"

"You were one of the few people to know the full facts.

177

This inquiry is to establish whether through careless talk or . . . or other reasons you passed the information on."

"I assure you I did not, Herr Major. Not only did I not pass any information on, I had none to pass. This is the first I've heard of such an attempt."

Like most born liars Oberleutnant Kapp was totally convincing in his denial. If the trap had not been baited with such care Breithaupt would have been inclined to believe him.

"I see," he said. "Hauptmann Weiss?"

"This Council does not believe the Oberleutnant's last statement," said Weiss. His one good eye stared at Kapp coldly, like that of a hangman measuring his victim for the rope. "For the last two weeks I have personally been responsible for the rumor of the sick bay attempt reaching you. I have used only those officers whose loyalty I trust implicitly and they told no one other than you of the rumor. Note the word *rumor*, Oberleutnant. It is used advisedly. There was no attempt from the sick bay last night, nor is one planned. The place was chosen deliberately to see if the *Tommis* would appear. As you well know, they did, and they could not have been there unless they had information. That information could only have come from you."

Heinrich Weiss rubbed his eye in an effort to stop it twitching. Since the crash it always did that when he was excited, and he was excited now. So far as he was concerned Kapp was as guilty as sin, and the quicker he was put where he could do no more harm, the better. In his opinion the Council was a complete waste of time, but he was wise enough to know that Breithaupt would not sanction lynch law. To get the verdict he wanted he would have to play within the rules.

"We're waiting, Oberleutnant," said Major Breithaupt.

"Waiting for what, Herr Major?" Kapp took off his spectacles and polished them vigorously. "Hauptmann Weiss is saying in effect that I am guilty of a treasonable rela-

178

tionship with the British. I resent that imputation, and I repeat that I knew nothing of the sick-bay escape plan until a few minutes ago. I would furthermore remind the Major that this Council is illegal. You have no right to try me."

"You suggest we hand you over to the British?" asked Heydt.

"I suggest we terminate this farce here and now and that you allow me to go about my business."

"No doubt with Captain Thorogood," sneered Weiss.

"That's a damned lie!"

Breithaupt rapped on the table with his pencil.

"That will be more than enough, gentlemen," he said sharply. "You will remember that in spite of the location you are German officers and that this, whatever Oberleutnant Kapp says to the contrary, is a properly constituted court."

He picked up a document from the table in front of him. Kapp was almost convincing, full of plausible indignity, but the words written down were incontrovertible evidence that he was not telling the truth.

"You say, Oberleutnant, that you had no knowledge of the escape until just now. Yet I have here a signed statement from two officers whose honor cannot be impugned that you were told the day before yesterday that an attempt was to be made at 2100 last night."

"Name them," demanded Kapp.

Breithaupt gave him the names of two *Oberleutnants* who assisted Weiss with camp security.

"They too are lying," snapped the artillery officer.

"Both of them?" queried Mohr.

"Both of them. I recall no such conversation and I would again remind the senior officer that this Council is illegal."

"I can have the two officers brought in," said Weiss generally.

Kapp hesitated. "That will hardly be necessary. For some reason unknown to me they will only repeat in per-

179

son the same lies they have already put their signatures to."

"Why would they do that?" asked Heydt.

"I don't know. Perhaps I've done something to offend them. It is not unheard of for some individuals to use a public court for private vengeance."

Weiss pounced. "Then you accept the legality of this body?"

"I do no such thing," blustered Kapp. "But since I appear to have little choice in the matter I insist upon being allowed a defense."

"Another officer?" asked Mohr.

"Another officer, one chosen by myself with the power to examine witnesses. It would only take a day or so to arrange—"

"No," said Breithaupt. "If we permit you to leave here you will go straight to the British for protection."

"You're assuming me guilty," cried Kapp. He was sweating badly now. As fast as he cleaned and polished his spectacles they misted up again.

"We're simply examining the evidence."

Which they continued to do for a further ten minutes, though really it was a monologue. With hardly a pause for breath Kapp kept on denying that he was a traitor and protested that he was being treated unjustly.

Weiss could see that Breithaupt wanted a confession. Although the evidence, apart from the man's attitude, pointed overwhelmingly to Kapp's guilt, Weiss knew that the Major was the sort of individual who wanted every *i* dotted, every *t* crossed. He therefore offered Kapp an escape route that was not really an escape route at all.

"Perhaps the Oberleutnant made a mistake earlier when he professed not to have heard of the sick-bay attempt," he said cunningly. "Perhaps, unwittingly, he was guilty of no more than careless talk and is now frightened to tell us."

Kapp committed the fatal error of seizing this straw. Had he stuck to his original denial he might have got

180

away with it, because the evidence against him was at best circumstantial.

"Hauptmann Weiss is right," he said after a moment. "I didn't want to say anything before, because I was afraid matters would go badly for me. But yes, I do remember the conversation with the two officers concerned and I also remember talking about it."

"To whom?" demanded Heydt.

"I don't recall." Kapp wiped his palms on his tunic. "Another officer, I think, outside the Pig Pen yesterday morning. I was excited at the prospect of another escape being made and I wanted to see what others thought. There were several NCOs nearby and I think the guard known as Harpo was also in the vicinity. He could have overheard me, or the NCOs—"

"You disgust me!" Breithaupt hammered the table with a fist in sudden anger. "To save your own neck you're willing to malign some nameless NCO or fellow officer. Why did you do it, Oberleutnant? Money, better rations, some promise or other?"

"Herr Major, I swear to God—"

"You'd swear your own mother's life away if you thought it would save your treacherous hide." Breithaupt was white and shaking. Mohr had never seen his friend so angry. "There are men out there, Kapp, brave men, officers and NCOs, who suffer deprivation gladly rather than rat on their comrades. Treason is far too kind a word for what you've done, because I've no doubt that if we looked hard enough and dug long enough we'd find that the other failed escapes were the result of your collaboration. God knows, if I had a gun I'd shoot you myself here and now. Oberleutnant Emke!"

Theo Emke came to attention and clicked his heels. "Herr Major?"

"Get this man out of my sight and see that he talks to no one. If he tries to run for it or call for help you are to break his neck instantly. I'm sorry to burden you with such a responsibility with the inevitable consequences, but I

181

want you to tell us here and now, so that Oberleutnant Kapp can hear, that you accept it."

"I accept it, Herr Major. If Oberleutnant Kapp so much as sneezes without my permission, it will give me great pleasure to kill him."

"Thank you, Emke. Let Oberleutnant Herburg know where you'll be so that we can recall you when we have finished our deliberations. Now get him out of here."

Kapp opened his mouth to protest, but Emke's hand on his collar soon silenced him. He went through the door as meek as a lamb.

Breithaupt heaved a long sigh. "I'm sorry about that outburst, gentlemen."

"You were too easy on him," said Weiss. "You should have ordered Emke to kill him right away."

"This is still a properly constituted court, Herr Hauptmann. There'll be no sentence until we've had the verdict, though I take it there's no disagreement on that."

"None," said Heydt. "Guilty."

"Guilty," said Mohr.

"Of course, guilty." This from Weiss.

"And my vote makes it unanimous," said Breithaupt. "The question is, what do we do with him?"

"Do with him?" Weiss was quite frankly astounded. "What do we do with him, Herr Major? We dispose of him as quickly as possible, as a warning to others who might be inclined similarly."

"And what do you suggest we do with the corpse?" asked Breithaupt. "Don't misunderstand me; I've no intention of going soft on Oberleutnant Kapp. But now we've found our traitor I'm more interested in the living than the dead. If we execute him it will almost certainly be impossible to hide the body. When the British find it they will institute an inquiry, and they will know that such an execution could not have taken place without at least my consent. In their eyes the Council of Honor is illegal and therefore not competent to pass the sentence of death. We will in effect have committed murder and we'll be tried accordingly under British law. And let none of us doubt what the verdict of that court will be. We will not even be given the choice of a firing squad. The sentence will be death by hanging."

"Otto—Major Breithaupt is right," Mohr broke in before Weiss could protest. "And don't think for a moment it's only his own skin he's worried about. As senior officer he's automatically involved, but let's not fool ourselves for a second; Captain Thorogood may not have proof that the four of us in this room constitute the Escape Committee, but he could hazard a pretty good guess. It would mean the rope for all of us."

"Ridiculous," said Weiss angrily. "Are you trying to tell me that four German officers cannot find a way to make the death of one criminal look like an accident? Like you, gentlemen, I have no wish to give the British hangman employment, but I would rather have it that way than let Kapp go free. Good God, what was the point in trapping him if all we do is pat him on the head and tell him not to do it again?" He turned to Kapitaenleutnant Heydt for support.

"I don't believe I heard Major Breithaupt suggest any such thing," said Heydt. Breithaupt looked at the naval officer with new respect. "Under normal circumstances we would, of course, march Kapp directly outside and put a bullet through his head. But these are far from normal circumstances. With the twelfth so close we can't afford to take unnecessary risks—"

"You can't maybe."

"—and neither can Kapp simply disappear. If he is not seen around, Captain Thorogood will add two and two together and assume the worst. Neither can we execute him, hide him in the Rabbit Run, and make it look like an escape. With Kaehler and Preiss already missing Thorogood would tear the camp apart to find Kapp. We were lucky once; we can't expect the cards to fall for us again."

"They had a similar problem at Grizedale Hall a year or two back," said Mohr. "A naval officer accused of cowardice. They gave him the choice of running for it and not coming back, or being killed."

"I remember it." Heydt had begun his POW career at Grizedale Hall. "The *Tommis* caught up with him but he kept on running. They shot him in the back."

"Unfortunately that wouldn't work here," said Breithaupt. "If what we suspect about Kapp is true, he just about threw his weapon down at Dunkirk and volunteered to be taken prisoner. He's not the sort to take that option. If we give him a choice between running and being executed he'll run all right—but to Thorogood."

"Which leaves his immediate dispatch the only solution," argued Weiss.

"Not necessarily," said Breithaupt. "I've been thinking about this carefully. I can see one or two obvious objections, but what about using Kapp ourselves? What about giving him the choice between having his neck broken or taking orders from us? Thorogood thinks he has an informer in our midst; very well, let's see he gets all the information he can use—but tailored to our own needs."

"Absurd!" snorted Weiss. "Insanity. If we let Kapp go, the first thing he'll do is ask the adjutant for a transfer, telling him why."

Breithaupt did not agree. "Perhaps not. I think I can persuade Oberleutnant Kapp that we can track him down no matter where he goes, which is not so far from the truth. Using the Doenitz code we can let the High Command know that Kapp is a collaborator and see that they pass on the message to the other camps. It would take time but it's more than possible."

"Nonsense." Weiss could see his victim slipping away. "Kapp would know that all he's doing is buying time. When the war's over he'll be tried by a properly constituted court-martial, which will undoubtedly sentence him to death. He might live this year, but next year he's a dead man."

Breithaupt and Mohr glanced at one another, but neither bothered to point out that such a court-martial would depend very much on who won.

"Perhaps you're right," acknowledged Breithaupt, "but an eleventh-hour reprieve is always welcome. In any case, I don't see we have much choice. No matter what you say, Heinrich, killing the wretched man is out of the question. We agreed earlier that a majority verdict on the sentence is one we should all accept, but I'd prefer it to be unanimous. I'm therefore willing to spend a little more time trying to persuade you that getting Kapp to work for us is the most sensible decision to take.

"We had a stroke of bad luck the day before yesterday with Kaehler and Preiss getting caught in the Rabbit Run. To the best of our knowledge Thorogood thinks they've gone under the wire. But the one thing we can do without is him suddenly becoming inquisitive again. The *Tommis* overlooked the chapel last time; maybe next time they won't. So let's say we brief Kapp to tell Thorogood that, although he made a mistake last night, he's heard that a mass break-out is being planned for the middle of January and that Kaehler and Preiss have already gone to test the route. He doesn't know yet how they escaped, but he expects to find out over Christmas. Knowing the way Thorogood's mind works he'll be quite happy to leave us alone until the second week in January. He won't even bother to look again for Kaehler and Preiss. And by the second week in January, gentlemen, a dozen German officers should be sending us picture postcards of Berlin."

"Beautiful," said Franz Mohr delightedly, and even Heydt managed a rare grin.

But Weiss was still far from happy.

"And after the middle of January? Or rather, after December 12—because on December 13 Captain Thorogood will know for certain he's been made a fool of."

"After December 13, Hauptmann Weiss, I don't think Kapp will have much credibility left as an informer. We all know that Thorogood hates Germans and I doubt if the good captain will worry one way or another what happens to Kapp once his usefulness is at an end. An accident as you suggested, perhaps? It shouldn't be difficult to arrange."

185

As far as Heydt and Mohr were concerned, the matter was decided. But Breithaupt wanted his unanimity and he waited anxiously to hear from Hauptmann Weiss.

"Very well," said Weiss finally. "I agree. But I want it made quite clear that what happens to Kapp after the twelfth is my business and my business alone."

"Of course," said Breithaupt.

They had Kapp brought back. Hangdog and sweating profusely in spite of the temperature, the bespectacled *Oberleutnant* listened with growing astonishment as he learned that he was not to be executed on the spot. With an alacrity that was shameful, he agreed to everything Breithaupt suggested, though the Major was careful to omit the actual date and place of the fictitious escape. As far as Kapp was aware, something was being planned for the middle of January and he was part of a diversionary tactic.

"And make no mistake," Breithaupt concluded. "You are being offered your life only because you can be useful to us. If we suspect that you are still collaborating with the British, that you are passing on information which does not emanate directly from this committee, you will surely die. Wherever you try to hide, we shall find you. Take him out, Emke."

Hauptmann Weiss's one good eye followed Kapp to the door. Major Breithaupt could say what he liked, but Weiss had already made up his mind that Kapp would not survive the night of the twelfth.

Part III

Twelve

DECEMBER 9

Korvettenkapitaen Dieter Stieff was as cheerful a character as any of them had ever come across. A native of Kiel, he looked about nineteen, though Christian knew this could hardly be the case. Even in a war where the promotion system had gone beserk, the German navy did not give that sort of rank and command of an expensive U-boat to nineteen-year-olds.

Obersturmbannfuehrer Kirdorff was also something of a surprise. Christian had been expecting a much older man, but Kirdorff turned out to be a couple of years younger than thirty. He greeted Christian's party on coming aboard, and that was more or less the last anyone saw of him. He took his meals alone and slept in a tiny cabin next to the radio shack.

After embarkation from Lorient dead on time on the morning of the seventh, there was nothing to do for the two days it would take to reach the northwest coast of England. Stieff took the long way round, coursing well to the west of the Ile d'Ouessant and heading out into the Atlantic. Sailing through St. George's Channel and up into

189

the Irish Sea was asking for trouble, he explained. At longitude 12 degrees he swung the U-boat north and followed the Irish coast.

On the morning of the second day, while cruising at periscope depth, they spotted a large convoy heading east. The urge to take a pot shot at the merchantmen ferrying foodstuffs from Canada and the United States to England was almost irresistible, but Stieff overcame his natural inclinations. "There'll be plenty of time to play hide and seek with the *Tommis*."

The most hazardous part of the journey took place on the ninth, going through that stretch of water between the northeast coast of Ireland and the southwest coast of Scotland, the North Channel, from the Mull of Kintyre down to the Mull of Galloway. Stieff openly confessed that these were unfamiliar waters and that he proposed to make part of the run in daylight and on the surface.

Christian was not in the least happy at the prospect of being picked up on coastal radar and meeting up with the Royal Navy or a Mosquito of Coastal Command. "I thought the whole idea of a U-boat was to travel underwater."

"That's the theory," said Stieff nonchalantly, "but I'm one of those people who likes to see where he's going. You can stay topside and watch if you wish. If there's any danger we've always got a minute or two."

Christian took one look at the choppy seas and the heavy clouds hanging over the Scottish mainland and felt threatened enough.

"No thanks," he said.

Although the German navy was not usually so democratic as to quarter the officers with the men, Stieff was no slavish disciple of protocol. "As you'll be working together you might as well eat and sleep together," he said in Lorient, and promptly turned over his second in command's cabin to Feldwebel Schelling and Obergefreiter Schultz. Christian himself bunked with Stieff, and all four men took their meals together, apart from the other officers and crew.

In spite of the cramped conditions it proved to be an admirable arrangement. Stieff was an excellent host and raconteur and a fine mimic. His impersonations of Germany's leaders had the other three in fits of laughter, though Schelling and Schultz were a little embarrassed at first and kept looking over their shoulder for Kirdorff.

Leaving Stieff to the business of getting them safely through the North Channel, Christian sought out his men. He found them in their cabin, making a final equipment check.

Apart from the clothes they stood up in and a spare set of civvies in a rucksack for von Stuerzbecher, they were taking a three-man tent, cooking utensils and food (with British labels), and iron rations. Christian was to carry the Luger, a compass and, after much private debate, a large-scale map of the area. He had pondered the question of a map at great length and eventually decided it was indispensable. Although after much study he was fairly certain he knew the topography of the area, its hazards and pitfalls, there was always the unexpected to be reckoned with. They might not be able to come out the way they went in, and it would be the height of irony if they succeeded in all other aspects of the venture but could not find their way back to the rendezvous before Stieff was compelled to abandon them. Christian hoped they would not be seen, but if they were he intended passing the group off as hikers, a not unlikely pastime for the British even in the depths of winter. Hikers carried maps, so a map became part of their kit.

In a side pocket of Christian's waterproof jacket were the sealed orders that Standartenfuehrer Weil had given him in Berlin. As they were so close to landfall he was tempted to break the seal now, memorize the contents and destroy them. But Weil had decreed otherwise, and Christian decided to play it by the book.

He had examined himself for nerves and found none. He was feeling better than he had felt for months. Weil might have selected him because he knew England and the English and was a close friend of von Stuerzbecher's, but the *Standartenfuehrer* was not to know he had more or less saved Christian's life. The drunken days in Cologne and elsewhere seemed no more than a distant nightmare, and he hadn't touched more than a couple of glasses of beer in over two weeks. He had lost the excess weight too, and was now not far short of perfect fitness, mental as well as physical. He had something positive, worthwhile, to do, and it made him feel good.

"Everything all right?" he asked.

"It will be when I get out of this can," growled Schelling. "Christ, how these people put up with it for weeks on end is beyond me."

"Look at it from their point of view. Imagine us crawling around England in the depths of winter when we could be as snug as bugs under fifty fathoms of ocean."

"Are we on schedule, Christian?" asked Wolf Schultz. Neither he nor Schelling had been on deck since Lorient and the U-boat could be in the Pacific for all they knew.

"As far as I know. Stieff expects to be somewhere off the lower end of the Solway Firth, between Maryport and Workington, by nightfall, but it'll be 2100 or thereabouts before we're ashore. Do you want to go over the whole thing once more?"

Neither Schelling nor Schultz was the nervous type, but it was still good military practice to keep a man's mind occupied until it was time to go.

"Might as well," answered Schelling. "If Wolf gets lost it'll be useful if he knows where to surrender."

"Balls. The only way I'll get lost is looking for you."

Christian grinned and spread open the map.

"As near as possible Stieff wants to stand offshore just south of Maryport, but that will depend very much on enemy activity. However, there's not much of strategic importance in this part of the world so it shouldn't be a problem. He'll heave to as close as he dares, and we'll be rowed ashore by dinghy.

"From Maryport or wherever it is, we strike due east. I'd

like to go cross-country, avoiding roads, villages and towns, but that will depend upon conditions underfoot. If we're forced to use roads we'll go via Broughton Moor, Dovenby, Bridekirk, Blindcrake and Bewaldeth, skirting Bassenthwaite Lake to the north and going down its east side to the camp. It's about twenty miles or thirty-one kilometers door to door, so I don't expect to be at the objective much before dawn. In fact, I'd like to work it that way, get somewhere within the vicinity of the camp by daybreak. It'll probably take the rest of the day to reconnoiter and figure out a way to let Stuerzbecher know we're here, but I've got a couple of thoughts on that subject. I'll tell you about them later.

"The next part's the easy part." Christian smiled. "We liberate Stuerzbecher and take him home."

"With half the British Army chasing us," grunted Schelling.

"And with only a couple of days to do it in," added Schultz.

"Nobody said it was going to be easy, but I think we're agreed that if we can't find a way to free Stuerzbecher in a couple of days, we'll never find it."

"Doesn't matter anyway," said Schelling. "If we're not back by the evening of the fourteenth we've got a long swim home."

"Precisely." Christian folded up the map and put it away. "Tomorrow's the tenth, and by tomorrow night we should know if the job's possible. Strictly speaking that only leaves us two whole days to get it done, because if we're to rendezvous with Stieff on the night of the fourteenth at the latest, we'll need to travel back during the dark hours of the thirteenth and hole up during the day. If we can't get Stuerzbecher out on the eleventh or twelfth, we can't get him out at all."

Wolf Schultz grinned mischievously. "Maybe that's how we should play it. Take a stroll through the English countryside for a few days then come back and report failure. No one's going to blame us for trying."

"We're not going to fail," said Christian seriously. "That's the last thing we're going to do."

Later on in the day Stieff came below to report that they had just rounded the Mull of Galloway without incident and that darkness had fallen ten minutes ago; that the weather was atrocious upstairs and that it didn't look much better over the mainland; that they were making a steady eight knots on the surface and that he expected to be in position between 2000 and 2100.

"I must say I don't envy you," he commented. "If it's not snowing it'll be sleeting, and if not sleeting, raining."

"We've seen worse," said Christian. "If this were Russia we'd think it was spring."

"You look the part anyway." Not wishing to leave anything until the last moment, all three were dressed to go. "If I didn't know differently, I swear I'd shoot you on sight as British spies. I particularly like the hair."

Christian smiled self-consciously. It was one of the details he was pleased to have remembered, instructing Schelling and Schultz to give the barber a miss. Fortunately neither of them wore their hair closely cropped, as British cartoonists liked to depict German soldiers, and Christian had always favored a style just above his collar. In the short time he had had, it wasn't really long enough to satisfy him absolutely, but all three were wearing it longer than would have been permitted in Germany.

"Thanks. I expect we'll be court-martialed for slovenly appearance when we get home."

"When you get home," said Stieff, "I doubt if anyone will mind if it's halfway down your back." Abruptly he was serious. "You're quite clear about the signals?" he asked Christian.

"Quite clear. We return to where you drop us, wherever that happens to be. On the night of the thirteenth or fourteenth, at exactly 2000, we flash two long two short, wait sixty seconds, then repeat the signal. Fifteen minutes later we do the same thing again. On neither occasion will you reply."

194

"It's safer. It's unlikely your signal will be seen, but a patrol could pick up our acknowledgment. But we'll be there, never fear. Your first signal will tell me you're ready to be taken off and your second will guide the dinghy in. I could also be there on the twelfth if you wish."

Christian shook his head. "No point. Even if everything goes like clockwork, to be at the rendezvous on the twelfth would mean traveling overnight on the eleventh, and there's no chance we'll be able to do that."

No one bothered to mention what would happen if the U-boat did not receive a signal on the fourteenth; that would have been tempting fate.

"All right, then." Stieff stood in the companionway. "I'll get back upstairs and start driving this crate. I've instructed the galley to prepare the biggest and best meal they can muster. It shouldn't be long."

"I wish he hadn't said that," muttered Josef Schelling, when Stieff had gone. "I remember what happens when the supper is gone."

Now observing full silent routine, Christian and his party scrambled over the side of the U-boat and into the waiting dinghy at 2050 hours. To prevent their civilian clothes getting too wet too quickly, Stieff had thoughtfully equipped the trio with oilskins and sou'westers. These would be brought back on landing by the crew of the dinghy.

His eyes not yet accustomed to the darkness, Christian wondered how the hell Stieff knew where they were, for looking east not a light showed anywhere. Even screwing up his eyes and adopting the ridiculous but usual landlubber's pose of leaning physically forward, Christian could see nothing. The night was moonless, the sky black and angry. It was still raining, though that could well be snow inland.

As the dinghy pulled away from the U-boat's side, glancing over his shoulder Christian thought he could make out Stieff in the conning tower. There was no sign of Kirdorff.

Neither was there any whispered "good-luck"; farewells and silent prayers had already been said below. All that could be heard now was the wail of the wind and the sound of oars.

Stieff had chosen the three biggest members of his crew to man the inflatable dinghy, but even so, Christian could sense that the prevailing wind and the run of the tide were pushing them further south than they wished to be. By gesture he managed to convey that his party would take a couple of spare oars, but the *Obersteuermann* in command shook his head and thumbed out into the darkness. Christian understood; the passengers would be better employed keeping an eye open for stray mines.

It seemed an hour but it was probably no more than twenty minutes before a darker patch of sky turned out to be coastline, and a change in the sound of the waves indicated they were nearing shore. Minutes later, the dinghy scraped the bottom.

Christian, Schelling and Schultz slipped quietly out of their oilskins. With Schultz carrying the rucksack and Schelling the harness which held the tent, Christian led them over the side. Again, from the sailors, there were no vocal incantations to the spirits of good fortune; either they would reunite with their passengers in a few days or they would not. That was all there was to it.

Under the lee of the cliff that towered ahead of them, Christian tried to calculate his bearings. Neither he nor the others watched the dinghy disappear into the night. They were ashore all right, but none of them wanted to hang around.

"We've got to find a way up," he shouted. It shouldn't be much of a problem; even if he was farther south than he reckoned, nowhere did the map show the cliffs rising above a couple of hundred feet. "Wolf, scout left, Josef right."

They found a path in no time.

"Take it easy going up," warned Christian. "The last thing we need now is a broken ankle."

Thirteen

DECEMBER 10

It was no longer snowing, but all the signs pointed to another fall before morning. In the meantime they had the cold to contend with.

They had been trekking for two hours, and Maryport and the coast were a long way behind them. Christian estimated they had covered five miles or so and he was quite happy with their rate of progress. Although they were using the roads, as a precaution he had set the phosphorescent dial of his British Army compass to ten degrees south of east. In an emergency that heading would put them on a collision course with the River Derwent.

The night had so far been uneventful—with one exception. On the outskirts of the hamlet of Dovenby they had come across a detached house standing in several acres of ground. As they were about to pass it, the stillness was suddenly shattered by the sound of a car engine and the driveway illuminated by headlights. In a panic they flattened themselves against the hedgerow. The car shot down the driveway and skidded to a halt before entering the main road. Christian could see the occupants quite clearly, a man and a woman. And a window must have been open because he heard the man say: "For the love of God we'll only be away five days, don't worry about it."

When his heart stopped thumping Christian filed the information. An empty house could well be useful on the way back.

Attempting to travel cross-country had proved to be impossible. In places the snow was two or three feet deep, and they had all sunk into it up to their knees before the idea was abandoned. The return trip might be a different proposition, but for the moment they hugged the sides of roads, ready to leap into a ditch at the slightest danger. Apart from the incident with the car, so far they had seen only one truck, full of singing troops, and a solitary motorcyclist; traveling at night had its advantages. It took time, of course, but even so they were beyond Blindcrake by one-thirty. Half an hour later Christian called a halt.

"If all England's like this," said Josef Schelling, gulping down a can of self-heating soup, "can anyone tell me why we want to conquer it?"

Christian massaged his calves while eating a bar of chocolate. "It's not all like this and not even this is always the same. You should see it in the summer, or in summers before the war, at any rate. The place is crawling with hikers and climbers—at least half of them girls," he added pointedly for Schultz's benefit.

"I don't think I'd know what to do with a girl if I was presented with one on a plate," said Schultz. "My privates have shriveled up and disappeared."

"I thought I saw something small drop on the road a while back." Schelling grinned in the darkness. "But it was such a pathetic little thing I didn't think you'd miss it."

Schultz made an obscene gesture with his fist. "Speak for yourself, Feldwebel. If anything drops off me the British'll think it's an air raid."

"Bury the cans," warned Christian. He squinted at his wrist watch, bought in Bond Street in happier times. It was two-twenty. With luck they should be through Bewaldeth by three-thirty and on top of the objective an hour or so after that. Sunrise in this part of the world for the time of year was a few minutes before 8 A.M. He wanted to be several hundred feet up Skiddaw with a good view of the camp before then.

They were level with the northern tip of Bassenthwaite Lake ten minutes the wrong side of Christian's e.t.a. Although in theory it was a straight run down the Keswick road now, Christian nevertheless reset his compass to read 150 degrees. They would only be able to follow the road so far and he wanted no guessing games when they left it.

Three quarters of an hour later, ahead of them in the distance, they were puzzled by a pattern of lights that got no closer. Static convoy? Air raid defenses? It took a couple of minutes to work it out.

"Stupid of me," said Christian. "They're the searchlights from the camp." He experienced a surge of elation; the first part of their mission was almost over.

As they left the road to make for the lower slopes of Skiddaw, it started to snow. But it was only a short-lived squall.

They were all desperately tired now, having covered the best part of twenty miles in something under seven hours. But they found reserves of energy from somewhere and by 5:15 A.M. they were a thousand feet up the mountain, looking down on the camp.

The searchlights made it as bright as day, and it was all pretty much as Christian had expected; row after row of wooden huts in the middle of the compound, and administrative and other buildings dotted around the inner perimeter wire. The searchlights appeared to function automatically, judging by the way they traversed in a regular pattern, though doubtless there were armed guards in each watchtower to operate them manually if there was a breakdown in the power plant. Anyway, there wasn't much more he could do until daylight, when the first item

199

on the agenda would be to establish the POWs' routine. In the meantime, rest, food and sleep.

"Put the tent up somewhere where it can't be seen from the camp," he told Wolf Schultz. "Over there by that rock face looks like a good place."

"Camouflage?"

"Yes, but not too much. We don't know yet whether this area is used by shepherds, and I'll lay odds the *Tommis* come up from time to time. I don't want to make it too obvious that we're trying to hide."

"I'll take the first watch until dawn," offered Schelling.

"All right. But if you see anything or anyone for God's sake wake me up. And keep a note of anything important that happens down there. Parades, roll calls, anything of that nature."

All three were really far too exhausted to eat, but they forced themselves to munch some hard tack and chocolate. Five minutes later, Christian and Wolf Schultz were asleep.

When Schelling shook them awake with the news that the camp was coming alive, it seemed as if they had only just closed their eyes. In fact, it was a few minutes after sunup. For a change the sky was almost clear and it looked as if they might get away without a snowfall for at least part of the day.

After a cold breakfast Christian insisted they all shave; if they were unfortunate enough to be spotted nothing stood out more than a man with a day-old beard. Afterward, while Schelling got some rest, Schultz kept watch and Christian settled down to the dreary business of establishing the camp routine.

He decided against using binoculars. It was always possible some sharp-eyed sentry would see lense reflections up on the mountain and wonder what the hell was going on. In any case, the POWs were almost close enough to touch, though he was still too far away to make out individual faces.

Morning roll call took place at precisely eight-thirty in a fenced-off section of the compound. He made a careful note of the time, the disposition of the prisoners, and how long the operation took, though that was the only note he made for three hours. It seemed hardly worth recording that after roll call the POWs split up and went their separate ways. Some strolled around the compound, others brought out a ball and batted it around the fenced-off section. But the majority disappeared back into their huts and into several buildings on the south side, to his far left. There was nothing to be gained by watching a ball game or men wandering aimlessly, so he switched his attention to the main gates. Short of a miracle, that was going to be his way in and out.

Like many others before him, Christian looked at the main gates and despaired when he realized that, with two notable exceptions, the inner perimeter gate was never open at the same time as the outer. Unless a man's business in the world beyond Skiddaw was accepted as legitimate by both lots of sentries, he was trapped in that stretch of no man's land which separated the fences.

The first exception was for men coming the other way, returning from leave or a trip to town or the thousand and one other reasons that mean constant activity at the entrance to any establishment containing the military. Less stringent precautions were taken here, the theory being, as Christian had worked out for himself, that while there were a couple of hundred Germans anxious to say goodbye to Skiddaw, only a lunatic would want to say hello.

The second exception was for vehicles, of all shapes and sizes, going in either direction. Heading out, anything larger or more suspicious than an open-topped jeep was searched thoroughly by the sentries on the inner gates. Once that was done, however, the vehicle was waved through both gates. Coming into camp, provided that the driver's papers were in order, there was even less formality. It therefore seemed that the only way in was on wheels. Christian had neither the papers nor the uniform to pretend to be a *Tommi*, and he could hardly hijack a military vehicle plus driver on the open highway. It followed that his method of entry would have to be via a civilian car or van.

For the remainder of the day he concentrated exclusively on civilian vehicles, paying particular attention to anything that might belong to a local tradesman. He was well prepared to spend the following day repeating the exercise, for if the same vehicle appeared twice at approximately the same hour it could mean a regular delivery service and worthy of further investigation.

But by the time the second roll call of the day was taken at 1600 hours, his list was far from impressive: four civilian private cars (three of them almost certainly belonging to camp personnel, as they came in from some overnight business but did not go out) and two vans. He had risked binoculars on the vans. One was an ancient contraption of nondescript color, seemingly held together by bits of wire and will power. And judging by the way the driver stood and talked and smoked a cigarette with a couple of *Tommis,* he was well known. The second was bright yellow in color and bore the legend Foster's Bakery. The driver of this turned out to be a woman, though from the distance it was difficult to tell her age. She drove up to what Christian assumed to be the guardroom, unloaded several wooden trays of loaves and handed them to a couple of *Tommis,* then drove off along the Keswick road, in the direction of that town. All in all, she was in the compound less than ninety seconds.

The time of entry of the first van was recorded as 3:20 P.M., that of the second as 3:55, just as the watchtower lights were being switched on and the POWs assembling for roll call.

By 4:30 the roll call was over, the POWs dispersed, and Christian had learned nothing more. And with the Germans now presumably locked up for the night, he doubted if there was anything more to learn—not that day.

He was also very tired. With only a couple of short

202

breaks for food and a slightly longer one for a session of violent exercise to prevent his freezing to death, he had kept the camp under surveillance for nine hours. Three hours' sleep after a twenty-mile-route march was hardly adequate preparation for that sort of vigil. Still, it was not something he could have delegated to his NCOs. They were good men, brave as lions and thoroughly reliable, but the ultimate responsibility for freeing von Stuerzbecher was his alone. They had been extremely patient all day, however, and it was high time he let them know his thoughts.

Over a heated can of soup followed by a surreptitious cigarette, he told them his idea of using a civilian vehicle. Neither was impressed by his apparently suicidal urge to get into the camp.

"It's too risky, Christian," said Schelling. "First of all you've got to steal a van, then pass yourself off as a relief driver. Even if you succeed in doing both without the alarm being raised, you won't get further than the guardroom, at any rate not much further. I was also watching the procedure. Deliveries are made just inside the inner gates. The *Tommis* are not going to risk letting a civilian driver have the run of the camp. God knows what might happen to him or his vehicle."

"And we don't see the necessity," said Wolf Schultz. "We're here to get Stuerzbecher out, not join him behind barbed wire or worse. I don't see why we don't steal a pair of cutters and go in through the fence."

But Christian negated that. "It wouldn't work. There are twenty-five or thirty huts in the compound and Stuerzbecher could be in any one of them. It might take us a week to ascertain which, and in a week the U-boat won't be waiting for us. On the other hand, if I could get in near roll call I could possibly do something to let Stuerzbecher see me. You saw where they held the *Appell,* in the fenced-off section where the men were playing ball?" The other two nodded. "It's only thirty or forty meters from the guardroom. If I was there around 0830 or 1600 and created a disturbance, Stuerzbecher would at least know help was at hand. Don't forget, we're old friends. He'd recognize me at once."

"Then what?" asked Schultz. "He's not going to run up and embrace you, jump in the van, and drive off with you into the setting sun."

"No, but he'll realize I wouldn't be showing myself unless I wanted something from him, some information. I wouldn't be such a fool as to drive into Skiddaw in broad daylight if I already had a viable scheme for freeing him. He's only been a POW himself a few weeks, remember. He'll be fully aware that our knowledge of Skiddaw is sparse."

"Go on," said Schelling.

"If he's as bright as I know him to be," Christian continued, "he'll work out some sort of signal for us. It could take any form, so we'll have to keep our eyes open, but if it tells us no more than which hut he's in or where he'll be at any particular time and day—well, that's at least more than we know at present. It may then mean taking up Wolf's idea about the cutters."

There was a long silence.

"It's pretty damned bare, Christian," said Schelling finally. "We're working on practically nothing. Christ, for all we know there might be a camp inspection by Churchill tomorrow."

Christian shrugged his shoulders. "I agree, but we're up against a deadline. If I had a month to plan it I'd not only get Stuerzbecher out but the rest as well. But—" He stopped and frowned as a sudden thought occurred.

"What is it?" asked Schelling.

"He's planning to use the pair of us as battering rams," suggested Schultz, who could already see the eye-whites of the firing squad.

Christian didn't hear him. He thumped his palm excitedly. "We're short of knowledge, right? We need more information than we've got, right? Now who in the world, in Germany, England or anywhere else you care to name knows more about the inner workings of a military base than even the troops themselves?"

"Civilian workers," said Schelling.

"Tradesmen," offered Schultz.

"Right," said Christian, "right both times. And where do civilian workers and tradesmen go when they're not working and they're not at home?"

"A concert?"

"A cinema?"

"A beer house?"

"Precisely," said Christian. "A beer house, a pub, there to discuss politics, lament the day's events, and gossip. Gentlemen, I regret you cannot accompany me, but I'm going for a drink."

When Christian saw the yellow Foster's Bakery van parked outside the tiny pub a mile down the Keswick road, his pulse rate shot up thirty points. Careful now, he cautioned, don't get so bloody excited. And for God's sake don't walk in and order a glass of *Schnapps*.

The pub was no more than two ground-floor rooms of a private house, converted into a single bar when the owner got a license, an occurrence not uncommon in the north of England and something Christian had seen scores of times during the prewar years. Before the advent of Skiddaw Camp it had catered only to the occupants of the dozen houses which made up the tiny hamlet, but now it was used by off-duty soldiers as well.

There were three of these at the dartboard when Christian walked in, but they gave him no more than a perfunctory glance. That was how it should be. As far as he was concerned he passed muster. His boots, clothes and rucksack were the accouterments of a hiker, and in physical appearance he looked more Irish than German. If there was any flaw in his accent, which he doubted, a casual listener would ascribe it to Hibernian influence. In any event, it seemed most unlikely that any of them could envisage a former Waffen SS officer turning up in their pub.

205

Apart from the soldiers, the only other customers were two old men playing dominoes and a woman propped up by the counter. He quickly surmised that she was the bakery driver, but he needed confirmation.

"Does anyone own that yellow van out there?" he asked.

The woman turned on her stool. Close up, she was far prettier than a distant view via binoculars had suggested. Dark hair cut quite short, big hazel eyes, and a more than generous mouth that needed no gilding of the lily by the addition of lipstick. In spite of the fact that she was wearing a chunky sweater, an open parka and slacks, he guessed that underneath it all she was quite slim. Her age he estimated as middle twenties.

"I don't own it, but I'm driving it," she said. Her words were slightly slurred; the gin in front of her was evidently not the first of the evening.

Christian had been out of England for many years, but he remembered an educated voice when he heard one. It didn't make any sense, a woman like this doing a bakery round.

"Is anything the matter?" she added.

"I saw someone trying the door as I walked up," Christian lied. "He ran off when he saw me, but I thought you should know. He didn't look more than a boy."

"One of the local children, I expect. They're always hoping that I'll leave the back open and a tray of cakes inside." She rattled her keys, which were lying on the bar. "But I never do. Thanks anyway."

The barmaid was hovering now, a blowzy, overweight creature in her forties. "What can I get you?"

Christian flashed her one of his best smiles. What he really wanted was to get closer to this woman who drove for Foster's, but that would have to be done *pianissimo*, in the English fashion.

"A whisky if you've got it, a pint of beer if you haven't."

"No whisky, sorry."

Christian understood. The whisky allocation would be small and saved for regulars.

"Try the gin," suggested the woman driver. "It's noth-

206

ing like the prewar variety, but it'll get the circulation going again." She indicated the rucksack, which Christian had placed on the floor beside him. "You look as though you need it."

"Fine—if you'll join me."

The woman hesitated before shrugging her shoulders and nodding. "Thanks."

Christian pocketed his change and sank half his drink in a single gulp. "That's better. I was beginning to think my blood had deserted me."

Now that the ice was partly broken the woman seemed more inclined to chat.

"Have you come far today?" she asked.

"From Cockermouth," answered Christian, sticking close to the truth. "I had hoped to get as far as Keswick before it got dark, but I couldn't get a lift and the roads were worse than I thought." He decided he had nothing to lose by firing his opening shots early. The Keswick address of Foster's Bakery was emblazoned under the proprietor's name on the side of the van. "Still, that's my own fault for setting off so late."

"And for hiking in this part of the country at this time of year," said the woman.

"True enough. But I had a couple of weeks leave due and anything's better than spending that in London. The Americans have taken over everything."

"That's what my husband used to say."

"Used to?"

"He's been a prisoner of war for six months."

"I'm sorry to hear it."

"Thank you, but there are many other wives much worse off. At least he was fortunate enough to bail out of his Halifax and land unharmed. From what I can gather unofficially, all but one of the rest of the crew didn't make it."

Christian's mind was working overtime. He didn't much believe in luck, but here was a situation which could readily be exploited.

Sheer chance had put him next to a woman who was a

grass widow as a result of the war. She drove—for reasons he had still to ascertain—a van that had access to Skiddaw. That she was lonely and drank too much was obvious; attractive young women did not sit by themselves in pubs for any other reason. The next move was his.

"Perhaps he'll manage to get out," he offered. "It's been done before."

"I'd rather he stayed there. You know what the Nazis are like. If any of those dreadful people from Skiddaw escape and are recaptured, they're simply put into solitary confinement for a while as punishment. That much I know for certain. If one of our men is recaught, he's shot."

Christian moved in for the kill, though really, he couldn't help thinking, it was the height of irony that the wife of a captured R.A.F. flier could—might—assist him in freeing Kurt von Stuerzbecher.

"Look," he said, lowering his voice, "I shouldn't be telling you this and obviously I can't reveal what my job is, but conditions in German POW camps are not as bad as the general public is led to believe."

"I can't accept that. We read and hear all the time about the appalling way the men have to live."

Christian tried to act like a British officer whose only motive was to help a lady in distress.

"Those things have to be said and written, you must understand that. The propaganda war is as vital to eventual victory as Bomber Command. But—" He paused deliberately—"But I've said too much already."

"No, please." Unthinkingly she put a hand on his arm. "Please don't stop there." The hazel eyes begged for reassurance.

Christian feigned momentary reluctance. "All right," he said finally, "but let's move over to one of the tables. And let me refill your glass while I'm about it."

One hour and three gins later, they were on a first-name basis. She was Anna Newfield, he Charles Kay, the identity on his forged papers.

He knew much more about her now. The combination of gin and a sympathetic ear had broken down what remained of her reserve. Foster was some sort of distant relation of her husband, and she had taken the delivery job both to help him out and to keep herself occupied.

"Otherwise it's too much of this."

She held up her empty glass. Christian took it as a cue and refilled it before she could decline, although she was already half drunk. The barmaid eyed him knowingly as he paid. He got the impression that, if he left with Anna, it would not be the first time she had gone out with someone.

At half-past nine, just as the darts-playing soldiers were leaving, he decided to push her a little harder. Somehow he had to get his hands on the delivery van and find a legitimate reason for visiting Skiddaw tomorrow, but as yet he had only the vaguest idea of how that could be accomplished. The key was Anna.

"Don't you have to be up rather early?" he asked.

"Not tomorrow. Tomorrow I only have to do that wretched camp. You see, for the next two days we don't deliver at all, except locally in Keswick, so the camp takes three days' supplies at once. The whole of Mr. Foster's output, for that matter. I try to do it before midmorning, which gives me the rest of the day off, but it really doesn't matter when I arrive." She paused, her lips hovering over the rim of the glass. "What about you?"

"All I have to do is get to Keswick. I could sleep under canvas, but I'm afraid somebody might have to dig me out in the morning. I'll try to find lodgings."

She hesitated just a fraction too long for her next words to be anything other than calculated, gin-induced or not.

"I live in that direction, about a mile outside town to be exact. I could take you part of the way." She looked at him steadily, judging, assessing, wondering if he could see through her act, her pitiful need for company. "Better still, I could put you up for the night. You won't find it easy getting lodgings."

"I wouldn't dream of asking you to do such a thing," protested Christian.

"Nonsense. In any case, you didn't ask, remember? I

209

offered. You've been very kind and it's the least I can do in return. It's only a small cottage, I'm afraid, so it'll have to be the sofa."

Bull's-eye, thought Christian.

Outside, he held her arm as the cold night air hit her like a sledgehammer.

"Would you like me to drive?"

"Not at all. I've done this trip a hundred times. The van knows its own way home."

The cottage was a one-story building set well back from the main road and apparently isolated. From the front door a narrow hallway led into the sitting room, which was furnished tastefully and, to a degree, with little regard for expense.

While Anna went away to fetch blankets, Christian quickly examined his surroundings.

Near the telephone, the drinks table contained a full bottle and a half-empty bottle of gin, three quarters of a bottle of whisky and a bottle of some very old brandy. On the mantelpiece stood a framed photograph of a young man wearing the uniform of a R.A.F. flight lieutenant. Next to it was a small box. One glance at the label was enough to tell Christian that there were occasions when Anna Newfield needed barbiturates to help her sleep.

He replaced the box when he heard her returning, but already the germ of an idea was beginning to form.

She insisted on making sandwiches and coffee for both of them, and they chased the snack with a small tot of brandy apiece.

The signs were more obvious now. Over the brandy her expression made it quite clear that the slightest gesture from him that he found her attractive would not be rejected. But it suited his purpose more if the advances came from her.

Shortly before midnight she said she was going to bed, that he could help himself to another drink if he wanted it. He said no, that he was tired too.

He stripped down to his shorts in the sitting room, switched off the lights, and climbed under the blankets. There he waited.

A thin sliver of light shone through a crack in her bedroom door. Whatever she was doing, she wasn't going to sleep.

Midnight struck on the softly chiming wall clock; then the half hour. It must therefore have been close to 1 A.M. before he heard the click of a latch being lifted.

He inclined his head slightly. She stood in the bedroom doorway, wearing a flimsy nightdress through which the light beyond shone, framing her naked body beneath.

"Charles?" It was no more than a whisper.

"Yes?" he answered.

"I need holding, Charles. I need to be close to someone."

She proved to be far above average in bed, although Christian was experienced enough in the ways of women to realize that her apparent eagerness had more to do with desperate loneliness than inbred lust. Nevertheless, she responded to his every thrust and showed no shyness or reluctance when he turned her over and mounted her from the rear.

Afterward he let her sleep for a while though he himself took great care to do no more than cat nap.

He heard 3 A.M. strike, and woke her gently. This time he concentrated on leaving her just short of orgasm. It was important to his scheme that she was aroused. He wanted her awake for a few minutes.

When it was over he lit cigarettes for both of them.

"I could use a drink," he said.

"I'll get it."

"No, I know where it is. You too?"

"Perhaps a brandy."

He padded naked into the adjoining room and flicked on the lights. He poured a small brandy for himself and a much larger one for her. This done, he took the box of sleeping tablets and crushed four into her glass. The normal dosage, according to the label, was one or two. He stirred the mixture with his finger until the powder was as dissolved as it would ever be.

The sheets pulled modestly across the breasts, she was sitting up when he returned. He passed over her drink and perched himself on the edge of the bed.

"You've left the lights on," she said.

He had done so deliberately, as well as leaving the bedroom door half open. He wanted to make sure she drank every drop of the drugged brandy.

"I'll fix it in a minute."

She stared at him silently, almost reproachfully, clutching the glass tightly with both hands. He couldn't be sure but he thought, at some point, she had been crying.

"I don't want you to think I make a habit of doing this," she said.

"Don't talk about it. Drink your brandy and go to sleep."

"I just want you to understand."

"I do. Don't think about it. It'll all look different in the morning."

He touched his glass to hers. She swallowed the brandy in a single gulp. If she was not already an alcoholic, she was well on the way. In spite of himself and his mission, he felt sorry for her.

She pulled a face. "God, that tasted awful."

"We've both had too much tonight."

"Of everything," she said.

Within twenty minutes she was asleep and breathing evenly. If he left her alone she would probably not wake for a dozen hours. But he had no intention of allowing events to proceed in that manner.

It was a few minutes after 4 A.M. when he rinsed both glasses under the kitchen tap, taking particular care with hers. By this time Schultz and Schelling would be worried sick, but they were both well enough trained to stay put until he either returned or they judged him to be in captivity. With any luck, they would be reassured in a few hours.

Climbing into bed alongside Anna Newfield, Christian set a mental clock for 6:30 A.M. In spite of his tiredness and the amount of drink he had consumed, he knew he would be awake within a few minutes of that hour.

Fourteen

He shook her at 6:45. He was already dressed and shaved, and he had taken a look around outside. Although it was still dark with some ground frost about, it wasn't snowing.

He held out a mug of freshly made tea. It was heavily sugared to disguise the taste of a second helping of barbiturates, only two on this occasion. He just wanted her out, not dead.

Drugged as she already was, it took a considerable effort on his part to get her to open her eyes and grasp the mug. She was still only semiconscious when he reminded her that she had a delivery to make.

"Can't do it. Christ, I feel awful."

"You asked me to wake you early."

"Did I? I don't remember."

"Drink this. It'll help."

She gulped the tea eagerly and the immediate effect was to brighten her up a fraction. But he knew this state of affairs wouldn't last long. The combination of the pills he had fed her during the night together with the present

215

dose would render her comatose in a few minutes. And she had a job to do before that if he was to arrive at the camp for morning roll call.

"What time is it?" she asked.

"Coming up to seven."

"God, I've got hours yet."

"The way you look you'll be asleep for the rest of the day."

She was already finding it difficult to drink the tea without spilling any, and he had to steady her hands.

"I've got an idea," he said, as though it had only just occurred. "Why don't I make the trip for you? You give Mr. Foster a ring, tell him you're feeling ill but that you've got a friend to help you out. Don't worry, I know where the camp is because I passed it yesterday. And I won't run off with the van. I'll even leave my rucksack here to prove I'll be back."

She was in no fit state to argue and even had to lean on him while he led her to the telephone.

He stood over her while she made the call. She certainly sounded ill, and Foster did not seem to care one way or another provided that she would vouch for the substitute driver and that the delivery was made.

Thirty seconds after she replaced the receiver she was back in bed. A minute later she was fast asleep again.

Christian left the house at 7:05. The body of the yellow van was covered with a light mantle of snow and frost, but it started at the first attempt. Choke half out, he pulled onto the road and headed for Keswick.

Foster turned out to be a surly individual in his fifties. He expressed no surprise that Anna Newfield's surrogate was a good-looking young man. Perhaps he had seen it all before.

There were ten dozen freshly baked loaves, in wooden trays, destined for Skiddaw, and Christian was well ahead of schedule when he left the bakery—so much so that a couple of miles outside Keswick he parked on

216

a grass verge and smoked for a while. It was getting lighter now, the road busier, but no one paid him any attention.

He waited until precisely 8:15 before switching on the ignition. If he drove steadily he should be outside the camp at 8:25.

At 8:20, in Hut 9, Franz Mohr said: "Come on, let's not give the *Tommis* any excuse to put us all in the brig."

"You've got a damned alarm clock in that head of yours," called Theo Emke. To Hans Baum, with a slight gesture, he indicated that it was time for roll call.

On the bunk once occupied by Emil Naumann, Kurt von Stuerzbecher, fully dressed, decided he would indulge himself for two more minutes in the comparative warmth of the hut. Though probably, he told himself, it's not the warmth that interests you at all; it's the unwillingness to face another boring day, compounded by the fact that tomorrow's the twelfth.

In twos and threes and occasionally alone, the POWs made their way over to the Pig Pen. Probably not more than half a dozen saw the yellow van come to a halt outside the main gates.

The *Tommi* guard walked round to the driver's side, his expression one of cautious puzzlement. "Foster's?"

It was an idiotic question, but Christian knew what he meant. He also knew that the military had little time for the civilian population, and vice versa.

"If that's what it says on the side of the van, that's where I'm from."

"All right, pal, keep your shirt on. I was just wondering where Anna was."

"None of your bloody business. Now open the gates, will you? Foster told me to make you first on the list because some bugger's been complaining. But I can't hang around all day. Either get the gates open or I'll leave you till this afternoon."

217

"All right, all right. Christ, anyone would think you owned the bakery."

The guard waved an arm and both sets of gates swung open. Christian drove in slowly. Ahead of him, no more than forty or fifty yards away, he could see the POWs assembling for morning *Appell*.

From his previous day's observations Christian remembered that Anna, once through the inner gates, had turned sharp left and pulled up tight against what was obviously the guardroom. But he was a new driver, wasn't he? Any fool could see that. He would be forgiven if he didn't park in the right place.

Instead of parking with his near side adjacent to the guardroom, he drove the van in a wide arc so that the nose was now facing the gates; the rear doors, out of which he would remove the bread trays, were directly opposite the Exercise Yard. It brought the van and the POWs ten yards closer to one another. Given more time that ten could have been twenty, but he wanted to start his performance before the *Tommi* NCOs, already consulting their lists, began calling the roll.

A corporal and two privates descended the guardroom steps. Christian opened the rear doors.

"Where's Anna?" asked the corporal to Christian's back.

"Still in bed, where I left her." Christian decided there was no harm in being coarse. "Any more questions?"

The corporal was the belligerent type. "Yes. You're early."

Christian turned to face him. There was an immediate flicker of recognition in the corporal's eyes.

"I know you, don't I? I've seen you somewhere before."

Christian could have given him time, date and place, but it was better that it came from the *Tommi*.

"I've got it. You were in the pub last night, you and Anna." He leered openly. "So that's the way the land lies."

"That's the way it lies," agreed Christian. "Now let's get this stuff unloaded so that I can get back to bed." He beckoned the nearer of the privates. "Here, grab one end of this."

218

The *Tommi* took one end of the tray while Christian took the other. Suddenly the contents were on the ground, in the snow and slush.

"You bloody fool!" yelled Christian. His words echoed throughout the compound. "Now look what you've done!"

The *Tommi* protested that it wasn't his fault, that Christian had let his own end slip. But Christian would have none of that, and he continued to rant.

In Hut 9's rank Theo Emke and Fritz Uhde grinned at each other when they saw what was going on. Serve the *Tommis* right. All that fresh bread and not a morsel of it for the POWs. They would get the stale stuff, yesterday's leftovers, last bloody week's leftovers. The way the van was parked they could not only see the loaves, they could smell them. A couple of hundred mouths watered.

Von Stuerzbecher stood on tiptoe and peered over Franz Mohr's head to get a better look. The loaves on the ground between them, the driver seemed about ready to take a swing at one of the *Tommis*. To make matters worse, some of the nearer prisoners were now jeering raucously, and the driver, in his anger, turned round to give them a vicious V-sign.

The blood drained from von Stuerzbecher's face. Unless his eyes were going, the man now glaring at them all from less than forty meters away was his old friend Christian Eicke.

"Are you all right?" asked Emke anxiously. "You look as though you've seen a ghost."

"I'm fine." Von Stuerzbecher's mind was racing. "Theo, I don't think I've ever felt better."

The corporal from the pub had hold of one of Christian's arms. He wasn't at all happy with the situation. This driver had biceps like iron.

"For Chrissake take it easy! What's a few lousy loaves of bread?"

"They may be a few lousy loaves to you—" Christian was still shouting—"but it means I've got to make another trip back here this afternoon. If I give you what's left there'll be nothing for anyone else."

"I thought we were the only ones on your round today."

"Then you thought wrong."

"So you make another trip, then. It's not the end of the world."

"And who's going to pay for the stuff on the deck?" Christian gave one of the loaves a kick.

"The Army will. Just tell Foster to book it out to the camp. And for Christ's sake get a hold of yourself."

Christian decided it was high time he did exactly that. Judging from the jeers, just about every German on parade had witnessed his histrionics.

"All right. But don't expect me back before midday. You can wait for the rest of your stuff until then too. If you're short of bread in the meantime, blame him." He gestured toward the unfortunate private, who was still protesting that it wasn't his fault.

Leaving the loaves where they lay, Christian got behind the wheel. The guards at both gates had seen the incident and waved him straight through without a search.

"Bloody madman," swore the corporal. "I wish I had him in my platoon for a couple of weeks. You two idiots, pick up those loaves and get rid of them."

High up on Skiddaw, Wolf Schultz and Josef Schelling had also witnessed the whole performance through their binoculars. Somehow Christian had got hold of the baker's van and gained access to the camp. Sooner or later he would return and they would be told everything, but for the time being they could relax.

"You're sure?" asked Major Breithaupt.

"Of course I'm sure." Von Stuerzbecher thumped the table with his fist. "Good God, I spent most of the thirties with the Eicke family. I was going to marry Christian's sister. I know him as well as I know myself."

Immediately after roll call von Stuerzbecher had sought

out Otto Breithaupt, who in turn called an emergency meeting of the Escape Committee. They were now in Hut 5, trying to figure out the significance of Christian's presence, assuming it was Christian Eicke.

"A man's memory can play peculiar tricks," murmured Kapitaenleutnant Heydt, "especially in a place like this. You were some distance away, the light was poor. You'll forgive me, I know, but it seems almost unbelievable that a German officer appears on our doorstep just weeks after you were shot down."

In spite of their inevitable doubts all four members of the Escape Committee were looking at von Stuerzbecher with renewed interest. He was a very senior officer, they knew, but it wasn't uncommon for even senior officers to exaggerate their own importance. If he hadn't made a mistake, however, he was as valuable to the Reich as he had hinted, for the presence of a German officer disguised as a British civilian could mean only one thing.

"I tell you it was Eicke," insisted von Stuerzbecher. "Look at that ridiculous business of the bread and the trouble he caused. And look how he made certain that everyone within earshot would know he was coming back at midday. It was play-acting, pure and simple. He arrived at roll call and created a disturbance because he wanted me to see him. He knew damn well I'd recognize him, which is no doubt why he was selected for the mission. And he's coming back at noon in the hope that I can get a message to him."

Franz Mohr admitted it made sense. "If he had found a way to get you out—I assume that is his intention—he'd have had no need to take the risk he did. I just hope to God it isn't his intention to smuggle you out in the back of that wretched van."

"That won't be necessary." Otto Breithaupt was now convinced that von Stuerzbecher's eyes had not deceived him. "By one of those absurd coincidences that happen in war, Herr Eicke has arrived at precisely the right time. He won't have to find a way to free you. Tomorrow night you'll be free in any case. I take it you'll now accept the last place in the Rabbit Run?"

Von Stuerzbecher wasted no time on false humility. "I will."

"Then that's settled. But it leads us to the problem of letting Eicke know our intentions. This is not just for your sake," he told von Stuerzbecher, "but for everyone's. If Eicke isn't told of our plans he might try something on his own, and that could ruin Rabbit Run for everyone. Any ideas?"

Heinrich Weiss had one, and he massaged his one good eye while he mulled it over. Eventually he said, "With Eicke expecting some kind of signal a dozen methods could be used. But I think his choice of vehicle has provided the answer for us."

The other four listened as Weiss outlined a tentative scheme. When he had finished Heydt remarked: "I hope for all our sakes this is not a question of mistaken identity. If it is, we are going to have on our hands one very surprised British driver and no tunnel."

It was five minutes before noon when Christian neared the camp for the second time. He had spent the intervening hours back at the cottage. Anna Newfield was still dead to the world when he left.

The outer perimeter sentry recognized the van and gave the signal for both sets of gates to be opened.

Bloody fool, thought Christian, hitting the horn in acknowledgment; I could have a dozen stormtroopers with Schmeissers in the back.

Obergefreiter Willi Braune and Unteroffizier Hans Geith were lounging near the Pig Pen when Christian pulled up by the guardroom. And if the camp staff had been paying attention they would have noticed that many more spectators than usual, officers and other ranks, were watching the volleyball game. Even more significant, the whole group, some twenty or twenty-five strong, sauntered forward as Christian opened the van's rear doors.

The corporal he had rowed with earlier, the same two privates in tow, descended the guardroom steps.

"We'll do the unloading ourselves this time. Any more foul-ups, I want someone I can blame."

"Please yourself."

But events never got that far. Led by Braune and Geith, a score of POWs made a sudden dart for the van, calling rapidly to each other in German. Although he had been expecting something to happen, Christian was unprepared for this, and he found himself shoved to one side as dozens of hands reached past him and into the van for the freshly baked bread.

The *Tommis* were transfixed with bewildered horror. They didn't even make a move for their rifles. Neither did the watchtower guards nor the other British personnel in the vicinity have an opportunity to raise more than a feeble bleat of protest before what became known as the Great Bread Raid was over, with POWs dashing in all directions, clutching their spoils.

Christian thought he caught a glimpse of von Stuerzbecher's face in the melee, grinning fiendishly, but everything happened so fast he could easily have been mistaken. Nevertheless, he felt something thrust into his pocket.

"Jesus Christ." The guard corporal stared bug-eyed at a score of disappearing backs. "Jesus Christ on a bicycle."

Christian knew he'd be expected to throw a fit. "What the bloody blue blazes was all that about?" he raged. "Look at the mess!" The area around the van resembled a battlefield, and what had not been filched was unrecognizable as food. "What am I going to say to old man Foster? Don't you feed these people, for the love of God?"

The corporal could see his stripes disappearing like straw in a gale and he was happy to hand over the whole matter to the CSM, who had come out of his office to see what all the noise was about. It was one of those days when the commandant and the adjutant were away simultaneously, and CSM Purser took it upon himself to defuse the situation. After reassuring Christian that full restitution would be made for the damaged and stolen foodstuffs, he asked that the matter be kept private.

"It won't do the war effort any good, lad, for half the population of Keswick to know what went on."

Christian promised to say nothing. It wasn't often a British senior NCO apologized to an *Oberleutnant,* and that in itself was reward enough.

When Major Mitchell returned and was told of the incident, he summoned Otto Breithaupt. Breithaupt professed not to know the names of the perpetrators; it had all happened so quickly. Though doubting the truth of this, Mitchell accepted it. There was little else he could do. He was, in any case, more concerned about the apparent inefficiency of his staff than about a few loaves of bread. It could have been the armory under siege and not just a delivery van. But Breithaupt was told that although no individual would be punished, the POW community would pay a collective fine amounting to the cost of the damage.

Breithaupt agreed that this was probably the best solution and left the commandant's office feeling greatly pleased with himself.

The note from von Stuerzbecher was direct and to the point. In block capitals it said simply:

TUNNEL BREAK-OUT TIMED FOR 2200
DECEMBER 12. STRUCTURE EXTREME
WEST SOUTHERN PERIMETER.

Christian remembered the building. It was in the far left-hand corner of the compound from where they were bivouacked. The POWs must have been working on the tunnel for months, long before Kurt was shot down. But while it solved one problem, it created another.

Von Stuerzbecher would not be coming out alone, and his fellow escapers were Germans too. Nevertheless, they were not his concern, and he hoped von Stuerzbecher had made it clear that they could not tag along. It pained him to abandon them, but there was nothing else to do. It might be the morning of the thirteenth before the escape was discovered, but then all hell would break loose, with the coast a prime target for the pursuers. Getting there with just four men was going to be difficult; more than four was asking a miracle.

It crossed his mind to use the van, but he quickly dismissed that notion as too risky. If it was not back in its place when Anna woke up, the police would be informed.

No, he must return it, pick up his rucksack, and get the hell out. If Anna, when she recovered, put his disappearance down to the fact that he had really wanted no more than a bed and a bedmate for the night, that was too bad. It doubtless wouldn't be the first time.

As it happened, it wasn't to be this time, either.

She was sitting in an armchair when he got back, legs tucked under her, a dressing gown over her nightdress. In one hand she held a mug of black coffee, in the other a cigarette. On the table beside her was the box of sleeping pills, its contents in a neat row. She couldn't have been awake long, but long enough to empty his rucksack. His changes of clothing, emergency rations and the rest were on the floor beside her.

He closed the door behind him.

"Why?" she asked.

He tried to bluff it out. "I should be asking you that question. Do you usually go through your guests' private things?"

"Only when they try to kill me."

"*Kill* you? You're delirious."

"No, Charles—if that really is your name—I'm not delirious." Her voice was quite steady though the hand which held the mug was shaking. "I woke up twenty minutes ago. I think it was the phone ringing that did it, but I can't be sure. Anyway, I woke up. It took me a while to surface because I was suffering from a barbiturate hangover. I know what they're like; I've had them before—but I didn't take any pills last night. I never do when I've been drinking or when I've got a man with me. I don't need them then."

She indicated the box and the row of pills.

"I always keep a careful count of how many I have left. I'd hate to run out if I really needed one. There were twenty there yesterday; now there are fourteen."

"You obviously miscounted." He made his voice hard. "Alcoholics frequently forget things."

"Thank you," she said bitterly, "but in this case I know you're wrong. You drugged my drink last night and probably my tea this morning. I want to know why. You're obviously not a thief or you wouldn't be here now. But neither are you a hiker. You said last night that if you couldn't find lodgings you would sleep under canvas, yet I don't see a tent among your belongings."

"It was a subterfuge," lied Christian. "I knew you'd invite me home. I never sleep under canvas. I generally find lodgings or someone like you to spend the night with."

"And do you usually drug them and do their jobs for them? It doesn't make any sense unless . . . unless you needed a reason for entering the camp. . . ."

The black coffee was doing its work now. Her eyes widened and her expression changed from one of accusation to one of fear as the truth struck her.

"You're a German."

Christian ignored her and cursed his ill luck. He should have ripped out the telephone cable before he left. Another few hours and all of her suspicions would have amounted to nothing. She would not even have called the police, because what could she have said? It would have meant admitting that she had spent the night with a stranger, one who had had the courtesy to help her out. She would have put down the missing pills to a lapse of memory. Alcoholics, potential or actual, suffered frequently from amnesia as he remembered to his own regret.

226

But that was academic now. Even if she hadn't guessed the whole truth, he couldn't leave her behind and alive. There was no telling what she might do.

"A pity," he said, kneeling to repack his gear in the rucksack. "A great pity."

She lit another cigarette. "You're going to kill me, aren't you?"

"No." She was innocent and pitiful, and he was not the sort of man to cold-bloodedly murder such people. There were other ways.

"No, I'm not going to kill you, but as soon as you've finished that cigarette you're to dress in your warmest clothes—what you had on last night should be adequate. After that, you're to take a further three barbiturates."

"Which will probably be enough to kill me anyway."

"Don't be hysterical. A fatal dose is twice as much."

"And if I refuse?"

"That would be most unwise."

She nodded dully and he wondered, in passing, what sort of woman she had been once upon a time.

He waited until it was dark before bundling her into the van. She was unconscious again now; he had stood over her while she took the pills, to make sure she truly swallowed them.

He drove north, passing the slip road leading to the camp at a steady 30 m.p.h. A mile further on he pulled off the main highway and dumped the van up to its axles in mud in a copse, covering it as best he could with fallen branches. Come morning, it would be on someone's missing-vehicles list, but with any luck it would not be found for weeks.

Anna was a lightweight and Christian had no difficulty, in spite of the cumbersome rucksack, in slinging her across his shoulder in a fireman's lift.

The lights from the camp were some distant aid to direction finding, but even so it was another hour before he stumbled noisily upon Schelling and Schultz.

227

"Jesus Christ," swore Schelling, "where the hell have you been and who's that?"

Thirty minutes later they knew the whole story, though Christian could see that Schelling, at least, was far from happy with Anna's presence.

"What happens tomorrow?" he asked. "We won't be able to leave her behind. The second they find out there's been a break, the *Tommis* will be all over these hills. If she's left alive to tell them she was held prisoner by three Germans, they'll know the escape was organized from the outside."

"We'll take her with us, release her on the coast. She'll be quiet."

"And if she isn't?"

"Then we might have to think again."

There was a moment's silence. "I'll do it," offered Schelling, leaving Christian in no doubt what "it" was.

"If anyone's going to do it it'll be me. But I don't think it'll be necessary."

Later, with Anna still unconscious, they fed themselves and settled back to the dull if dangerous business of waiting a further twenty-four hours. Although physically tired after his long day, Christian was still very much mentally alert and he volunteered to stand the first watch.

They had already decided that with so much illumination emanating from the camp it was quite safe to smoke, and Christian lit up. It was desperately cold, too cold to snow, and there was a vicious wind blowing from the northeast. For no reason at all he thought of the survival manual, where he remembered reading that for every knot of wind on wet clothes the body temperature dropped by one degree.

Replacing the cigarettes in his breast pocket, his fingers touched the sealed orders given to him by Weil. Abruptly he decided to disobey the *Standartenfuehrer*'s instructions by opening them immediately. Christ knows what would be happening this time tomorrow night.

The single sheet of paper was couched in official lan-

228

guage and signed by Reichsfuehrer-SS Himmler himself. But in effect it read that if there was any danger of Generalmajor von Stuerzbecher being retaken alive by the British, Oberleutnant Christian Eicke was to shoot him himself.

Fifteen

Throughout the war, with one or two notable exceptions, troops selected for prison camp duties were of a caliber far inferior to those with fighting units. Like Major David Mitchell, many of the officers had suffered wounds rendering them unfit for active service though not totally incapacitated; others were too old; still others, such as Adrian Thorogood, had had their papers temporarily slotted into the wrong pigeonholes.

If it can be said that repetition dulls the senses, the Skiddaw guards were totally blunt, for anyone with half an ear attuned to atmosphere would have sensed, during the twelfth, an air of suppressed excitement among the POWs. Even those who were not in on the break knew that something was imminent. Willi Braune summed it up. "If we have a full complement of prisoners by the end of the week, I'll apply for a commission in the R.A.F."

All over, last-minute preparations were being made. Civilian clothes were checked, money counted, counterfeit papers stashed away, prayers said. The prayers would be needed most of all. Of those due to make the break, only

231

Franz Mohr and one of the naval officers spoke a little English. Apart from von Stuerzbecher, of course.

There was to be no choir practice this day and no work on the tunnel. As far as anyone could estimate they were through now, under the trees on the south side. An hour's digging upward, less than a cubic meter of earth, and gravity would do the rest. They would be out. Not least of those to heave a sigh of relief at the prospect were Leutnants Kaehler and Preiss.

Apart from being unutterably filthy, the two junior officers were not much the worse for wear—in much better condition than anyone could have expected a week ago, although they were completely disorientated. Time had become meaningless. They slept when they were tired and stayed awake when they were not. Bone-chilling cold was a major problem, but that was partly alleviated by the extra blankets Breithaupt had smuggled to them and the increased rations. By far the worst part of their stay underground was the unavoidable smell of their own bodily functions. Johann Preiss, at least, knew he would never forget that.

They passed part of their waking hours in physical exercise, paying particular attention to the legs. There wasn't enough room, or oxygen, for running on the spot, but they each managed five hundred knee-bends a day and one hundred push-ups. When they wearied of that they tried elementary isometrics. It says much for the feeling of friendship they had for each other that at no time did either lose his temper.

During their nonactive hours, which were in the majority, they played guessing games or described in detail a seven-course meal, right down to the last cup of coffee and the positioning of the silver. To begin with, they invented a different meal each day, but Kaehler's descriptions were so spectacularly graphic, so mouth-wateringly accurate, that Preiss decided he didn't want to hear any more.

Sometimes they read, but flashlight batteries were at a

premium and this activity was limited. In any case, their favorite pastime, one that did not require light after the initial stages, was going over their escape route.

On the second day of their incarceration Major Breit-haupt produced a torn-out page of a school-atlas map of northern England. "I'm sorry I can only let you have this overnight, but you'll appreciate it's in great demand."

The scale was too small to be of much practical use on the outside, but they memorized the major roads and towns thoroughly.

It was a convention of escapes from Skiddaw, as it was from most other camps, that routes were never discussed except by those who were traveling together. Neither Kaehler nor Preiss, therefore, knew if anyone else would be going their way. On balance they doubted it. The obvious places to head for were the ports of Workington and Whitehaven. From there, with luck, an escaper could stow away on a coastal vessel sailing for Liverpool; and it was a simple matter, in theory, to find a ship going from Liverpool to neutral Eire. The trouble was, what was apparent to the POWs was equally apparent to the British, and both ports were always closely watched, particularly after a break-out. It was certainly quicker to get to the west coast than to anywhere else in the British Isles, but it was pointless arriving if the coast was crawling with *Tommis*.

"We'll fox the bastards," exclaimed Peter Kaehler. "We'll take the main road to Carlisle and then head for Newcastle."

Preiss traced the route with his forefinger. "There are ports galore on the east coast. If we can't steal some kind of boat we don't deserve to get out."

Neither considered the difficulties, the almost insurmountable obstacles to be overcome before they reached German-occupied territory. Like their counterparts in German camps, if they had sat down to calculate the odds against them they would never have made a move.

"While the *Tommis* are running around in circles on the west coast, we'll be hundreds of kilometers away."

233

"And we'll be home for Christmas."

Oberleutnant Theo Emke felt more or less the same way, but with the advantage of four or five years in age over the two young lieutenants, he was more realistic about his chances. Still, the important thing was getting out, as Major Breithaupt had impressed upon all the Luftwaffe officers. "Look upon it as a bombing mission. You don't expect to hit the target every time and there are always some losses. But you have a nuisance value far out of proportion to your chances of success. While the *Tommis* are looking for you, they can't be doing the thousand and one other things they should be doing."

Theo Emke was traveling alone. Earlier in the month Werner Herburg had made a tentative suggestion that they make the run together, but Emke had brushed him off as politely as he could. It was not that he disliked Herburg, far from it, but he felt his chances would be enhanced going solo. About the only person he would have taken was Hans Baum; but that, of course , was out of the question. It was hard to know if Baum was even aware of what was going on, though as morning became afternoon Emke was aware that Baum's eyes were always on him, like a dog who is being left behind on a summer walk. It became too much for Emke finally, and he went out into the compound, casting an anxious glance skyward as he did so.

He wasn't the only one worried about the weather. It hadn't snowed for the last couple of days, not more than the occasional flurry, and Fritz Uhde knew that the difference between success and failure depended upon whether it snowed heavily their first night out.

For Uhde there was no question of not getting back to Germany. Although he had told no one in the camp, the reason he wrote so often to his young wife was that he was uncertain of her fidelity. At the end of the week in which they first met, she had made it quite clear by word and gesture that she wanted to go to bed with him, and the night that followed gave him more pleasure than he thought humanly possible. There was nothing she wouldn't do, no experiment she wouldn't try. And while he was with her and she was his, he was the happiest man alive.

But he was wise enough to realize that while he was the immediate object of her sexuality, if he were absent for any length of time she would find it difficult to sleep alone. She wasn't a whore, but she had basic needs that had to be satisfied. If he wasn't there to provide an outlet, sooner or later someone else would be. He had to get home, that was all there was to it.

The naval officers under Kapitaenleutnant Heydt were to travel as a pack. They knew there were risks in this—if one was recaptured they all were—but they considered the risks worth taking. For them there would be no nonsense about stowing away on a boat to Eire or anywhere else. There were five of them and they were fully experienced in all matters of the sea. If they couldn't steal a ship, any sort of ship, and sail it to Brazil if necessary, they didn't deserve their badges of rank.

"The trouble with pilots," Heydt was fond of saying, "is that they have no stamina for long missions. Take away their airplanes and breakfast in the Mess and they're lost."

To a man the naval personnel agreed with him. (It's no secret that in the armed forces of any nation the air branch is thoroughly disliked by the army and the navy, who see air crews the way a marathon runner sees sprinters—they take risks, surely, but only for an hour or two each time, and then it's back home for tea and a medal; an hour in the air does not compare with weeks at sea or months knee-deep in mud.)

On his stroll around the compound Theo Emke came across Werner Herburg, who looked up hopefully. But Emke merely smiled and walked on.

Herburg shrugged philosophically to himself. He couldn't blame Emke for wanting to go it alone, but it would have calmed some of the butterflies now racing around his stomach to know that he would have a companion on the break.

Werner Herburg was a realist and knew he had been included in the dozen for Rabbit Run only because of the money found in the chess set. He had put it all into the escape fund because that was his nature; he had certainly not expected Major Breithaupt to reward him with a place on the break. Moreover, if he were honest with himself he knew he should have told Breithaupt at the beginning that he'd far rather the place went to someone else, someone more deserving; for he didn't really want to go, as he had never really wanted to be a flier. That the High Command thought him ideally suited to the job of piloting a bomber didn't alter the fact that he was of the opposite opinion. Every mission—and they had been few enough before the Spitfire got him—had been preceded by bouts of physical sickness. But somehow he had got the aircraft off the tarmac and brought it back, all but once. If the truth were known, however, he was not unhappy in the camp. He didn't even really want to go home. Home meant a domineering mother (who ideally should have taken his place in the Luftwaffe) and the horrific thought of further missions.

Still, he was stuck with it now and, as he had done throughout his life, he would try his best.

For different reasons Franz Mohr, now playing chess in the German Mess with Otto Breithaupt, was also determined to try his best. He couldn't afford to do anything else. Another twenty-eight days in the cooler would finish him.

Major Breithaupt moved a knight and successfully forked Mohr's remaining rook and bishop.

"You'll notice that with my customary chivalry I'm taking advantage of your preoccupation to beat the hell out of you."

Mohr smiled at him. "It'll be the last time."

"Let's hope so."

Mohr opted to save his rook and moved it out of reach. Breithaupt studied the board keenly.

"You're all set, of course. I mean, I'm not keeping you from anything?"

Mohr's outside clothes were already bundled up, papers and money in the trousers pocket. Emergency rations, mostly chocolate, were in a waterproof wrapping. It would take him under five minutes to prepare. "Nothing."

"Good. Don't forget to send me a postcard."

"I just hope it's from Berlin and not the London Cage."

"It will be—from Berlin, I mean. I have a good feeling about this one."

After much deliberation Breithaupt took the bishop.

"It'll be your turn one day, Otto."

"Not me." Breithaupt grinned cheerfully. "I'm indispensable here, haven't you heard? Besides, with you and Heydt both going that means two spare seats on the Escape Committee. If I went too, Hauptmann Weiss would fill them with his cronies and run the camp like a reform school."

"It still seems terribly unfair." Mohr decided that attack was the best form of defense and swooped down on Breithaupt's back rank with his queen. "Unless the *Tommis* are fortunate enough to capture an *Oberst*, you'll remain senior officer until the end of the war."

"The penalties of organizational brilliance, dear boy. In any case, I'm only senior officer technically. Karl outranks me so much that a day's pay of his is equal to a month's of mine."

"Only for another few hours."

"With luck." Breithaupt moved a pawn to give his king an escape hatch. "You know, I still can't get over it—yesterday, I mean. It's just as well I hadn't offered the last place to someone else."

"He could always have tagged on the end."

"And make thirteen? No chance. There'd have been a riot."

"Another would have made fourteen."

Breithaupt shook his head. "We discussed that at the beginning if you remember. In theory there's nothing to

237

prevent the whole wretched camp going out, but those watchtower lights, in spite of the automatic traverse, don't make it easy. Even with the trees as partial cover, if a guard turns round at the wrong moment you're all in the soup."

"It's the first man out who'll have the greatest burden," said Mohr. "He'll be going up blind, unable to see which way the guards are facing."

"There's nothing we can do about that; it's one of the hazards of the business. It'll be you, incidentally, the first man."

"Me?" This was the first Mohr had heard about the escape order.

"I can't send Emke, he's too big, and Heydt insists that the navy go out together. Kaehler and Preiss I'm leaving until last. There won't be much light coming down that hole, but it'll get them used to the outside again. They'll be as blind as bats otherwise. Uhde's too young to trust in the vanguard, and I'm a bit worried about Oberleutnant Herburg. Oh, he'll be all right, I'm not suggesting anything different, but he's rather timid. That leaves you or Karl. I can't send him first becaue I don't know what orders the people on the outside have been given. It may well be that they're to get him to hell out of it above all else, and it'll be necessary for the first man to make sure the coast's clear for the second man, and so forth. Which leaves you. Karl will go second. If they whisk him away immediately it'll be up to you to wait around for the third man. Sorry and all that, but noblesse oblige."

"It's all right. A minute more, a minute less, it makes no difference. Unless we get a whole night's start they'll catch up with us anyway. You're in check, incidentally."

Breithaupt moved a bishop between Mohr's queen and his own king. "I'm calling a final briefing immediately after this afternoon's roll call," he said, "but there's no harm in telling you now that you'll all move across to the chapel in escape order, which means you first, beginning at twenty hundred hours. Five-minute intervals between

238

each man. Even allowing for delays, you should all be inside the tunnel by twenty-one hundred."

"The door will be open, of course?"

"I've arranged that. I was going to do it myself, but I want to be last across. I'm using Braune and Geith. As they seem to spend most of the dark hours flitting between their huts and the boiler room, they might as well make themselves useful. They think we're having some sort of meeting there."

"He's a good man, Willi Braune."

"They both are. I was most impressed with the way they handled that bread business yesterday."

Mohr moved his rook horizontally. It was now in the column adjacent to his queen with a free run down the board.

"You said you'll be last across. Does that mean Hauptmann Weiss won't be coming to wave goodbye?"

"Correct. He says his one eye isn't really good enough for moving around unseen in the dark, but frankly I suspect a trace of envy. It's all very well him saying he doesn't want to go home because of his injuries, but it must be hard, watching others take advantage of your own planning."

"It's the same for you."

"No, it isn't." Breithaupt eased forward a pawn to threaten Mohr's rook. "We stay for different reasons. I admit that when I slide the altar back into place I'll feel a twinge of something, but it won't be envy. Uncertainty probably. Perhaps even a touch of despair. I won't know anything, won't even know whether you're alive or dead or on the high seas until I get a postcard or a message or they frog-march you back through the gates. That will be the hardest part, not knowing."

"You'll also have to arrange for a new chess partner," said Mohr slyly, his finger on the rook.

"True enough."

"Though perhaps you'll choose someone nearer your own weight next time. Checkmate."

Franz Mohr pushed forward the rook. Otto Breithaupt stared at the board in disbelief before bursting into gales of laughter.

Christian gave the order to strike camp and pack up a few minutes before 8 P.M. Although it was still two hours to break-out time, they had to get down the mountain and skirt the camp far to the south before coming in through the trees opposite the tunnel exit. Now all that remained was the vexatious question of Anna Newfield.

"We can't leave her, Christian," said Schelling urgently, "and neither can we take her with us." Normally a kind and generous man outside battle, Schelling was also the archetypal realist. "If we leave her she'll either die of exposure or be found by the *Tommis*. If we take her she'll slow us down."

"She goes where we go," said Christian firmly. "We'll release her on the coast."

"You're a fool, Christian."

Christian remembered the *Vernichtungslager*, the extermination camp, and his argument with Standartenfuehrer Weil. Either he had meant what he said then or they were the self-righteous excuses of a drunk.

"I'll thank you to remember who you're talking to, Feldwebel," he said coldly.

Schelling stiffened to attention. "As you wish, Herr Oberleutnant."

Christian shook his head sorrowfully and walked across to where Anna, her hands lightly bound, was propped up against a tree. She was fully recovered from the effects of the barbiturates now, and she looked at Christian with hatred. She understood no German, but she sensed that the two men had been arguing about her.

"In a minute or two we'll be leaving here and taking up a position opposite the camp," Christian told her. "You'll be coming with us. At ten o'clock some German POWs will be making an escape bid and from you I want to hear not a sound. We'll be very close to the wire, but if you make

240

the slightest attempt to attract attention, by word or gesture, you'll be killed. Is that perfectly clear?"

"Go to hell," said Anna.

Part of her could not have cared less if they shot her right away. She had been used by this man, a filthy German. What was worse, she had enjoyed it. She was his prisoner until he decided what to do with her. She was freezing, hungry and had no privacy; she was kept under guard even while performing her natural bodily functions.

Christian gripped her shoulder so hard that she had to bite her lip in order not to cry out.

"Listen to me, you bloody little fool," he said. "Do as you're told and you'll be released some time tomorrow, possibly the next day. You will be unharmed. I might add that the decision to keep you alive is mine. At least one of the others and probably both would have you killed here and now, so don't upset them. More important, don't do anything to upset me. I may have lost their trust by allowing you to live, but I won't hesitate to win it back if you so much as breathe out of turn."

"How do I know that you'll really let me go tomorrow?"

"Because I could have killed you back at the cottage if I really wanted you dead."

"Ready to move," called Schultz.

"Okay," said Christian, "let's go."

At approximately the same time as Christian and his team began making their way down the mountain, Willi Braune broke into the chapel while Hans Geith kept watch for patrolling guards. It was an ordinary padlock and presented no difficulties, though Willi was careful to rearrange the broken mechanism in such a way that a perfunctory examination would reveal no trace of damage.

This done, they hid in the shadows until the searchlight beams swung past them before heading back to their hut. There was no card game this night; Lance Corporal Cade was on duty. But there was one scheduled for tomorrow, and they were both looking forward to it.

At 2000 hours Oberleutnant Franz Mohr took a last look around Hut 9 and slipped out into the compound. Over his shoulder, in a sack, he carried the clothes and accessories Peter Kaehler and Johann Preiss would wear for the break.

Situated in the second row of POW accommodations, Hut 9 was two hundred yards from the chapel and almost diametrically opposite it. But this was a help rather than a hindrance as Mohr could glide from row to row, north to south, before making a final dash for the shadows of the German Mess on the southern perimeter wire. From there it was simply a matter of following the wire, behind the Mess and behind the M.T. Pool, until he reached the chapel. The watchtower between the Mess and the M.T. Pool presented no problems, thanks to the automatic traverses the *Tommis* insisted upon using. In theory no section of the compound should be unilluminated for more than ten seconds, but in practice it didn't work out that way. The machinery was old and malfunctioned from time to time; rather like a domestic clock, it went faster or slower as the mood took it. The idiosyncracies of each searchlight were well known to the POWs, though in any case ten seconds was more than enough time to move from building to building.

One . . . two . . . three . . . four . . . Mohr made the shelter of the central watchtower without difficulty. He experienced a moment's panic when he heard voices, but he realized that they were coming from above his head, inside the tower itself, and that he was out of the guards' range of vision.

One . . . two . . . three . . . four . . . The whole length of the M.T. Pool during the seconds of darkness, a quick breather, then on to the chapel.

They had all realized weeks ago that getting from the rear of the chapel to the front and in through the door was going to be the most risky part of the maneuver. In sequence, the chapel door was illuminated by two of the searchlights on the north side of the compound. The one in the northeast corner swung counter-clockwise from north to south and back again. Ten seconds after it began its return trip the central light, whose main function was to illuminate the southern wire, lit up the same door. But because of a faulty cog somewhere in the mechanism, one time in four the central light was only six seconds behind. After that, things got back to normal. But as even ten seconds was barely enough to get to the front of the chapel, open the door, go inside and close the door again, it would obviously be fatal to make the attempt when the interval between the lights was only six.

Mohr hugged the wall and counted. One to ten. Wait. One to ten again. Wait. One . . . two . . . three . . . four . . . five . . . six . . . Wait. Northeast light coming back . . . and vanishing. Go.

Clutching his bundle, Mohr raced for the door. Three . . . four . . . He saw the lock and froze. Five . . . six . . . Christ, hadn't Willi Braune . . . Seven . . . eight . . . He wrenched at the padlock. It came away in his hands. No time to do anything about that now. Nine . . . He threw himself inside and pushed the door shut behind him, leaning against it breathlessly, his heart pounding.

Ten . . .

But no shouts in the distance, nothing to show that the watchtower guards had spotted anything out of the ordinary.

Although the uncovered windows let in some light, he waited a minute to allow his eyes to become accustomed to his surroundings before moving quickly toward the altar and putting his back against it. It moved an inch or two, then a couple of feet. Below, Preiss and Kaehler stiffened at this new and threatening noise.

"Peter? Johann? Are you there? Shine your flashlight, will you? I can't see a damned thing."

The dim beam lit up Mohr's anxious face.

"Franz? Is it really you? Is it time?"

Mohr tossed down the bundle. "It's me and it is. Your clothes are in there. Get into them as quickly as you can. This place is going to start filling up."

One by one at the predetermined interval of five minutes the remaining POWs followed Mohr into the chapel and down into the Rabbit Run.

Next came von Stuerzbecher with Fritz Uhde hot on his heels. Uhde had miscalculated and allowed only a three-minute gap. After Uhde, Werner Herburg arrived, panting like a man with a heart condition. The naval officers came next, with Kapitaenleutnant Heydt bringing up the rear. At a quarter to nine Theo Emke's big feet and broad shoulders appeared.

"Christ, there's a smell down there. Haven't you been washing your socks, young Kaehler?"

"Shut up, Theo, and make yourself useful," said Mohr. "Take something to dig with and start making a hole. The rest of you, you all know the order of escape so let's keep it organized."

Major Breithaupt was last to arrive, at three minutes to nine. Franz Mohr was waiting for him when he dropped through the floorboards beneath the altar.

"Is everyone here?"

"All except Emke. I've sent him up ahead to begin the hole."

"Good."

Breithaupt peered into a darkness only partly relieved by Kaehler's torchbeam. He didn't want to make a speech, but the Rabbit Run, the mere existence of it, was a major achievement and he couldn't let the occasion pass without saying something.

"I can't stay to see you off," he began, "because that altar has to be replaced before someone discovers the chapel door's been forced and decides to investigate. But it goes without saying that I wish all of you all the luck in the world. Have a drink for me when you get home, but *get* home."

There were murmurs of thanks and vows that they would.

"One other thing. Most of you will have guessed by now that Karl is not who he purports to be. I mention this only because he has some people waiting for him on the outside, though as he's number two they'll probably be on their way before the rest of you are out. But if you see them, ignore them, keep your distance. Don't try to join forces. That's it. Good luck."

And then he was gone. A slight touch on Franz Mohr's shoulder, and he was up through the floorboards. The heavy altar was pushed back into place.

"Kaehler, shine the torch that way," said Mohr. "Let's see how Emke's getting on."

Once within the area of the huts, Otto Breithaupt made no show of furtiveness. If anyone asked, he was on his way to the heads. Near Hut 7 he thought he caught a glimpse of Hauptmann Weiss, but he could have been mistaken. In any case, there was no reason why Weiss shouldn't be on the prowl.

Christian's team were in position opposite the chapel at 9:40. Sixty or seventy yards into the copse, they nevertheless had a more or less clear view of the southwest section of the compound.

Nothing moved save the trees. The wind was picking up, blowing roughly north-northeast. There was undoubtedly more snow on the way, but Christian refused to think about it. If it came, it came. He would worry about it when it happened.

He held up five fingers three times. Schelling, over to his right, and Wolf Schultz, standing guard over Anna, signaled their understanding. Fifteen minutes to go.

At 9:48 Theo Emke returned through the tunnel in a state of great excitement. "I'm through. I just got an avalanche of snow on my head."

Mohr took the sharpened mess tin they were using as a shovel. In spite of the fact that he was trembling with anticipation, he issued the final orders coolly and concisely.

"Right, you all know the exit procedure so stick to it. We'll be a bit low on oxygen in there so no more than three people in the tunnel itself at any one time. The man in front will have the torch. Two flashes means he's under the hole. The next man can then come up. A single flash means wait. Good luck, everyone."

On his hands and knees, the torch in his right hand, Mohr crawled the length of the tunnel, only stopping when he could go no further. He looked up and almost wept with exultation. Emke and gravity had done a magnificent job, and for the first time it was possible to stand up in the Rabbit Run. A foot or two above his head was a hole six inches in diameter, ready for widening. Through it and beyond he could see the lights from the camp. They were free.

"Look."

Schelling pointed, Some forty yards away and over to their left, a figure was emerging from the ground.

Christian motioned the others to stay where they were and ran forward at the crouch. "Over here," he whispered.

Franz Mohr crawled toward him. They shook hands, both feeling faintly ridiculous.

"Franz Mohr, Oberleutnant."

"Christian Eicke, same. Where's Stuerzbecher?"

"Right behind me."

It was two minutes before von Stuerzbecher's head appeared. Christian was beside him in a flash. There was no danger; the trees took care of that.

The German major general shook himself like a dog.

"What the hell are you doing here, Christian?"

"Getting senior officers who can't fly airplanes out of trouble. Come on, let's get to hell out of here. There are three others in my party, two NCOs and a prisoner. I'll explain it all when we're a million miles away."

More than a little envious, Mohr watched them disappear into the darkness. It was quite an advantage, having rank. Oberleutnant Eicke would undoubtedly have their escape route well planned.

"Can I come out now?"

Mohr almost laughed out loud in spite of himself. Fritz Uhde sounded like a small child playing hide and seek.

"Yes. Shake it up." He waited until Uhde was beside him. "See you in Germany," he said, and was gone.

One by one the Rabbit Run escapers emerged from their burrow. After Uhde came Herburg, who felt he had been waiting an hour before the first of the naval officers appeared. But he was a quarter of a mile away—determined to put as much distance as he could between himself and the camp before morning—when Kapitaenleutnant Heydt joined his men.

Emke had to widen the hole. Two feet six inches was adequate for the others, but it was at least six inches too narrow for him. It took him valuable minutes, but then he was on his way, heading west.

Blinking, Peter Kaehler came out ahead of Johann Preiss. The filigreeing effect of the trees made the camp lights barely sufficient to read by, but that was for men who hadn't been in almost total darkness for a week.

Once on level ground they each tested their legs, each their balance. The exercises had paid off. Apart from a slight feeling of giddiness they felt ready for anything.

"The hole," whispered Kaehler.

"Oh Christ, I almost forgot."

Breithaupt had asked them to fill it in with snow as best they could. It was unlikely the deception would last long, but it was always possible.

"That should do it."

They took a last look at the camp, sleeping peacefully now.

"Good-damned-bye," said Preiss.

Major Breithaupt lay awake in his bunk, fearfully listening for any sound that would tell him the escape had

247

failed. He heard nothing. An hour passed. Then two. They had made it.

A few minutes after midnight, more due to nerves than anything else, he found it necessary to go to the head. In one of the shower sections he came across Oberleutnant Kapp. The artillery officer had been hanged, and his executioners had made a mess of it.

Breithaupt now realized the significance of Weiss's presence in the compound, and he had to admit that his security officer had been clever about the whole affair. No one would suspect murder, certainly not Thorogood. To all intents and purposes an informer had taken his own life for failing to tell the *Tommis* about an escape before it happened.

Part IV

Part IV

Sixteen

The blizzard hit them with the vengeful suddenness of an assassin's dagger. One minute they could see the dark outline of Bassenthwaite Lake over to their left; the next they were blinded by a million icy flakes, racing before a northeaster.

In the van of the tiny column Christian cursed out loud and glanced over his shoulder. Next in line, von Stuerzbecher was struggling; a month of POW regimen had left him far from fit. Behind him, Anna, her hands unbound now, was also feeling the pace. Bringing up the rear, Schelling and Schultz were going easily, but the entire quintet could travel only as fast as the slowest.

Christian beckoned von Stuerzbecher to join him.

"It's going to be tougher from now on, but we've got to keep going." He shouted to make himself heard. "We have to be within striking distance of the coast by morning, before they start setting up road blocks and covering the countryside with troops."

"How far d'you think we've come?"

Christian knew the answer to that without referring to

251

his map. They were still on the Keswick-Carlisle road. The next objective was Bewaldeth, where they would swing west.

"About a quarter of the way, perhaps a little less. If it wasn't for this cursed snow we'd make it easily."

"Perhaps it'll go off."

But it didn't, and their rate of progress dropped to a snail's pace. Even when they left Bessenthwaite far behind and a bend in the road brought the prevailing wind slightly to their right, they were still averaging less than a couple kilometers an hour.

At 1 A.M. Christian came to the conclusion that he was tiring von Stuerzbecher needlessly. If they kept going and the blizzard blew itself out at dawn, the major general would be too tired to go any further.

He raised his arm and called a halt. "It's no use, we've got to get out of this. If my calculations are correct Bewaldeth's just up ahead."

Schelling remembered it from coming in, a tiny hamlet, a cluster of twenty houses or so, and a solitary general store. Because there had been lights showing in two or three downstairs windows, they had given the place a wide berth by cutting across the fields. "There was a barn or something in one of them."

They left the road and were immediately knee deep in snow.

"Over that way," called Schelling, but they had only covered a few yards before Wolf Schultz yelled at them to stop.

"Listen. . . ."

They listened; nothing but the howl of the wind.

"I could have sworn I heard . . . There it is again."

"Cows," said Christian. "Well done, Wolf. You're not going to find cows out on a night like this."

They struck off at a tangent and found the barn after five minutes' searching. It was open on one side and a dozen or so cows were huddled together miserably against the far wall. Nearby were twenty or thirty sheep, who eyed

252

the newcomers nervously. The stench was appalling, but at least they were protected from the storm.

"Up there."

A ladder led up to an open loft. One by one they trooped up it and flung themselves down on the straw.

Schelling slipped the rucksack from his broad shoulders. "There are still a few cans of that self-heating soup left."

"Warm them up. Keep an eye on her, Wolf."

Christian jerked a thumb at Anna, who was shivering.

"Are you all right?" he called over.

She was far from all right, but she realized the futility of complaint.

"I'm all right."

Von Stuerzbecher beckoned Christian to one side. "I hope we're not taking this break because of me."

There was no point in making him feel any worse. "No, we all need one. But I had hoped to get a lot further tonight."

"The snow will delay the *Tommis* as well."

"I wouldn't bank on it. The blizzard may well have blown itself out by morning, in which case they'll have a clear run. Don't forget they have transport, we haven't; they can travel by day, we can't."

"What do you think they'll do?"

Christian had thought of virtually nothing else for the last two days. Like a criminal who has masterminded a bank robbery, he knew that the easiest part was getting into the bank and out with the money. Far more difficult was getting somewhere where the money could be spent.

"Well, we have a little time on our side, at least for the moment. They're unlikely to discover you've all skipped until morning roll call, and then they'll spend an hour double-checking, because I doubt if they'll believe it themselves at first. After that, if I was in command I wouldn't waste much time scouring the immediate area; I'd take all my troops directly to the west coast. Sooner or later we'll have to go toward them, and they know it."

253

"That stretch of coastline is pretty massive; they can't comb it all."

"Agreed. But they'll almost certainly concentrate part of their force around Maryport, and just below Maryport is where Korvettenkapitaen Stieff is to pick us up." Christian realized he was painting a pretty gloomy picture and it wasn't really as black as all that. "However," he went on, "we have one advantage I didn't know about yesterday; it's not just you they'll be looking for. With eleven others on the run the *Tommis* are going to be spread pretty thin on the ground. It's my guess they'll descend like flies on Workington and Whitehaven, which are the obvious exit routes and quite a few miles from Maryport. There's another advantage too. Because they'll be searching en masse we should see or hear them coming miles away, especially at night."

"If we can move at night."

"We've *got* to move at night." Christian fisted his palm in emphasis. "It would be suicidal to try it by day."

"Literally," said von Stuerzbecher. "I was forgetting. If they recapture me and still fall for my false identity, as an official POW it's just twenty-eight days' solitary confinement. If they take you it means a brick wall."

Christian shrugged. "We'll just have to make sure we're not caught. Regardless of weather conditions, we're moving out of here at 3 A.M. We might not get very far, but we will get farther. I can't risk hanging around. If we're not at the rendezvous by the fourteenth, Stieff has his orders. He'll leave without us."

Christian didn't bother to add that if Reichsfuehrer Himmler's directive was obeyed to the letter, there would be no prison cell for von Stuerzbecher. It wasn't only his own party's necks that made it imperative they get home, though if it didn't work out that way there was no question of shooting his old friend. Himmler could throw a thousand fits, but if they were retaken he and Schelling and Schultz would be somewhere the Reichsfuehrer couldn't reach them.

254

Von Stuerzbecher shook his head at Christian's offer of an English cigarette. "It was a hell of a risk to take, Christian, and I haven't thanked you properly for it yet."

Christian waved him away. "Forget it." He smiled mischievously. "If the truth were known I was virtually blackmailed into it, or at least bribed. Restoration of my former rank and perhaps the oak leaves to go with my Ritterkreuz. If you want to thank anyone it should be Feldwebel Schelling and Obergefreiter Schultz. They were in a cozy billet in Russia before I pulled them out."

"I'll see it's done properly when we get back to Germany."

"Which we will, provided that we keep our heads and do nothing foolish. How's the soup coming along?"

"Almost ready," said Schelling.

Unknown to Christian, four hundred yards south of the barn Leutnant Fritz Uhde was about to do something incredibly foolish.

After Franz Mohr said, "See you in Germany," Uhde waited only to see Werner Herburg's head emerge from the tunnel before setting off in hot pursuit of Christian's party. At that time he had no idea how many it comprised, but judging by Major Breithaupt's warning, and including the mysterious Karl, there had to be at least three of them.

Away from the camp searchlights it was unbelievably dark, but he guessed correctly that the group would begin their escape by heading north along the main road. Ten minutes' hard running and he had the rear man, Wolf Schultz, in sight. His eyes now accustomed to the darkness, he found that by walking along the bank on the opposite side of the road he could make out the silhouettes of the men up front against the snow without getting any nearer than a hundred meters. There was no chance that anyone would see him if they suddenly turned around.

In spite of Breithaupt's caution, Uhde didn't question the morality of his actions. In any case, he didn't intend to join forces with the group, merely follow. And if they had,

255

as they surely did, a ship or a U-boat or even a plane waiting somewhere for them, they could hardly refuse him a ride if he turned up unexpectedly.

It was all very well for Breithaupt to lay down the law like a schoolmaster, but he, Fritz Uhde, had as pressing a need as anyone for getting home. Besides, in officer training they called this sort of thing initiative.

At midnight they were still on the main road, but Uhde deduced that they would swing west when an opportunity presented itself. On reflection it had to be a ship or a U-boat. There was no way anyone could land an aircraft in total darkness in this sort of country.

Fifteen minutes later he felt the first of the snowflakes on his face, and quickly he tried to close the gap. But quick as he was he was too late. The storm was upon him.

As he stumbled into Bewaldeth he knew he had lost them. They had either left the road to seek shelter or changed direction. In either case, short of a miracle he wouldn't find them again.

Despairing, he crouched in the doorway of the general store. Although he was an officer in Goering's Luftwaffe and in consequence regarded as a superman by his family and friends, he knew he was a perfectly ordinary young man with no more courage and tenacity than most. He was not cast in the heroic mold of Emil Naumann, for example, and as the minutes ticked by and he found himself unable to make a decision, he would have given a lot for a companion, someone to talk to and share his predicament. For that matter, he would have given a hell of a lot for a square meal.

With a start he realized he was standing within a few feet of as much food as he would need in a week; probably more than he had seen in a year. Behind a pane of glass was the answer to at least the problem of hunger. It was a general store (the English lessons given in Skiddaw by officers who spoke the language told him that much), but it would undoubtedly stock quantities of food in tins, as well as biscuits, butter and bread.

He stepped out into the street and looked up. If anyone lived over the store he was asleep. And with the wind howling like a hundred Loreleis they wouldn't hear much even if they were awake.

It was against all his instructions, of course. Breaking into a house or shop was a sure giveaway. He could hear Major Breithaupt giving the lecture now. "Whatever you do don't start stealing from shops or private houses. If you're hungry, take something from a field. If you're thirsty, drink water or suck snow. The *Tommis* will only have the roughest of rough ideas which way you're heading. But if a householder or a shopkeeper reports a broken window or a forced door to the police, you might as well leave a map of your route."

But that was all theory. In the comparative warmth of the Mess on a snowy afternoon, it sounded perfectly reasonable. Out here, at God knows what hour in the morning and with a gale blowing, it was a different matter.

Suiting the action to the thought, he withdrew his fist into the sleeve of his jacket and punched the glass in the shop door, just above the lock. The first blow failed so he tried again, full force. This time the pane shattered with what seemed enough noise to wake the whole hamlet, and a jagged edge tore through the sleeve and into his arm. But his nerve ends were partly anesthetized by the cold and he scarcely realized he was bleeding.

Holding his breath until he thought his lungs would burst, he put his hand through the broken glass, slipped the latch, and entered.

A few miles farther north disaster struck Leutnants Kaehler and Preiss shortly after they passed through one of the small villages on the road to Carlisle.

Although last away from Skiddaw they had covered a greater mileage than any of the others by the time the blizzard blew itself out at 4 A.M. Unlike Christian's party, they had no rendezvous to make, no need to conserve energy for another day. Their only concern was to get as far away as possible as quickly as possible, and their enforced stay in the Rabbit Run had done them no harm at all. The exercises had toughened them and their peculiar rest hours had found them still asleep at 6 P.M. the previous day. Even though the packed snow dragged at their feet and for four hours they had been marching straight into the storm, at 4 A.M. they were fifteen miles from the camp and less than that distance from their first objective, Carlisle.

"Bastard." Johann Preiss swore at the wind, which had dropped without warning. The snow thinned. "Now why the hell couldn't it have done that hours ago?"

"It's a *Tommi* plot." Peter Kaehler was feeling good. Morale was high even though they were both soaked to the skin and cold. For most of the last hour they had been singing, in particular *Wovon kann der Landser denn schon traumen* ("What does the soldier really dream of?") inventing obscene choruses that would have shocked the composers, Plucker and Richartz. At that hour in the morning and in those conditions it was unlikely anyone would hear them. "Time we started looking for a burrow anyway."

Neither possessed a wrist watch, but even if they had known that dawn was still four hours off they'd have come to the same conclusion. They didn't want to be caught out in the open, and it was better to be safe than sorry.

The most risky period for any escaper was the first twenty-four hours. The majority were recaptured within that time because the search parties could assess almost to the last quarter mile how far a POW would have traveled from roll call to roll call. The pursuer's main problem was guessing direction, and Kaehler and Preiss felt they had foxed them on that. All they had to do now was keep out of sight during daylight for a few days; after that, human nature being what it was, the hunt would lose its intensity.

"Backward or forward?" queried Preiss.

Kaehler debated it. The village they had just passed through didn't hold out much hope; a few houses, shops, a garage, something that looked like a school. There would doubtless be a farm across one of the fields, but farms were always dangerous.

"Let's press on."

They continued walking, keeping well to the side of the road.

Now that the wind had dropped, the night was uncannily quiet, and they had only covered a couple of hundred yards before Kaehler, who was in the lead, stopped and held up his hand. "Listen."

Preiss did so. Somewhere up front he heard a peculiar clanking noise. He knew he should be able to identify it, but his memory refused to work.

But it was getting louder and therefore closer.

"What the hell is it?"

Kaehler shook his head worriedly. "I don't know, but . . ."

And then it was on top of them, a horse-drawn milk cart, the horse's footbeats deadened by the snow, the empty milk churns rattling in the back. There were no lights on the cart. The driver—they could just make out his muffled shape as they dived through the hedge—evidently trusted the animal to follow a well-worn path.

Preiss felt his ankle go as he jumped. He was off balance as he made the leap, and he experienced a jab of excruciating pain. He bit his lip and clenched his fists to resist crying out.

The sound of the milk cart receded. Kaehler got to his feet and dusted himself off. "Christ, that was close." Preiss didn't move. "Are you all right?"

"My ankle."

"Oh Jesus. Here, let me feel."

It wasn't broken but it was already swelling from a sprain. And judging by his muted grunts of agony, Johann wasn't going any further that night or for several nights thereafter.

259

Preiss swore for fully a minute. "Of all the stupid things to happen. You'll have to go without me, Peter."

"Don't be a damn fool," Kaehler protested. "You'll be all right in a day or two. We'll hole up until you're ready."

"Hole up where?" Preiss tested the ankle and winced.

"Back there in the village. It's less than half a mile. I can carry you that far."

"And then what? Knock at the first house we come to and ask them to put us up for a couple of nights?"

"No, in the school," Kaehler said. The idea had only just occurred to him but it made sense. "It's the middle of December, right? If English schools are like German schools the kids will have broken up for the holidays. No arguments, Johann. We'll manage."

Kaehler hoisted Preiss to his shoulders, ignoring his protests, and retraced their steps to the village. The school was just off the main road, the iron railing which had once surrounded it long since part of a Lancaster.

Preiss stood one-legged against a wall while Kaehler circled the one-story building, looking for a way in. A door at the rear seemed best, and he wasted no time breaking the glass and slipping the bolt. Unlike Fritz Uhde, Kaehler wouldn't have considered taking such action, in spite of Preiss's ankle, if the building had been a shop or a house. But if his guess was correct, no one would come near the school until January.

He chipped out the pane completely. From a distance it would be impossible to see that anything was broken.

Once inside one of the classrooms, Preiss removed his boot. The ankle had swelled considerably.

"You're a fool, Peter," he said from the darkness. "A nice fool but a fool nevertheless. I won't be walking on this for a week."

"Then we'll stay for a week."

"And what will we do for food?"

"We'll survive. Christ, we got out, didn't we? That was the hardest part. Who'd have thought yesterday that tonight we'd be free and sleeping in an English school?

260

Takes me back ten years. I suppose schools everywhere have a smell of their own."

"Don't change the subject. This time tomorrow you could be in Carlisle. Ten days from now you could be home."

"And what would I tell Hannah? 'Yes, of course Johann came out with me, but he injured his foot so I left him.' She'd be very proud of me. I intend to marry your sister, Johann, and I don't see her marrying someone who'd leave her brother to rot."

"I wish to God you would—marry her, I mean."

"It's the first order of business when we get home."

"If we get home."

"Christ, what a pessimist you're becoming in your old age. Of course we'll get home. It might take a little longer now, but we'll make it. Providing we keep out of sight for the next couple of days, the *Tommis* will assume we're out of the area and call off the hounds. After that, we proceed as planned."

"You make it sound like an afternoon stroll through the Black Forest."

"Much less dangerous; no wolves. At least, I don't *think* there are wolves in England."

"You're a good friend, Peter."

Kaehler was embarrassed. "I'm only doing it to impress Hannah. Now shut up and get some sleep. We'll see to your ankle in the morning."

Toward 7 A.M. it became apparent to Christian that they would still be four or five miles short of the coast at daybreak. They had just passed through, or rather round, Bridekirk, and Dovenby, where the man and wife in the car had almost run them down, was a mile or so further on. An empty house wasn't the safest place in the world to shelter for a whole day, but as it was nearing the time when the first of the tradesmen would be starting his rounds, his options were limited.

"Let's step it up," he called over his shoulder.

All in all they hadn't done too badly, in spite of two wasted hours in the barn, and he was confident that the night would see them safely aboard the U-boat. With luck. Any enterprise such as this needed luck and so far they had had it. But so far, of course, the *Tommis* in Skiddaw had been fast asleep. In a little over sixty minutes they would be very wide awake and hopping mad.

Christian was wrong in that assessment by several hours. Long before morning roll call the CSM was given the news that Oberleutnant Kapp was dead, found hanged by the neck in the bathhouse. Purser immediately called the adjutant, who experienced a stab of unease. Any other German found dangling from a rope would have pleased him hugely, but this was Kapp, his own man. If Kapp had committed suicide, assuming it was suicide, something must be seriously wrong.

"See that he's cut down, Sarnt Major, and tell the M.O. I want the fullest report. Never mind, I'll call him my-self. Let's hope to God it's not going to be one of those days."

Apart from Kapp, the ensuing head count, accurate for once, revealed a discrepancy of ten. CSM Purser knew that that was ridiculous, that his NCOs, still sleep-sodden, had miscounted. But when a second check, inaccurate this time, showed Skiddaw to be eleven POWs short, he began to get alarmed.

"Absurd," snapped Thorogood. "Out of the question. Take a proper roll call and teach your NCOs how to count."

Nevertheless, Thorogood knew in his steadily sinking heart that there was nothing wrong with their addition. He didn't believe in coincidences; there had to be a con-nection between Kapp's death and the shortfall.

By 9:25 he knew the truth. CSM Purser had checked and double-checked. There was no mistake. There were ten POWs missing. Including Kaehler and Preiss, he had lost a dozen in a week. It just wasn't possible, but figures couldn't lie.

"What the bloody hell is going on around here?" he screamed. "Am I surrounded by incompetents? Doesn't anybody keep guard, keep watch? Every man on sentry duty last night is on a charge! How the hell can ten bloody Jerries disappear overnight?"

CSM Purser stood his ground. "Perhaps it's some sort of trick, sir—to get us in a flap."

"Trick, Sarnt Major! Are you out of your mind?" Thorogood snatched up the list of missing men. "Look at the names. Heydt and Mohr, two of the seniors officers and up to their necks in any dirty work that goes on around here. That sort don't play tricks. Oberleutnant Stuerzbecher. Good Christ, the bloody man's only been here a couple of weeks. Emke, Herburg, Uhde . . . Are you seriously suggesting that these officers are playing some lunatic game of hide and seek?"

"Perhaps not, sir."

"Perhaps not, sir! I'll tell you bloody certainly not! They're over the bloody hills and far away. Ten of them, Sarnt Major. While you and that idiotic bunch of men you call NCOs were snoring your heads off, ten Germans calmly walk out of this camp as though it were an hotel."

"That's unfair, sir—"

"Unfair, is it . . ."

Thorogood slammed down the list and took a grip of himself. It was a far cry from being unfair, but screaming at Purser would get him nowhere. He was going to need the CSM now, need him as he had never needed anyone before.

"Perhaps you're right." It took a supreme effort, but he managed to calm down and apologize. "I'm sorry I addressed you in that fashion. We're all to blame, every last one of us. They've got away, but they won't get far. You're to turn this whole camp upside down. I want last week's hunt for Kaehler and Preiss to be nothing by comparison. Every available man. I don't care if they're off duty or about to go on leave. I want to know how those people got out and I want to know it fast."

The CSM snapped to attention. "Yessir." He hesitated. "Have you . . . er . . . told Major Mitchell yet, sir?"

Thorogood shuddered at the prospect. "No. That's next on the agenda, after I've phoned the police and the Home Guard."

Major Mitchell didn't believe it either. He had already received a brief report from the M.O. on the death of Oberleutnant Kapp, but that matter paled into insignificance compared to this. When it finally sank in, however, he hit the roof.

"Ten of them, Adrian?" He was having trouble with his vocal cords. *"Ten of them?* Are you sure?"

"As sure as we can be."

"But how? When?"

"I've got the CSM on that now, sir."

"The CSM?" Mitchell's face went purple with anger. "Camp security and discipline is *your* job, Captain Thorogood, not Sarnt Major Purser's."

"With due respect, sir—"

"With due respect nothing! I've let you have more or less your own way since you got here—special roll calls included. And what have you achieved? Precisely nothing! You treat the prisoners like dirt, the good ones and the bad ones alike, and they respond the way men of character should: they try to get home.

"Let me itemize the last few weeks for you. Oberleutnant Naumann shot in very sinister circumstances; Leutnants Kaehler and Preiss escaped. Your own informer Kapp found hanged in the showers. And now ten more Germans missing. So much for your methods! Have you any idea what this is going to look like when written down formally?"

"Every idea, sir, but if I might say so this is no time to be discussing it." Considering Mitchell's mood, Thorogood knew he was taking a terrible risk of being accused of insubordination. "I'm more than willing to assume full responsibility for what has occurred at the inquiry. But right here and now we have to find the escape hatch—in case some other bright bastard thinks of using it—and then get after them."

"If you mean what I think you mean there'll be none of that. The escapers are now the responsibility of the civilian police, the Home Guard, the Military Police, and any other units in the area who can be spared. Our job is keeping the prisoners inside Skiddaw, a task at which we are becoming inefficient to the point of derision."

Thorogood stared at the C.O. with disbelief. "You can't be serious, sir. They've escaped from our jurisdiction. It's up to us to get them back."

"Wrong, Adrian. The areas of responsibility are clearly defined."

But not for Adrian Thorogood. This was a personal matter now, nothing to do with the war. Heydt and the rest had stuck out their tongues and he was determined to see them lopped off.

"I don't think you've considered the implications, sir. Losing ten men, twelve if we include Kaehler and Preiss, is bad enough, but if we allow the civilian police or the Home Guard to bring them back we'll be a laughing stock."

"What the devil d'you think we are now?"

"Sir—" Thorogood was becoming desperate—"You and I both know that we've foiled any number of escapes. This was just bad luck. But it won't read like that on paper."

"Nevertheless, I can't have half the garrison chasing their tails throughout Cumberland."

"I wasn't thinking of half the garrison. Let me take CSM Purser and half a dozen men in a one-tonner. I won't ask for more than that."

Mitchell considered it. Now that he had thoroughly reproved the adjutant, he was feeling better; better but somewhat ashamed at the uncontrolled outburst. Thorogood's suggestion could do no harm, but he doubted it would do much good either.

"You won't get very far with a handful of men and a

265

one-tonner. Ten prisoners are on the loose and they've probably gone in ten different directions. It'll be like looking for a needle in a haystack."

Thorogood sensed the C.O. weakening. "Not entirely, sir. There was a hell of a storm last night. That will have slowed them up. In any case, they'll be heading for the coast—Workington, Whitehaven, Maryport. They always do. And to get there they've got to pass through or near Cockermouth. If I leave within the hour I stand a chance."

Mitchell sucked at the stem of his pipe.

"Very well; the CSM and half a dozen men. But before you go I think we'd better have Major Breithaupt in."

Thorogood heaved a sigh of relief.

Otto Breithaupt found it difficult not to look smug; the ill-tempered interview with Major Mitchell was the first solid confirmation he had received that the twelve had actually made it. Missing names at roll call were one thing; a dressing-down from the commandant was quite another. There would be jubilation in the German lines this day.

There was only one note of disappointment. Toward the end of the session CSM Purser came in to announce that the tunnel had been found. A sharp-eyed sentry on patrol outside the wire had spotted the exit hole. The snow Kaehler and Preiss had packed in to disguise it had simply fallen down into the tunnel proper.

Adrian Thorogood went across to see for himself. He cursed vilely when he realized that the excavations obviously began somewhere under the chapel. Those damned choir practices!

"All right, Sarnt Major—house of God or no house of God, strip the blasted thing."

It took less than five minutes to find the entrance. Moving around in the dark the previous evening, the POWs had left muddy footprints near the altar. When it was moved and the broken floorboards revealed, Thorogood had no doubt that down there was where Kaehler and Preiss had been concealed for a week. He would have somebody's head for overlooking such an obvious hideout, but not now.

"Organize a one-tonner, will you, Sarnt Major, and round up half a dozen men, a Bren team among them. I want to get going as soon as possible."

Lance Corporal Cade saw the CSM coming and suspected something unpleasant in the offing. He disappeared at top speed. Harpo Cook wasn't so lucky and found himself included in the CSM's half dozen.

Minutes before Thorogood was due to leave, Major Mitchell received a call from the police.

"They say a general store in a little place called Bewaldeth was broken into overnight. The only thing missing is food. Sounds like one of ours."

Thorogood checked his map. Bewaldeth was too far north for that POW to be making for Workington or Whitehaven. Most likely his destination was Maryport. Bewaldeth, Blindcrake, Bridekirk, Dovenby, Maryport. That was the probable route.

Seventeen

Taking a leaf out of Franz von Werra's book, Oberleutnant Mohr had left Skiddaw dressed as a Dutch airman. Dutch papers were among the easiest to forge, and those in his breast pocket proclaimed him to be Captain van Nuy of the Royal Netherlands Air Force. He fervently hoped he would not be asked to produce them. They were adequate, but they wouldn't stand up to much scrutiny. Neither would his command of the English language. He had enough, heavily accented, to ask for directions or the time of day, but far too little to engage in a long conversation. Which was one of the reasons he had chosen to travel as a foreign officer rather than a British civilian.

Mohr's uniform was the Skiddaw version of what a Dutch captain wore: a pair of navy-blue trousers and a castoff naval jacket, tailored to fit at the waist. To each sleeve were sewn three strips of white tape. On his head he wore a German naval officer's white peaked summer cap. Woven with painstaking care in red and white cotton, the emblem on this was a cross between a shield and a rectangle. The whole ensemble bore no resemblance to a

Dutch officer's dress uniform, but Mohr knew there were so many different uniforms in England nowadays that one more would attract little attention. At least he hoped not.

A final touch was the addition of a small cardboard suitcase. There was nothing inside it save shaving gear and a change of underwear and socks, but he felt it added legitimacy to his appearance.

As a veteran of several escape bids Mohr was determined not to make the mistakes of his last break. Then, like so many others in his position, he had headed for the west coast and hoped for the best. This time he had a plan, one which seemed to be going well as he approached the outskirts of Penrith soon after 10 A.M.

Unlike Christian Eicke's party, once away from the camp Mohr had swung south, along the main road to Keswick. On the other side of Keswick he found the Penrith road without difficulty and got as far as the hamlet of Scales before the blizzard broke. Not wishing to look as if he had slept rough all night, a sure giveaway for a supposed officer, he took shelter until the storm subsided.

Six A.M. found him just west of Penruddock, where he rested up and shaved in a creek before tackling the last five miles to Penrith.

As he neared the town he was feeling well pleased with himself. Half a dozen vehicles had passed him, going in the opposite direction, but evidently no one thought it strange to see a uniformed officer trudging along the main road, suitcase in hand. Going for a train, probably. Which was precisely Mohr's intention.

In the months since the Rabbit Run became a viable proposition, Mohr had given a lot of thought to his route. Remaining anywhere in the Lake District for too long was obviously suicidal; it invited recapture. So too, in his opinion, was traveling south down the west coast. The only thing to do was to get to hell out of the area as quickly as possible, and that meant some form of transport. Stealing a vehicle was too risky; that left trains. Trains were speedy, fairly regular when the Luftwaffe wasn't creating havoc on the lines, and anonymous. The nearest mainline station, as far as he could judge from Breithaupt's map, was Penrith; and from Penrith to London was a mere three hundred miles. In London he would be safe until he could reach one of the Channel ports, from where Occupied France beckoned.

He had money, more than enough for a ticket, but he did not intend buying one at the station. That might involve producing an authority to travel, which he didn't have. None of the Skiddaw forgers had ever seen one. Instead, when tickets were inspected on the train, he would pay then, pleading in broken English that he had been in too much of a hurry to purchase one earlier. If that didn't work . . . But he refused to consider that eventuality. Whatever happened, he was not going to be retaken, with twenty-eight days in solitary the automatic punishment.

Theo Emke felt much the same way. This was his second time on the run and he had no intention of there being a third.

Twenty miles southwest of Penrith in the village of Grasmere, he was leaning against a wall opposite the church, watching a young man fiddle with his motorcycle. Like Mohr, Emke had come to the conclusion that transport was essential. Unlike Mohr, he was not opposed to stealing a vehicle. He had little choice. His English was virtually nonexistent. For him there could be no question of taking a train or any other form of public transport. He would only have to open his mouth for the police to descend like dogs on a bitch. If he were to make it down the west coast to Liverpool or North Wales, he had to be mobile.

Because of his bulk Emke was an imposing figure, even after a night in the open. He had shaved and washed, and the dyed greatcoat, now a sodden wreck in the bag at his feet, had absorbed the worst of the storm. The good people of Grasmere were accustomed to seeing burly men, up from the filth of the cities for a week's hiking or climbing, and they paid him scant attention.

He drew in several deep breaths. Christ, but it was beautiful country. Under different circumstances he could have spent many happy hours here, just wandering aimlessly from fell to fell, lake to lake. The trek down from Keswick hadn't tired him in the least. With the blizzard at his back and his head tucked deep inside the greatcoat collar, he had felt about sixteen.

The young man opposite was having trouble with the fuel feed. Emke watched him carefully. There was little profit in stealing a motorcycle that would break down on him a mile farther on.

People passed him, going about their business. One or two smiled; he smiled back. He had an easy manner, he knew that, and people generally liked him for it. He wondered if they would feel the same if they knew he had dropped hundreds of tons of bombs on their towns.

He sighed to himself. He was no philosopher, but people were pretty much the same wherever you found them, whatever their nationality. Some good, some bad. Whatever Goebbels and his idiotic *Voelkischer Beobachter* might say, there wasn't much difference between the average German and the average Briton. It was a great pity it took a war to find that out.

A little later two teen-age girls threw him a glance of more than casual interest. He did what all young men do in the circumstances; he tipped them a big wink. They giggled at one another and hurried on.

The youngster was still fumbling inexpertly with the fuel tap and Emke wished to God he would hurry up. Sooner or later the BBC would be carrying news of the escaped POWs, and from then on any stranger would be suspect.

Another five minutes elapsed before the problem was licked. The youngster climbed aboard and kicked the starter. The engine fired first time. Emke strolled over.

Two bright-blue innocent eyes looked up inquiringly.

272

Emke smiled and pointed at the front wheel. The youngster's head went down and Emke chopped him across the back of the neck—enough to stun, no more.

One or two passers-by shouted in protest, but by this time Emke had opened the throttle and was heading out of the village. In passing, he wondered how the others were getting on.

Werner Herburg was doing very nicely. Although neither of them knew it, and in fact would never know it, he had passed within a hundred yards of Theo Emke not half an hour earlier.

After getting no farther than a mile outside Keswick when the blizzard struck, he had sheltered as best he could for the rest of the night. Dawn found him cold, wet and hungry, and he was half prepared to walk straight into the nearest police station and give himself up. But that same spark of character that had got his bomber into the air and over the target when logic told him to report sick would have none of it. So he continued walking, without a concrete plan, without much idea where he was going or what he would do when he got there.

To pass the time he thought of new and original ways to curse his mother and the one hundred and fifty pounds in British notes she had smuggled in. Christ, she'd be delighted when she heard her efforts had paid off, that he had made a break for it (though he wasn't quite sure of the procedure for that).

Dear old Mutti.

He was jolted from his reverie by the sound of an engine behind him. Oh Christ, he thought, here we go.

But it was a lorry, not a military vehicle or police car. Its open back was piled high with secondhand furniture, and the driver pulled up beside him.

"You want a lift, mate? I'm going to Preston."

Herburg had no idea what the words meant, but it seemed pretty obvious that he was being offered a ride. Which was out of the question.

And then the luck that had smiled upon him as a pilot smiled again. The lorry driver pointed over his shoulder and then down into the cab. Wedged between the passenger seat and the floorboards were half a dozen panes of glass. The meaning was obvious; there was no way a hitch-hiker could squeeze in there.

"You'll have to climb up back." Herburg would not have understood the thick Lancashire accent even if he spoke English. "It'll be draughty, but it's better than walking."

Herburg gave the thumbs-up sign and scrambled over the tailboard. Within seconds he was ensconced in an armchair. The fact that it was minus half its stuffing was of no consequence.

At 9:30 they were passing through Grasmere, where Theo Emke had just spotted the motorcyclist. But Werner Herburg was blissfully unaware of this. He neither knew where he was going, nor did he care. His head thrust up toward the clouds, he fell fast asleep.

Kapitaenleutnant Heydt and his naval officers were the first casualties of the escape, a couple of miles east of High Lorton in the Vale of Lorton. Had it not been for an adulterous wife returning home early after a drunken row with her lover they might have made it to the coast, and who knows after that? On such tenuous happenings do fates hang.

The affair that Molly Hankin, married woman of Braithwaite, was having with Jack Angus, bachelor of High Lorton, was a year old. She was not a bad woman, she frequently reassured herself, simply a young one with normal physical desires that needed satisfying. And with her husband serving overseas, Jack Angus was the man to satisfy them. Sometimes. Other times he drank too much, and then they quarreled as they had done earlier. Still, quarrels between them were nothing new, and it had come as quite a shock to be picked up bodily and tossed out of the house.

There was no chance of a lift at that hour, 6 A.M., and it

274

was a long haul from High Lorton to Braithwaite, up one side of the Whinlatter Pass and down the other. The overnight blizzard had made the going difficult, too, but she would see herself damned before she asked Jack Angus to run her home. They were finished, however contrite he might feel when he had slept it off.

At the top of the Pass she paused for breath and was astonished to hear, in the incredible silence of early morning, the sound of voices coming the other way. Quickly she ducked out of sight, and she remained out of sight when five figures, trudging one behind the other, loomed up out of the mist. The words they spoke were unfamiliar, foreign, but she thought no more about it until later.

She did not arrive home until 7:30, much in need of a long hot soak in the bath. In consequence it was not until nearly 10 A.M., with a cup of tea and a slice of toast in front of her, that she switched on the wireless for the morning music program. Ten minutes later the announcer interrupted with a news flash. Some German prisoners of war—he didn't give the number—had escaped from Skiddaw Camp overnight and were believed to be still in the area. All civilians were warned to be on the lookout and to report anything suspicious to the police.

But by the time he got that far, with nary a thought that the police might wonder what she had been doing out so early in the morning, Molly Hankin was through the door, heading for the nearest phone box.

The emergency call was recorded in the log of Cockermouth police station at 10:14, precisely thirty-two minutes after a previous entry advising of the breakout from Skiddaw.

As far as the officer in charge was concerned there was only one place the five alleged Germans could be, now that it was daylight, and that was Thornthwaite Forest. They wouldn't risk using the roads again until it was dark.

The forest was a good-sized place, of course, but if he used dogs and deployed half his force to beat down from the north and east while he and the remainder moved in

275

from the south and west, the Germans should be in hand-cuffs by lunch.

And so it proved to be.

Months of living on an inadequate diet topped by a sleepless and freezing night in the open had sapped the strength of Heydt and his men. But, more than that, their morale took a hammering when they heard the dogs. It seemed unjust that luck had deserted them so soon.

But there was no way out of the trap. In order to escape the *Tommis* in the south they had to retreat farther and deeper into the forest, which drove them straight into the arms of the force descending from the north.

Long before midday they were completely surrounded, and only Heydt, older and tougher than the others, decided to go down fighting, dogs or no dogs. He got in a couple of punches, but he was no match for a brace of fit young policemen. And finally a short-handled truncheon put an end to the matter.

In the manner of these things news quickly filtered through to the POWs that Heydt and his fellow officers had been retaken. Few were surprised, but the naval *Obersteuermann* who attempted to make book that the others wouldn't last the day was severely beaten up.

Major Breithaupt was informed officially by the commandant ten minutes after he had been informed unofficially by Hans Geith. He accepted the news with good grace and silence. Seven out of twelve were still free; it wasn't over yet.

In the endless game that was played between the POWs and their captors, the position at the moment was generally considered to be a tie. Only the next twenty-four hours would decide the over-all winner.

Corporal Napley was particularly pleased that five of the bastards were back in the can. Escapes were a bloody nuisance. They meant more work, a tightening of discipline, more aggravation for everyone. And James Napley had had as much aggravation as he could handle. His bigamous Carlisle wife was now demanding that he take her to London on his next leave "or she would think he had something to hide." Damned right he had something to hide.

In a foul and filthy mood, exacerbated by the fact that it was too cold to be NCO in charge of the compound guard, he went looking for trouble. He knew exactly where to find it. Getting Lance Corporal Cade stripped of his chevron and a couple of Jerries tossed in the cooler would make him feel a lot better.

Drinking tea in the boiler room with Harry Cade, Willi Braune and Hans Geith were in high spirits. By some freak in the postal system they had both received earlier that morning a letter from Lottie Kreipe, the blond barmaid from Berlin. The information in each letter was identical: Lotti was getting married.

"Good riddance," said Hans Geith in German, raising his mug of tea.

Willi clinked cups in a toast. "You can say that again. Christ, I pity her husband. The minute he turns his back she'll be in bed with someone else."

Hans didn't like the sound of that. "Did you ever get her into bed?"

"No." Willi opted to tell the truth. It was all over now, anyway. "I didn't even get my hand inside her dress. You?"

"A kiss and a cuddle, that's all. She kept promising but never delivered."

"Bitch."

"Prick-teaser."

"Can we play some cards now," asked Harry Cade, "or do you two want to carry on this private conversation?"

Willi winked at Hans. "He'll never learn, will he? Deal," he said in English.

The game was five-card draw poker and Cade got no further than dealing a single card to each of them before the boiler-room door shuddered under the impact of a kick.

"Open up, you bastards. Open up before I break it down."

The two Germans got to their feet in a hurry at the sound of Napley's voice, but Cade motioned them to stay where they were.

"Take it easy. If Napley wants to start something I'll beat the shit out of him."

He removed the iron bar which served as a lock.

Corporal Napley stood in the doorway, grinning with malicious delight. To judge by the way he was holding his rifle, he meant business.

"Well, well, what a cozy little scene. Caught in the act, Cade, fraternizing with the Jerries. You won't be seeing daylight for a few months. Let's go."

Cade stood his ground. "Don't be so bloody wet. We're not doing any harm."

"The C.O. can be the judge of that."

"You mean you're arresting us?" Cade couldn't believe his ears.

"Damn right. Now let's move it. You know where the guardroom is."

"Bollocks." Cade sat down on a box. "I'm not moving an inch, Napley, and you'd do well to remember that the Jerries might have something to say to the C.O. if you're stupid enough to go on with this. It's no secret to them who let Naumann through the gate. You're digging your own grave."

Napley hesitated, but he had gone too far to back out. Besides, it was only their word against his on the Naumann business. "We'll see about that. Now get moving, I won't tell you again."

He slipped off the safety catch and jabbed at Cade with his rifle.

"You mad jerk!" shouted Cade. His face white with anger, he leaped at Napley.

Braune and Geith looked on with fascinated horror as

278

the two NCOs struggled to gain possession of the rifle. Napley had much the better grip on the weapon but Harry Cade was stronger, and it seemed, by twisting the rifle through a vertical plane, that he must quickly disarm the corporal. Which made the shot, when it happened, all the more surprising.

Within the narrow confines of the boiler room the sound was deafening. But it had been heard on the outside too, and soon guards and POWs alike were running in the direction of the noise.

Clutching his chest, his useless fingers covered with blood, Corporal Napley staggered and fell on a mound of coke. "You . . . silly . . . bloody . . ."

Which was all he said. Along with his marital troubles, James Napley's life was over. And although they didn't know it yet, so were the lives of Willi Braune and Hans Geith.

Eighteen

Police forces and army units as far north as Gretna Green and as far south as Lancaster, west to the coast and east to the Pennines, had been alerted to be on the look-out for the fugitives, and at various major junctions roadblocks were in the process of being set up. But Theo Emke was blissfully unaware of these facts as he dropped down a gear to cross Troutbeck Bridge. To his right lay Lake Windermere, and the town of Windermere was just ahead. He would have avoided both like a plague had it been possible, but unfortunately they straddled his route south.

It could have been imagination, but as he passed through the town itself he thought he saw one or two people staring at him with more than normal interest. That was the trouble with being so big. He looked like a circus bear on a child's scooter. On the other hand, in the time it had taken him to get from Grasmere, no doubt the theft of the motorcycle and a description of the thief had been circulated by the police. It wouldn't take them long to deduce that he was a POW on the run and in which direction he was heading. At Ambleside he had had a choice of two routes and only two.

Still, all he could do was keep going until the fuel ran out and hope to get as far as he could. He had money for petrol but no stamps or coupons or whatever the British called them. On the plus side, however, these little machines were very economical. On the minus side they weren't very fast.

Once through Windermere he opened the throttle. The engine spluttered but didn't die. Emke muttered a prayer that the rightful owner had managed to correct the feed problem.

If the information he had gleaned from the school map back in Skiddaw was accurate, in English terms of measurement it was around a hundred miles from the camp to Liverpool; call it eighty from Grasmere. Two hours, given luck and fuel. After that, Ireland and home. And Frau Baum first on his visiting list.

He had made up his mind about that. In spite of earlier misgivings, he had made a tacit promise to himself overnight that he would see Baum's mother, if he got back to Germany. It wouldn't be so difficult, telling her about her son. She would want to know anyway, and she had that right. One day the war would be over and Hans would be going home too. It would be a terrible shock for his mother if she hadn't been prepared in advance. Perhaps she could make arrangements to book him into a clinic or put pressure on the Red Cross to have him repatriated. It was better than doing nothing.

No one had challenged Franz Mohr walking onto the platform of Penrith Station without a ticket, and nobody challenged him now. But he nevertheless felt conspicuous and as naked as a newborn babe as he waited for the London train. Which was late, of course. He had learned that as much by studying the faces of his fellow travelers as by listening to their conversations, only one word in three of which did he understand. Due in at 10:40, the train already was thirty-five minutes late.

It was the first time he had seen so many Englishmen (and a sprinkling of English women) close up, and in spite of the precariousness of his position he found himself staring. Most of the would-be passengers were soldiers, sailors and airmen, and the majority of these were NCOs and other ranks. The handful of officers were gathered, as if by predetermined arrangement, at the far end of the platform. No doubt, as in Germany, some sort of rank segregation system operated on the railways, but Mohr couldn't risk getting too close to men who held commissions. He wouldn't stand a chance of fooling them with his ersatz uniform.

They were a healthy-looking lot, the *Tommis*, he thought, pretending to be interested in a timetable. Their physical condition was obviously first rate; no shortage of food here. It was a point worth remembering, as the High Command would undoubtedly quiz him on such matters when he got home. Their morale, too, was unquestionably high. Sitting on kitbags reading newspapers and magazines or playing a quick hand of cards, not a man among them looked as if he considered the war lost. Well, maybe they were right. Only time would tell.

"Did you hear about those Jerry prisoners getting away from Skiddaw?"

Mohr stiffened at the word "prisoners." The speaker was a hard-looking sergeant wearing the flashes of a Scottish regiment.

"Heard it on the wireless just before I came out. They just strolled through the gates or something."

"How many?"

"Didn't say. But one of the blokes in the billet said it was fifty."

"Don't be bloody daft. If there were fifty of them on the loose they'd have hauled us in."

"That's what I heard."

"Where the hell's Skiddaw, anyway?"

"Carlisle way, I think."

"Probably why the train's late. Bloody Jerries have hijacked it."

283

The Scottish sergeant roared with laughter at his own wit. As he did so he looked straight at Mohr. His eyes narrowed, puzzled, as they took in the strange uniform. At a complete loss, but knowing it would be fatal to turn away, Mohr smiled broadly, as though he too were enjoying the joke.

The sergeant nodded curtly in acknowledgment but did not smile back. Mohr moved a few yards farther down the platform.

Christ, this was worse than waiting to go on a mission, a thousand times worse than sitting in the Rabbit Run. Where the hell was the bloody train?

"Excuse me?" Mohr turned with as much aplomb as he could muster. The Scottish sergeant was holding an unlit cigarette. From their kitbags his friends watched him curiously. "Have you got a light . . . sir?"

The "sir" was definitely an afterthought, but the question was well within the compass of Mohr's knowledge of English.

"I do not smoke." He had matches in his pocket but they were the Skiddaw variety, each match split into three for reasons of economy. He could hardly produce those.

"Oh, foreign, are you?"

"Captain van Nuy, Royal Netherlands Air Force." Mohr thanked God he'd got out of the habit of automatically clicking his heels.

The sergeant toyed with the unlit cigarette, his eyes never leaving Mohr's face. But eventually he seemed satisfied.

"Thought that was it. I was telling my mates that the uniform was either Dutch or Polish. But you should be at the other end of the platform, sir. They usually put on a special coach for officers."

Mohr missed most of this, but he caught "special coach" and "officers." Taking a deep breath he summoned up his reserves of English.

"In Netherlands officers and men travel together. What is good enough for men is good enough for officers."

284

"Bloody good," said the sergeant. "I mean, that's the way it should be, sir. But if you're going all the way to London with that accent, I'd advise you to keep your papers handy. Some Jerries have escaped from a POW camp."

"They have been captured, sergeant. I hear someone say they have been taken."

"Oh well, that's all right then. See you on the train maybe."

Mohr's legs were quivering like harp strings by the time the sergeant rejoined his friends.

Arriving in the one-tonner just as a uniformed police sergeant was in the act of leaving the general store, Captain Thorogood wasted no time in making his authority felt. Strictly speaking, this was now a matter for the civilian police, but Thorogood was having none of that and fortunately the sergeant was the cooperative type. If the army was willing to do his job, that was all right with him. The police were shorthanded as it was.

"He won't have got far, sir. From what I can make out he must have lost quite a lot of blood."

"Blood?" This was the first Thorogood had heard that one of them was wounded.

"Blood, sir."

He showed Thorogood the broken pane in the door and the trail of blood leading to the shelves. A flour sack had been torn apart, the sacking evidently to be used as bandages. An elderly man whom Thorogood took to be the owner was making notes in a cash book and muttering something about "bloody soldiers who couldn't do the job they were paid for."

"Of course, it doesn't necessarily have to be one of your chaps," said the sergeant. "It could be an ordinary burglary."

"What was missing?"

The sergeant consulted his notebook. "Cigarettes, biscuits, butter, cooked meats, a few tins."

"Then it's a Jerry, sergeant. What else have you got?"

"There were one or two drops of blood leading away from the shop, which means he certainly didn't leave until the small hours, probably later." The sergeant preened himself, pleased with his detective work. "The storm didn't blow out until 4 A.M. and we had another local shower around 6:30. Even if he left straight after that, he'd look for somewhere to hide out before it got light. It's my guess he's not more than two or three miles away."

"Direction?"

"I'd say toward the coast, sir. That's the way the buggers always go."

Thorogood wasn't too happy with the "always," but he let it pass. "So would I. Well done, Sergeant. We'll keep you posted."

CSM Purser was acknowledging a signal from Skiddaw on the one-tonner's wireless when Thorogood returned. He told the adjutant that the police had already picked up five of the runaways in Thornthwaite Forest. Thorogood hoped they would leave something for him.

"All right, Sarnt Major, let's move out—west toward Blindcrake and Bridekirk. I'll explain as we go."

If prayer was the common denominator among the surviving POWs that morning, Fritz Uhde had done more than his share.

He knew he should be moving from his hiding place in the ruins of the crofter's cottage, but somehow he couldn't find the energy. The gash was deeper than he had at first supposed, and blood was still seeping through the bandage he had fashioned from the flour sack.

He would move out in fifteen minutes, he resolved. He was quite safe for the moment. Across the field, through a gap in the fallen masonry, he had a clear view of the road. He would see any danger long before it saw him. And as he had taken great care to walk in the tracks made by early morning cattle, he had left no telltale footprints.

His arm throbbed painfully and he pressed a handful of snow against the bandage. Characteristically, Uhde

286

didn't blame himself for his misfortune. It was the fault of rotten bloody luck, something intangible over which he had no control.

Seven miles to the west, on the outskirts of Dovenby, Christian Eicke was also feeling, but without self-pity, that he had temporarily lost control of events.

He had posted a guard at the front and rear first-floor windows of the empty house, and from his own position he could see the coast and the sea beyond, a frustrating three or four miles away. Somewhere out there Stieff was playing a dangerous game of tag and waiting for dusk, which was five hours off. Christian felt privately that they were likely to be five of the longest hours he had ever spent.

Werner Herburg's luck continued to hold. Ten minutes after the furniture lorry passed through the town of Kendal, the police threw road blocks across all roads leading south and east.

Heading in roughly the same direction as Herburg, but fifteen minutes behind and by a different route, Theo Emke wasn't so lucky.

Entering the hamlet of Winster on the Cumberland-Westmoreland border, he saw, sitting at the curbside, a red-headed little boy of seven or eight playing with a mongrel puppy. Instinctively he touched the brakes, but seconds before he drew abreast of the child and the dog, he knew that the dog was going to run at him and that he was going to hit it.

There was a sickening crunch and a strangled yelp, and Emke came off the motorcycle. The boy, tears already forming, hadn't moved, but the puppy's back was broken. It was still alive, but only just.

Emke let out a cry of angry despair as he picked himself up. He was unharmed, and the motorcycle, its engine still running, appeared no worse for wear. But other ears had heard the crash, and from the house opposite a young woman in her late twenties, also with red hair, came running, her face as white as the surrounding snow.

"I'm sorry," said Emke in German, and pulled the motorcycle upright.

The woman shouted for him to stop, but he paid no attention. Glancing over his shoulder as he slipped into gear, he saw her bend over the body of the dog and knew it would be only minutes before she telephoned the police.

There was no doubt about it, they were checking papers. Mohr stiffened with horror and edged his way farther down the platform.

He hadn't seen the two redcaps at first. Because he had moved far away from the barrier and, since his brush with the Scottish sergeant, was keeping close to the wall, he hadn't spotted the two military policemen until they were less than thirty yards away. Whether they were looking for escaped POWs or simply making a routine check for deserters was immaterial. Unless he could get off the platform or the train arrived within the next few minutes, he was in serious trouble. MPs would not be fooled by his phony Dutch papers. At the very least they would haul him in for further questioning, and that would be that.

Leutnants Kaehler and Preiss knew all about trouble. By midmorning Preiss's ankle had swollen to twice its normal size, and it was obvious he wouldn't be walking anywhere for a long time. It would have been impossible to move, anyway. Since 10 A.M. a gang of children had been playing a scratch game of football in the schoolyard, and from time to time the ball thudded against the outside of the classroom wall. Kaehler's assessment that school had broken up for the Christmas holidays had proved correct, but that didn't mean that the yard was not used. In spite of the snow, it was the obvious place to play.

"Maybe we could offer our services as goalkeepers," whispered Kaehler, and grinned reassuringly. He could see that his friend felt guilty and depressed and was determined to keep his spirits up.

"They'd stone us as soon as look at us," muttered Preiss. "I don't know, Peter, but the kids seem worse than the adults. If it's like this in Germany, God help the next generation of both countries. They'll never recover from this war."

Kaehler nodded his understanding and looked at the reasons for Preiss's disenchantment, which were hung up on all four walls of the classroom. As well as childish paintings of Christmas scenes, many of the artists had depicted scenes of war. The most common were rough drawings of German planes, either in flames or in the act of crashing, having been shot down by British aircraft, always shown at a superior height. Neither Willi Messerschmitt nor R. J. Mitchell would have recognized one of his own designs, but the swastikas and red-white-and-blue roundels painted on the fuselages left no doubt which side the losers were on. As Preiss said, it was depressing. Judging by the size of the desks and the standard of the artwork, most of the children couldn't be more than eight or nine.

"A thousand years ago they were probably painting Viking ships being burnt," offered Kaehler cheerfully.

"Which is precisely what I mean. The Vikings, the Bayeux Tapestry, the Hundred Years War, the Elizabethans, the Napoleonic Wars, the First War. It never seems to end."

"No," said Kaehler, "I suppose it doesn't."

"You should get some rest, Christian."

Christian turned away from the window. Kurt von Stuerzbecher was holding out a cup of coffee. One thing to be said about their present billet, there was no shortage of hot drinks.

"I'll sleep for a week when we're aboard that U-boat. Thanks." Christian sipped the scalding coffee gratefully. "Who's looking after the English woman?"

"I put her in with Schelling. They could use some sleep too. Schultz and Schelling, I mean."

"They're used to it. I've seen both of them travel across

289

some of the worst country in the world for forty-eight hours nonstop. And with nothing more to eat than a bar of chocolate."

"They're first-class men. Strange, isn't it, that we should be losing the war with men like that."

"The *Tommis* have their own fair share. So do the Ivans."

"Yes, it was a mistake to take on both at the same time."

Christian smiled. "Treason, Herr Generalmajor?"

"If it is, half the Luftwaffe are guilty of the same thing. The army and navy, too, I shouldn't wonder. If it eventually goes against us, I suppose only the SS will fight to the last man. Sorry, Christian."

Christian shrugged it off. "That's all right. I'm no longer SS."

"But you will be when this is over. Restoration of your former rank and with a crack division is the least they can do."

"Perhaps."

"You'll be needed, Christian," said von Stuerzbecher seriously. "Not everyone holds the opinion that all SS are thugs and bullies. You'll be needed in the east if not elsewhere. If it ever becomes a question of losing, it will be better to be overrun by the British and the Americans than the Ivans. Every SS man will be needed to hold them back."

"To save the Reich for others who couldn't do their jobs properly?" asked Christian. "No offense intended."

"And none taken. You're right. The Luftwaffe didn't command the skies the way Goering promised, and the navy didn't sink enough ships. But that's not the reason we're on the defensive."

"What is?"

"As always, leadership. The wrong men in the wrong jobs for the wrong reasons. Once in power, the Fuehrer should have sacked all the old gang and started from scratch. Mark my words, Christian, when historians come to write about this they'll say exactly that; that the fighting was left to politicians instead of soldiers, that good men were killed or removed from office because they held the wrong political views, while lackeys were promoted to the highest positions."

Christian thought of the sealed orders signed personally by Himmler.

"I can't argue with that," he said.

The redcap military-police corporals were only feet away, examining the travel documents of the Scottish sergeant and his companions, when Mohr heard the whistle of the train. The passengers surged forward en masse, all anxious to be first to board.

Mohr sidled to his right, toward the barrier, to put himself beyond the MPs, among those whose authority to travel had been passed as legitimate.

"All right, you, not so fast."

Mohr kept going. The speaker made a move toward him, but the Scottish sergeant was having none of that. He snatched his paybook and warrant and thrust them into his breast pocket as the train shuddered to a halt.

"Haven't you buggers got anything better to do?" he demanded belligerently, and barged to the front of the crowd, using his kitbag as a battering ram.

Mohr had one hand on the door handle when he felt a shove in the back.

"Come on, sir," pleaded the sergeant. "You won't get back to Holland that way."

Seconds later, Mohr was aboard.

Thorogood had been of half a mind to head straight for the coast and beat back from there, but two factors militated against that. The first was the obvious one; that whoever had broken into the store couldn't be far away, certainly nowhere near the coast. The second was that the area around Whitehaven and Workington was already crawling with troops and police. Two companies of Paras had been diverted from an exercise on Scafell Pike and the police covered the ports as a matter of routine. As far as he could see, no one except his small group was following the obvious route via Bewaldeth to Maryport, which was the way he wanted it. With five prisoners already in the bag, the next success had better be his or he would want to know the reason why.

"Pull in here, driver."

The one-tonner skidded to a halt. Thorogood scanned the surrounding countryside with his field glasses.

"What do you make of that, Sarnt Major?"

CSM Purser took the glasses. Two fields away was what appeared to be a derelict cottage or lean-to. The CSM wasn't impressed. Since leaving Bewaldeth they had searched a variety of farm outbuildings, including, although he didn't know this, the barn where Christian and his party had holed up during the night. They had found nothing, no trace of illicit occupancy.

"Not a lot, sir. It's got no roof and not much in the way of walls. He'd freeze to death before the day's out."

"Maybe, but take one man and have a look anyway."

Through a gap in the masonry Fritz Uhde gave vent to an oath of despair when he saw what was happening. From this distance he couldn't make out whether the two men now climbing through the hedge were troops or civilians, but he'd have laid long odds that they weren't hikers on a ramble.

He had to get out. Behind him was a dip that led down to a stream. Beyond the stream were trees. If he could hide there until they completed their search . . .

Swiftly he gathered up his belongings.

By common consent among his teachers, Michael Wills was the biggest troublemaker in the school. Not yet ten years of age, whether it was lifting the girls' skirts to see what color bloomers they were wearing or setting a booby trap of a bucket of water above a classroom door, Michael Wills was usually at the bottom of it. And now, as he trapped the football expertly and prepared to shoot, he knew exactly what he was going to do; he was going to put the ball straight through the window. He would make it look like an accident, of course, and no doubt there'd be hell to pay when the holidays were over. But that didn't deter him.

He evaded a clumsy tackle and put the full force of his boot behind the shot. The other children watched awe-struck as the ball sailed into the air. They could see per-fectly well what was going to happen before it did, and it came as no surprise when the window pane shattered and the ball disappeared into the classroom within.

"You idiot, Wills! What did you want to do a thing like that for?"

"It was an accident."

"Accident my arse. You did it deliberately."

"I did not."

"He'd better get it back anyway." This from a bigger boy. "It's the only ball we've got."

"Give us a bunk up then. Let's see where it is."

Standing on the shoulders of the bigger boy, Michael Wills peered into the classroom—straight into the shocked eyes of Peter Kaehler.

Unkempt as they were, seeing Kaehler and Preiss gave Michael as much of a fright as it gave them, and he jumped down quickly.

"There are two tramps in there," he said.

Nineteen

Fritz Uhde was the next casualty of the break.

Following the progress of CSM Purser and Harpo Cook via the field glasses, Thorogood spotted the movement in the derelict cottage before Uhde had taken three steps. His pulse racing with sudden excitement, he quickly adjusted the focus screw. There was no doubt about it. He couldn't make out the man's features, but there was someone over there who didn't want to be seen.

He cupped his hands to his mouth to shout a warning, but the CSM's old-soldier's eyes didn't miss a thing, and he and Harpo were already proceeding at the double.

Uhde might still have got away, or at least remained at liberty a little longer, if he had not concluded that the angle of the bank leading down to the stream was too steep immediately behind the cottage. Rather than add a broken leg to his other problems, he looked for an easier descent. But to find one he had to leave the shelter of the ruins and run across open ground.

CSM Purser was not a man to waste time on subtleties.

His own personal weapon was a Sten, useless at this distance, but Cook had a Lee-Enfield .303, standard issue.

"All right, son, put a couple of rounds over his head."

"Me, Sergeant Major?" Never in his life had Harpo expected to be ordered to shoot at someone.

"No, Greta Garbo, you damn fool. Shake it up, he's getting away."

Harpo didn't move. He had shot on the range, at cardboard dummies, and barely obtained a passing grade. He knew only too well that if he aimed over someone's head, the likelihood was that he'd hit him between the shoulders.

In the fraction of a second it had taken him to work this out, Uhde was almost out of sight.

"You bloody half-wit!" screamed Purser, and let fly with the Sten.

Uhde heard the shots and instinctively flinched. But experience told him he was being fired upon by an automatic weapon, of low caliber at that, which was unlikely to do any damage at this range.

Slipping and sliding he stumbled down the bank. His injured arm caught a jutting rock and he cried out in pain.

The stream was wider than he had at first supposed, but if he could make it to the trees . . .

Behind him he heard a couple of rifle shots. If they had done that in the first place . . .

The water came up to his thighs and was cold, bitterly so. The weight of the pilfered provisions threatened to throw him off balance. But he had to hang on to those. Literally, they meant life or death.

Only a few more meters now. The bare branches opposite beckoned like sirens.

His arm was bleeding again, but he ignored it, did not even feel it.

He had to get away. If they caught him now, there would never be another chance. He had to get home. His wife needed him. No, wrong—he needed his wife. He would willingly fly a hundred more missions, a thousand, if once in a while he could share her bed. The war, the bloody war ruined everything. It wasn't just being killed or maimed that was so dreadful about war. It was the other losses, the unseen ones; those no one remarked upon because they were hidden inside.

I hear your wife's been to bed with half the Luftwaffe, Uhde. You're well rid of her, Fritz. Never trust a woman who, sober, is too interested in sex. Have your fun, certainly, but don't spend the rest of your life paying the bills for her hats and dresses. Find yourself a nice dumpling who's content to make the meals and bring up the kids.

What Uhde intended doing when he reached the other side of the stream, whether he thought a few sparse trees would hide him, became academic. As he was about to take the last couple of steps, the CSM and Harpo appeared on the slope behind him. But this time the CSM had the Lee-Enfield and Harpo was carrying the Sten.

For good measure Purser put a shot into the trees, though only fifty feet separated him from the German. Uhde turned slowly, dreams over, hands raised, pale and shaking from his night in the open. He was, thought Purser, not much older than David.

The driver of the furniture lorry ferrying Werner Herburg south was a burly individual named Tom Walsh, who had a special reason for taking the long way round, via Kirkby Lonsdale, to Preston. But Herburg was unaware of this and awoke with a start as the lorry pulled off the A65 and on to the forecourt of a transport café.

As far as he could see they were approaching a town, but which town? Judging by the distance of the Cumbrian Mountains, way off in the northwest, they had covered quite a few miles in the last two hours.

He heard the driver jump down from his cab and the door slam. He shut his eyes, feigning sleep.

Walsh poked his head over the tailboard. "Pit stop. Time for something to eat."

Herburg grunted and tried to indicate that he was all right where he was.

"Please yourself."

Walsh went into the café. His "special reason" was standing behind the counter, every voluptuous inch of her making some sort of impression in the thin white overall. There were some who said that Janet Higgins, a widow, was over the top at thirty-eight, but he knew different. Feed her a couple of gins and she was hell on wheels. Her nineteen-year-old daughter Jean, who now tipped him a big wink, was going the same way too. It had crossed his mind to take up with her when he tired of the mother.

He fought his way to the counter. Food rationing never seemed to worry Janet, which was one reason the place was always jammed to the gills with drivers. The other reason was the woman herself. Many a man would have given a month's pay to be in Walsh's trousers. Or out of them.

"Hello, Tom. Are you stopping or should I put bromide in the tea?"

"I've got an hour. But food first."

Janet Higgins felt a tingling in her loins. An hour with Tom Walsh was what she needed. Although big and strong, outwardly he was a mild-mannered man—until he was aroused. Then he was vicious, and lately she had become very fond of viciousness.

"I'll get Jean to bring it over. I've saved you something special so it'll be a few minutes."

Walsh helped himself to cutlery and found a vacant place at a table near the window. The other three occupants were all men he knew well and they didn't interrupt their conversation to greet him. The talk was inevitably of the war.

"Of course we're bloody winning." This from a wiry individual hovering over a forkful of beans. "Rommel's had the shit beaten out of him in North Africa and the Russians are doing the same in Stalingrad."

"I didn't say we weren't winning, you daft bugger. All I said was there's no point in taking prisoners if we can't hang on to them. We might as well shoot them on the spot."

"Can't hang on to who?" asked Walsh.

"The Jerries that got out of Skiddaw last night. The wireless didn't give the exact number so you can bet your life there are hundreds of the bleeders on the run. My argument is that we might as well put a bullet through them if they're going to cause trouble later."

Tom Walsh hadn't heard the newsflash, and his knowledge of geography was minimal, but as a medium-distance lorry driver plying the route between Carlisle and Preston three times a week, he knew he had seen the name Skiddaw somewhere.

"Where exactly is the camp?"

The man with the beans told him, adding that the police had issued a bulletin warning motorists to be on the lookout for anything suspicious—such as strangers hitching lifts.

Walsh's knees turned to jelly. Jesus Christ, no wonder the bloke in the back hadn't said anything. Half the police forces in the north of England looking for Jerries and he had been coolly ferrying one out. If that ever got out he'd be a laughingstock. Tom Walsh, the driver who runs a travel service for POWs. Neither Janet Higgins nor her daughter would look at him twice after that—unless, of course, he could turn the situation to his advantage.

"I wonder if they give rewards for capturing one," he said casually.

"Shouldn't think so. Why d'you want to know?"

"Because I picked one up a few miles up the road."

The other three stared at him. "You must be bloody joking!"

"I'm not. Take a gander."

They looked out of the window. Werner Herburg's head was just visible in the back of Walsh's lorry.

"That's a *Jerry*?"

"Sure. I knew it as soon as I picked him up. I was just waiting for a chance to deliver him to the local coppers."

"But Christ, he might have made a run for it as soon as your back was turned!"

299

"He's got nowhere to run to, mate. Besides, I can see him from here. That's why I sat by the window."

"You're a cool bastard, Tom."

Walsh shrugged modestly. "You want to take a closer look?"

The man with the beans fished a heavy bunch of keys from his pocket. "I want more than that," he said grimly. "They're all Luftwaffe at Skiddaw, and those buggers have been bombing the shit out of us for three years."

Werner Herburg saw them coming. News had quickly spread throughout the café that Tom Walsh had "captured" one of the escaped POWS and everyone wanted to get in on the act. Some twenty or thirty hard, heavy men, as well as Janet Higgins and her daughter, were now marching toward the lorry. At their head Walsh was angry at his own stupidity, and irrationally his anger was directed at Herburg. The bloody Jerry had almost made him look a complete fool.

Herburg knew the game was up. It was a pity; in the last five minutes he had started to take his bid for freedom a little more seriously. But if it wasn't to be, it wasn't to be.

He stood up in the back of the lorry and raised his hands.

"Come on down from there, you bastard!"

There was no mistaking the command, but Herburg wasn't sure he wanted to obey it. Some of the men were carrying iron bars. He backed away, but half a dozen hands reached for him and pulled him over the side of the lorry. Within seconds, feet and fists were flying, and what should have been a mild roughing up turned into a brutal beating.

Herburg was pulled upright and pushed from one man to another. Those who couldn't reach him shouted encouragement at the others and begged for a turn. The two women—like mother, like daughter—experienced almost identical excitement in the face of so much violence and both were among the most vocal in their exhortations to "kill the bastard."

Somebody, somewhere saw what was going on and, not knowing the reason, telephoned the police. By the time they arrived Herburg was almost unrecognizable. His face was a mask of blood, his jaw was broken; both arms and four ribs were fractured. Later, in the hospital, it was diagnosed that he had suffered multiple internal injuries. His bruises and minor lacerations were too numerous to count, and it was three weeks before he could even talk.

The police arrested no one. There was no doubt a law somewhere that covered such affrays, but nobody could be bothered to dig it out.

Later on in the day, under the pounding weight of Tom Walsh, Janet Higgins experienced the most intense orgasms she could ever recall, and at approximately the same time as Herburg was having wire inserted in his jaw, her daughter Jean joined the couple in the big double bed.

"Do we take him back, sir?" asked CSM Purser.

Thorogood looked Uhde up and down. "No, we damn well don't. I'm not wasting valuable daylight getting him to a doctor. If ne bleeds to death, that's his hard luck. Do what you can with a field dressing, but we're pressing on."

Theo Emke was also pressing on, just as fast as the prewar bike would carry him. The speedometer was laid out in m.p.h. and the needle was pointing at sixty.

Several miles away the red-headed child's mother had already called the police, who had flashed a signal to divert cars from the Kendal roadblock to the junction of the A5094, Emke's road, and the A590.

With the cold wind bringing tears to his eyes, Emke pushed the motorcycle to its limit. The needle edged toward seventy. There were side roads, minor roads, but God knows where they led. His recall of the map of England was sketchy, but he knew that somewhere around here the northwest coast jutted out into the Irish Sea. If he took one of the right-handers he could well find himself trapped in Cumberland.

Curiously, only part of Emke's mind was on his immediate plight; the rest was on the boy and the dog.

Like many German pilots, on first being captured he had been astonished by the hostility that confronted him. In the early days of the war it was British government policy not to conceal captives, especially pilots, from the prying gaze of the public as they were transferred from camp to camp. In Emke's case, after interrogation in the London Cage he had been sent north by rail, and the attitude of British civilians at Euston Station had both bewildered and frightened him. Fists clenched, voices raised in anger. He thought at first he was going to be lynched.

On the drive across London he had seen some of the devastation Luftwaffe bombs had caused, but didn't the British realize that the same thing was happening to German cities? Night after night the R.A.F. dropped thousands of tons of high explosive, though it was doubtful if more than a handful of *Tommi* pilots consciously wanted to kill German civilians. Their deaths were an inevitable consequence of war. The British might call the Luftwaffe Nazi murderers, but surely they knew that the German expression for the R.A.F. was terror fliers.

It saddened Emke to think that somewhere in England a young boy would grow up believing that all Germans were heartless puppy killers. In the way of these things, time would distort the incident out of all proportion to the facts. The boy would become a man without ever realizing that his dog's death had not been an act of malice, had only been the result of a single German pilot seeking his liberty.

In the trickle of seconds it had taken to think these thoughts, Emke had traveled a mile. The faster police cars coming from Kendal had covered slightly more ground and were already pulling across the T-junction when Emke was still five hundred yards away.

He cursed when he saw what was happening, but there

302

were no slip roads to escape down. He had to go on. The two cars did not block the entire road, although the gaps were being filled by uniformed constables. They would move, however; they would move when they realized he had no intention of stopping.

Four hundred yards, three hundred, two hundred . . .

He gave the throttle a final twist, and it was then that fate took a hand. The engine spluttered, roared to life momentarily, and died as the last of the fuel was exhausted.

The policemen linked arms. Three of them were on his side of the road. He was close enough to see that panic was their common expression. But they stood their ground.

Fifty yards, forty, thirty . . .

Brave bastards, he thought, and wrenched the handlebars to the left. Even without power he was still traveling at almost seventy miles an hour when he hit the front wing of the nearest car.

There was an ear piercing crunch of metal, and Emke was flung over the handlebars and over the hood of the police car. His neck snapped the instant his head touched the ground. Almost his last thoughts were of the boy and his dog. His very last were of Hans Baum.

Twenty

DECEMBER 13: 1330–1600 HOURS

Young Michael Wills's father hated Germans with an intensity that exceeded anything felt by Adrian Thorogood, though in his case there was a more tangible reason.

One of the last to be taken off the beach at Dunkirk, Frank Wills had suffered for five days under the ferocious dive-bombing of the Stukas. Some said he was lucky to be invalided out with nothing more than total deafness in one ear; others had lost their lives or at least a limb. Wills disagreed. Long after he was safely home he knew he would live forever with the memory of the JU 87s' sirens, the screams of the wounded, the feeling that death was but minutes away.

His hostility toward Germans in general was surpassed only by his loathing of the Luftwaffe in particular. So when his son ran in with the news that he had seen two tramps hiding in the school, Frank Wills didn't treat it as a practical joke or a wild imagination. He knew precisely who they were and what he was going to do.

He should, of course, contact the police immediately; that was what the wireless had said. But the police would

305

merely rearrest them and return them to Skiddaw. That wasn't good enough. Luftwaffe personnel lived like lords in the camps, or so he had heard; they wanted for nothing. The two in the school would be punished mildly, rapped across the knuckles, and in a few weeks would be trying the same thing again.

No, sir.

"Have you told anyone else?" he asked his son.

"Well, the others were there."

"What others?"

"Billy Barnes, Andy Craig, quite a lot."

"Then run and tell Mr. Barnes not to do anything until he's seen me."

He would see Andy Craig's father himself. Bert Craig had lost a sister in the Coventry bombings.

But before leaving the house he took his 12-bore, a gun he normally used for poaching, from its rack and filled his pockets with cartridges.

"We've got to get out," said Preiss for the umpteenth time.

He was on his feet, staring futilely at the shattered window pane and the football, lying like a severed head between the desks. It was quiet outside now and had been for half an hour.

"Don't be a bloody fool. How far d'you think you'd get with that ankle?"

"All right, *you've* got to get out."

"Not by myself," said Kaehler calmly. "We'ye been over this a dozen times, Johann. Either we both go or we both stay. That's all there is to it. Besides, we don't know that the child will tell his parents or that his parents will believe him or add two and two together. We're as safe here as we would be anywhere."

Preiss lost his temper. "Of course he'll tell his parents. He'll want his ball back if nothing else. You've got to go, Peter. Please," he pleaded. "You've got a few minutes. How the hell do you think I'm going to feel if we're recaptured because I was clumsy?"

"Would you go if the situation were reversed?"

"Of course I would. It'd be my duty."

Kaehler smiled. "You're a liar, Johann, and a bad one. We'll sit it out."

The train was bursting with troops returning from leave or in transit. As it had started its journey in Scotland and had stopped at Carlisle en route, obtaining a seat was impossible. Mohr found himself standing in the corridor, sharing the same few cubic meters of what passed for oxygen with the Scottish sergeant and his friends. The sergeant's breath reeked of stale beer and tobacco, but Mohr wasn't complaining. The way they were packed, with kitbags, suitcases and rifles taking up any spare space, a ticket collector was going to have one hell of a job getting through.

"Told you you should have gone up to the officers' end," grinned the sergeant. "I'll bet it's not like this in Holland."

"Not now," said Mohr, catching the drift.

"Never mind, we'll kick the Nazis out one day and you can have it back, windmills and all."

There was another side to the coin, of course, thought Mohr. Spending hours on a train as close as this meant that his homemade uniform was under constant scrutiny, especially the cap. It might be a good idea to take it off. The weakest part of his disguise was the wretched hand-sewn badge, and at this range the sergeant or one of his companions could well notice that it didn't represent anything.

He removed it and tucked it under one arm.

"You want to watch that, sir. If it drops on the floor it'll come up the color of a coal miner's neck."

Mohr smiled uncomprehendingly.

In the back of the one-tonner Harpo Cook knew he was in big trouble for disobeying the CSM's order to shoot at Uhde. Fourteen days in the brig was the least he could expect and maybe it would be a lot more. But even fourteen days was bad enough because it would include the

Christmas period. If he was put on C.O.'s orders first thing in the morning, the punishment would take him up to the twenty-eighth.

Christ!

Up front, sandwiched between Captain Thorogood and the driver, CSM Purser said: "Bridekirk coming up, sir."

Thorogood nodded sourly in acknowledgement. He was feeling thoroughly disgruntled. After recapturing Fritz Uhde he had thought that this was going to be his day, but since then they had found nothing, not even a trace. They had searched every conceivable hideout between Bewaldeth and Blindcrake, Blindcrake and Bridekirk. Barns, byres, farm buildings, even hedgerows. Zero. After Bridekirk there was, on the main road, only Dovenby before Maryport. Perhaps he was on a wild-goose chase. Perhaps only that idiot Uhde had been coming this way. Perhaps . . . Perhaps there was only one real way to find out, and that was to interrogate Uhde without being too fussy about the methods used. But he couldn't do that with the CSM and the men around.

"Stop the truck," he said suddenly.

The driver applied the brakes. The one-tonner skidded to a halt.

Thorogood pointed through the windscreen with his cane. "You see those fields over there, Sarnt Major?" The CSM said he did. "I want you to beat across them."

"Across the fields, sir?" Purser looked bewildered. There was nothing across the fields except more fields and nowhere a man could hide.

"That's what I said. Look for tracks. According to the map there's some sort of bridle path leading toward Gilcrux. See if it's been used recently."

The CSM had seen the map too and knew that if anyone was making for Maryport they wouldn't be going by way of Gilcrux. But it was a direct order and he wasn't going to argue on that score.

"Very good, sir."

"And take all the men, the driver as well. You'll be able to cover a greater area of ground that way."

Thorogood waited until they were a couple of hundred yards away before climbing into the back of the one-tonner.

"And now, Herr Leutnant, you and I are going to have a little talk," he said in German.

Christian switched off the radio and went to relieve Schelling. The weather news was better than he had any right to expect. Gales were forecast for the Irish Sea and further heavy snowfalls for Cumbria, but neither was due before midnight.

"Has she eaten?"

"Enough for six," answered Schelling. "I thought fear took away a person's appetite."

"Maybe she isn't frightened."

"Then she's the only one in the house who's not. Can I bring you anything?"

"No, thanks. Leave the Luger."

Schelling placed it on the dressing table and left the room.

Christian shook a cigarette from the Players packet and offered one to Anna. She seemed about to decline, but eventually reached out and took one. Although Schelling had had to watch the road and the prisoner simultaneously, he had not bothered to tie her hands. There was nowhere she could run to. She looked exhausted.

Christian lit both cigarettes. He saw that Anna's eyes were on the dressing table. Maybe she was frightened after all.

"Don't worry, I'm not going to shoot you. Neither is anyone else."

He turned to the window. The house was at the eastern extremity of Dovenby—a quarter of a mile outside the village, to be accurate—and from his vantage point he had a more or less clear view of the road as far as Bridekirk. Wolf Schultz was watching the west, but Christian knew that trouble, if it came, would come from the east or northeast.

"I don't understand it," he heard her say, and there was a different tone in her voice.

Christian faced her. "You don't understand what?"

"Why I'm still alive. I'm in your way, somebody's always got to be awake to make sure I don't escape, and I'm slower than the rest of you. During the night, the big man who just went out even helped me keep going. I don't understand any of it. We're at war. England and Germany are at war."

"I'm a soldier," Christian said. "English soldiers are fighting German soldiers. We don't kill civilians." At least most of us don't, he added silently.

"That's not what you hear," Anna hurried on. "You hear . . . I mean, *we* hear on the wireless and read in the newspapers that the Germans are murderers, that you kill women and children."

Christian looked her straight in the eyes. "We're told the same stories about the English and the Americans," he said. "So now we both know somebody's lying."

"And you're really going to let me go?"

"Later tonight if all goes well. You can't do us any harm then."

"I doubt if I would anyway." The words were out before she could stop them, and she seemed as surprised as Christian at their implication.

He smiled at her. It seemed the natural thing to do. "You're learning."

"I doubt that also. I don't know what the hell this war's all about."

"I wish I could tell you," said Christian, "but I'm afraid I can't."

At the other end of the house, carrying two mugs of coffee, Schelling kicked open a bedroom door. Kurt von Stuerzbecher turned at the sudden noise.

"I'm sorry, Herr Generalmajor," apologized Schelling, spilling some of the coffee as he tried to come to attention. "I thought Wolf . . . Obergefreiter Schultz was in here."

310

Von Stuerzbecher pointed to the bed. "So he is."

Schelling looked across. Schultz was lying on his back, mouth wide open, dead to the world.

"But if that's coffee you've got there, I could use some. I'm sure Obergefreiter Schultz won't be needing it for a couple of hours."

"Of course." Schelling passed over a mug. "If the General would like to get some sleep also I can keep watch here."

"No, thanks. It's your turn. I've done precious little to earn my keep up to now, and it's high time I started. There are three or four other bedrooms. Take your pick." He smiled. "Pretend it's a first-class hotel, the war is over, and you've just inherited several billion Reichsmarks."

"If the General will forgive me," said Schelling, "I'd like to add just one item to that list."

"A woman?"

"No—that the waiters speak German, not English."

"Amen to that," said von Stuerzbecher.

Thorogood brought the cane down sharply for a third time on Fritz Uhde's injured arm. The German cried out with pain.

"I'm trying to help you, Herr Leutnant. You know very well what will happen if Major Breithaupt finds out you broke into that store. It's against everything you've ever been taught, isn't it? Whatever you do, don't leave a trail. I'm sure the good Major must have spent hours drumming that into your thick skull."

"Go to hell," muttered Uhde. His arm was bleeding freely now.

Thorogood ignored the remark and the blood. "But Major Breithaupt need never know how you were captured. You can say it was bad luck and I won't tell him anything different. However, one favor deserves another. Are you listening to me, Uhde?"

The question was punctuated with another blow.

"You bastard. You sadistic bastard."

"Wrong, Uhde. I'm not like your lot. Bastard I may be

but sadistic, never. I'm not enjoying this if that's what you're thinking. You have information, I need that information. Beating it out of you is just an expediency. If I had more time I'd use other methods."

"It'd be a wasted effort either way. I don't know anything."

"Wrong again. You might be lying or you might just think you know nothing. But I'll be the judge of that. Just tell me everything that happened from the moment you got out. Which way you went, who you saw. Don't leave anything out. I'll give you five seconds to make up your mind and then I'll really start on you."

Only two-thirds conscious because of pain and loss of blood, Uhde nevertheless knew that Thorogood wasn't joking. It was useless quoting the Geneva Convention or pleading the laws of common humanity to a man like this. He would get what he wanted, one way or another.

Fritz Uhde was a realist. Theo Emke or Franz Mohr would have spat in Thorogood's eye, but he wasn't Emke or Mohr. It was a matter of balancing immediate pain against what he knew, and really he knew very little.

Thorogood raised his arm to strike again, but Uhde had had enough. "All right," he said quickly, "I'll tell you."

Thorogood relaxed. "That's better. Now you're using your head. Begin at the beginning, from the moment you were on the outside."

"A cigarette first."

Thorogood gave him one and took one for himself. He lit both. Uhde inhaled deeply. The events of last night seemed a long time ago, and it took a while to recall the sequence.

"Major Breithaupt had decided the order of escape," he said, finally, "and I was number three."

"Who were the first two?"

"Oberleutnants Mohr and Stuerzbecher. Behind me came Oberleutnant Herburg and then Heydt and his naval people, I think."

"Go on."

312

"Well, it was around ten when I got out. I guessed the others would be going north, so I ran and caught up with them. At least, I kept them in sight."

"Mohr and Stuerzbecher?"

"No, Stuerzbecher and the others."

"Wait a minute, wait a minute. Stuerzbecher and *what* others? You said he and Mohr were the only two out."

Uhde hesitated. To hell with it. He was committed now and it couldn't do any harm. "Stuerzbecher had some people waiting for him on the outside."

"*People?* You mean *Germans?*"

"Yes. Only Breithaupt and Mohr and perhaps a couple of others knew who Stuerzbecher really was, but he wasn't an Oberleutnant in the Luftwaffe."

Thorogood experienced a surge of adrenalin. Jesus Christ, he had stumbled on more than he knew. But it made sense. It had puzzled him from the beginning why Stuerzbecher had been included in the break. The man had only just arrived in Skiddaw and in the normal course of events would have been way down the list. Now it was becoming clearer. Not only was Stuerzbecher important enough to have been given a major place in the tunnel, the Germans had sent someone in to fetch him, take him home.

"If Stuerzbecher wasn't an officer in the Luftwaffe," he asked Uhde, "who was he? A civilian?"

"I don't know."

Thorogood decided not to labor the point. "All right, what happened next?"

"I followed them until the storm broke, then I lost them."

"You keep saying 'them.' How many of them were there?"

"I couldn't see exactly. I didn't want to get too close. Four or five."

"And when the snow came you lost sight of them?"

"Yes. I tried to close the gap, but I think they must have taken shelter somewhere. I never saw them again."

313

"And that was in Bewaldeth?"

"I don't understand."

"That was in the village where you burgled the store."

"Just outside it, yes."

Thorogood lit a second cigarette from the stub of his first and added up what he had learned.

Three, possibly four, German commandos had been sent in to rescue this mysterious man Stuerzbecher. By a coincidence they had arrived on or near the day an escape attempt was to be made. Somehow Stuerzbecher had got a message to them and they had been waiting for him outside the wire.

They would undoubtedly try to get out the same way they came in, and that meant a ship or a U-boat. An airplane was out of the question. The terrain was too rugged for an illicit landing, and the weather too unreliable. So either a ship or a U-boat, with the odds heavily in favor of the latter.

Judging by the route they were following before Uhde lost them, they were making for Maryport or somewhere in that region. But as they had evidently taken shelter when the blizzard broke, it stood to reason they would have remained in hiding near Bewaldeth until it blew itself out, which was at 4 A.M. They wouldn't risk traveling in daylight and from 4 A.M. to dawn was insufficient time for them to reach the rendezvous. Therefore they had holed up somewhere until dark, when they would make their way to the coast. And somewhere off the coast, when darkness fell, a U-boat would be waiting to ferry them home to Germany.

But not if he could help it.

He should, he was well aware, radio Skiddaw, tell Mitchell what he had deduced and ask for assistance. Had he been working entirely in the dark he would probably have done just that. But Stuerzbecher and his rescuers were under cover somewhere between Bridekirk, where the one-tonner now was, and the coast around Maryport. It was simply a question of searching every possible bolt hole, by no means a daunting task in such a rural area, before nightfall. If he failed to find them he would make for Maryport and patrol the coast road. Sooner or later there would have to be a signal flashed between the shore party and the U-boat, and then he would have them.

In the meantime, there was Uhde to be considered. Thorogood doubted if anyone would examine his methods too closely if he were successful, but failure had to be anticipated also. Uhde would complain to Breithaupt about ill-treatment and there would be an inquiry. He couldn't risk that. In any case, Uhde had now outlived his usefulness. A little accident, a recaptured POW making a run for it; that was the answer.

Thorogood's side arm was a Webley, and he was in the act of unfastening the holster, watched by the suddenly frightened German, when the CSM's face appeared over the tailboard of the one-tonner.

"No one could get far across those fields, sir. The snow's three feet deep." He became aware that all was not as he had left it and looked quickly from the adjutant to Uhde, who was nursing his bleeding arm. "What's going on here?"

"Prisoner decided he didn't like my company." The lie slipped easily from Thorogood's lips. "I had to rap him across the knuckles. Patch him up, will you, then get the men aboard and join me up front. I've had a couple of ideas about what we should do next."

Thorogood jumped down and vanished round the side of the truck. He would deal with Uhde later.

The CSM examined the young German's arm. Uhde could speak no English, but it wasn't hard to guess what had happened.

"Bastard," muttered Purser, and fished in his tunic for a fresh field dressing.

Someone had produced a few bottles of beer and the troops around Mohr were busily drinking and singing.

315

"Come on, sir," said the Scottish sergeant, "give us a song in Dutch."

But Mohr smiled politely and shook his head.

Johann Preiss heard them first. "Listen."

Kaehler cocked an ear and heard the sound of footsteps crossing the schoolyard, heels crunching in the snow, and the buzz of excited voices, adult and child.

He scrambled onto one of the desks and peered through the window. "Christ," he said, and ducked down.

"What is it?"

"Looks like a lynching party. About a dozen men and the same number of kids."

"Armed?"

"One of them has a shotgun, the rest sticks and spades." Kaehler grinned. "We're a bloody dangerous bunch, you know. I don't think they quite realize how well you can fight with that foot of yours."

In spite of himself Preiss grinned too. But after a moment his eyes clouded over. "Looks like we've had it."

"So it would seem. Maybe next time."

"She'll wait, Peter."

"I never doubted it. It'll be something to tell the children anyway; how daddy and Uncle Johann spent the war."

"Come on out, you bastards. We know you're in there."

The words were meaningless to the two Germans, but there was no mistaking the sentiment.

"We'll do it in style this time," said Kaehler, "through the front door."

"It's out of here and to the left, I think. Help me up."

Leaning heavily against his friend, Preiss hobbled from the classroom.

If the people in the schoolyard were expecting two proud young eagles to emerge, newsreel Germans resplendent in Luftwaffe blue and jackboots, they were doomed to disappointment. The pair now coming through the main doorway looked scarcely old enough to be out of school. Their clothes were tattered, their eyes tired, their faces

316

unshaven. A good meal would not have gone amiss with either of them.

The one who was limping tried to smile, but as he was descending the steps he missed his footing and pitched forward. The other made a quick movement to save him, but it seemed to one or two of the bystanders that he was going to make a run for it, run through the crowd. It was at that moment that the shotgun went off.

After shouting for the Germans to show themselves, Frank Wills had broken the 12-bore and made sure that both barrels were loaded. Satisfied, he snapped the gun shut and flicked off the safety.

"They won't come out by themselves, you know," he told Bert Craig. "We'll have to go in and get them."

"Don't be bloody silly, of course they'll come out. And watch what you're doing with that gun. You're not Annie bloody Oakley."

Wills realized he couldn't rely upon Bert Craig to back him up. Only to be expected, of course; Craig hadn't been in the Forces. But you'd have thought you could have counted on a bit of support from a man who lost a sister in the bombing.

Wills was disappointed when the school door was unbolted and the two young Germans appeared at the top of the steps. They might at least have put up a fight. He moved a few paces forward.

"They're only kids," someone said—which was when Preiss slipped.

Years later Wills still wasn't sure whether he had pulled the trigger deliberately or whether it was a reflex action. But in either case, the right-hand barrel went off with a devastating roar.

Only a dozen yards separated Wills from the Germans at this point, and in trying to break his friend's fall, Peter Kaehler took the full blast in the face. Bits of gristle and lumps of flesh flew everywhere, but he made no noise as he landed at the foot of the steps.

In the sudden shocked silence afterward, only Wills could be heard, bleating feebly. "I thought he was going to run for it." No one believed him.

Because it was likely to be a unique event in the annals of the village, someone had brought along a camera. The photograph, when later developed, showed Johann Preiss cradling Peter Kaehler in his arms. It was hard to tell, because the exposure wasn't right, but it definitely looked as if the surviving German was crying.

The train had been rattling along rapidly for a couple of hours and the scene in the corridor was becoming rowdier by the minute. In addition to the beer, someone had dived into a kitbag and produced a bottle of whisky. The abandon with which it was being passed from man to man in the Scottish sergeant's group seemed to indicate that no one had paid good British currency for it. Mohr was forced to take a turn. He tried to decline, but the sergeant would have none of it.

"Come on, sir," he roared, "it's free."

Mohr took a mouthful and almost threw up. With one or two very minor exceptions, it was the first hard liquor that had passed his lips in almost two years.

"That's the way. Here, don't drink the bloody lot."

Mohr wiped his mouth. Not for nothing, he thought wryly, do they segregate the officers from the men in any army.

The songs were seemingly endless. The soldiers had been through "Bless 'Em All," "Roll Out the Barrel," "The Good Ship Venus" and were now into "Four-and-Twenty Virgins." The sergeant had a nice line in original verses for this one, and the train rocked with merriment.

> The vicar's daughter, she was there
> She had us all in fits
> Jumping off the mantelpiece
> And landing on her tits . . .
> Singing balls to your father. . . .

"Come on, sir—you're not singing."

Mohr wondered what they would do if he broke into a couple of choruses of the Horst Wessel song.

There was horseplay, too. One of the soldiers had stolen the sergeant's Glengarry and was wearing it back to front, the ribbons over his face. The sergeant was trying to get it back. It was all good-natured lunacy and might have remained that way if, after unsuccessfully snatching for his headgear, the sergeant hadn't collided with Mohr, knocking the Oberleutnant's own cap to the floor.

The Scot apologized and picked it up. Mohr reached for it quickly, but the sergeant had drunk enough not to care. He put it on and faced his friends.

"Look, lads, I'm an officer." The men hooted. "Now fall in in three ranks and say sir when you address me."

Mohr began to panic. "My cap, please," he said stiffly.

Realizing that he had gone too far and that Dutch officers doubtless had the same power of life or death over other ranks as British officers did, the sergeant prepared to hand it back. But as he took it off his eyes fell upon the cap badge. He knew he was drunk, but he wasn't that drunk. As he had thought on the station platform, there was something very fishy about that badge.

"Bloody peculiar, this," he muttered, and picked at the emblem with a dirty fingernail. The cotton started to come away.

"My cap, sergeant!" Too late, Mohr realized his voice had gone up an octave. The men shuffled their feet uneasily.

"Give him his cap back, for Christ's sake, Jock," someone urged. "You'll land us all in it."

"In a minute. . . ."

The sergeant was a regular soldier, not "hostilities only," and he had seen and handled enough cap badges, both officers' and enlisted men's, to know that they didn't unravel if you picked at them with a finger.

"Look at this." The cotton was coming away in handfuls. "Look at this bugger." One or two heads peered over his shoulder. "This isn't a cap badge at all. It's been sewn on."

Mohr edged toward the compartment door, a few feet away. The train was traveling at sixty miles per hour, but it was an unconscious reaction, a flustered brain seeking a way out. It was all over now, thanks to these drunken fools.

The sergeant focused his bloodshot eyes. "You know what I think we've got here, lads? I think we've got one of those bloody Jerries. Say something in Dutch . . . sir."

Mohr didn't get a chance to say anything. At the mention of the word "Jerries," one of the soldiers reached up and pulled the emergency handle. The train decelerated instantly, throwing everyone to the floor.

It seemed an age, but it was literally only seconds before Mohr was among the first to regain his feet as the train shuddered and screeched to a halt. His hand gripped the door handle until his knuckles were white. The *Tommis* all had rifles, but did they have ammo? It was unlikely, in transit, but one never knew. In any case, what did it matter? Running and taking a bullet in the back—wasn't that preferable to twenty-eight more days in solitary, going slowly out of his mind staring at the walls? He had told Otto Breithaupt weeks ago that he'd rather be shot than spend another month in the cooler, but Otto hadn't believed him. In his book, a man stayed alive and carried on fighting as long as he had breath in his body, even if fighting meant nothing more laudable than surviving. The alternative was the act of a coward.

The *Tommis* were getting up now, the Scottish sergeant to the fore. They didn't rush him, however. Curiously, they stood stock still, waiting.

Slowly, Mohr felt his whole body relaxing. He loosened his grip on the door handle. Perhaps it was the thought of the bullet or perhaps it was wondering what Breithaupt would say, but he knew he couldn't run away. It wasn't in his nature. So what the hell was twenty-eight days anyway? He had done it before; he could do it again.

320

He shrugged his shoulders philosophically and drew himself up to his full height. In English he said: "Oberleutnant Franz Mohr, Luftwaffe, at your service."

He expected to be floored then. They were *Tommis* and he was, to them, a Nazi. He expected them to beat him, land a few kicks and punches before the M.P.s were summoned. What he wasn't prepared for was the Scottish sergeant's half-smile to become a grin, which quickly turned into laughter. Nor was he prepared for the others to join in, and it was with something close to amazement that he watched the tears roll down their cheeks.

The Scot put his arm around Mohr's shoulders. "You cheeky bastard," he spluttered. "You almost had us fooled. Where's that bloody whisky?"

Someone thrust the bottle forward. Like all good soldiers, in any crisis they protected the booze first and foremost.

"Here, take a swallow before the redcaps come along to see what's happened."

Thoroughly bewildered, Mohr accepted the bottle gratefully. He wasn't quite sure what lesson he had just learned, but he knew that, whatever it was, it had nothing to do with the color of his uniform.

Dusk wasn't far off. It was time to be getting ready.

Christian called them all to the bedroom on the east side of the house. The map was unfolded on the dressing table.

"We're here," he said, "and we want to get here." He jabbed a finger at a spot on the coast equidistant between Flimby and Maryport. "We'll be using the back roads, so I estimate it will take us a couple of hours. However, we don't know what sort of a reception committee they'll have waiting for us on the coast or whether we'll meet roadblocks or other obstacles. So let's add an hour to that for safety."

He checked the time on his wrist watch.

"It's now coming up to 1600, and it will be dark enough to move in another half hour, which should put us on the coast at 1930. Stieff will be waiting for our first signal at 2000. If he doesn't see it he'll go away and come back tomorrow. Except I don't think much of our chances of remaining free, outside this house, for another twenty-four hours. It has to be tonight."

"You're cutting it very fine, Christian," said von Stuerz-becher.

"I admit it, but we're restricted by sunset."

"That's not the only thing we're restricted by." Feldwe-bel Schelling was doing a stint at the window. "Come and see this."

Christian crossed the room in three strides and peered through the curtains. Coming slowly down the road, looking as if it had every intention of stopping, was a British Army one-tonner.

Part V

Twenty-one

It was almost dark now.

"They're not moving." Wolf Schultz had taken over at the window. "They're set for the whole night."

The one-tonner was parked in the road at the end of the driveway and had been for ten minutes. Christian recognized the CSM immediately and asked von Stuerzbecher to confirm that the troops were from the camp. Von Stuerzbecher borrowed Christian's field glasses to get a better look.

"Yes, they're from Skiddaw. The one on the radio is the adjutant, Captain Thorogood. I remember some of the other faces too." He handed the glasses back. "Do you think he suspects something and is calling for reinforcements?"

"I don't know."

"Maybe they'll go away," said Schelling hopefully, but they didn't. And as the ten minutes became fifteen and then twenty, Christian began to worry.

"We're going to have to find out what they're up to," he said finally.

"How?"

"By going out and talking to them. Me going out, that is."

"That's madness, Christian," protested von Stuerzbecher.

"No, it's the only way. Look at it like this. If they are summoning up reinforcements, the one Luger we have between us isn't going to be very effective. We're all dead. But if they're hanging around out there for some other reason, it's up to us to move them." He tapped his wrist watch significantly. "It's four–twenty-five. Unless we're out of here and on our way in the next quarter of an hour, Stieff will think we're not coming."

Von Stuerzbecher accepted the logic of the argument. "What do you intend doing?"

Christian picked up the rucksack. "I'll slip out the back door, come up the road behind them, and pretend I'm a hiker. If I get the opportunity, I'll tell them I saw something fishy earlier in the day. That should get them moving."

"The Company Sergeant Major knows you," von Stuerzbecher reminded him. "Won't he think it somewhat odd to see you once as a van driver and once as a hiker?"

"I'll take the English woman with me. They know her of old. If there are any queries, I'll say that as a result of the bread business the other day old man Foster fired us both."

Von Stuerzbecher shook his head. "It's flimsy, Christian."

"And staying here is suicide. Have you got any better ideas?"

Von Stuerzbecher hadn't. Christian walked across to Anna.

"There's a squad of British soldiers at the end of the driveway," he said, "and you're going to help me get rid of them. We'll be alone, so you might think it an ideal opportunity to raise the alarm. That would be exceptionally foolish. I'll be taking the Luger and I'll have nothing to lose by killing you. Is that understood?"

"Yes."

"Good. Please keep it in mind at all times."

Thorogood had pulled up outside the house because it was the first in the village and the obvious place to park. And he had been stationary for the best part of half an hour because the C.O. had ordered him to return to camp. At least, the duty officer, Second Lieutenant Tom Hastings, had passed on Major Mitchell's message. But Thorogood wanted none of it. He refused to move unless ordered to do so by Mitchell in person, and he had dispatched Hastings to find the C.O. and bring him to the radio room. Until that happened, he was staying put.

"Someone coming, sir," said CSM Purser.

Christian and Anna hove into view, Christian wearing the rucksack. One or two of the soldiers had their rifles at the ready, but they were relaxed when they saw that the newcomers were hikers.

"What's going on?" asked Christian.

"Never mind that." Thorogood scrutinized Christian with all the suspicion of a butcher buying a bargain calf. "Who are you two and where are you going?"

Christian explained that they had hiked up from Keswick that day and were on their way to Dearham, a mile or two up the road, where they would spend the night with friends. He was all the time conscious that the CSM was studying him closely, trying to place his face.

"Hello again," he said.

The CSM got it then, especially when Christian casually pulled back the hood of Anna's anorak.

"You're from the bakery."

"Not any more." Christian smiled feebly. "Neither of us. Thanks to that business the other day we both got the sack—me for allowing the load to be stolen and Mrs. Newfield for recommending me in the first place."

"I said I'd speak to Foster about that."

"Wouldn't make any difference. A dozen customers didn't get their orders, thanks to those Jerries."

This was all going too fast for Thorogood.

327

"Wait a minute. You know these people, Sarnt Major?"

"They work for Foster's Bakery, sir." He jerked a thumb at Christian. "This one was the driver of the van that was involved in the rumpus the other day. I put the report on your desk."

Thorogood lost interest. The matter had been dead and buried by the time he got back to Skiddaw.

"Which way have you come today?" he asked.

"Across Whinlatter Pass."

"Spot anything unusual?"

"If you mean did we see any sign of those escaped POWs, the answer's no, nothing like a dozen anyway. But we did see a couple of suspicious-looking characters."

"That's near where the police copped Heydt and his cronies, sir," said the CSM.

Thorogood nodded. "Did you report it?"

Christian took his cue from the CSM's last sentence. "Called the police at Cockermouth."

Thorogood was less than interested. Whinlatter Pass was a long way from Dovenby.

"C.O.'s on the radio, sir." The soldier who had been given the job of listening watch on the wireless poked his head out of the one-tonner.

"I'll be right there. If you see anything suspicious on the way to Dearham," he said to Christian and Anna, "don't ring the police, ring Skiddaw Camp. Tell whoever you talk to to get the message to Captain Thorogood."

"Okay," said Christian, "we'll do just that."

Thorogood left them to have it out with Major Mitchell. Christian decided it was safe to stick around for a little while longer. He made a move toward the one-tonner, but the CSM barred his way.

"That's far enough, lad."

"I'm not going to steal it."

"You're not going to do anything with it."

"You've got someone in there?" It was impossible to see into the depths of the truck, but the CSM's attitude made it apparent that they had recaptured at least one of the

328

POWs. Poor bastard, thought Christian. "Is he dangerous?"

"He's a man, just like you. Maybe better than you. Now clear off."

Christian hesitated. "Because if he's not dangerous you couldn't give us a lift, could you, as far as Dearham? The last couple of miles are always the worst."

"No, we couldn't. We're not going that way, in any case. Now beat it before I have to do something I'll regret."

That was as far as he had any right to push his luck, Christian thought, and was about to move off when Thorogood called out. There was no mistaking the white-hot rage in his voice.

"We're going back, Sarnt Major. Get the men aboard."

Christian waited until the truck had completed its turn and was out of sight before running for the house, urging Anna along in front of him. Von Stuerzbecher opened the back door.

"They say they're going back," panted Christian, "but I wouldn't bank on it. I made a big mistake when I was talking to that captain and I'm wondering how long it'll take him to realize it."

As the one-tonner rounded Bassenthwaite Lake and headed down the Keswick road, Adrian Thorogood tried to work out what had been bothering him for the last hour. It wasn't the peremptory summons from Mitchell to return to Skiddaw or the fact that he would have to explain Leutnant Uhde's condition when he got there. Regarding the former, there was still plenty of time to have it out face to face with the C.O., explain his deductions, and be on the coast by 7 P.M. As for the latter, it was only Uhde's word against his. No, there was something else.

For the fourth or fifth time he went over everything he had learned from Fritz Uhde. A squad of German commandos had landed with the object of rescuing this man Stuerzbecher; Stuerzbecher was not who he purported to be; the commandos had arrived on or around a day when an escape was already planned, and Stuerzbecher had got a message to them; they had waited for him outside the wire and were now on their way to rendezvous with a U-boat.

What the hell was wrong with that?

He sat bolt upright, almost hitting his head on the roof of the cab. One thing was very seriously wrong and he had ignored it before because he couldn't find the answer. In order for Stuerzbecher to get word to the commandos about the date and time of the escape, there would have to have been some contact between them, a message passed physically from someone on the inside to someone on the outside. Yet physical contact between the POWs and anyone except the guards was impossible. Except, except . . . Except that during the bread riot the day before yesterday, dozens of POWs had been within inches of the van driver, the man they had seen at Dovenby . . . And the commandos would obviously include a man who spoke fluent English . . .

In an instant he had it, the thing that was troubling him. The so-called van driver had said he had seen no sign of Jerries. "Nothing like a dozen, anyway."

The news bulletins had made no mention of the number of escapers. Mitchell had insisted on that from the start. Even if they had, the figure would have been ten, not twelve. Only someone who knew about Kaehler and Preiss hiding in the tunnel would call it a dozen.

The driver nearly went through the windscreen as, in response to Thorogood's sudden shout, he slammed on the brakes.

"But Major Mitchell, sir," protested the CSM when he realized Thorogood intended going back.

"Damn Major Mitchell. As of this moment this call sign is off the air."

Twenty-two

DECEMBER 13: 1945–2030 HOURS

The U-boat had surfaced fifteen minutes earlier, at 1930, and was riding the choppy sea half a mile off shore, as close as Stieff dared approach. The forward machine gun and the conning-tower searchlight were manned as a matter of routine. The dinghy party, under the command of an *Obersteuermann,* was ready to push off at a moment's notice.

Stieff huddled deeper inside his duffle coat. Apart from the danger of coastal radar, he knew he was taking a hell of a risk. Although the sky was overcast, it was far from pitch dark. Behind the clouds, scudding before a north-easter, a sliver of moon was doing its best to shine through.

Beside Stieff, Obersturmbannfuehrer Kirdorff scanned the coast with night glasses. "Tell your men to keep their eyes peeled. It won't be much of a signal, if and when it comes."

"They're watching. They're well trained."

"Do as I ask, please, Herr Korvettenkapitaen. We want no mistakes."

Stieff resented being told what to do on his own boat, but he relayed the order via a runner. Kirdorff had made it quite clear that he was in command—until the U-boat was under way or in peril.

Five minutes passed.

"Maybe it won't be tonight."

"It'll be tonight," said Kirdorff. "I have that feeling."

A quarter of a mile inland, Christian was far from certain that it would be this night or any other night. To get to the path, any path, which led down to the beach, it was necessary to cross the road and the railway line, which ran parallel with the coast, and the two *Tommis* who were patrolling this sector were there to make sure no one did. Christian would have walked straight into them if he hadn't spotted their silhouettes as a match was struck and if he hadn't heard the crackle of a wireless.

Schelling tapped him on the shoulder. The *Feldwebel* drew his hand across his throat in an unmistakable gesture. Christian shook his head and thumbed over his shoulder. Move back. They retreated to the edge of the field they had just crossed. After reaching the outskirts of Flimby they had abandoned the road as being too risky.

The others were waiting in the shadows.

"What's the matter?" whispered Schultz.

Christian told him. "Though the fact that one of them's carrying a portable wireless means that they're probably spread pretty thin on the ground."

"You're thinking of going round them?" asked von Stuerzbecher.

"I'm thinking we might have to. What worries me is what the hell they're doing here in the first place. POWs wouldn't head for a remote part of the coast such as this, so why the patrol?"

"Perhaps Thorogood's already rung the tocsin."

"I don't think so. If he had, the road would be littered with troops and we'd have seen the lights of their vehicles for miles. No, I think it's more than likely a day patrol waiting to be picked up."

"If you'll forgive me Christian," said Schelling, "we haven't got time to debate the point. It's six minutes to eight."

Christian nodded decisively. "You're right. Let me have your knife, Wolf."

Schultz handed it over reluctantly. "Schelling and I could do it."

"No, we know exactly where they are."

"Take care, Christian," said von Stuerzbecher.

"It's my middle name."

It was seventy-five yards from the edge of the field to the road. Schelling and Christian moved forward at the crouch, keeping several feet apart. Years of training ensured that their approach was noiseless.

When they were fifty yards away they could hear the *Tommis* talking. A few seconds later they saw them clearly. Both were looking out to sea.

Christian put the knife between his teeth and waved Schelling down. The Feldwebel needed no telling. The last few yards were to be covered on their bellies and the executions carried out silently, just in case Christian had made a mistake about the *Tommis* being thin on the ground.

Twenty-five yards . . . twenty . . . fifteen . . .

Christian could hear the conversation now.

"She doesn't look much, but there's nothing she won't do for a bloke."

"Yeah, any bloke."

"Come off it, she hasn't been with anyone else since she started going with me."

They sounded very young.

Because their faces were only inches from the snow, neither Schelling nor Christian saw the headlights in the distance. Schultz did. "Oh Christ," he whispered. But there was nothing he could do.

They were at the edge of the road, only feet separating them from the exposed backs of the *Tommis*. Out of the corner of his eye Christian saw Schelling push himself to his feet for the final rush. He began to do the same and

333

simultaneously caught sight of the headlights as the truck rounded a bend. Like a rabbit hypnotized by a torch beam, for a fraction of a second he froze, as Schelling froze, lost in that no man's land between decision and indecision. Then they hit the ground together and lay absolutely motionless, two dark shadows among other shadows.

They heard the truck grind to a halt. A voice called out: "Come on, you pair, we haven't got all night."

Neither German moved for a full half minute, until long after the truck had moved off with a clash of gears and the sound of its engine was a diminishing hum in the distance. When they did, each was surprised to discover that he was shaking from head to foot.

"There they are."

In the conning tower of the U-boat Stieff grunted with satisfaction. Three minutes earlier, after seeing the headlights going down the coast road, he had been prepared to accept that his cargo wasn't coming. But there was the signal. Two long, two short—over to the right. A pause of exactly sixty seconds and the same again.

"Get going, Obersteuermann," he called out.

But the dinghy was already over the side.

On the coast road, less than a mile away from where Christian's party were waiting on the beach, Adrian Thorogood had parked the one-tonner with its lights off just south of Flimby. Remembering that the so-called van driver had said that he and the woman were making for Dearham, northwest of Dovenby, Thorogood had headed due west, assuming correctly that Dearham was a red herring. He had wasted no time searching side roads. The game was too far advanced for that. His only hope now was to watch for the signal the Germans would inevitably make or catch sight of the U-boat. To this end he had two men on the beach, looking inland to the cliffs for lights. CSM Purser and the remainder were spread out at intervals of two hundred yards along the road. It was the best

334

he could do. If it didn't work and it became known, as it surely would, that he had failed to pass on vital information, the brass would pillory him.

"Truck coming, sir."

Thorogood stepped into the middle of the road and flagged it down. A Para sergeant stuck his head out of the window.

"Need any help, sir?"

"No, thanks. Where are you people going?"

"Back to Workington. It's as quiet as a grave up coast."

Thorogood waved them on.

He glanced anxiously toward the sky. Snow had been forecast for later on, and snow was the last thing he needed now. What he did want was for that bloody moon to try a bit harder, if only for a few seconds.

A quarter of a mile north of the one-tonner, at the extreme right of a line of lookouts, Harpo Cook stamped his feet to keep warm and stared miserably out to sea. Unaware that at this moment Harry Cade was in the guardroom cells under close arrest, he had made up his mind to see his friend as soon as he got back to camp. Harry would know what to do about the CSM's charge of disobedience.

Harpo Cook was a shy, humble individual, very uncertain of himself and his role in society; a young man who had achieved nothing of note in his life and never expected to. So when the sudden, momentary break in the clouds occurred and the thin crescent of moon briefly illuminated the sea, he wasn't sure whether or not he had seen the upper superstructure of a U-boat. It all happened so fast. One minute he was screwing up his eyes in an endeavor to see beyond the immediate blackness, and next he was staring at a German submarine, half a mile out and roughly twice that distance northwest of his position. A second after that there was only blackness again.

Harpo had never seen even a photograph of a U-boat, but he knew what a submarine looked like, and the CSM had told them to watch out for submarines. But had he

335

seen one? What if he hadn't? What if it was his imagination playing tricks? If he sent the whole patrol off on a wild-goose chase, the CSM would have his hide. No one else had apparently seen it. It was probably better to say nothing.

But Harpo's mind didn't work to the rules of self-preservation, and a moment later he was racing down the road, shouting as he went.

Crouched near the water's edge, Christian willed the second hand of his wrist watch to move faster. He could hardly believe it was only twelve minutes since Schultz had flashed the first signal. It felt more like twelve years. Come on, you bastard. Faster.

A few yards behind Christian, in the shelter of the rocks, Anna was experiencing her first feeling of panic for almost two days. They weren't going to let her go. They were either going to kill her or take her to Germany. She'd been a fool to believe the English-speaking officer. All that talk about soldiers only fighting soldiers had been a ruse to keep her quiet.

She shuffled her feet nervously. Feldwebel Schelling placed a restraining hand on her arm and said something to her in German.

The minute hand of Christian's watch moved on to the quarter hour.

"Flash them again, Wolf. Now."

"You're absolutely sure?" demanded Thorogood.

"Yessir." Harpo was more sure than ever. "About a mile up coast and half a mile out."

Thorogood had no option but to believe him, and he issued his orders calmly and precisely. However lacking were some of his other qualities, he knew how to direct a section attack.

The driver of the one-tonner was told to motor for exactly one mile on his odometer. "Not a few yards more nor a few yards less unless I tell you otherwise. After the rest

336

of us debus, turn your vehicle so that it's facing the sea and switch on every light you've got. Bren team, I'm not sure how these people are armed, but if they start shooting back with anything I want them silenced. I'd prefer them alive, but I'm not fussy."

"What about Leutnant Uhde?" asked the CSM.

"Damn, I'd forgotten about him. All right—driver, as soon as you've done your business with the lights, get round the back and stand guard over the prisoner. If he tries anything ambitious, shoot him. Okay, Sarnt Major, get the men aboard."

In the conning-tower of the U-boat, Stieff was first to see the headlights of the one-tonner as it began moving.

"It may not be relevant," commented Obersturmbann-fuehrer Kirdorff. "There's nothing we can do about it, anyway. But tell the machine gun crew to be ready, just in case."

They could see the outline of the dinghy now, the three men straining at the oars. It was still a hundred yards off shore and about twice that distance down coast. At the same time, above the roar of the waves, they heard the sound of the approaching one-tonner and saw its lights.

"Shake it up," shouted Christian.

"What about the English woman?"

"Bring her with us."

This conversation was conducted entirely in German, and all Anna knew was that she was being hurried along in the direction of the dinghy.

In the one-tonner the driver counted off the tenths on the odometer and braked when precisely one mile showed. Being an intelligent man, he didn't wait for Thorogood and the squad to debus but swung the vehicle in a wide arc and pulled up facing the sea. There was still the railway line between the road and the cliff top, and had Christian's party been sheltering within the lee of the cliff, the

337

lights would have been ineffective. But they weren't; they were at the water's edge, waiting for the dinghy. And to make matters worse, Anna Newfield chose that moment to scream.

In the U-boat Stieff and Kirdorff knew instantly that this was no passing truck, that it was a pursuit vehicle with a damn good idea where the fugitives were. Even as they watched they saw Thorogood's squad pile out of the back.

"Christ, they've only got a pistol."

Kirdorff evidently knew that. "Then we'll have to give them some help, won't we. Give the order to switch on the searchlight and tell the machine gunner to fire at will."

Stieff hesitated. "We'll have every *Tommi* plane and ship in the area down on us."

Kirdorff turned to face him. "Herr Korvettenkapitaen, let me remind you once more that I am in complete command of this operation until the U-boat is in danger. At the moment there is no danger. In ten minutes that situation may have altered, at which time you will be in command and may do as you think necessary. But until then kindly do as I say."

Suddenly a whole area of beach was flooded with light. Blinded until he turned his head away and half closed his eyes, Christian looked desperately for cover. There was none save a few small rocks. The dinghy was still fifty yards from shallow water, the oarsmen momentarily shocked into immobility. It was either a question of wading out to meet it or not getting there at all. A quick glance over his shoulder revealed a squad of men scrambling down the cliff path. It was a million to one they weren't armed with pea shooters.

All this took less than a second to register. The next five seconds were filled with devastating noise as the world went mad and the U-boat's machine gun opened up.

The machine gunner was no newcomer to this business, and he did not have to be told what his primary targets

338

were. His first sighting burst was 'way off, but then he got the range. The next twenty rounds shattered the lights on the one-tonner and decapitated the driver, who was in the act of climbing from the cab to stand guard over Uhde. Traversing right, the gunner selected the lead men on the path for his next burst. He hosed the path from bottom to top. Really, it was like swatting flies on a wall.

The CSM was the first to die. No longer a young man, he nevertheless knew that it was both his right and his duty to be in the vanguard of the assault on the beach. Once down there, it would be his job to keep the enemy occupied with his Sten while the Bren machine-gun team got into position and tried to do something about that bloody U-boat. But he was still fifty feet from the bottom when two of the machine gun's shells tore his chest open and flung him against the cliff wall like a discarded rag doll.

Immediately behind the CSM the Bren team were caught in the same upward hosing action. Hampered in their movements by the gun and the spare magazines, their chances had been almost zero from the moment the machine gunner squeezed the trigger. And what little they had was lost when neither man attempted to take cover. Instead they kept running, slipping and sliding in their anxiety to get to the beach. It was not so much that the machine gunner shot them; it was more a question of their running into the bullets. As the number one died he let go of the carrying handle. The Bren fell twenty feet before becoming wedged in the rocks.

The duration of the skirmish was still being measured in seconds when Thorogood realized that it was a rout. Not only had he lost the CSM and the Bren team, he was about to lose the Germans, who were now wading out toward the dinghy. At least three of them were. Two were still at the water's edge. One was on his knees, firing back with a pistol; the other was standing bolt upright, as though paralyzed.

"Aim for the bloody dinghy!" he screamed.

339

Safely behind cover, three of the riflemen opened up in unison, and one of the oarsmen collapsed over his blade. A moment later, it seemed as though another was hit. But Thorogood knew he needed the LMG to become even marginally effective.

"You . . . come with me . . . we're going to get that Bren."

"Me, sir?" Harpo shuddered at the thought. He hadn't fired a shot yet. He had found himself a big rock and was determined to keep his head down. The ear-splitting noise being made by the U-boat's machine gun was terrifying, and spent bullets were ricocheting off the cliff face in all directions.

"You! At the double before I have you shot!"

Harpo almost laughed in Thorogood's face at the absurdity of the statement, but like so many youngsters who never quite knew why, he got to his feet.

Knee-deep in water, Christian winced and ducked involuntarily as bullets from the *Tommi* rifles thudded into the bodies of the two oarsmen. The dinghy was only feet away now. They'd make it, providing the machine gunner kept playing his music.

Where the hell was everybody? He glanced around quickly. Kurt was there, just behind him, his eyes bulging with effort. So was Wolf Schultz, the water almost up to the little man's waist. But where the hell was Schelling? Christ, not still on the bloody beach!

Feldwebel Schelling heard Christian's shout but chose to ignore it. Only fifty yards separated the water's edge from the base of the cliffs and he could see the *Tommi* officer scrambling for the Bren gun. If he reached it and managed to set it up behind cover, Christian and the others would be sitting ducks.

Slipping a fresh clip into the Luger he ran forward, weaving as he went. Behind him Anna, tears streaming down her face, was screaming. *"I'm English, I'm En-*

glish!" But above the roar of the Lee-Enfields and the machine gun, no one could hear her.

Stieff was first to see the headlights of vehicles coming down the main road from Maryport.

"How long have we got?" asked Kirdorff.

Stieff did not like to think about it. "Five minutes, ten. Fifteen at the most."

Kirdorff nodded his understanding. When Stieff turned to speak to him again, the *Obersturmbannfuehrer* had clambered out of the conning tower and was standing next to the machine gun, directing operations.

Thorogood reached the Bren while Schelling was still climbing up through the rocks. Sweat dripping from his forehead, he wrenched it free and ducked as the Feldwebel loosed off a couple of snap shots. Frantically he pulled at the cocking piece. But it was jammed, damaged in the fall.

"For the love of God shoot him, man, shoot him!" he raved at Harpo.

As Schelling saw it, he had two choices. Either to kill the officer first, or kill the rifleman. If he disposed of the officer, the rifleman would undoubtedly kill him immediately afterward. If he dealt with the greater danger of the rifleman first, there was a possibility that he could dispatch the officer before the man succeeded in unjamming the Bren. One decision meant certain death, the other gave him a chance.

Schelling was an ordinary mortal who just happened to be in an extraordinary situation, a man who wanted to live if he had the chance. He made the wrong choice. He was not to know that Harpo Cook had never shot anything more lethal than a rabbit in his life, and never would. So he killed him first. Steadying himself against a boulder, he took aim with both hands. The single shot from the 9mm pistol took Harpo in the throat, severing the jugular. He died with the safety catch still on.

But by this time, with an effort that made his hands bleed, Thorogood had freed the cocking piece. Schelling saw the barrel of the Bren swing toward him and knew he had no chance. The *Tommi* officer was smiling. His last thought before Thorogood fired the shots which tore him in half was that the man was undoubtedly insane.

Thorogood was on the beach, racing for the sea, before Schelling stopped moving. On the way, firing from the hip, he put a final burst into the stomach of the woman who was screaming at him. It sounded like ". . . English . . ." But it could have been anything.

Christian saw him coming, bullets from the U-boat's machine gun kicking up sand and spray at his feet. At that moment he would have given five years of his life for a loaded rifle. Of the two sailors who had been hit, one was only wounded but the *Obersteuermann* was dead. Christian heaved him over the side before yanking von Stuerzbecher into the dinghy.

"Grab an oar!"

Wolf Schultz was the last to scramble aboard.

"What happened to Schelling?"

Christian was already rowing. "Hit," he said curtly. "I saw him fall."

"Bloody fool," muttered Wolf. "He never could look after himself."

As Thorogood reached the sea, the Bren stopped firing. A magazine contained only twenty-eight rounds and he had fired all twenty-eight.

Throwing the now useless weapon to the sand, he pulled out his Webley. With hardly a break in his stride he began wading after the dinghy.

Standing next to the U-boat's machine gun, Obersturmbannfuehrer Kirdorff totted up the odds. The action had lasted less than five minutes, but that was five minutes too long. The headlights of the vehicles from Maryport

342

were growing brighter by the second, and it could surely not be long before the Royal Navy and the R.A.F. decided to take a hand. At a rough guess it would take at least a quarter of an hour, rowing against the tide, for the dinghy to reach the U-boat. Long before then, Korvettenkapitaen Stieff would have reassumed command and given the order to dive.

"Why have you stopped firing?" he demanded of the machine gunner.

"The *Tommi* is too near the dinghy, Herr Obersturmbannfuehrer."

"Never mind, continue."

The gunner was a veteran of a thousand surface and subsurface battles and was not afraid of the SS. He stepped a few paces back from his weapon. "I regret, Herr Obersturmbannfuehrer, that I must disobey that order."

Kirdorff pushed him to one side. "You'll be dealt with later."

It was not the first time Kirdorff had handled this sort of weapon under these circumstances. He drew a bead on the dinghy and held it in the machine gun's sights. He too had his orders.

While the gun crew looked on with horror, he raked the dinghy from end to end. One in six of the machine gun's bullets were of the tracer variety, and there was no chance he could miss such a simple target. He saw the *Tommi* fall, cut down in mid-stride. Two of the dinghy's occupants stood up, waving their arms, facing the U-boat. Then they too fell.

Though mortally wounded and with the U-boat's machine gun still tearing lumps off the dinghy, Christian understood it all now. Either Himmler or Weil had not trusted him to carry out the sealed orders if there was a danger of recapture. That was why Kirdorff was aboard. It had to be the *Obersturmbannfuehrer* doing the shooting. Stieff would never have permitted it.

Not that it mattered any more. The remaining two crew

men and Wolf Schultz were already dead and there was a gaping wound in von Stuerzbecher's chest.

Christian crawled over to him. He was still alive, but only just.

"Why, Christian, why?" There was blood foaming from von Stuerzbecher's mouth.

"You said it yourself—the wrong men in the wrong jobs."

"But not you." There was a flicker of a grin.

"I always was a fool—Schelling told me that."

Von Stuerzbecher nodded slowly, coughed once, and died.

Christian struggled to stand up, and failed. He had been hit by three, perhaps four, heavy-caliber bullets, and he knew he had only seconds of life left. That didn't matter either. Long ago he had told the woman in the pretty little house out east that he did not expect to survive the year. Well, he had been proved right in that respect.

He sensed rather than saw the U-boat's searchlight go out and heard the wail of the emergency klaxon. Then he too was dead.

Major Mitchell arrived just before midnight. The beach was filled with light and frantic activity. Officers far senior to himself tried to attract his attention, but he ignored them. Dazed, he wandered over to where the bodies lay, laid out in a neat row, waiting for identification and the medics. Some he recognized, some he did not.

At the extreme right of the line, stiff in death, was Adrian Thorogood. His mouth was half open, parted in a snarl. Or it could have been a smile.

344

Epilogue

Operation Hammer, Generalmajor Kurt von Stuerz-becher's plan for the mass escape of German POWs, never did take place, though an updated version of it was tried from Devizes Camp in December 1944. Details of the plot were revealed to the British before the attempt could be made, however, and the ringleaders were transferred to Comrie Camp, in Scotland. There, a Council of Honor was instituted in an endeavor to ascertain the name of the traitor, and suspicion fell upon two men. One was quickly exonerated of all blame, but the second, Wolfgang Rosterg, was executed by his fellow POWs for his apparent part in the betrayal and his anti-German sentiments.

Five men were eventually tried for the death of Rosterg: Pallme Koenig and Jupp Mertens; Kurt Zuelsdorf, Heinz Bruelling and Joachim Golitz. All were found guilty of murder under British law, and they were hanged.

It may be argued that they were executed not so much for the murder of Rosterg, guilty of treason in German eyes, but because they had proved themselves to be thoroughly intransigent. What, for example, would have been the attitude of British officers in, say, Colditz, if one of their own kind had ratted to the Germans on the eve of an escape? What the Devizes POWs had tried once they might well try again, with greater success. When examining the crimes, and they were many, perpetrated by the Nazi regime, it is as well to sit back and reflect that not all the men in the black hats were on one side.

Of those who survived the events of the thirteenth of December, Leutnant Fritz Uhde made no further attempts to escape. Nor did he complain of the ill treatment he had received at the hands of Captain Thorogood. With Thorogood dead he thought it best to keep his mouth shut. Doing otherwise would have meant an inquiry in the course of which his burglary of the Bewaldeth shop, the first link in the chain which led Thorogood to the coast, might have been revealed.

When the war was over, Uhde was among the first to be repatriated and was quite surprised to find his wife waiting for him, loving as ever. Try as he might, he could find no evidence of infidelity.

Oberleutnant Franz Mohr survived his twenty-eight days in the cooler and indeed made one more (unsuccessful) attempt to escape before the war's end. This time he got as far as Liverpool before being recaptured, but he decided that was his last throw of the dice. Completely bald before his thirtieth birthday, a fact he attributes to the camp diet, he now lives in Düsseldorf, where he is the proud and somewhat corpulent grandfather of three girls.

Johann Preiss became an inveterate troublemaker during the rest of his time in Skiddaw and an incurable alcoholic soon afterward. When he can think clearly, which is rare these days, he blames his drinking partly on a feeling of guilt for Peter Kaehler's death and partly on the death of his family, who were all killed in the Dresden bombings. In a way, he is glad Hannah Preiss did not survive long after Kaehler.

Otto Breithaupt was promoted to *Oberstleutnant,* in his absence, in 1943, and continued to head the Escape Committee until that body was no longer needed. But security, under a new commandant, tightened up after the night of

December 12–13, and an escape attempt on such a scale was never again feasible.

When he returned home in 1946, it was to a son, now aged eleven, who didn't know him, and a wife who had lost five stone and aged twenty years. Whatever they had had together, both in bed and out, had been eroded by the war, and they were divorced in 1950. Frau Breithaupt died soon afterward.

Otto Breithaupt remarried and was fortunate in the fact that his new wife got on famously with her stepson. But talents acquired in the Luftwaffe and in Skiddaw were not much use in the new Germany, and Breithaupt found it difficult to earn a living. In 1952 he emigrated to Australia, where he still lives, the owner of a small restaurant, the old days forgotten.

Heinrich Weiss could not forget the old days and could not become accustomed to living in a Germany where the Third Reich was but a distant, unpleasant memory. Because of his scars he divorced his wife without ever seeing her again and set sail for Argentina. There, until he died of a heart attack in 1968, he lived among Germans who still thought as they had done during the great days of the thirties, who believed that only a battle was lost, not a war. It wasn't the perfect end to a career, but it was better than democracy.

Kapitaenleutnant Heydt went into politics. A born opportunist, he began his career as a right-winger but quickly realized that extreme conservatism was a thing of the past. With an adroitness that left opponents and allies alike gasping with admiration, he joined the Christian Democrats and now wields considerable influence in Bonn. Walking the corridors of power he occasionally comes across a face he recognizes, a face that once peered at him from beneath a peaked cap, but both men studiously ignore their recent history. It was as if yesterday had never happened.

Werner Herburg recovered completely from his beating and, as he had expected and dreaded, was feted by his

347

mother when he arrived home. She knew nothing, of course, of his escape attempt; but to hear her talk, her son would have won the war singlehanded if only that fat oaf (no longer the dear Reichsmarschall) Goering had seen fit to promote him to the general staff.

Herburg stood it as long as he could, which was nine months, then wangled himself into America. From New York he went to Los Angeles and Hollywood, where he started writing screenplays. His first few efforts were rejected as hopeless, but showing that quiet determination that had always been a characteristic, he persevered. Nowadays, on either the big screen or television, his name is frequently among the credits.

Oberleutnant Hans Baum never recovered from the effects of seeing his crew die in flames. The newest techniques, the most brilliant specialists, even a handful of quacks—they all tried their luck and failed. Hans Baum hasn't spoken to this day, and lives in a state-run home on the outskirts of Munich. His mother, now in her eighties, never forgave Theo Emke for deluding her. It is her private opinion that Emke lacked guts.

Major David Mitchell, M.C. was removed quietly from the post of Commandant of Skiddaw after the debacle of the thirteenth of December. The escape record of the camp was not good, and it was decided by the brass that tougher measures were needed. Mitchell was given an unimportant desk job in Whitehall, which bothered him not a whit. As soon as he was out of uniform he returned to his civilian occupation of accountancy and quickly prospered. With masses of new fiscal legislation coming in right after the war, anyone with half a mind for figures was at a premium.

He now lives in a large detached house in Surrey and once in a while some event, a book or a film, will bring back memories of Skiddaw. To this day he doesn't know what possessed Adrian Thorogood to do what he did with a mere handful of men.

Lance Corporal Harry Cade, Unteroffizier Hans Geith

and Obergefreiter Willi Braune were tried for the murder of Corporal James Napley. In vain did Cade protest that not only was Napley's death a grisly accident, Braune and Geith had been no more than innocent bystanders.

The court was unsympathetic. Too much had happened in Skiddaw that day, and the result had been the death of a British soldier. There was circumstantial proof that Geith and Braune had had a hand in the escape, and it seemed possible that Corporal Napley had discovered their complicity and was going to challenge them when he met his end.

All three were sentenced to be executed, though Cade was later reprieved and imprisoned for life. Not so Willi Braune and Hans Geith. On the morning of March 24, 1943, bewildered and frightened, they paid the ultimate price.

It is hard to believe that the young men who tunneled their way out of Skiddaw and who suffered the hardships of being on the run in a hostile country are now in or approaching their sixties. War may take its toll, but the fee is small compared to that demanded by time. But that applies to all of us.